FOLLOW APOLLO
A Levi Hart Thriller

Excerpts from "The Hollow Men" and "Little Gidding" from *Collected Poems 1909–1962* by T.S. Eliot. Copyright 1936 by Houghton Mifflin Harcourt Publishing Company. Copyright renewed 1964 by Thomas Stearns Eliot. Reprinted by permission of Houghton Mifflin Harcourt Publishing Company.

Published by Hellgate Press
(An imprint of L&R Publishing, LLC)
PO Box 3531
Ashland, OR 97520
email: sales@hellgatepress.com

Book design: Michael Campbell
Cover design: L. Redding

ISBN: 978-1-55571-849-7

FOLLOW APOLLO

A LEVI HART THRILLER

. . .

RICHARD CRAIG
ANDERSON

WHAT OTHERS ARE SAYING ABOUT *FOLLOW APOLLO*

"*Follow Apollo* is a tale of covert operators—men and women motivated by loyalty with appetites for the extreme. I'd say Rick Anderson got it right." —*Michael R Shevock, retired undercover special agent*

"*Follow Apollo* is a gripping thriller with a kick-ass protagonist. I'd trust Levi Hart and his team to have my back any day." —*Janice Gable Bashman, Bram Stoker nominated author of* Predator

"Rick Anderson puts you at the scene in this smart and suspenseful account that reflects an authenticity that only someone who has been there can capture. It's all real in this story: the team play, the black bag ops, the dangers and the seductions. F*ollow Apollo* is a page-turning winner." —*Craig "Sawman" Sawyer, combat-decorated Navy SEAL, actor, and tactical consultant*

"In *Follow Apollo*, Rick Anderson's highly anticipated follow up to *Cobra Clearance,* hero Levi Hart embodies the spirit of James Bond into the twenty-first century in this edge dancing thriller that breaches the limits of the genre and brings Levi to the mystical edges of life itself." —*Matthew Pallamary, author of* Night Whispers

"*Follow Apollo* sent me on a thrilling adventure and a deeply emotional journey. I lived every minute of it. More, Rick Anderson! —*Nancy Holder, bestselling author of* The Rules

This story is dedicated to Phil Lynch.

It is also committed to the memories of
Richard K. Bailey and Riddick Earl Wilkins,
Senior. They served their country, loved
their families and honored their God.

•   •   •

*The end of all our exploring will be
to arrive at the place where we started
and know the place for the first time.*

T.S. ELIOT

PART I

. . .

May 22, 1969
20:35:02 UTC
In Close Proximity to
Apollo 11's Future Landing Site

CHAPTER ONE

· ·

EVEN THE AIR seemed to hold its breath as he returned to the Lunar Excursion Module. Except there was no air beyond what he and his fellow Apollo 10 astronaut carried on their backs. Pausing amid the silence of barren moonscape, he stared at the boot print he'd made moments earlier when he first stepped off the LEM's ladder. During the interval of stepping off and returning, he'd come to accept the reason why fewer than a dozen people could ever know that he'd become the first man to step foot on the moon. He absorbed the image of his print, knowing that in the absence of air it would endure for millennia.

A twinge of regret passed over him. But the mission profile left no doubt. The world could never learn that Apollo 10's LEM had done more than perform a highly publicized practice descent toward the moon — that it had in fact secretly landed so its crew could examine an abnormality that was already forming the biggest government conspiracy ever conceived. But the plot wasn't meant to convince the world that man had landed on the moon. Instead, it was meant to conceal the fact that someone had walked on the moon *before* that other guy took a giant leap for mankind.

TWO MONTHS LATER, Neil Armstrong took manual control of Apollo 11's LEM during the final moment of its lunar descent. But he didn't do it to avoid a sudden boulder field, although that's the reason he gave Houston's flight controllers. The maneuver's real purpose was so highly classified that only the Flight Director knew that Armstrong had to park the LEM within walking distance of Apollo 10's earlier, not-to-be-discussed landing site. This way he and Buzz Aldrin could put on a televised performance for a worldwide audience, and then bounce as if on a trampoline to a structure near the discarded lower portion of Apollo 10's LEM.

And bounce they finally did, bringing along the specially designed tools that their predecessors said were needed to open the vault-like cavity inside the edifice. Armstrong and Aldrin performed their task in a calm professional manner, their breath coming short only when they pried the cover from the vault and saw its contents.

Working against time, they brought the precious items to their LEM and stowed them. Next, they took from the LEM a plaque that read, *Here men from the planet Earth first set foot upon the Moon, July 1969 A.D. We came in peace for all mankind.* They put it near the American flag they'd planted earlier and prepared to leave. Soon after, an estimated half billion people watched the televised ascent during which the LEM's blast knocked over the flag. Breaking free of the subdued lunar gravity, the men rendezvoused with the command capsule that was being piloted by Michael Collins.

When the capsule splashed down in the Pacific days later, the astronauts were placed inside an isolation trailer.

Contrary to what the world was told, the quarantine hadn't been implemented to protect their health. Rather, scientists were anxious to isolate potential alien organisms that may have been lying in wait within the recovered objects, for although the scientists held advanced degrees and were published extensively in their various fields, they felt a primal need to ensure against releasing a genie that might prove impossible to return to its bottle.

Forty-Six Years Later

The wail of police motorcycle sirens split the air, startling the ever-present tourists as Vice President Mark Cohen's limousine and its Secret Service follow-up car drew closer to the White House. Inside, Cohen was sandwiched between two agents with MP-5 submachine guns at the ready, while the follow-up carrying more heavily armed agents hugged the limo's rear bumper.

Once past the gates the limo screeched to a halt. Doors flew open. Agents formed a phalanx around the tall, athletically trim vice president and hustled him through a door flanked by Uniformed Secret Service officers. Once inside the Oval Office he stood before a federal district court judge and raised his right hand. Then as aides and a gaggle of Senators and Representatives looked on, Cohen repeated the oath after her, speaking the final words in a strong voice, "… and will to the best of my ability, preserve, protect and defend the Constitution of the United States."

Within an hour following the violent assassination of America's second black president, America's first Jewish

4 · RICHARD CRAIG ANDERSON

president held talks with the Congressional leadership followed by a quick confab with the Chairman of the Joint Chiefs of Staff. Finally he turned to the National Security Advisor. After a grim exchange of greetings, the advisor raised an eyebrow and pointed at the others. The new President pressed his lips tight but ushered everyone out. Settling into one of two facing sofas separated by a teak coffee table, he said without preamble, "Proceed."

The advisor gave Cohen crash briefings on classified items of immediate priority. They included military, geo-political, and practical issues. Cohen interrupted at times to seek clarification. Otherwise he listened with a calm but alert demeanor until the National Security Advisor closed the final briefing book. But he wasn't done. Not yet. Reaching for a locked briefcase, he pulled out a black notebook and after glancing around even though they were alone, he leaned forward. "Now I must disclose to you a matter of paramount importance. What I'm about to reveal is passed along to each new president by whoever holds my position. This is done to insure its delivery." He offered the book.

Cohen took it, his thoughts racing. *What could this be?* Sitting erect, he read the title: APOLLO—1969. He began turning pages. At times he shook his head. It wasn't until he reached the analyses that his eyes grew wide and he sat even straighter. But when he saw the conclusions that had been drawn, he breathed in a whisper. "Oh my God."

Fourteen Months Later

The Senior Cardinal Deacon stepped onto the balcony overlooking Saint Peter's Square and proclaimed to the throngs of worshipers, *"Habemus Papam!"* The crowds cheered. Among them was a man with a Boston accent who translated for his fidgeting young son, "We have a pope!"

Within minutes the new leader of the world's Catholics appeared and greeted his followers. After praying with them he turned to the *Camerlengo* of the Holy Roman Church—the Church's Chamberlain—and whispered into his ear. "Tomorrow I wish to pay a visit to the Secret Archives. Please alert the Documents Protection detail."

The Vatican Secret Archives serve as the repository for all acts promulgated by the Popes. But the name is misleading. The term *secret* is more closely associated with a term from antiquity that refers to *privacy*. And this new Pope had a private matter—a profound curiosity, really—one that for decades he'd yearned to satisfy.

THE NEXT morning, following prayers and a light breakfast, the new Pope met with his predecessor's staff and advisors. After thanking them, he caught the Camerlengo's eye and waited while the plainclothes protective detail formed around him. Two of the men in the detail wore suits. Two others wore priest's habits. All were armed. When a pair of Swiss Guards in colorful Renaissance uniforms also fell into place, the men walked along a series of hallways toward the Vatican Library. Going past it, they went through the *Porta di S. Anna in via di Porta Angelica* before turning into the Archives, which smelled of old stone and lingering traces of incense. A portly middle aged man in a dark suit stepped toward the Pope and bowed his head.

"Your Holiness. I am a Documents Protection agent, here to serve you."

"Thank you. I am interested in a particular document." He told the agent what he wanted, then followed him to a monastic-like chamber that contained a simple desk and wooden chair. As the Swiss Guards posted themselves outside the door, he sat to wait while the agent retrieved the papers.

Not just papers, the Pope said to himself. *A file.* And not just any file, for the new Head of the Catholic Church was an old hand at palace intrigue. Long schooled and experienced in dealing with complicated and momentous information, this strong-willed and well-read leader had sophisticated views of the world, along with a religious focus on the next world. He also had friends, and over time he'd heard rumors of a concern that could affect all mankind. He had also learned that it involved the first moon landing.

The Documents Protection agent reappeared and handed over a simple file folder. "I must remain at its side," he explained without apology, and after taking two steps back he stood against the wall and folded his hands in front of him.

Opening the folder, the new Pope found a highly prepared report entitled Apollo Moon Mission Findings – 20 July 1969 A.D. He began reading. When he finished, he looked up at the blank wall in front of him and made the sign of the cross. He sat quietly before turning to the agent, only to find his face deathly pale and his eyes darting wildly while tugging at his collar with one hand and clutching his head with the other.

Bolting from his chair just as the agent collapsed, the Pope rushed to his side while calling to the Swiss Guards for help. One of them stepped inside, followed by the Camerlengo and a bodyguard .

"He has suffered a cerebral vascular accident," the Guard said after checking the agent's eyes. "A stroke. See? One pupil is dilated. The other? It is like the pin-point. We must get him to a physician quickly if he is to survive." Taking charge, he motioned to the protective detail to help him carry the DP agent to the infirmary.

"I will go with this poor soul," the clearly moved Holy Father announced.

Seconds later the men were hustling the agent out of the Archives and through the *Porta di S. Anna in via di Porta Angelica* while the Pope hovered over him, leaving only the lone Swiss Guard to keep watch over the document.

The young Guard, known to friends as Johan, had gone through years of training in austere, difficult conditions at great personal sacrifice. What the friends did not know was that he'd become disgruntled to the point of rage after learning that he was going to be dismissed. The reason? His alliance with the former Commandant of the Pontifical Guard, a man who'd been shamed out of service. Johan saw this as not only unfair, but being Swiss he felt it would bring disgrace to him and to his family. In his resentment he'd taken to excessive drinking.

So once the others vanished around a corner he dashed inside the room. The file lay open. Fluent in five languages, he scanned the pages. When Johan reached the end his breath caught. Though stunned, he had the presence of mind to glance over his shoulder before removing the last three pages and tucking them inside his tunic.

Four Days Later

Levi Hart closed the Top Secret briefing paper and let out a long, low whistle, then sat in silence while he assimilated what he'd read. Finally he looked up at the only other person in the room and said, "Mr. President, what would you have us do?"

CHAPTER TWO

. . . .

LEVI HART left the White House through a tourist exit, noting autumn's tang to the air, but haunted by insider knowledge and by T.S. Eliot's words:

> *This is the way the world ends*
> *This is the way the world ends*
> *This is the way the world ends*
> *Not with a bang but a whimper.*

Troubled or not, he had a job to do. First though, he glanced up at the bright noon sky and squinted, as if by peering hard enough he might see the moon. Then he got going. Slender and angular, with a tapering swimmer's build and lean face, the former FBI supervisor had on a beautifully tailored black pinstripe, gleaming Bally shoes, and a rakishly knotted blue tie that matched his eyes. The sum of the parts let him blend with the throngs of tourists, staffers, and myriad government workers. Two of the workers, attractive thirtysomethings in smart skirt-and-blouse ensembles, smiled at him. The taller one even winked. Levi ignored them. At first. Then he wondered if they could somehow read his thoughts, and were now mocking the distress he felt over the key meeting with the president and the earth-shaking information he had to act on.

He told himself, *Okay, I'm getting warped. Hell, they can't possibly know where I was, or why.* Turning south on 15th Street he strode to E Street, where he turned left toward a public parking lot three blocks away.

But as he approached the lot he found the entrance blocked by an ancient Buick slanted over a low rear tire. A white-haired woman with dark parchment skin crisscrossed by thin lines resembling a waffle grid stared at it in dismay. Levi had to get moving, but he couldn't go anywhere fast until he took care of the car.

He offered to help, and after taking off his suit jacket he rolled up his sleeves. *I've just been with the President of the United States, but a year ago I was deep undercover and clearly looking the part of scum.* He wondered what she would have thought if she'd seen the tattoos that had adorned his arms—not to mention the Swastika on his forehead. Just then a gust caught his heavy auburn hair, which he'd grown back to conceal a shaved scalp. *No, I don't think she'd want a skinhead helping her.* When she handed him the key he popped the trunk and rooted around. *Come on, where is it? All seniors carry 'em.*

While searching he thought about the tatts. They'd been removed. All but the big barbed wire one that still shack-led his left ankle. He'd kept it as a token but now regret-ted the choice, especially when ladies got around to asking about it. For some, curiosity took deeper root. "I checked around," they'd say. "Your tatt symbolizes the ball and chain of someone who's done hard time. So... should I be afraid?"

They always looked at him differently afterward. Some even took a skewed interest in his years behind bars.

Craning his neck in search of the item he wanted, he wondered what he could have done with his life if the undercover assignment hadn't meant getting involved with the white supremacists. He might've married again; had children. He'd have had a chance to break away from the nightmares of his once-upon-a-time family. But he'd accepted the job that forced him to sink into the life of a thug. Why? Call it a sense of duty. At least he got out alive—that's if ending up hooked on heroin was the better option over death. In any event the assignment was done. Behind him. Now he clung to hope—hope for an end to the excruciating pain he still felt over his lost family; hope for a chance to find love again and start over. Hope. It's what drove him these days.

Finally pushing aside a wool blanket, he found a white aerosol can with a blue label: *Fix-A-Flat*. Much easier than crawling around, getting his clothes dirty. He went to the tire, crouched, and made a mental note of a silver Taurus that slowed as it passed by.

He inflated the tire and after a quick check he found a nail embedded between its worn treads. An easy repair. He gave her directions to a nearby service station. But the look on her face spelled p-o-v-e-r-t-y, so he reached for his wallet and pulled out a fifty. Pushing it into her hand, he helped her into the Buick and waited while she sorted through several items in her purse, adjusted the rear-view mirror, and inched closer to the wheel before finally starting the engine. The instant she drove off, he entered the lot.

His candy-apple red '67 Mustang Fastback stood out among the other cars, and after getting in he reached beneath the steering wheel and found the SIG Sauer P-229 pistol loaded with .357 SIG magnum hollow points. He slid it into a leather shoulder holster and put it on, then covered it with his jacket. Next, he retrieved a pouch with two spare magazines and attached it to his left hip. Finally, he pulled a Special U.S. Deputy Marshal badge from a pocket and clipped it to his belt. He was a deputy in name only. His real missions were classified, but didn't require being armed inside the Big House.

He started the car. The big block 390 cubic inch V-8 rumbled to life and after letting out the clutch, he drove to the attendant's booth where he paid with cash to avoid leaving a paper trail. Turning east on E Street, he drove toward 10th.

Eyes scanning, he spotted a portion of Ford's Theater, then routinely checked the rearview mirror for anything in his six o'clock position. A silver Taurus caught his eye. "Not a Bureau car," he mumbled while passing the nearby FBI Headquarters. The Taurus was too old to be a G-Ride. It also had an unlevel fender and its windows were tinted. An image of the car that crept by when he went to the old woman's aid popped into mind. He goosed the accelerator. The Taurus kept up.

Watching the mirror, he flew down E Street toward 7th Street NW. But the intersection was packed, cars and pedestrians everywhere. The light changed. Green, to amber. He glanced in both directions, jammed his foot against the accelerator, then made a sharp left. Angry motorists leaned on their horns. He checked behind. Saw the Taurus.

What the hell's this all about? Who's chasing me? Could it have anything to do with my meeting? But who would even know about it?

Levi roared down the road, the 320 horsepower engine with its Holley four-barrel carburetor running wide open. He blasted past a stopped delivery van, hung a hard right onto a side street, and burned rubber as he sped off, leaving a wide-eyed businessman in a blue cloud of foul-smelling smoke. He eyeballed the mirror. Saw the Taurus rounding the corner. Double-clutching, he downshifted into a narrow alley. Stomped on the gas. Dodged trash cans at high-speed. Burst onto a main road. Then took off.

He thought he spied the Taurus again but couldn't be certain. He pressed on. At Mount Vernon Place he negotiated a tricky turn onto Massachusetts. For once, luck favored him. Green lights all the way. He checked his six and frowned when a silver Taurus popped into view. Who could it be? He'd made enemies over the years and some had vowed to kill him. He felt the pistol's weight in the shoulder holster and sped up, whizzing past tortuously slow-moving cars, letting off the gas only when he approached DuPont Circle. Sticking to the outer lane, he fumed when forced to stop for a group of jaywalking teens bent on disrupting traffic.

Spotting a popular bar nestled between New Hampshire and 19th, he used the landmark to gauge his next turn: Connecticut Avenue. Dead ahead. He hit the gas. Smoked the tires. Spun the wheel left. Scooting past a lumbering delivery van, he stomped on the gas again, slid past rows of popular gay bars and checked his mirror. The pursuer was nowhere to be seen. He drove on for two more blocks before slowing to a sane, sensible speed.

HALF AN HOUR later he turned into the long driveway of a stately two story red-brick home in Chevy Chase, Maryland. After backing into a spot alongside a stand-alone garage, he killed the engine. Its ticking sounds as it cooled cluttered the quiet. Levi sat for a moment, willing tense muscles to relax while examining his surroundings. He'd always believed that detached garages lent a certain dignity to a home—especially homes like this one, built in the early twentieth century. He noted the quality of the craftsmanship, the equal spacing of brick and mortar and the evenly edged roof tiles. There was a permanence to this place. He reflected on the word. Permanence. Damn. What a fleeting thing that can be—especially now.

But Levi hadn't come here to muse. In pursuit of dignity in all things, he spurned the convenient rear door and trooped around to the formal front entrance. He reached for the wrought-iron knocker, about to use it when the door swung open.

A burly, tweed-clad man with a ruined potato sack for a face glared. "What the hell do you want?"

Levi clenched his hands and fired back. "I'm here to kick your ass, old man."

"Humph. In your dreams." The man's ferocity melted into a smiling face. "How about joining me for a drink, even if it is a bit early?"

"Thought you'd never ask." Levi cracked a smile. "Make it a scotch and I'll gladly accompany you on your journey to Perdition."

Heath Baker threw his large head back and laughed. Then he swept a hand the size of a bear's paw toward his home's warm interior.

BAKER SHOWED Levi to a first floor library of dark wood and brown leather. A fieldstone fireplace glowed from a whispering flame even on this seasonally mild day. When Levi removed his suit coat, the firelight glinted against the badge on his belt. Pointing to a pair of leather wing chairs, Baker said, "Take a load off." Then he excused himself and vanished, only to return a minute later clutching two crystal glasses in one hand and a bottle in the other.

Levi leaned forward. "Wow. A twenty-five year old *Bunnahabhain*. From Islay. North Shore, if I'm not mistaken." He knew the bottle cost at least $350.00.

After Baker poured a half inch of the single malt, Levi held the glass to the light and studied its contents while the older man poured a drink for himself.

Baker raised his glass and tilted it toward Levi. "Here's to us and those like us."

"Absent companions…"

"…Fond memories."

They touched glasses. The *ping* of the crystal hung in the air as each man took a healthy swallow. Then Baker put down his glass and plucked a briar pipe from a rack. It was the *GBD Tapestry* he'd bought during a long-ago visit to Great Britain. He packed its bowl, then pulled a kitchen match from an interior tweed pocket and flicked a fingernail against its white phosphorous end. It flared with a sharp *whooosh* and he puffed the tobacco to life while exhaling a blue cloud that rose to the ceiling.

Sniffing pointedly, Levi smiled. "Vanilla. Some things never change."

"Permanence is a key to contentment."

There was that word again, Levi thought. *Permanence.*

Baker raised his glass slightly. "I'm not supposed to be indulging. Or smoking. But—" He puffed at the pipe. "How did it go?"

"Before I start—" Levi described being followed. When he finished he said simply, "We're going top secret now."

Baker nodded once. "You know the drill."

"The President has given us a job. I assured him that Dragon Team's up to it."

Baker said around the pipe stem clamped between his teeth, "Concur." The retired Green Beret bull colonel had been on his third tour in 'Nam when he chose a young Jewish officer to infiltrate a mountainous region. The task: recruit Montagnard tribesmen in the fight against the Viet Cong. The two men forged a lifelong friendship. That officer was now President Mark Cohen.

After returning home with a Silver Star, a Bronze Star with a V-device for valor, and a Purple Heart with two oak leaf clusters, Baker studied law at Harvard and started a lucrative practice in Chevy Chase. But in the wake of the 9/11 attacks the government issued a clarion call for operatives. He answered it by creating *Vanguard International* as a side venture, and forming two dozen teams of eight men and women along the lines of Special Forces alpha teams. They performed surveillances, provided protective details, and did other tasks for private clients. But Vanguard also entered into contracts with the feds, and when terrorists had assassinated President Melchior the year before, Vanguard accepted a contract that called for Levi to infiltrate the gang of ruthless white supremacists who had taken part in the assassination.

The job almost cost him both his sanity and his life. But he prevailed and prevented an attempt on Cohen's life.

Baker closed his eyes and asked, "What's the word?"

Levi shifted, causing the leather chair to creak. "Top secret, Heath. And S.C.I."

SCI, or Special Compartmented Information, is a security clearance that trumps top secret. Information can only be shared with the select few who not only hold a similar SCI clearance, but also have the required 'need to know.' The particular SCI for Baker's people even had an assigned name—Cobra—and both men held Cobra Clearances.

The older man nodded. "Very well. Then I'm officially notifying you that I have a need to know, that I've scanned this room for listening devices prior to your expected arrival, and in keeping with protocol you will now conduct your own scan."

"Yes, sir." Levi got to his feet and retrieved a small electronic device from his suit jacket. After turning it on, he swept the device across the bookshelves, the desk—even the crackling fireplace, before turning it off. "I confirm that I've also scanned the room."

Baker puffed serenely at his pipe, sending another scented cloud of smoke toward the ceiling. "Acknowledged." When Levi handed him a non-disclosure statement, he signed the document and returned it.

"Sir," Levi began as he put the paper away. "The President sends his regrets that you're still recovering and therefore unable to attend today's meeting."

Baker inclined his head. "Carry on."

"You're no doubt aware of the conspiracy theorists who insist that man never walked on the moon—that Apollo 11 and the subsequent landings were filmed on a Hollywood sound stage. Of course, you and I both know that a conspiracy to deceive the public into believing we landed on the moon does not now, and never has, existed."

"I am aware of the various social phenomena. Please continue."

"However," Levi began carefully, "I've just learned that, in fact, a government conspiracy does exist."

Baker's eyebrows formed triangular arches. "Interesting. Proceed."

"The thing is, this conspiracy isn't designed to make it *appear* that we landed on the moon. Its purpose is to conceal the fact that we landed there *before* Apollo 11."

"Before? Holy hell." Baker pulled his pipe from his mouth and examined the carved piece of briar as if he'd never seen it before.

"It started in the 1960's with NASA's Ranger Program—the robotic flights meant to photograph the moon up-close and personal. The goal? Find suitable landing sites for future manned missions. But the first six Rangers turned out to be duds."

"I watched the televised launches," Baker said. "Big events... back then."

"Ranger Seven produced the first photos. But by then there were mounting social pressures against sending men to the moon. Regardless, the Ranger flights were already funded, so NASA launched number Eight. It turned into something special." He stopped and met Baker's eyes. "Its photos revealed an anomaly. NASA sent Ranger Nine to corroborate the earlier sighting. It did. This... *unearthing* is the real reason why the Apollo program got pushed forward."

Baker grunted and said around his pipe stem, "*Rushed forward is how most analysts describe it. It's why we lost Grissom, White, and Chafee.*"

"Yes, sir." Levi picked up his drink. "Then you undoubtedly recall that Apollo 8 proved we could reach the moon, circle it, and return safely. Then came Apollo 9. It remained in Earth orbit to practice extracting the LEM, docking with it, and testing its critical systems." Levi brought the drink to his lips, paused, then lowered it. "Apollo 10's mission was billed as a dress rehearsal. The crew extracted the LEM while in Earth orbit. They traveled to the moon and achieved lunar orbit. Two of the crew boarded the LEM, descended to within eight miles of the moon's surface, and rejoined the command module. That's the official version."

"I see where this is going."

A poker faced Levi took a drink. "Yes. You're right. Apollo 10 landed. Neil Armstrong was not the first human to step on the moon. Nor was he the second."

Levi described the crew's initial findings. "Now then. As to what Apollo 11 found during its follow-up landing, and the conclusions that were drawn..."

Five minutes later, Heath Baker's jaw dropped. But he managed to catch his pipe neatly in one large hand as it fell from his mouth.

CHAPTER THREE

. . . .

LEVI WAITED until Baker regained his composure. "These facts were compromised four days ago." He described the Pope's documents that also contained this information, their theft by the Swiss Guard, and his subsequent disappearance after a surveillance team filmed him at a local cafe having lunch with the disgraced Commandant of the Pontifical Guard. "They left the cafe and drove to a regional airport where they flew off in a private Cessna. The team couldn't follow. The aircraft's been located near Paris. Informants say the men reached Luxembourg City and are offering the papers to the highest bidder."

"I take it we are to retrieve those documents 'no matter what.' After all, as private contractors we're disposable. No post clean-up if things turn south."

"Of course." Levi waited a heartbeat. "No need for bizarre legal opinions that say it's okay to launch a cruise missile against a single terrorist, but it's not appropriate to put a bullet through their forehead, since that reeks of assassination."

Baker shrugged as if to say, *All right. I get it.*

Levi paused in acknowledgment of the silent message, then continued. "Naturally, the two Apollo crews and a few NASA technicians and scientists know what went down. Most of it anyway, and of course they've been sworn to secrecy. But even they're not privy to what's contained *within* the items that were found—*and* the ramifications." He swirled the contents of his drink and said as if reading a jury's decision, "As of this moment you and I are now the only two people other than Cohen and his security advisor, plus Roberts and Sullivan who have total knowledge. I can brief my team on many of the facts, but not on what's been predicted to occur." He paused. "An end. To everything."

Although he was a large man, Baker got up with surprising agility and went to the fireplace. He faced the flames. "Roberts won't whisper a word."

Levi nodded vigorously. "I agree. I met him a few times during my days with the Bureau. Helluva guy. He was an assistant director at the time."

"As for Sully—" Baker turned and faced Levi. "He runs Langley as if it were his private fiefdom. Never have trusted the man."

"That's good to be aware of."

Baker waved a hand. "So. We have a world-shaking mission on our hands."

"Yes, sir. And it's about as bad as it gets."

"But you and Dragon Team are good. I have total confidence in your ability to carry out your assignment." He tapped the ashes of his now-dead pipe into a sculpted marble ashtray. "When do you see your team?"

"I called them before I left the White House. We'll meet tomorrow morning."

"Excellent." Baker regarded Levi in silence while the fire popped faintly in the background. Finally he asked, "How's your health."

Levi had anticipated the question and wasn't offended. "I'm ten months out of rehab and thirteen months clean." He hesitated. "Not a day goes by that I don't consider doing it, though. But I'm good. Hell, I'd better be. Michael's on me like a hawk. He'll kick my butt if he even thinks I'm in search of a fix."

Baker chuckled in a manner that tried to downplay sensitive topics. "I'm certain Mr. Bailey would fulfill his threat, too." He returned to the wing chair and his scotch.

Levi said, "Heath? It was your duty to ask. I have no problem with it."

"Nor do I have a problem. Neither does the occupant of 1600 Pennsylvania."

"Yes, sir." Levi's face was a blank slate as he got up and stood in front of Baker to offer his hand. "Even so, I want to thank you again."

Baker held onto Levi's hand. "Nonsense. You're the one who deserves a ration of gratitude. Why? Because of what's inside you. Cohen saw it as well. It's why he regards you as a son."

"All because I knew how to say a Kaddish. And I'm not even Jewish."

Baker released Levi's hand. His face darkened. "I knew his son. You're identical to him in every aspect, except looks."

Left unmentioned as Levi put on his suit jacket was what Cohen gave him to cement their special relationship—the simple Star of David that belonged to Cohen's murdered son, and was now hanging from Levi's neck.

At the door, Baker said, "Keep me posted. Meanwhile, I have an appointment with a dialysis machine." Scowling, he opened the door and peered outside. "That's if my damn driver makes it here in time."

Levi checked the elegant Patek Phillipe strapped to his left wrist, recalling as he always did the day his wife gave it to him. "Speaking of time, I need to get going."

CHAPTER FOUR

. . . .

YURI BOGROV glanced at the million-and-a-half dollar Vacheron Constantin *Tour de l'Ile* timepiece that was attached to his left wrist by a thin alligator strap. Spurning the hour and minute hands, he checked the sunset indicator instead. It told him he'd better get going. Hawking up a lunger, he spit it to one side and moved on.

Gray clouds hanging tenaciously over the cemetery prevented the damp chill air from going anywhere except deeper into Bogrov's bones. In any event he'd spent enough time wandering this burial site for German soldiers who'd been killed in Luxembourg. It was gloomy even on the brightest days, but he'd still toasted his father with two glasses of vodka while standing, albeit unsteadily, near the headstone. The first drink had been for himself. Then he tossed back one for the father who could no longer enjoy a drink. Yuri Bogrov performed this act religiously whenever he flew to Luxembourg—and he'd had no intention of canceling the ritual on this of all days.

But today's visit was different, the motive simple: despite the six billion dollars he'd amassed since the U.S.S.R. ceased to exist—along with the secret police who had so effectively squelched major criminal enterprises—Bogrov didn't think his father would have approved of the manner in which he'd acquired his fortune. So he had come here to tell his father that he, Yuri Bogrov, distant relative of Boris Pasternak and son of a Russian peasant taken prisoner by the Germans and forced to serve as a soldier—that he had a plan, one that would compel his father to sit up in his grave and take notice of him for the first time ever.

Turning to go, he sank his hands into the deep pockets of his long, black leather coat and hunched his shoulders against the soggy weather before trudging through slick grass toward the waiting ZIL-41052. He'd bought the 1988 armored limousine—this icon of the Communist state—and had it shipped to Luxembourg to facilitate his visits. Boxy and cumbersome, the black beast matched both his coat and his mood. Drawing closer to the car, he nodded to Slavko. The hulking chauffer stood at the rear door in his trademark black suit. Slavko had a wandering eye, he pulled double-duty as a bodyguard, and he towered over Bogrov—a contrast that the short, thickset billionaire resented but had long ago resigned himself to.

Bogrov got in and sat next to the dark haired woman who had accompanied him. Reaching for a half-eaten bagel, he tore into it to absorb some of the alcohol while she touched long, tapered fingers to his pockmarked face. "It's good that you visit your father," she said with genuine feeling. "Family is everything."

"Shut up," he snapped. Wiping his mouth on his sleeve and leaving a smear across the fine leather, he glared at her.

"I know what is good and what is not. I need no guidance. Especially from someone such as yourself."

Slowly easing her fingers away, she settled deeper into her seat. "How stupid of me. Please forgive my pretentiousness."

Bogrov ignored her and told Slavko, "Take me to the fortifications."

Luxembourg City's ancient fortifications are a series of casements and fighting positions that surround the city. They were designed to repel invaders and are connected by tunnels. But now its casemates serve in vain, impotent even against the unruly tourists who flocked to the city—which is why Bogrov chose the tunnels for his rendezvous with the former Swiss Guard and his discredited commandant. It's also why he gave thanks for habitually visiting the fourteen twisting miles of tunnels, because his appearance on the surveillance cameras would be consistent with the former pimp billionaire's interest in historic sites, rather than an irregularity which might catch an investigator's interest.

"Remain inside the automobile," Bogrov told the woman. "I will not be long." Getting out, he glanced at the gray remnants of daylight and grimaced. Then he turned to Slavko. "Let's go. You have a torch?"

The large man pulled a penlight from a pocket and displayed it.

"*Khorosho.*" Bogrov patted a pocket containing his own penlight, then started off with a lopsided swagger for the yawning opening of a tunnel. Slavko fell in behind him. As they stepped inside, the cool air smelled of mold and human exhaustion. Then as they descended a stone stairway, their footsteps echoed against the massive rock walls before mixing with faint tourist voices from further down.

Bogrov stopped when the tunnel branched into three passages. In keeping with the layout of ancient fortifications, the tunnels were a maze meant to confuse invaders. But Bogrov and Slavko had explored this one yesterday, and they'd selected a suitable site for today's meeting—one that served his dual needs of encounter, and escape.

As they ventured further inside the labyrinth, Bogrov imagined a narrowing of the walls. He knew they weren't really closing in, yet his stomach flip-flopped. But he could never let Slavko know, so he strutted on until they reached the juncture he wanted. While coming to a halt he tilted his head toward a dim passage. Slavko brushed past him without a word. Seconds later the dark swallowed him whole.

Bogrov waited until Slavko's footfalls faded before nestling himself within a dark alcove chiseled into the wall centuries ago. Glancing warily at the confining spaces, he hunkered down inside his coat as an all-pervasive gloom enveloped him. At least the men he'd come here to see should arrive shortly.

Soon enough— much to his relief—he heard footsteps. Two sets. Leather soles. One had a higher pitch. He emerged from his hiding place as two figures materialized—a tall lean young man, and the older but still physically imposing ex-Commandant of the Pontifical Guard. The men stopped several paces away and showed no signs of fear.

Getting down to business, Bogrov asked, "What have you brought?"

The older man smiled in a way that said, *you don't impress me*. Then he spoke. "I have pages taken from the Vatican's Secret Archives." He jutted his jaw at the young man. "Johan removed them while the new pope was distracted. Although their absence has since been discovered, the Vatican has chosen to remain silent on the subject."

Bogrov skewered him with his eyes. "Why do they say nothing?"

The older man gestured toward his colleague. "Perhaps to avoid alerting us. But you see, we spotted the detectives sent to follow our trail. Hence, one may assume the Vatican knows they're gone. Once you see what the papers reveal, you will appreciate the Vatican's reluctance to publicize their absence."

"Absence? Not, stolen?" Bogrov glowered. "Do not mince words with me. Say what you mean, damn you."

The older man hesitated, then bobbed his head submissively. "Johan took the papers without authorization. That makes him a thief. But a thief of the highest caliber."

Bogrov stepped nonchalantly toward the former commandant until they were almost shoulder-to-shoulder, which put him in a position to block their escape. "You have brought the documents with you, *da?*"

Patting a jacket pocket, the old man smiled.

"*Khorosho,*" Bogrov said. "Very good. Now let me examine them." When the disgraced man produced the papers, Bogrov pulled a penlight from a trouser pocket and shined its narrow beam on them. Like most Europeans, Bogrov was multi-lingual and he readily deciphered the Latin. But when he came to the end of the last page his breath caught and his eyes got wide. "*Fuck.*"

The commandant smirked. "Quite. With this information, a man of your brilliance can control the destiny of the entire world. At least what will remain of it."

Bogrov's chest swelled with vain glory, but he needed time to absorb what he'd read. Finally he said to the older man, "Tell me how you came to be involved in this."

The ex-commandant described Johan as a devout Catholic and rising star of the Swiss Guard, one whose impeccable military record and good looks prompted the older man to lavish extra care and training on him. Then he uttered a brittle laugh. "You are no doubt aware that I stood accused of a rather tawdry incident. Untrue, mind you." He paused to let this sink in. "After the Vatican made an issue of Johan's allegiance to me, they told him he would be dismissed. So he took the pages as a guarantor of sorts. But upon reflection he chose the wiser course, which was to offer them to me." All at once the old man's hands became fists. "Now I shall have my revenge."

"How much?" Bogrov asked.

"Forty two million. In Euros. For you see, I wish to live in luxury until... then."

Bogrov scoffed. "You are quite insane. Why, that's... that's fifty million U.S. dollars. No, my friend. We must negotiate." Bogrov flicked his eyes at Johan. "But I am not accustomed to having others hover about while I conduct business." Pointing down the dark tunnel where he'd sent Slavko, he told Johann to step away while they talked.

Johan shook his head and didn't budge.

The Russian glared. "What do you wait for?"

The commandant said, "Perhaps he hesitates because your man is nowhere to be seen." Narrowing his eyes, he took half a step forward and dropped his voice an octave. "You see, Johan and I arrived well before our scheduled meeting.

We watched you enter the tunnel in the company of another. Your bodyguard, perhaps?"

Bogrov had anticipated this. The pair standing in front of him might have been dismissed from the Vatican, but neither of them had achieved their positions without intelligence and cunning. So Bogrov threw both hands into the air and all but shouted, "Of *course* my man accompanied me. But only into the tunnel entrance. I left him behind to guard against intruders. Surely you saw him back there."

"No," Johan began slowly. "We did not."

Bogrov frowned. He couldn't fool them after all. That meant he had to act, and act now. So he gestured toward the escape route and said triumphantly, "Ah. He approaches us even now... and from the very place I said he has been." With that, Bogrov boldly stepped to one side and waited until they gazed back the way they'd come.

It was all over in seconds.

Johan's eyes became saucers as Bogrov drove a knife into the base of his skull, just above the spinal column where it was softest. He twisted the blade viciously, but as Johan's lifeless body fell with a thud, the old commandant aimed a fist at Bogrov's chin.

Bogrov ducked. Snarled. Swept his knife in an arc.

Slavko appeared. While the old man's eyes followed Bogrov's steel blade, Slavko sprang into action and drove his own knife into his prey's temple with brutal force. The commandant gasped and dropped to the cold stone floor like a pallet of bricks, landing next to his erstwhile protégé.

Bogrov slid the papal pages into a coat pocket. Then he grabbed the old man's hair, and in one quick motion he drew the knife across his neck and severed the jugulars and both carotid arteries. Bright red blood jetted forth, spraying the walls.

Once the spurting stopped, Bogrov growled, "Get to work."

Slavko grunted and donned surgical gloves. Then he bared Johan's chest and shoved the knife into his left armpit. After making a cut all the way to the bottom of the sternum, he made a similar incision on the right side. Then as distant voices bounced against the walls, he sliced the skin from the sternum to the pubic bone—the 'Standard Y' incision that pathologists use when conducting autopsies. Next, he yanked the muscles apart to expose the underlying tissues, rib cages, and abdominal cavity. Using the knife, he removed the intestines, the stomach, and the liver. The gallbladder, kidneys, and pancreas were next. Tossing them aside, he methodically cut off Johan's reproductive organs and stuffed them inside the dead young man's mouth.

Then he went to the commandant's body. After exposing the belly he grasped the distal end of the intestines and started down the tunnel. He didn't stop until he'd pulled thirty feet of bowel from the body, which he let plop against the cold stone floor. The bowels, still warm, gave off a feint steam. Nearly at attention now, he waited until Bogrov joined him.

Neither spoke as they proceeded at a leisurely pace toward an even deeper tunnel juncture, where they turned right. A short time later they came out unscathed, unharmed, and uncaring. Turning cold reptilian eyes back to where they'd come, Bogrov prodded Slavko's arm. "Now let the investigators amuse themselves. Let them pursue their Jack the Ripper." Patting his pocket, he laughed for the first time in weeks, for he now held a secret that would plunge the world into a panic that promised to be far greater than any plague ever known, or any nuclear war that might erupt. Laughing again, he asked, "We did a bang-up job, did we not?"

Slavko was about to answer when an ear-splitting shriek erupted from deep within the tunnel.

CHAPTER FIVE

· ·

LEVI BAILEY—also known within the family as The Kid to distinguish him from Levi Hart—swept past the sleek, floor-to-ceiling ledgestone fireplace to where Michael Bailey lay sleeping on the couch. Gingerly taking hold of his father's bare ankle, the teen got ready to leap aside in case his father came up swinging. Then he tugged. "Dad. Nap time's over. You need to get your butt moving."

Michael Bailey jerked awake and sat up. After a cavernous yawn he said to his sixteen-year-old son, "Thanks." Stifling another yawn, he unraveled his long lanky frame and stood.

Levi's girlfriends almost always gasped when he introduced them to his blond-haired father. "Oh my God," they'd blurt. "He's gorgeous! He… he could be your twin!" Levi, who had his mother's brown hair but took after his father in every other respect, thought only that his dad's striking unspoiled face contradicted a cruel childhood combined with forty years of bold living. Now his father had been called to duty again, and Levi felt a tumble of emotions while watching him prepare to leave.

At least the routine never varied, for it provided the tall young man with a degree of reassurance: Michael would tell Levi to wake him on time, then stretch out on the couch for a nap. Upon getting up, Michael would pluck his shirt from the couch and proceed to the front door, where he habitually left his shoes and socks.

Now grabbing his shirt and padding to the door, Michael dressed and attached a badge to his belt near his right hip. Next, he fastened a holstered SIG Sauer P-229 pistol to the same hip. Finally, he grabbed his carry-on bag.

Levi got his father's larger suitcase and followed him from the coziness of their Maryland seashore home to the crisp autumn air outside.

After placing the bags in the trunk of the green 750 BMW that Uncle Levi had talked his father into buying, the Kid glanced at the spot where last year a bullet had nearly severed his father's carotid artery. Don't go, he wanted to say, but knew such a plea would do no good. So he tilted his head and squinted. "Take care of yourself, okay?"

Michael locked eyes with him. "Water polo season will be here before you know it, son. I know you're getting straight A's. And going to dances and spending time with your girl-friends is great." He held up a finger. "Even so, don't miss practice."

"You'll swim laps with me if you're back in time?"

Michael playfully cuffed the back of his son's head. "Don't I always?"

Levi opened his mouth to say something, then clamped it shut. After worrying a loose stone with the tip of his shoe he said, "Dad? Give Uncle Levi my best. Also? Tell him I said thanks." His mouth became a straight line and he didn't resist when Michael pulled him close and kissed the top of his head. Nor did he recoil in teen angst when his father released him and asked, "Know who gave me the greatest compliment ever?"

Levi knew the answer but deadpanned with, "Jennifer, when she told me I had a wicked-cool old man?"

Michael chuckled. "Well, that works. But you know what I mean."

Levi shrugged. "Hey, I'm just bustin' your balls." He grinned, but then his face darkened as memories flashed—his dad lying so still in the hospital bed; President Cohen coming into the ICU and saying that he, his younger brother Nick, and their mother were living proof that his dad had done well in life.

Michael finally looked sidelong at him to signal the ritualistic prelude to saying farewell. "Listen, try not to pick your nose in public."

"Try showering more often," Levi teased back.

"Try not to wear it out before you turn seventeen."

Levi fought to maintain a poker face. But then the sun broke out in his eyes and he smiled disarmingly as a blush broke out across his cheeks. "I guess ya got me there."

"A regular stud, huh? And modest at that." Michael play-punched his son's shoulder before turning serious. "Look after Nick. Take care of your mother."

"Aw, *dude*. Gimme a break will ya? Why do I gotta—" He flashed a grin. "Don't worry, Dad. I have his back. Mom's, too."

Michael drew his son into his arms again. This time he kissed his cheek. After Levi kissed his father's in return, they each took a step back and shook hands. Then Michael got into his car and drove off.

Levi Bailey watched him go. Just before the green car blended with the summer's residual foliage and faded away, he raised a hand in farewell, confident that his father was still watching in the mirror.

CHAPTER SIX

· ·

GRISLY MURDERS committed in high-density tourist attractions don't sit well in most places. But in the tiny Grand Duchy of Luxembourg, the *Tunnel Rippings*—as the media were already calling the slayings—surpassed any challenge the authorities had ever faced short of Germany's invasion. So great were the shock waves that rippled tsunami-like through Luxembourg City, that the Grand Duke himself summoned his Minister of the Interior, who in turn called the Director-General of the Grand Ducal Police, who then placed Pierre Roland in charge of the investigation—and the trim, thirty year veteran detective didn't like what he saw deep within the normally dark dank tunnel that was now lit by brilliant floodlights.

It wasn't the horrific crime scene that troubled Pierre Roland, nor the manner in which the bodies were positioned. It was his gut that caused his anguish—and not from gastritis. Squatting next to the deceased ex-commandant, he looked up at his assistant and muttered, "This was not a boat accident—and it wasn't Jack the Ripper."

The assistant's dark, angular eyebrows rose a trifle. "Sir? Boat accident?" She turned her head sideways, her conservatively rouged lips partly open.

Roland waved a dismissive hand. "'Boat accident.' From that great American motion picture, *Jaws*." He rubbed the end of his nose. "Something is not right, Hannah."

"Yes, sir. I understand." Hannah Dieter then said in a clipped manner, "You always stress, 'trust implicitly what one's body feels.'"

"Yes. *Exactement*." He stood and caught a crime-scene specialist's attention. Flicking a finger at the bodies, he said, "We are done here." While turning to go so the technicians could do their work, he pulled a silver cigarette case from his coat pocket and removed a non-filter *Gauloises* cigarette—a brand he had shipped from Spain after a lawsuit closed down the French manufacturer. He lit it with a silver Zippo, snapped the lighter closed with a flick of his wrist, took a deep drag, and exhaled. The strong aroma of dark Turkish tobacco made his nostrils flare. As the smoke drifted in blue coils toward the gloomy ceiling, he told Hannah, "No. This is not what it has been made to appear."

"How is that, please?"

"Simple. Two grown men. Forget for a moment that we've already determined who they are… who they once protected. From their identity cards, both saw military service. The younger man was stabbed from behind. And yet what does the older one do?" Roland raised his palms toward the tunnel ceiling. "Does he intercede while his companion is being attacked? Does he attempt to make his own escape? No. He does neither of these things. Why? Because there were two attackers." Turning as if to shield himself from an attacker, Roland said the rest of it. "*Voila.* He has no chance to run. The other assailant blocked his path. And this is when the killers commit their first error. For you see, sexual deviates almost *always* operate alone." Pointing at Johan's defiled body, he said quietly, "These two were not killed by a sexual predator. They were made to appear as if they'd been. This detail opens a wealth of possibilities." He dragged on the cigarette, then blew out a gray cloud.

CHAPTER SEVEN

. . . .

MICHAEL BAILEY made good time, arriving in Georgetown three hours after leaving his seaside home. Turning onto 35th from Prospect, he pulled into a strip of reserved parking spaces near a row of upscale townhouses. After looking for the jet-black Mustang 5.0 and the red '67 Mustang but seeing neither, he parked his luxury Beemer in a guest spot and pulled his bags from the trunk.

The air smelled of blazing autumn leaves, bans against burning be damned. That's the way of the world, he thought as he walked toward a white brick townhouse. Built in 1876, the stately two bedroom, one bath rental was a bargain at $4,500.00 per month. It was close to the nightlife and also near the house where they'd filmed *The Exorcist*.

At the door he turned and faced south. The Key Bridge fairly leaped into view. It spanned the Potomac and separated Georgetown from Arlington, and the Key Marriott just beyond the bridge loomed large atop a small plateau of prime real estate. Although it had been over a year since President Melchior's gruesome assassination at the hotel's entrance, people still stayed away in droves.

Finally fishing a key from a pocket, he opened the door only to wince when a shrill burglar alarm sounded. Hurrying inside, his long fingers danced across the alarm panel's keyboard. The screech ceased at once.

It was late afternoon, and topography and flanking buildings put the townhouse in shade, forcing him to flip a light switch to check the living room for anything amiss. He'd come to love this place. The air smelled to him of lemon-scented wood polish. The furnishings were masculine yet elegant. Silver-framed photos of Levi, his wife Anita, and their eight-year-old son adorned a fireplace mantel. But the photos were four years old. There were no current ones.

Other framed pictures sat on tabletops or hung from walls. There were shots of him and Nadia with their two boys. In a place of honor at the base of the stairs was Anita's favorite: a portrait of a scrawny, long-haired eighteen-year-old Levi Hart and a somewhat older Michael, the two of them in Speedos posing with their college water polo team. Here and there were more photos: Levi and Michael in police uniforms, or next to the sleek and swift 6-seat airplane Levi once owned. There were also gold-framed shots of Michael's two sons riding horses with their Uncle Levi.

Finally there was *that* photo—the one of a grinning, twentysomething Levi Hart holding Michael's future wife Nadia in his arms. At the time she was the love of Levi's life, and the photo had been taken when the brilliant brown-haired Russian Jewess shared a house with Michael and Levi. She had a Yale MBA but worked as a cocktail waitress and both men loved her. But when her greater feelings for Michael could no longer be denied, Levi stepped aside. Three years later he married Anita and they had a son whom they named *Michael*. Now there was only Levi. Michael closed his eyes, willing the dark thoughts away. Then he closed the door to *that* compartment and locked it.

Satisfied that all was well, he shed his shoes and socks and carefully positioned them next to the door, having learned long ago to be ready to run on short notice. Next, he unholstered his pistol and placed it on a simple chair of dark walnut. Finally, he took off his shirt and draped it over the chair. Now bare-chested and barefoot, he took his bags to the guest room, and after dropping them he went to the kitchen where he grabbed two bottles of a robust India Pale Ale.

Uncapping both bottles, he carried them to the living room and plopped onto the couch to watch ESPN. He'd just grabbed the remote when the rumble of a Mustang 5.0 engine reached his ears. Seconds later the front door burst open. Michael glanced at the DVR's clock and said without looking at Levi, "You're a minute late, brother."

"Wrong, donkey breath. *You're* early."

"Where's the other 'Stang? The '67?"

"Parked it inside a friend's garage. More on that later."

As Michael stood, Levi crossed the room in three quick strides and gripped his outstretched hand, then accepted the beer being thrust at him. After clinking the bottles together, they took healthy swigs.

"You've got great taste in beer," Michael said from the side of his mouth.

"So do you. Especially when I'm the one paying for 'em." Levi gave him a cop's once-over. "I see some things never change."

Michael glanced at his lean bare torso. "You know how it is."

"I know how it *was*. But you're not a street kid anymore. I believe you're worth what, six mill now? I'm thinking it means you can stop stretching pennies."

"I know, I know. Nadia says the same thing. And before you say it, yeah—there's also *that*." He flicked his gaze toward the shoes he'd placed next to the door.

Levi frowned. "I repeat, you're not on the streets. Your step-dad's dead. There's no need to fight off predators. *Or* make quick exits. Not anymore."

Michael wagged a finger. "Old habits."

About to reply, Levi hesitated. Then, "It's good to see you, Michael."

"Nadia and the boys send their love."

"Thanks. Give mine to her, as always." Tugging at his shirt collar, he said, "Give me a minute." Without waiting for a reply, he dashed upstairs and returned sixty seconds later, having changed into a black T, blue jeans and sneakers.

Michael's eyes instantly darted to Levi's exposed arms, like a guy checking out another guy in a public restroom.

Holding out his arms for inspection, Levi said, "I'm clean brother. Or do you also feel a need to check between my toes?"

"Should I?" When Levi frowned and began kicking off a shoe, Michael held up a hand like a traffic cop. "All right! Knock it off. Look, I care about you."

"Yeah? Well sometimes I get a little tired of all the concern. I—" Levi fell silent, then said with soft eyes, "Hey, forget it. I'm glad you care." Then he said while fixing his shoe,

"Did you know your boys called me every day while I was in rehab?"

"Yeah. They told me. The Kid also said to say thanks. Again." He shook his head. "That boy's got a knowing that's mature beyond his years." He fell silent and looked for signs of stress in his friend—along with clues to the call-out. Levi was cool and collected even in the worst situations, but Michael was picking up a different vibe. It wasn't like Levi to hassle him. Finally he asked, "Anything you wanna tell me about the callout?"

Levi's reply was short, sharp. "Whatever you need to know, you'll learn during tomorrow's reading-in." After an awkward silence he said, "Listen, I'm gonna order some Chinese. Why don't you break out the cards?"

"Sure. Let's make it gin rummy." Michael didn't say what he really thought—that he'd never seen Levi so rattled that he would change topics midstream, only to fall back on a card game to sidestep further discussion. He figured the element of *time* must have triggered the team's callout, a factor that lent a new sense of urgency.

CHAPTER EIGHT

. . . .

YURI BOGROV jerked awake, drenched in a cold sweat and with his heart thudding against his chest. Yet the woman at his side slept on peacefully. He wanted to smack her because of that, until he recognized the culprit responsible for his sudden misery.

Those damn papers.

Settling back, he wondered if he'd exercised wisdom in choosing where to hide them. The bedside clock read 3:41 AM. He'd have to wait ten more hours before the sun rose in Washington. Then he'd know if investigators had linked the tunnel deaths to the missing papers. But would Washington's officials tell the public what was in them? He doubted they would.

If the American officials didn't know—or if they did but had chosen to remain quiet—his task would be much easier. A world ignorant of the paper's revelations would increase his bargaining power, since he could threaten to use the facts contained in them to create global panic. After that, the island sanctuary where he'd stockpiled gold, food, and weapons would make him the most vital man on Earth—more vital than any pope or president—at least for the few months that remained before the world's demise.

As for those documents, he realized there'd be no more sleep for him until he checked on them. So he put on a silk robe and slippers and shuffled down a barren hallway to a guest room that never saw any guests. Switching on a ceiling light, he went to a chest of drawers and retrieved an old leather bag.

It wasn't much to look at. His father had carried his schoolbooks in it. There were places where the leather had flaked away due to age. But he'd done nothing to preserve it, letting it disintegrate instead—much as his father lay moldering inside his coffin.

Besides, the bag's decrepit condition should deter a closer inspection of its felt lining, where he'd secreted the papers that had been worth fifty million dollars to the ex-commandant. Bogrov scoffed; if only the fool had realized they were worth a hundred times more. Not that it had ever mattered. Bogrov would've killed him anyway.

He pulled out the documents and read them again. One raw fact remained clear: they made a claim that could not be proven. But like any agnostic who wants to cover his bases, Bogrov wasn't prepared to ignore it.

Replacing them, he gripped the bag as an emotional rollercoaster of feelings about his father washed over him. *Bah, he would never approve of what I'd done to get them. Yet he would respect what I'll do with them. That is a given—I'd have his respect.*

Unbidden memories of his own son abruptly surfaced. Anton was so young when his stupid mother put him inside the car and turned on the engine without opening the garage door. The fool woman then returned to the kitchen to retrieve the boy's coat, and while there she made a phone call, forgetting that her son was in the car with the motor running. Half an hour passed. By then it was too late. Tasteless, odorless and colorless, carbon monoxide lulls even its most alert victims into sleep before it kills. In this case, the gas left his son's sweet, chubby cheeks the color of a bright shiny cherry.

At the time, Bogrov thought he would die, too. He hadn't of course, though his heart had atrophied. So he'd slipped sleeping pills into his wife's tea after they buried his son, and once she was dead he summoned the police to report the tragic suicide brought about by inconsolable grief. If Bogrov already hated women when he married her, his venom had known few bounds since.

A wave of hot anger washed over him. He didn't need this—not right now. Tossing aside the bag, he returned to bed and shook the woman awake. As she rubbed her eyes, he demanded sex—a demand she certainly wasn't prepared to ignore.

After he finished with her, he decided to give her to Slavko for his own, distorted amusement. Following that he would eliminate her, as he'd eliminated his wife.

CHAPTER NINE

. . . .

NESTLED BETWEEN Georgetown and the Pentagon, Crystal City's streets are studded with stores, banks and business establishments. Scattered among them, there are nameless office buildings that provide secure sites where certain types of personnel can meet in secrecy. Since these buildings also house classified information, procedural methods are used to keep secrets secure. Intel professionals refer to these Sensitive Compartmented Information Facilities as SCIFs.

Traffic had been snarled since dawn but Tommy Wilkins eventually pushed past a glut of cars and delivery trucks to reach one of the SCIFs. At the entrance he showed his ID to an armed security officer and handed over his cell phone, then opened his briefcase and extracted two thumb drives, which he turned over to the officer.

"Do you have any other media that could carry information from this facility?"

"No, sir."

"Very well." After the officer passed it through an airport x-ray machine, he tilted his head toward a glass-topped pedestal.

Tommy placed his palm against it, opened his fingers wide, and held still until a small green light glowed. When a muted *beep* concluded the verification process, the officer passed him through a hardened door. Tommy then ventured down a series of sterile passageways before reaching *Room Eight* and pushing through its heavy wooden door.

It opened into what he thought was a richly appointed room, one of dark wood paneling, an elliptical conference table and deep leather chairs. Two men and a woman were there and he greeted them in turn: "Hack, Wild Bill; Monica." Placing his attaché case near the head of the table, he said, "Show me the coffee." When Monica pointed to a service tucked in a corner, he lurched for it and after pouring a cup he took a tentative sip.

It was hot stuff—Navy stuff—and somehow appropriate, for he'd handled lethal naval ordnance when he was a sailor. Spotting a bowl of creamers labeled, *Irish Cream,* he dumped one in and stirred until the coffee matched the color of his broad, round face. Raising the cup to his lips, he closed his eyes and took in the rich aroma before gulping some down. It was good and he groaned with pleasure.

Tommy was all about pleasure—both the giving and the receiving. But he was no people-pleaser. As his ex-wife once told him, "You're like Israel. Small and affable, but nuclear capable." Not that he was diminutive. He wasn't short but neither was he six-feet tall. Neither slim nor obese, he had what many politely called a husky build. He loved to fly but feared heights. Tommy had an open heart, and a receptive brain that boasted a keen intellect and near-flawless analytical abilities. He was also Levi's ATL.

He'd felt uncomfortable when Levi offered him the assistant team leader job. Levi had been Dragon Team's ATL. When he moved into the TL slot, everyone thought he'd give the ATL job to William "Wild Bill" Dentz. The tall rawboned retired SEAL had the credentials, and his moustache and resemblance to the actor Sam Elliott added to his qualifications—though everyone admitted that the movie star looks were just superficial indices. But Levi knew and respected Tommy Wilkins for what he'd once been—a hard-charging cop who'd worked the mean streets of Nasco City, a town on the Mexican border whose inhabitants referred to it as *Nasty* City.

Today marked the first time Tommy had been called out in his new role. But he wasn't nervous about how the others might perceive him, for as his beloved grandfather once taught him: *take your job seriously, but don't take yourself seriously.*

He was tasting the coffee again when Monica Mastronardi approached. Her unblemished skin lay taut over high cheekbones. Hair the color of midnight framed sea green eyes, and brushed the back of her neck like a whisper. Poised and confident and thirty years old, the former Hollywood F/X expert was lethal in any *dojo*. And last year she shot a terrorist to death. She asked Tommy, "What can I do to help?"

He ran a mental checklist. "I brought the non-disclosures for everyone to sign. If you wouldn't mind scanning the room for bugs, we'll be ready to proceed."

"Will do." She was about to turn away when she paused and looked sidelong at him. "Must be a helluva show coming for Levi to tell us to get our butts here pronto. I was in Kauai with my boyfriend." She rolled her eyes. "Well, ex-boyfriend now. But damn. I barely reached LAX in time to snag the redeye to Dulles."

A tiny man of Congolese descent stepped next to her and said in the relaxed rhythms of the Virginia Tidelands, "I had me the same issue." Quenton Jones — dubbed *Hacksaw*, or simply *Hack,* because he'd worked as a locksmith to put himself through William and Mary — had a masters in English lit, was fluent in Farsi, and could outshoot everyone on the team except Levi. He continued, "There I was, *forced* to endure *hordes* of Yankee motorists swarming the Dwight D. Eisenhower *interstate* highway system. Yes sir — and ma'am. They were like *hornets* with their *stingers* at the high ready." His eyes narrowed. "Something's up, guys. I got me a bad feeling. Why, I..."

Tommy held up a hand when he found Levi and Michael standing in the door. He shook his head. "You bastards — I'm damned if I heard you guys come in. And I was *listening* for that door." Peering closely at Levi, he cocked his head and wondered what had the TL looking so somber.

Wild Bill asked as he handed cups of coffee to them, "What's the word, boss?"

Levi grunted. "A big word, that's what." He shook hands all around, but upon reaching Monica he embraced her. After they shared some private words he kissed her cheek. All this could open him to charges of sexual harassment in most places. But these were high-speed operators whose bond permitted a higher degree of affection. Besides, he and Monica had a history — *and* she'd helped him quit heroin.

As Levi turned away, she rushed into Michael's open arms and kissed his mouth. They weren't lovers — not now or ever — but they did enjoy a deep friendship.

Levi finally announced, "We're it. Sawyer and Bedelia won't be joining us."

Hacksaw Jones said, "I shudder to think that either has fallen into disfavor."

"Sawyer's recovering from an appendectomy. Bedelia's pregnant." Levi flipped a palm back and forth. "I could've asked other teams to provide bodies, but it'll be better to proceed with just the six of us." He paused. "Once I read everyone into the mission I think you'll agree." Reaching into a pocket, he produced a thumb drive that must have been certified for entry and inserted it in a recessed USB slot atop the table. Then he caught Tommy's eye and inclined his head.

The ATL clapped his hands together. "Seats."

CHAPTER TEN

. . . .

BOGROV PUSHED away the lunch plates and checked his watch. It was 1:30 PM local time. That made it morning in Washington. If the Americans had connected the tunnel murders to the documents by now and decided to publicize the facts, the news agencies should begin reporting within the hour. Luxembourg by contrast was already a hornet's nest. Local media had done little more than babble *ad nauseam* about the Tunnel Rippings. But confident that the investigators would never trace the slayings to him, he decided to remain in town and conduct business as usual. Then he would return to Russia, and if by chance a Luxembourg detective did manage to tie him to the crime? He didn't care. Russia's current leader would rip an extradition request to shreds.

•   •   •

At that same instant Pierre Roland was guiding his unmarked police car down a narrow street. Glancing at Hannah, he raised a palm. "Tunnel surveillance photos suggest everything, yet nothing. None of the several dozen men, women or even children among the throngs of tourists appear suspicious."

Dieter shifted and straightened the pleats of her black wool skirt. "Yes, sir."

"The few people who did catch the photo tech's attention are easily accounted for. The usual suspects. No more, no less." He frowned as traffic slowed to a crawl. "Nothing extraordinary. Even so, the tech earmarked six people for further scrutiny. But they're all in business attire. None appear to be anything other than a person of *business* rather than a person of interest."

She nodded. "I agree, sir."

Drawing a deep breath, Roland recalled how the hairs on the back of his neck prickled each time he'd looked at the name of one businessman in particular: *Yuri Bogrov*. "Naturally we will pay a visit to each of them. But first we must see an old acquaintance of mine."

CHAPTER ELEVEN

· ·

LEVI SETTLED into his leather chair at the head of the table and said, "Tommy?"

"Yes, sir." The ATL opened a thin notebook and turned to the face page. "Okay, folks. We're going top secret in a moment." He made a tic mark inside a small box on the page. Moving to the next box, he intoned, "Everyone here has a Cobra Clearance and the required need-to-know."

He waited until each person acknowledged this before checking the box. Next, he gave the mandatory security lecture. It was clear, concise and simple: violating the terms of an SCI clearance posed potential penalties of fines, imprisonment, and even death.

"The terms of this SCI specify that the information we're about to receive cannot be disclosed for a period of forty years from today's date." After making another tic, he distributed non-disclosure agreements. It was routine and the Dragons barely glanced at the papers before signing them. Tommy gathered the papers, marked another box on his list, and looked at Levi—who'd signed his agreement at the White House.

"Thanks, Tommy. We're now top secret. Maintain OPSEC from here on." Once the team verbally acknowledged his call for operational security, he leaned back in his chair and propped his elbows on the arms. "If all life on Earth ended today, within thirty thousand years virtually all traces of human existence on our planet will be wiped clean. Buildings will have crumbled and become dust, their steel and iron supports dissolving into powder. Soil and vegetation would cover entire metropolitan areas. The pyramids? Even they will be no more, eroded by wind; swallowed whole by desert sands. The last vestige would most likely be the granite heads on Mount Rushmore." He scanned their faces. "So unless some intelligent life finds one of the *Voyager* probes with its sounds and images, there'll be no record of human existence on Earth."

Raising an eyebrow, he related most of what he told Heath Baker the day before, beginning with the Ranger recon missions and ending with the revelation of Apollo 10's moon landing. As the room stirred he leaned forward. "The reason behind the intrigue? It wasn't to beat the Russians to the moon for political purposes, although that did remain a part of the proposal to go forward. No, it centered on what the Ranger missions found and Apollo 10 confirmed. I'll now reveal the object that the crew examined."

Levi's chair squeaked as he pressed a button next to the recessed USB. A hidden projector came to life and displayed on the wall behind him an overhead image of a rectangular box. There were evenly spaced dots along the sides. A pair of what looked like giant domino *double six* tiles were laid end-to-end within the box.

"This diagram depicts a bird's-eye view of what was found, minus its roof."

Everyone leaned forward.

Michael peered at it and said, "Whoa."

"Whoa is right," Levi said. "This structure is seventeen and a half feet long by seven wide. It's built of titanium. Extremely light and durable."

Wild Bill said at once, "Meteorites contain titanium."

"They do." Levi pointed at the image. "The straight lines are the tops of its walls, looking straight down. The dots are the tops of columns. Analysts were understandably puzzled at first, until someone with a history degree realized it was an exact scale model of the floor plan for a temple in Corinth, Greece."

A ripple of excitement ran through the room as he pressed the button again. An overhead image of the Corinth temple appeared on the wall next to the diagram.

"The Greeks built this temple in the 6th century BC to honor Apollo, whom the ancients regarded as both an oracle and a sun god. The temple's dimensions are 174.86 feet by 70.07 feet. Run the numbers. The lunar object is a dead-on 1/10th scale version."

Hacksaw Jones pushed forward in his seat with a nervous energy. "There's a term for the manner in which the columns line up. They're called *pteron* columns."

"Yes," Levi said while pressing the button. The images shifted until the temple was superimposed over the lunar image. "As you see, the columns and the dots form an exact match."

"Damn." Hacksaw slowly shook his head.

Levi pressed the button again. The other images faded and were replaced by a grainy black & white close-up of a sphere about the size of a soccer ball. There were lines resembling Earth's continents etched on its surface. But the continents were a bit askew, and something resembling a polar ice cap covered much of the northern hemisphere. As a final point, the sphere itself was precisely centered within the temple-like structure.

Dentz peered at the image and tilted his head. "Calling card of some kind?"

"Yes. And, more." He pressed the button. An enlarged image appeared. "Take a close look at the sphere. Especially the area near present day Greece."

All five leaned forward as one. Hacksaw spotted it first. "A keyhole."

"Good call." Levi pulled up a better image. "It's a point of entry to the sphere. There's also a reason why it's near that cradle of civilization now known as Greece."

"The keyhole first," Michael chimed in. "What about it?"

"The Apollo 10 crew discovered the sphere but couldn't open it with what they had available. So special tools were engineered for Apollo 11."

Dentz snorted. "That's one small step for man, one giant turn for a screw*driver*."

Levi frowned. "Knock it off. None of this is amusing." He paused to let this settle in. "Armstrong and Aldrin opened the sphere. Inside were hundreds of glass rectangles similar to microscope slides. The slides had etchings. The first ones provided primers for the translation of another language. On subsequent slides are the words, and the words are breathtaking."

The only sounds in the room were the muted air vents and the hush of five people unconsciously holding their collective breath.

"Okay," Levi said. "Here it is. An ancient and exceedingly advanced civilization once thrived in the Mediterranean region. They first appeared on present-day Crete. They evolved rapidly and reached a point of development somewhat beyond our current level. And they did this some 250,000 years ago. Before an asteroid wiped 'em out."

Monica's voice carried above the others. "Mother of God."

LEVI WAITED for the shock to subside. "The *Ecos* as they're now referred to differ little from us in size or appearance. Here's an image that they etched onto a slide." He pressed the button. A representation of a man, a woman, a boy and a girl appeared.

The others drew sharp breaths almost in unison.

"They look like modern-day Greeks," Tommy said. "Only taller. Finer-boned." He squinted. "Spartan. Almost ascetic. I—" Tommy fell silent. Shaking his head, he admitted the obvious. "Sorry, guys. Guess I'm more than a little fucking overwhelmed."

"No more than I was," Levi told him. He hit the button. Another image from the etchings appeared. "They built aircraft, overland vehicles, and ships. They also built at least two spacecraft. But for reasons yet to be determined they never ventured far from the Med. The best guess is that too much of Earth remained locked in the final stages of an ice age. An add-on theory holds that spiritual or even mystical beliefs kept them close to home. One thesis posits that this was their Garden of Eden… possibly *the* Garden of Eden of both legend and the Bible.

"This argument has the added merit of the name given to them. *Eco*, short for ecology, much like today's Green Party. Turns out the slides are filled with references to environmentalism. For example, they didn't use fossil fuels."

Tommy shifted in his seat. "What'd they use for propulsion? Or energy?" He scoffed. "Electro-magnets?"

"Yes." Levi's quiet response commanded instant respect. "I can't vouch for the electro-portion. However, they were clearly advanced enough to harness magnetic force fields. It also appears that nothing went to waste. They were all about reusable resources. Visualize Native Americans using every part of an animal they've killed." He ran a hand across his face. "Other theorists think they did explore beyond their region, but backed off upon finding less developed humans—possibly for fear of altering their evolutionary development."

"Yeah," Hack said. "After all, are we not still discovering Amazonian tribes that remain locked in the Stone Age? For that matter, I could say the same thing about how the home of my heart in that grandest of all dominions, the Virginia Tidelands, remains locked in time." He squinted at Levi. "You said the Ecos were wiped out by an asteroid."

Levi watched his team exchange uneasy glances. "Yes, and it's the *raison d'être* for today's meeting. It's also what led the Ecos to the moon." He took a deep breath and slowly released it. "Back to those glass slides. The Ecos etched pictograms that were readily translatable. Even so, NSA's top cryptographers were given a crack at 'em as part of a double-blind experiment. Their findings were spot-on with the initial translations."

He wiped a hand across his brow. "According to the slides, the Ecos detected the asteroid while it was in deep-space. Their calculations nailed its diameter at four miles. Somewhat smaller than the Chicxulub asteroid that hit sixty-six million years ago."

"The one that formed the crater in the Gulf of Mexico," Tommy said.

"And killed off the dinosaurs," Michael added.

"Yes. So imagine this. They detect the asteroid. They develop and launch their version of the Hubble. And it saw a *lot*. More than they might've wanted to know." He grimaced. "Their space-borne observatory confirmed their calculations. The upshot was that things didn't look good. Naturally, they care about their children. They also want to perpetuate their bloodlines. Unfortunately, they see no escape. So they decide to leave something behind that says, 'Hey, we were here.' Hence, the sphere. Their version of *Voyagers I* and *II*." Seeing everyone nodding, he continued. "They assume Earth's total destruction. They build a rocket capable of bringing this record of their existence to the moon, and they deposit it safely for future explorers to find."

Hack said, "But the asteroid obviously did not wipe out our true-blue planet."

"No. But it wiped out the Ecos, while leaving the proto-Neanderthals unscathed."

"Why?" Monica asked.

"That's another big question. One theory has the asteroid carrying a deadly bio strain that killed the finely-developed

Ecos, but not the hardier Neanderthals. Or, that in the nuclear-like winter that followed, the less-developed humans took refuge in caves. One thing *is* certain. The Eco civilization did exist. This was proved after our research subs scoured the bottom of the Mediterranean…"

"Where they found magnetic evidence of an asteroid strike," Monica said.

"Yep. And years later, NASA sent the Challenger shuttle on a radar topography mission. As you might've already deduced, it located a prehistoric ocean basin created by the asteroid's impact. It's not as big as Chicxulub. But the asteroid strike still caused massive tsunamis, along with that nuclear-like winter." He paused. "They also found traces of their buildings… along with a rocket launch facility."

"There's more," Tommy said. "Gotta be."

Levi jabbed a finger at him. "There is."

CHAPTER TWELVE

· ·

"PLEASE. NO. What have I done? I love you, Yuri." The woman edged away, seeking refuge at the far end of the ZIL's back seat. As Slavko turned onto an even more dismal rural back road, she struggled against the leather restraints that bound her wrists and ankles. "Tell me what it is I've done," she wailed.

Bogrov's eyes snapped. All at once he slapped her and pointed a finger in her face. "If you open your mouth one more time, I will shut it for you." Glancing at Slavko's back, Bogrov wished he'd drive faster.

But she was not to be silenced. "Bastard! You used me. You gave me to that... that *thing* in the front seat. That *pig*."

"That's it!" The Russian's hand was a blur as he pulled a knife from a pocket and put the blade against her throat. "You doubt my word?"

Her breath caught. A foul stench filled the car as her bowels let loose.

Bogrov snorted like an enraged bull and yelled, "Pull over! This is far enough."

Slavko grunted and brought the lumbering machine to a stop next to a small field. Sprinting to the rear door, the huge man yanked it open and waited. The instant the woman opened her mouth, he jammed a handkerchief in until she gagged.

Both men working together pulled her bodily from the car. Then while Slavko retrieved a pair of shovels from the truck, Bogrov dragged the woman by the hair into the tall grass. He looked around. No people, no traffic; the only sound coming from the wind blowing through a copse of evergreens.

Slavko tossed the shovels aside, and while one eye wandered he called to his boss and pointed at the woman with a questioning look.

Bogrov said as if discussing the weather, "No. I'll do it." Getting out his knife, he pulled her head back. Then as he'd done countless times since he was a boy and given the honor of killing the family pig for Orthodox Christmas dinner, he slit her neck open from ear to ear.

The woman gasped for breath and flailed as her severed arteries spurted staccato streams of bright red blood. Finally she lay motionless.

Bogrov and Slavko quickly buried her, then tossed grass, branches and other detritus over the earthen mound.

Shuddering against the chill weather, Bogrov mumbled, "I cannot wait until we reach the island."

Slavko nodded. "Yes. The warmth will be most welcome."

The Russian wagged his eyebrows and jabbed the big man's arm in a rare show of camaraderie. "I could do with some coffee. How about you?"

CHAPTER THIRTEEN

· ·

IT TOOK everyone a few moments to process the information before Levi could continue the briefing. "In the wake of Apollo 11's mission, Nixon placed everything under ultra-tight security. But he had the foresight to establish a protocol to inform each ensuing president of the findings. However, acting unilaterally and possibly on impulse, Nixon, although a Quaker, revealed everything to Pope Paul VI."

"Why?" Tommy asked.

"Nixon concluded that proof of a previous advanced society would send shock waves throughout the world. There were religious implications. *Did* God make man in His image? Did the Ecos even believe in God as we know Him? Or did they worship a deity similar to Apollo? Their temples seem to suggest that the latter might've been the case, and since it's possible—not probable—but *possible* that pockets of Ecos survived, they might have passed along their beliefs to others… along with the designs of their temples. On the other hand, the designs are mathematical. Someone eventually would hit on the classic shapes. That's the more likely case."

Tommy perked up. "Sure. Even if the Ecos accepted their imminent demise, the instinct for survival prevails. Panic would've set in. They'd have taken to their planes, their ships." He worried an earlobe and said, "They'd have headed for the hills."

"That's the hypothesis," Levi said with a touch of admiration. "And since they had ships, it doesn't take a great leap to speculate that people must've trooped aboard one or more of 'em. They would've brought livestock along. Such a ship, caught up by the huge wave generated by the asteroid's impact and carried far inland, might even have triggered legends that are the source of Noah's ark."

"Or of Apollo," Monica replied.

Levi waved a handful of their non-disclosure agreements and dropped them to the table, then arranged them as a way to buy time before proceeding. Pushing the last paper into place, he looked up. "There's more. There are geo-political and ethnocentric issues at stake. Entire nations are unified under various mantels. Geographic in the case of Pacific Islanders. Cultural in the case of the Japanese. Religious..."

"In the case of Arab nations," Hack said.

"So if word of the Ecos' leaks," Dentz began, "whole cultures could implode."

"Which leads us to why we're here." Levi paused. "Five days ago a Vatican Swiss Guard discovered these facts in the Vatican's Archives and took them. The Pope himself notified Cohen at once. But too late. The guard had vanished. However, three days ago he and an accomplice offered unspecified priceless papers to the highest bidder. Now here's the thing. If word of a previous civilization is made public before people have a chance to assimilate this revelation, the world might go nuts."

"So Dragon Team's been given a task," Tommy said.

"You bet your ass we have. The Bureau and every alphabet agency you can name are searching for this pair. Once they're found however, our boys can't just waltz into another country and arrest them. However, *we* can snatch 'em. Why? Because we're government contractors and contractors are known to overstep boundaries." Levi then sank deep in his chair and said in a low tone, "We *must* find them."

Michael narrowed his eyes. "Must?"

Levi started to reply when someone knocked on the door. Dentz uncoiled his long legs to investigate. The door opened with a hushed squeal and when Levi smelled vanilla flavored tobacco, he said without looking, "Good morning, Mr. Baker."

The big man lumbered in and took off his overcoat, revealing layers of flannels and wools permeated with pipe smoke. He was a bit pale and his breathing was labored. "I've just left an urgent meeting with the National Security Advisor. One of the men who attacked the White House has escaped prison."

"*Whaaat?*" Levi sat forward.

"The one who drove the large truck..."

"Pete," Levi said at once. "Their tattoo artist. The one who inked me."

In order for the skinhead gang he'd infiltrated to fully accept him, Levi had to do drugs and get tattooed. Pete—who was also a gang enforcer—tattooed the barbed wire around Levi's ankle. Levi engineered an allergic reaction to the ink, but still ended up with a swastika on his forehead. Pete ordered hypo-allergenic ink, then covered Levi's body with henna tatts to give him the gang's "look." But the new ink didn't arrive before the gang attacked the White House—an attack that earned Pete a life-term in prison.

Levi asked, "How the hell did he get loose? And from Super Max of all places?"

"He faked a life-threatening illness. Pancreatitis. The prison doctor sedated him—or thought he had. Correctional officers were transporting him to a hospital when he overpowered them. This was two days ago, and yet we are only now getting word of it."

Levi frowned. "Wait. The car that followed me. It could've been him." He rubbed his chin. "Or maybe not. He respected me. Hell, he even liked me. My guess? He's gone into hiding." Levi then briefed the others about the quasi-chase.

"Remain alert." Baker told Levi. Then he said to Michael, "I've assigned *Blue Crew* to provide 24/7 protection to Nadia and your sons. Just in case."

Michael nodded at him in gratitude. The leader of Pete's gang had tried to kill Michael's family as pay-back for the failed White House attack. Blue Crew was one of Dragon Team's counterparts, and Michael knew it would cost Heath at least four grand a day, every day, to provide that level of protection.

Baker caught Levi's eye. "There's more. Finish your briefing. Then we'll talk."

Levi sensed a change in Baker since yesterday. The older man had become pallid, his breathing ragged and irregular—and yet his eyes revealed a new energy. Levi told him,

"I've just informed the team of our mission." Now he looked at his friends. "There it is. I wish I could tell you more, but you guys don't have the need-to-know."

"No. But they do need to be told this. The President crashed the meeting to inform me that our Swiss suspects have turned up dead. Someone else now has the papers."

Levi took a deep breath and blew it out. "Damn. That's a game changer, all right. This raises two possibilities. Criminals took the papers in exchange for a hefty ransom. Or, zealots have them and will use them to serve their own purposes."

"Precisely," Baker said. "We *must* recover those papers. However, there's nothing for this team to do until the European police identify the suspects. Our Bureau is working on the periphery—unofficially, of course. Once they have a clue?" He gestured at the team. "Then you'll move in for the kill. In the meantime rather than sitting idle, this team is going to Kwajalein." He looked around the room and waited.

"Kwajalein," Tommy said at once. "Central pacific. The world's largest atoll and site of a major WWII battle. It's now a U.S. base and is used to test the accuracy of our ICBM's. We also did much of the Star Wars work there." He looked at Baker.

"Our Navy veteran is dead on," the old man said. "*Kwaj* is populated by rocket scientists, technicians, and their families. Despite all this, it manages to remain a highly secure area. Hence, the brunt of the R&D on a major project is centered there. President Cohen thought it prudent for Levi to get an idea of the island's energy, for want of a better word." He exchanged looks with Levi, then shifted in his seat. "I talked Cohen into sending the entire team. You'll understand why at a later time. A much later time." He grimaced and wheezed. "Dragon Team will depart from Andrews tomorrow, but you'll be able to divert to Europe on short notice *if* a suspect is identified. Until the final travel arrangements are completed, I suggest we use the time to brainstorm."

Levi said, "Right." Facing the others, he pointed in the general direction of D.C. "Let's ask the same questions they're asking at the Bureau. First: what does anyone stand to gain through possession of the pope's documents?"

Dentz said at once, "He, she, or they are like art thieves. They wanna own the *Mona Lisa* even though they can never, ever tell a living soul about it."

"Ego," Michael chimed in. "A need to possess." He regarded Dentz with shrewd eyes. "Or... he, she, or *they* could be bent on blackmailing the Vatican." He waved a hand. "Occam's Razor. The simplest explanation is usually the best. The Church has big bucks. The bad guys want their share of it."

Hack edged forward in his seat. "Fix yer thoughts on this: I think it's one person. A psychopath. He—an' I'm sure it's a man—he didn't know what the Swiss guards were offering. But once he did? Boom. This guy *rocked* and *rolled*, baby. He didn't hesitate one damn *second* to kill *both* of 'em."

Baker coughed politely. "Nobody's yet asked the obvious."

Dentz said at once, "If the bad guy does sing, why can't the president simply disavow any of the claims."

"He could," Baker said. "Cohen is a fine man. He wouldn't care to deceive his constituency. But guarding a state secret is another matter. He'll deny the claims. The problem lies with the Pope."

Michael said, "I'm guessing he isn't eager to neuter the 'Thou shall not lie' clause of his contract. If the public confronts him, he'll concede the document's veracity."

Wiping his face with a handkerchief, Baker grumbled, "That's the thinking. Good job all around, Dragons. You've nailed the questions that were already asked." Exhaling loudly, he looked at the team. "Our people are working on a project. Call it a bunker-buster, if you will. It should stave off a global implosion even if word leaks. But more time is needed. There. That's the urgency." He grimaced. "They need at least a year to finish crossing their T's and dotting their i's."

"Got it," Levi said. Then he addressed the team. "You heard the man. We fly out tomorrow. In the meantime let's get back to asking devil's advocate questions." All of a sudden he stopped and stared at Baker, who was ashen-faced and tugging at his collar. Getting up instantly, Levi went to him. "Heath, what's going on? Talk to me."

"My fault, really. I might have contracted a mild sepsis. From the dialysis." Baker gasped. "Have a prescription but haven't found the time to fill it. I—"

"Do you have it with you?" Levi peered into Baker's eyes and was alarmed to see they'd lost some of their light of only moments ago.

Baker dug into a pocket and produced it. "Cephalosporin. An antibiotic." He opened and closed his mouth several times. "I'm not too proud to admit…"

"It's okay, Heath. Now's as good a time as any to call a break." Levi tugged the prescription from Baker's fingers. He considered sending Wild Bill but decided to clear his head with a short walk. While stepping away he told the others, "There's a mom and pop pharmacy two blocks from here. Take ten while I stretch my legs."

LEVI WAS leaving the pharmacy with the medication in hand when a silver Taurus with tinted windows slowed and then pulled to the curb a dozen feet ahead of him. Levi reached inside his suit jacket and gripped his pistol as yesterday's chase leaped to mind. His instant thought: it's Pete. And I'd better look for cover. Just in case.

The driver's window went down. Levi began to draw, but relaxed a bit when two hands appeared through the open window in plain sight. One hand manipulated the door handle. A rugged-looking white guy wearing an aging hippie's last-chance ponytail and a button down blue oxford shirt stepped out and locked eyes with Levi—and waited.

Levi studied him. *This guy's a professional. But a professional what? That show-the-hands bit is straight out of law enforcement. The question is, which side of law enforcement is he on?* He also waited.

CHAPTER FOURTEEN

· · · · · · · · · · · · · · · · · · · ·

"I'M HERE to discuss with you a matter of utmost urgency," Pierre Roland said to the elderly man who answered the door.

The man grunted. "Herr Roland. What do you want of me?" His skin was sallow and parchment thin. But his blue eyes had a fighter's light and he possessed a large frame that even the voluminous robe he had on couldn't mask. A simple silver cross hanging from his neck by a thin chain danced as he tilted his head toward Dieter. "Who is this?"

Roland said, "Forgive me, Herr Koehl. My associate, Frau Dieter. We have some questions to put to you." He gestured at the door. "May we?"

Koehl looked past Roland's shoulder, although there was little to see other than a tired street of overturned trash cans, patches of sparse grass, and a distant skyline of modern apartments. Koehl stepped aside wordlessly to let the investigators in.

Once inside, Roland paused. The apartment's main room was as spare as the street, and it smelled of dust and disinfectant. The walls were bare but for one, from which hung a huge Crucifix of ebony with an ivory Christ figure. Two large windows faced the street and Roland felt certain that Koehl sat next to them for hours, watching, looking; searching. But for what? Or for whom? Roland thought he already knew the answer, but good manners forbade him from going directly to the point.

"If you please." Koehl pointed to a pair of simple wood chairs set side-by-side. "May I offer a refreshment?"

"Yes," Roland said at once. "I will have a coffee." He turned to Dieter. "And you?"

"I don't know…"

Roland cut off the young assistant with an unseen jab of a finger to her ribs.

"I don't know… if you have tea. But if you should have a tin of Earl Grey, that would be most wonderful." She regarded Roland with a look that could only mean, *See? I know to accept our host's offer to share his meager resources.*

"Very well," Koehl said. "If you will excuse me."

After he disappeared inside the kitchen, Roland heard the muted clatter of a coffee pot, a tea kettle, and cups and saucers. When Koehl reappeared before anything could possibly be ready and begged his guests' indulgence, Roland watched him shuffle down a dim hallway before vanishing once again.

Koehl returned two minutes later dressed in a brown threadbare men's suit jacket over a white shirt that had yellowed from too many washings, and blue worsted-wool trousers with frayed cuffs that whisked the tops of ancient brown wingtips. He passed Roland and Dieter without a word and entered the kitchen. After another brief clatter of cups and saucers, he came back bearing coffee for Roland and tea for Dieter.

Brandishing the tea cup, he addressed Dieter. "Earl Grey. As you wish. Milk?" When she held up a hand and smiled, Koehl pivoted slightly and handed the coffee to Roland. "Two sugars, if memory serves."

"Two. Yes. How kind of you to remember." Roland waited while their host took the lone chair across from them.

Koehl sat ramrod straight, with feet flat on the floor and hands atop his knees.

Roland said, "If I may." Reaching inside his suit jacket, he pulled out a five by seven photo and held it up. "Do you know this man?"

Flicking his eyes at the photo for a micro-second, Koehl made a *tsk* sound. "But of course. He is Yuri Bogrov, billionaire Russian mafia scum."

"Quite so. Now then. You visit the fortifications often, do you not?" Roland sipped his coffee without taking his eyes from Koehl's face.

The old man frowned. "Yes. And to the next question you are about to pose, the answer is also yes—I see Bogrov often. He has a fondness for the ruins. The tunnels above all." He emitted an eerie laugh. "Above all. Get it?"

Roland showed no reaction as he took another sip. "I think perhaps I do not need to put to you my next question."

"No. Yes."

Dieter cocked her head. "No, we do not need to ask?"

"No, you needn't ask. And yes. I saw him there." Koehl's fingers tightened around his kneecaps. "I saw him directly before the murders, and shortly after." With a pained expression he added, "Now I suppose you wish to question me as to his demeanor, his appearance, and his... what not. I shall save you the trouble. He did it."

Roland raised the cup to his lips, paused, then lowered it. "Tell me why."

Koehl sneered. "You ask me *why*? You, of all people? Perhaps my friend, you should tell me *why* I know he is guilty of the crime."

Suppressing a smile while balancing cup and saucer atop his knee, Roland reached inside his jacket and produced his silver cigarette case and Zippo lighter. Holding them up, he arched his eyebrows.

"Of course you may," their host said.

"*Danke, mein Kapitän.*" Roland lit the cigarette, then dragged deep and exhaled through his nose, causing the smoke to flow down, then upward as a rank cloud. "You know he is guilty for the simple reason that you maintain ties with your colleagues of the 1960s. They in turn are aware of the whispers, the... mutterings of a grand theft from the Vatican. But a theft of what? That, nobody yet knows." He puffed at his cigarette and exhaled slowly and evenly. "However, you've heard even more beyond the whispers. Is that not so?" He looked shrewdly at Koehl.

"Have no fear, Herr Roland. You will not let slip anything I should not know." Sitting like the statue of William II atop his horse in nearby William Square, Koehl squinted at Roland. "I have heard about the dismissals. Of the younger one, whom I did not know. And of that... *fiend* who dared call himself Commandant of the Papal Guard." Koehl's eyes flared, and his hands turned to fists. "Commandant. Bah!"

"But you knew him," Roland prodded.

"*Natürlich.* We came at the same time to serve Paul the Sixth. I, with honor. He, with dishonor. He debased the very Guard which pushed him to prominence. Until..."

"Until he got caught, as the Americans say, with his pants down."

"Literally. On his knees, seeking to provide sexual gratification to a younger member of the Guard." Koehl's eyes burned. "An intoxicated, semi-conscious young man who had no memory of what had happened." Agitated now, he shifted and said, "What he does in his private life is of no concern to me, for as you've always known, I too am homosexual. But inside the Basilica? And to a helpless young man? No. That I cannot forgive."

Roland blew a steady stream of smoke toward the ceiling as he peered at Koehl. "Yes," he said. "The very type of devious human being whom our dear Bogrov would feel drawn to."

A curt nod, nothing more. Koehl pressed his lips tight.

While holding the cigarette between thumb and index finger, Roland asked, "So. You in your own way will assist me further, yes?"

Koehl's mouth worked soundlessly until he produced a clotted, "Of course."

ROLAND AND DIETER stepped onto the street five minutes later. It took that much time for Koehl to thank Roland once again for what he'd done as a young police officer conducting a foot patrol of the fortifications when he first encountered Koehl. The old man had been gazing at one of the casements as if transfixed, in clothes that were little more than rags. But Roland had touched his fingers to the bill of his cap and bade him a pleasant afternoon, before asking if he could assist him in any way.

The devout Catholic Koehl, who despite his family's great wealth had chosen a vow of poverty, never forgot the young Roland's offer—one Koehl had said could only have come from a pure heart, where God had intended such offers should originate. Later, Roland learned who Koehl had once been—a Swiss Guard since 1967 under Pope Paul VI, until 1991 under John Paul II. And not just any member of the Swiss Guard, but a stellar leader who never asked his men to do anything he'd not yet done. He'd led from the front—the hallmark of a true leader—before retiring to the rear lines, content to make his daily journey to the old city. At least that's how Roland explained it to Dieter. He fell silent, then added, "Koehl's insight validates what I already felt about this case. I think he will be useful later on... although I am not certain why this is so."

"I do know why," she said. "It is as you say. Trust one's instinct. I also believe he will be useful."

CHAPTER FIFTEEN

· · · · · · · · · · · · · · · · · · · ·

THE MAN kept both hands in sight as he moved away from the Taurus to the sidewalk. "Leo Ryan," he said. "I'm a reporter for the *Post*."

Levi squinted as he let go of the pistol grip. "The *Washington* Post?"

"Mr. Hart, you've nothing to fear. Not from me." He offered an affable smile.

"My name's not Hart. And you didn't answer my question, Mr. Leo Ryan."

"I'm with the *Post*, yes."

"Stop dicking around. Be specific."

"The *Washington Post*," Ryan said hurriedly. "Okay?"

Levi didn't believe him. "Show me your press credentials."

"They're in my back pocket." He raised an eyebrow. "May I?"

He had a pleasant face and a relaxed stance. Which is precisely why Levi remained on guard. "Sure."

Ryan produced a laminated card. "Here you go." As pedestrians jostled for position, he approached slowly.

"That's far enough," Levi said when Ryan was still six feet away. The edges of laminated cards can be filed to a razor sharpness and swiped across an unwitting victim's throat. Levi glanced at the credentials. "It says *Washington Post*. But with today's computers?" He studied Ryan more closely. Outdoorsy, despite the tree-hugger ponytail. Brown leather jacket over the blue button-down, but he also appeared capable of wearing a tuxedo with equal ease. "At any rate, whether it's genuine or not I'm afraid you've got the wrong person. My name's O'Toole."

"I know who you are, Mr. Hart. I…"

"Are you hard of hearing? My name's O'Toole."

Ryan made a show of drawing a deep breath. "Mr. Levi Hart. Your hair's grown back. The Swastika on your forehead's been removed. But the eyes are the same. Yep. The same pretty boy I saw at the Castle that day."

Levi instantly translated. *Castle* was the Secret Service code name for the White House. This guy talked the talk, but was he truly an insider? Or had he plucked it from the internet? Levi frowned. "Get to the point."

"I learned your name through my sources. I have sources in the Vatican as well. I heard about a momentous incident. Don't know what it is yet. But I will. Then who do I spot leaving the Castle yesterday? You. And you're an operative. Me? I'm a reporter. I saw a story. Tried to catch up to you. But you outdrove me." He smiled.

"Save the lube for some other guy's butt. What is it you want?"

Ryan rolled his eyes. "I told you. A story. It's why I staked out your home last night. Yeah, and I saw your colleague arrive. A certain Mr. Bailey." He leaned slightly forward at the waist. "It's why I've been circling the block while waiting for you to pop out of whatever SCIF you got to after I lost you in the rush hour traffic. You're involved in something. Something big. Aren't you?"

Levi could've fallen back on a lame reply — that he'd been to the White House for a social event. But he wasn't the type to be pushed into such a subterfuge. It would mean yielding to Ryan's determined questioning. Instead, he used a response that people with top secret clearances resort to. Executing an exaggerated shrug as traffic whizzed past, he said with a blank face, "I don't know what you're talking about."

Ryan snorted. "Sure you don't. And I'm the Easter fucking bunny."

Levi glared. "That's it. Outta my way, Bugs fucking Bunny." He started walking.

"It's a slow news day," Ryan said after him. "My editor's looking for filler. An item about missing papers and operatives from the shoot-out at the O.K. Castle popping up will catch his attention. I guarantee it."

Levi stopped and looked him over from head to toe. "Oh, I get it. So which one are you? Woodward? Or, Bernstein? Maybe a combination. Woodstein. Or Bernward." He scoffed. "Go play with your dick somewhere else." He started walking again.

Ryan called after him. "You know, Levi. At the end of the day you're gonna have to ask yourself if it was worth it to blow me off — especially after my piece hits the streets."

At the end of the day, if you knew what I've yet to tell my own team, you'll be lucky if I don't cause you to disappear from the face of this planet. "Sorry, pal. I get my news from the *Wall Street Journal*." He paused. "But if I do decide to switch allegiances, I know where to find you." He gave the reporter a look and added, "Mr. Leo Ryan—of the *Post*."

CHAPTER SIXTEEN

· ·

"PULL OVER here and park," Bogrov said. Slavko steered the bulky black ZIL toward one of the numerous tunnel entrances. "I have spotted a surveillance team. Now I shall screw with them."

The late afternoon crowds were unusually heavy for a day in which the damp chill caused their breath to frost. Yet the Tunnel Rippings still dominated the headlines and the event was drawing an abnormal number of visitors, since as anyone who's seen *Perry Mason* knows, killers like to return to the scene of the crime.

As Bogrov emerged from the limo a man muttered, "Euro trash." The Russian ignored the slur. Instead, he squinted at a wan sun peeking from behind leaden clouds. Hugging himself against the cold, he marched down a walkway along the ancient wall, stopping at times to read the historical placards.

After half an hour of this, he walked a circuitous route through growing crowds and even gloomier skies until he reached the limo. "Take me to another tunnel. Choose one at random. But take a route that will leave our shadows snarled in traffic.

Slavko's eyes—even the wandering one—appeared in the mirror as he nodded and started off. Luxembourg City's center area is a maze of twisting, turning roads and a hive of activity during the work week. He used the ZIL's intimidating bulk to elbow his way through the worst of the traffic. At one point the wandering eye was reflected in the mirror, followed by a deep grunt. "They are locked tight." Flashing a grim smile, he bulldozed through an opening up ahead, turned a corner and stopped at a tunnel entrance.

Bogrov uttered a harsh laugh as he got out and strutted down the sidewalk, aware of a surveillance vehicle hurrying past traffic and stopping nearby, but not before the Russian entered a familiar, waiting tunnel and dropped from sight.

CHAPTER SEVENTEEN

. . . .

PIERRE ROLAND had put in a long and arduous day. His stomach told him it was time for dinner. One glance at his office clock confirmed that it was indeed time to leave. So when there was a knock at the door he frowned and called out impatiently. "Yes?"

The door opened with a squeal. That much was normal. But he was taken aback when the Director-General of the Grand Ducal Police stepped inside, accompanied by a sixty-ish man in tailored clothing that all but shouted *American* to Roland's practiced eye.

"Excuse me," the Director-General said. Then he raised his eyebrows in a *may we enter* way that could not be refused.

Roland stood at once. "Please come in. Do be seated." He urged the Director-General toward a fabric covered chair.

But instead of sitting, his superior closed the door and stood still.

Roland asked, "May I offer you gentlemen coffee, perhaps?" An ancient service near his desk emitted a faint odor of too-old coffee. He'd have to make a fresh batch.

The Director-General bobbed his head. "Thank you. But no. We shall only trouble you for a moment." He pointed to the stranger. "May I present Mr. Stephen Boyd, United States ambassador to the Grand Duchy of Luxembourg." Shifting the introductions with practiced ease, he told Boyd, "Please meet Pierre Roland. He is my finest investigator."

Roland said while taking Boyd's outstretched hand, "I am pleased to make your acquaintance." He waited until his guests were seated before settling back into his desk chair. "To what do I owe the honor of this visit?"

Boyd sat with the ramrod posture of a British brigadier and pinned Roland with his eyes. "This visit is a matter of great importance. It must not go beyond this room."

Roland raised both hands. "But of course."

Boyd looked to the Director-General, who picked up the cue. "A team of American counter-terrorist operatives will arrive within a week's time."

Roland said, "The Tunnel Rippings, no doubt."

The Ambassador revealed a slight smile. "Your government assured me that you were the best. You've just confirmed their trust. Yes. The team has a task to perform."

"A task?" Roland leaned forward.

Boyd tilted his head to one side, his eyes wary. "Their mission is so highly classified that not even I am aware of their assignment. Nevertheless, I've been assured that their goal is of paramount importance. They will also be armed."

"This has been authorized by our government," the Director-General interjected.

Boyd offered a courteous smile. "The team will be at your disposal, and will assist in any way possible."

"But I am not to dismiss them out of hand. Nor am I to put national pride ahead of the larger goal." Roland rubbed his long jaw. *Just what I need. Experts from the Land of the Giant Waistlines.* "I am also to assume that if they question a suspect with, shall we say, uncommon dynamism, I am to look the other way."

Boyd said, "Thank you for sparing me the need to resort to dramatics." Then his face hardened. "Sir, make no mistake. Neither my government nor I would ever presume to ask so much of you and your sovereign nation had we not the need. I can only pledge to you that the person or persons responsible for the slayings represents a danger to the world that is of such a magnitude as to stun the imagination."

A shudder ran through Roland. He'd dealt with the powerful along with the meek all his life, and knew when officials were being pretentious and when they were being anything but. This Ambassador came across as *healthy*. He was also profoundly alarmed, but of what or by whom, Roland had no way of knowing. He made an instant decision and jumped to his feet. "I am at your service of course, Mr. Ambassador."

CHAPTER EIGHTEEN

· ·

SEVERAL TIME zones to the east, Michael studied Levi's gait as he entered the secure conference room. His guts might be doing flip flops over today's revelations, but as a retired police captain he saw things that untrained eyes dismiss as insignificant. "You're moving with the blinding speed of a sloth on Librium," he told Levi. "What'd you get into between here and the pharmacy?"

Levi said while going to Heath Baker's side, "On my way back a car tailed me." He gave Baker a direct look. "Took me a few minutes to check-out the driver."

"Needless to say, it wasn't Pete."

"No." Levi handed the antibiotics and a bottle of water to him. After Baker swallowed a capsule, Levi said, "Turned out to be the guy who ate my dust yesterday. Claims to be a reporter for the *Post*. He might even be legit. One thing's certain—he's caught wind of a story out of the Vatican. Another thing. He knows who I am and what I do. I tried giving him the brush-off. He didn't buy it."

Baker asked, "What's his name?"

"Ryan. Leo Ryan."

The old man barely disguised the disdain in his voice. "Leo Ryan. Son of the one and only Senator *Rand* Ryan. Jesus."

Levi all but sneered. "*That* nut job. Now it makes sense."

"Like father, like—" Baker made a face. "The son's a reporter, all right. A discredited one. Certainly not with the *Post*." He leaned back in his chair and said to the ceiling. "Police reporter. Some newspaper in Iowa. Good at his job. Wrote first-rate copy. Which is why it's so difficult to understand why he falsified a story."

Levi said, "I thought there was something fishy about him." He made a sound. "It explains why he's versed on police tactics."

"Why do you say that?" Michael asked.

"The way he approached me. He's nobody's fool. And he does have sources."

"Probably trying to hitch a ride on the comeback express." Baker sat straight and looked at the team. "This story would do it."

Tommy asked, "What do we do about him?"

"For now?" Baker paused. "Nothing. This team will be out of here by tomorrow. In the meantime, I'll alert the Bureau. They'll want to be aware of his actions."

"Bottom line," Michael wanted to know, "what if there's no controlling him?"

"We make him disappear," Levi said. "There's too much at stake. He—" Levi clammed-up. The others still didn't have all of the facts that he'd disclosed to Baker.

The older man said, "We're getting ahead of ourselves… although it's refreshing to note the level of dedication to the task. Now for another subject from this morning's meeting.

Our ambassador to Luxembourg is meeting with its law enforcement authorities about the murders. When you leave Kwajalein, you'll go there to assist them."

"Damn! We'll end up sidelined," Dentz muttered.

"Not if we charm 'em," Levi quipped. "All right, everyone. Let's brainstorm awhile longer. Then we'll get ready to deploy. Next stop: Kwaj."

Michael shook his head in wonder at his best friend's ability to remain calm and focused. But he'd known this about Levi since college, and from their days working the streets as cops before Levi moved on to the FBI. Later, Levi was in Baghdad's Green Zone one night when he came upon a former SEAL who was doing security work. Levi told him not to go down a certain street. The man didn't listen. When a terrorist popped out of a doorway and took aim at the dismissive operator, Levi put a 9mm slug between the bad guy's eyes. It turned out that the ex-SEAL worked for Baker, and after the men's tours were finished he introduced Levi to his boss. Levi in turn recruited Michael—and last year during an infamous shoot-out with terrorists, Levi shielded a mortally wounded Michael with his body while bullets ripped the asphalt around them. Meanwhile, Monica confronted the terrorist leader and shot him dead. Now here they were, on the cusp of an even greater event, and Michael wondered how he could ever look his family in the eye if he failed in his mission.

The mission. He renewed his vow to do whatever it took to protect his family from a world that might fall into chaos—and glancing at Levi, he saw his friend nodding at him as if reading his mind.

PART II

. . .

Kwajalein Atoll

CHAPTER NINETEEN

· ·

KWAJALEIN ATOLL is a remote chain of coral islands buried deep within Micronesia. It's a genuine tropical paradise whose islands possess exotic, textured names such as Omelek, Gagan, and Illeginni. Coconut palms sway in balmy breezes and furiously blue, green, and turquoise waters compete with talcum powder beaches for the eye's favor.

The islands are also a target. Once every two months or so, the United States test-fires an Inter-Continental Ballistic Missile—an ICBM—aiming it at Kwajalein where the tracking and telemetry equipment that sprout from beneath the palms possess equally alien appellations—Altair and Tradex and Super Radot among them.

Pacific atolls are named for their largest island, and at 800 acres Kwajalein takes the local prize for length and girth. Half of those acres are taken up by a giant runway. The remaining land houses 5,000 Americans. Located halfway between Hawaii and Australia and rising a mere five feet above sea level, the remote island supports buildings ranging from small homes to phased-array radar systems; from an elementary school to a senior high; from a fine-dining restaurant to shops and scuba facilities. Of the ninety-some other islands in the atoll, the U.S. controls nine and they serve as components in a ring of testing, tracking, and telemetry stations that surround the lagoon, becoming in effect a huge catcher's mitt designed to catch incoming dummy warheads.

Geo-politics aside, Kwajalein remains an isolated lagoon, and isolation serves to buffer probing eyes. It's why a super-secret R&D project that dwarfed Reagan's Star Wars had been moved there, so it could remain out of sight and out of mind.

Levi blinked against the harsh glare of a noon sun bouncing off coral sands as he stepped from the cold interior of a U.S. Air Force C-17 into a sauna—for that's how it felt with his first step onto a tarmac baking beneath the tropical sun. There was no jetway in sight, only a large all-metal stairway that could be positioned snug against fuselage doors for descending passengers, who then simply walk across the tarmac and into the terminal building. Or in the case of military transport aircraft, an internal set of steps is triggered, after which access to the terminal is equally straightforward.

Dragon Team entered the Arrivals Area where an armed security officer verified their paperwork. Following this, he issued temporary IDs granting unrestricted access to all areas of the atoll. Next, he delivered a security briefing during which he admonished them against taking *any* photographs. Finally he said, "Be careful until you're acclimated to this sun. It'll fry you within fifteen minutes." Then he showed them to another room where a tall tanned graying man in an aloha shirt, khakis and soft shoes waited with an open smile and an outstretched hand.

"Jeff Davis," he said. But after shaking each of their hands the smile vanished. "I've been given my marching orders: brief you on the 'gizmo' and give you face time with it. Beyond that I'm to ask zero questions."

It had taken Dragon Team twenty-two hours to reach the atoll, which lay on the other side of the International Date Line. Despite being hungry, haggard, and jet-lagged, Levi said, "Thank you, Dr. Davis. Shall we get started?"

Davis maintained a poker face. "Hmm. I didn't introduce myself as 'doctor.' You clearly did your homework." With that, he took them to a white van and drove along narrow roads teeming with bicycle traffic until they reached a white, two-story operations building built upon crushed coral and nestled between sheltering palms. Levi had it down by now: everything was painted white as protection from the all-invasive sun, people got around by bicycle, and motor vehicles were only used to move large loads—or large numbers of VIPs.

An armed security officer at the building's entrance examined their IDs despite Dr. Davis' assurance that they were "okay." Levi respected this level of professionalism. But when the guard finally let them inside, Levi's body seized-up. *Damn. I've stepped from a sauna into a meat locker.*

"Sorry," Davis murmured. "I should've told you to bring jackets. The a/c's kept low. Sensitive electronics and all that."

Davis spent twenty minutes explaining the systems integration studies that he and other teams were working on, before segueing into a discussion of rocket propellants, guidance systems, and the nuclear warheads—the *vehicles* as he called them—that can be fitted to ICBMs. Then he dropped his voice so low that the team leaned forward. "We're experimenting with laser-armed vehicles that could be used against large targets of great mass. An asteroid, perhaps. You know… just in case."

Levi knew what he meant. *Just in case* is a mantra known to all who stand a vigil against both external and internal threats. He also figured Dr. Davis might be privy to any hypothetical asteroids, if any, that could become the target of a laser—or nuclear warhead-equipped *vehicle*. He also trusted Heath's peculiar decision to send the team here.

Davis then drove them to the inter-island air terminal, where a specialist briefed them on safety procedures before guiding them to a waiting Lakota. Painted fire engine red—not white—the four-bladed, twin-boomed, twin-engine helicopter was already running, its two pilots watching idly as their passengers climbed in and buckled-up.

After a ten minute flight over small emerald-green dots of land set amid swirling ocean waters, they circled a thirty-acre island that was nearly devoid of vegetation. It was studded with buildings and antennae, and when Levi spotted a seventy-foot high, man-made hill with a flat surface, he guessed it was a concealed rocket-launch facility.

"Welcome to Meck Island," Davis said while the turbine engines wound down.

A white van awaited them. After a brief drive through sweltering heat, they stopped in front of a security gate. Two officers armed with M-16s huddled over Dragon Team's IDs before facing each other and making a thumbs-up. Levi figured it meant that unless both agreed, a single thumbs-down would deny them entry.

Once they were passed through, Davis led them through a solid gray steel door and then into the artificial hill, where Levi saw his hunch vindicated: it was a launch facility—and a rocket loomed ahead of them.

Davis described the shockingly small rocket as, "One of numerous super-efficient exoatmospheric kill vehicles of both the theater and ballistic interceptor variety. As you probably know," he continued, "exoatmospheric pertains to the nearby regions beyond Earth's atmosphere." He went on to explain the concept of testing and evaluation prior to building super-laser vehicles capable of reaching much further. Gazing steadily at Levi, he finished in a quiet voice, "Much further. Even beyond the moon—and we've reached a 55 percent success rate."

Levi deduced that a sense of urgency drove Davis and his colleagues to succeed. Levi wasn't surprised, for in the world of shadows and secrets, men and women accept their orders at face value and throw themselves body and soul into their work. Seeing all this, Levi abruptly understood the journey's purpose—to give him hope, and to let him appreciate a problem while remaining free of academic circles of pipe-puffing professors discussing theoretical probabilities and outcomes.

But it was a problem that only he among the team was aware of. He frowned. Baker had blundered by sending everyone here, for they were bound to ask him what the tour was all about—and he wasn't at liberty to tell them.

Thirty minutes later their helicopter landed back on Kwajalein. As Davis dropped them at their quarters—a government-run hotel for official guests that had been dubbed *The Kwaj Lodge*—he promised to pick them up for dinner.

Soon after, Levi and Michael walked a short distance to the island's swimming pool. It was Olympic-size, and as Levi got in he realized it was filled with filtered salt-water that clung agreeably to him. This small detail made sense in the sometimes crazy world he dealt with. It even provided him with a sense of peace, and once Michael finished his grousing about being pulled to the far side of the planet "for a dog and pony show," the former water-polo players began doing a mile's worth of laps. But because they were guys they ended up competing against each other. Michael's long arms and legs gave him the edge though, and he finished half a stroke ahead of Levi. Then it was back to their quarters to get ready for the evening meal.

Jeff Davis awaited them—and earlier than expected. Peering at Levi, he shook his head in wonder. "I don't know who you guys are. But a mission's been scheduled for tonight specifically for your benefit." He shook his head again. "Unbelievable. These things require months of prep and planning. We have to have assets in place. Telemetry and tracking people need to be airlifted to the outer islands. Hell, we even have to put a notice in the *Hourglass*... sorry, that's the island newspaper... warning everyone of an 'incoming' mission. I—" He raised his hands in despair. "But this one's going down on seven hours notice. Seven *hours*. Un-be-lievable."

Levi's eyebrows knotted together. "Mission?"

"Yeah. A mission." Davis' mouth opened and closed. "You guys have juice, is all I can say. Vandenberg's launching a missile at us later tonight. We're to destroy it before it re-enters Earth's atmosphere, using our exoatmospheric missile."

DRAGON TEAM was in front of the Ops Building a few minutes past six. Because they were so close to the equator, in the time it took to walk from the van to the main door, daylight had capitulated to a darkness so absolute that Levi could barely see his hand in front of his face. At the same time, stars fairly exploded in a night sky devoid of ambient light, revealing not only the Milky Way but the Southern Cross. It was as if a bowl of stars had been upended and settled atop the island, so that the stars dipped from horizon to horizon.

Inside the building and despite the muted lights, Levi and the others were forced to blink rapidly to get acclimated before Davis led them to a control room bustling with civilian technicians. The room resembled Houston's Mission Control, with numerous consoles with colorful computer displays. The men and women manning the consoles were leaning forward and studying their screens. "This way," Davis said as he directed them toward a well-appointed but musty-smelling viewing area of deep chairs and a stocked mini-bar.

At 1830 hours precisely, a small speaker in the viewing room crackled to life. "*Vandenberg to Kwajalein Operations... missile away.*" Davis pointed to a clock on the wall. "ICBMs normally require twenty-three minutes to travel the 6,760 kilometers to our lagoon. In about nine minutes we'll launch our Meck rocket to intercept it. Visualize trying to shoot a bullet nose-to-nose against another bullet that's travelling at 13,000 miles an hour, for a combined speed of 26,000 mph."

Hack whistled. "I'm impressed."

"Watch the screen once we launch. It'll take a few minutes to intercept the ICBM. The A.O.A.—sorry, the Airborne Optical Adjunct, a Boeing 757 specially outfitted with high resolution cameras—is flying a racetrack pattern 38,000 feet above the Pacific. Its cameras will actually see the strike."

A few minutes later, Davis said with growing excitement, "Okay. Here we go. And... yes! We have a launch."

Levi watched the screen. A pure white light burst forth from the Meck Island launch facility twenty miles to the north. All at once an even greater light overwhelmed the surveillance cameras as the missile took flight. Seconds later, a trail of thick brown rocket exhaust was all that remained as it sped into the night.

There were cheers from the control room, but as the incoming ICBM's re-entry drew near, the banter faded away. Almost on cue, the team turned their faces toward the main screen. The missile, launched from California's Vandenberg Air Force Base, was lost within the space clutter. Then an odd star suddenly appeared high in the screen. All at once another light streaked toward it. The Meck rocket. A split-second later, the images blossomed into a super-nova.

The techs and scientists were noticeably hushed—there were no "ooohs" or "ahhhs." Levi supposed that all the natural similes were there—that an angry Apollo had been roused from perpetual slumber, or that God Himself had thrust His hand into the great pickle barrel which mere mortals call "the Pacific Ocean."

A tentative burst of applause from the control room was followed by scattered radio reports blaring from the speakers. Tommy asked Davis, "What's it all mean?"

"Our rocket utilized a laser to destroy theirs. An extraordinarily powerful laser," he added with a direct look.

"Then it works," Levi blurted.

"*What* works?" Michael asked. Leaning into Levi, he locked eyes with him and asked in a guarded voice, "What the fuck's going on—*brother*? Why were we pulled all the way out here, when all the action's taking place in Luxem-fucking-bourg?"

"Yeah," Wild Bill wanted to know. "What is it you're not telling us?"

Levi chided himself for his indiscretion, his earlier fear that Baker had erred in sending them here confirmed. He clenched his fists. "Knock it off. Just trust me."

"Trust me?" Monica scoffed. "I've heard that line often enough—when I was sixteen and in the back seat of a boyfriend's car."

Jutting his chin while veins in his neck throbbed, he glared at her.

But even Hacksaw's eyes were hard. "What's going on—boss?"

Tommy jumped in. "We don't have the need-to-know, so can it. Like the man said. We trust, or we don't. Anybody has an issue with that?" He thumped his chest. "Come see me."

Levi's face remained set in stone as he looked from one team member to the next. "It'll all make sense. In time."

"The hell with time." Michael threw his hands in the air. "Tell us what's going on. 'Cause none of this makes any sense."

"You know me better than that, Michael." Levi opened his mouth to say more, but instead he stormed out of the room. Once in the hallway his mind went to work. *Sure. I'm*

in on the grand scheme. But they don't need to know... or do they?
He calculated the time zones. It was a little after 3:00 AM
in Washington. He swore beneath his breath, then found
Davis. "I need to call Washington. Now."

Davis studied his face. "I'm guessing you'll need a secure
line. Okay. This way."

Long distance calls from Kwajalein go through the local
operator. Calls following a mission are put on hold for three
hours. But Davis provided Levi with a password that caused
the operator to say, "Right away, sir."

"Heath," Levi began a few minutes later. "The team needs
to know."

Heath Baker wheezed, then said sleepily, "Yes. I realized after-the-fact that they'd ask questions, and got them
cleared. Okay," he said wearily. "Tell them."

"Yes, sir." Hanging up, Levi found Davis. "If you please.
I need a SCIF."

Davis rubbed his jaw, nodded, and showed them into a
Sensitive Compartmented Information Facility adjacent to
the control room. Closing the door once the team trooped
in, he walked off. Once they settled into plush leather chairs,
Levi slowly got to his feet. When he did, a murmur filled
the room.

Monica said, "This can't be good."

Levi spoke in a voice reserved for funeral homes. "There's
another reason why any revelations about the Ecos will cause
worldwide panic." In the silence that followed, the others
unconsciously leaned forward in their seats. Levi ran a hand
through his heavy auburn hair, drew an audible breath, and
began. "The Ecos predicted another asteroid. One that

dwarfs Chicxulub, which as you'll recall was seven miles wide. According to the Ecos' calculations, and confirmed by their space borne observatory, this asteroid is at least 25 miles in size. And its scheduled to hit Earth in eighteen months. When it does, every living thing on this planet will perish."

CHAPTER TWENTY

· · · · · · · · · · · · · · · · · · · ·

"WE'RE SCREWED," Tommy said. He started to say more, but couldn't.

Dentz gripped the edge of his chair. "We sure are."

Hack shook his head. Monica muttered something unintelligible.

Michael stared straight through Levi in stunned silence. His mouth opened and closed. He finally said in a near-whisper, "My kids. Nadia. Oh, *hell*."

Levi said, "None of this looks good. But there's hope. Not much, but it's there."

Michael looked up, anguish in his eyes. "What is it?"

"A project to divert the asteroid. It's what we saw demonstrated tonight."

"But?" Tommy asked.

"If those pages are leaked, the world will face a crisis of immortality that is without precedent. If all hope is lost there'll be no reason for people to live on. Or let others live. Experts agree on the eventuality: a virtual global feeding frenzy. However, the level of R&D that this project requires depends upon stability." He jerked a thumb toward the control room. "If word of the asteroid gets out and everyone goes bananas, there's no hope of success. None."

He explained it to the team this way. "Nixon quite naturally ordered feasibility studies on methods to stop or to at least divert the asteroid. But he lived under a perpetual dark cloud. His proposals were hampered by internal bickering and backstabbing. He also lacked JFK's charisma, which fueled the dream of sending a man to the moon in the first place."

"On the other hand," Dentz began, "Tricky Dick had an extraordinary grasp of international affairs. Unfortunately, he also had a tendency to step on his... dick."

"Leading to his downfall," Michael said, adding in an undertone, "Bless his tortured soul."

"Yeah. Bless him." Levi met Michael's eyes. If anyone knew torture, it was his closest friend.

Hack spoke up in the formal style he used when impassioned. "Despite Nixon's sometimes pathological behavior, he *was* a genius. Our nation has shamed him for his sordid activities. But we do owe him a debt of gratitude."

Tommy said, "What'd Nixon do about this damn rock?"

"Two things. First, he engineered a top secret framework to deal with the threat. It was a brilliant achievement. He added to the brilliance by putting his national security advisor in charge. That was Henry Kissinger. He got things going. Then as Secretary of State he took it to greater levels by hiding the project within his shuttle diplomacy. More on that later."

For the first time since the team demanded answers, Levi settled into a chair and crossed his legs, the professor holding court with his brightest students. "Ford picked up the fallen standard and made headway. But Ford crashed into a Chevy named Carter. The micro-managing Jimmy Carter not only managed to piss off most members of Congress, he offended the project's scientists. They'd been told only that they were working on a feasibility project. Had they been armed with knowledge of the ultimate goal, they might've pushed on despite Carter and solved the problem by now. Of course, we'll never know."

"I'll bet Reagan righted those scurrilous wrongs," Hack said.

"He did, Hack. Mr. Reagan got the asteroid-busting program back on course."

"And hid it under the mantel of Star Wars," Monica said with an edge of excitement that brought her to her feet. "Right here. On Kwaj."

"Correct. He had to fund the project without too many awkward questions. So he used the Strategic Defense Initiative to great effect, especially since the real purpose of the missile-busting laser program was geared toward that goddamn asteroid." He shook his head. "That it also scared the Russians into ending the Cold War was a bonus."

Pausing to gather his thoughts, Levi moved on. "Bush 41 and Clinton took the project to ever-increasing levels. One example was Hubble. You'll recall that it initially experienced funding problems. But they were contrived problems. The idea was to haggle over its price tag to deflect attention to the project. Development obviously did proceed, it did get carried into space, and when it malfunctioned, we damned sure repaired it."

Michael said, "To position it ahead of time, and validate the asteroid's existence."

"Yes. And it's done the job. Hubble spotted it." He paused as the others stirred restlessly. "That's among the reasons why the main project continues to prosper. But now ISIS is unknowingly posing a threat to it."

Furrows erupted across five foreheads. Levi got to his feet again. "This venture dwarfs World War II's Manhattan Project. The costs are astronomical. We can't do it alone. Even the combined surplus assets of our European and Asian trading partners pale in comparison to what's needed. The row of zeroes behind the dollar sign would stun the mind." He shifted from one foot to the other.

"To avoid suspicion by raising money through taxation, in 1973 we formed a secret fund-raising alliance with Saudi Arabia. The '73 Middle East War had ended. The combatants suffered terribly. But the war formed the pretext for a deliverance of sorts. You see, OPEC wanted to raise oil prices to punish us for backing Israel. Nixon, ever the astute politician, saw an opening that only his dark mind could envision, and he sent Kissinger to *urge* the Saudis to use our commitment to Israel as their excuse *not* to veto OPEC's plan to put a stranglehold on us."

The five faces were blank.

"What really happened is that the huge, steady siphoning of oil revenue profits to the Saudis were redirected under the utmost secrecy to fund the project." Levi pinned his audience with a hard look. "Nixon and the Saudis even designed market fluctuations to foster a sense of normal trading anomalies. The project's now nearing completion. But it requires increased funding."

"That explains the current plunge in Saudi oil prices," Michael said.

"Correct." Levi beamed. Michael had always demonstrated a keen mind. "Once again, they're using national animosities to their advantage, with all the trappings of logic behind it. You see, the public version of the market is simple: the Saudis hate Russia's leaders and Iran's zealots, so they dropped their prices to ruin those two country's economies. That's cleared the way for a release of the augmented funds that the Saudi king claims are a buffer for the lost revenue. Of course, that pretext allows him to divert the monies. Except they're not being sent to his nation's coffers, but to the project."

Monica cleared her throat. "We've informed them of the scheme's true facts?"

"To some degree. The Saudis are no different than us. The royal family wants to perpetuate its heredity. Even so, we haven't made a full disclosure. They know nothing of the lunar discoveries, only that there's a killer asteroid which our government claims to have discovered. We basically sold them a bill of goods, sorta like selling futures on the world market. Whether they suspect deeper levels of truth probably doesn't matter to them. Their goal is identical to ours—to save their children. They regard the fact that others will also avoid death as a warm and fuzzy."

"Not to mention that keeping others alive guarantees a steady oil export market," Tommy said.

Levi shifted uncomfortably. He needed to discuss the team's immediate tactics, and wanted their feedback and suggestions. "The thing to bear in mind is that there is hope." He held up a finger. "But there'll be no hope at all if talk of a pending doomsday leaks. Once that happens? Total chaos. The oil market will collapse onto itself and the crude will seep into the sands—along with funding and rational thought. Therefore our first priority is to find those stolen documents. Priority two is..."

"Wait," Monica demanded. "Remind me again. What the hell can whoever has the papers do with them?"

Michael squirmed in his chair. "Let's assume a single psychopath. The short answer is that he does nothing. At least not until he can establish a safe house from which to watch Armageddon unfold. Once he feels secure? He releases the info. Why? Because he'll have undeniable power which he'll use to get his kicks by telling the world what's in the papers. Then he'll get greater jollies by watching the ensuing feeding frenzy." He paused. "Psychopaths almost never commit suicide. At least not for the reasons others do. By that I mean, not out of a depressed mood after a romantic failure. But with sufficient booze coupled with an inherent moribund mentality? Taking everyone down along with him is the psychopath's ultimate act of power and control."

Hack rubbed his temples with his fingers. "We need more details. We need..."

"Screw the details." Michael slowly rose to his feet, a hard cast to his face. "We need to resolve this. We start by finding the bastards who grabbed those papers. Then we take 'em down. No matter if it means killing them."

MICHAEL SWEPT past the plain white sign that read, YOKWE YUK CLUB and entered the island's achingly cold night club. Dropping into a booth, he ordered two Guinness Stouts from the white-shirted, cummerbund-clad waiter who appeared as if by magic.

"You're expecting company?" the Pacific Islander asked.

"I'm expecting to get tanked," Michael replied.

"Very well, sir." The waiter left and returned moments later with two draft stouts and a bowl of pretzels.

Michael tossed down the first beer and reached for the second one. He was having trouble getting his mind out of denial gear and into fifth gear where it needed to be if he were to save his wife and sons. *And the world, by the way.* He laughed inwardly at his own dark humor, then downed the second beer. When he turned and found the waiter watching from afar, he held up two fingers and waited until the waiter nodded before plucking a pretzel from the bowl.

He was on his third beer when Wild Bill appeared and slapped his shoulder.

Michael returned the gesture. "Wild Bill! *Mi amigo!* Hey... let's order a pizza."

Wild Bill told the waiter, "I'll have two of what my friend's having, along with a large pepperoni pizza. Toss in some green peppers, please."

"An' make sure you give us *plenny* a peppah-roni," a glassy-eyed Michael added.

Monica plopped next to him. "Hi, Lover Boy. Getting hammered, are we?"

He draped an arm around her shoulders, and when she settled a hand on his leg and idly caressed it, they traded a private look and then he smiled and kissed her ear.

Once Hack appeared, the friends ate, drank and alternated between uproarious laughter and protracted silence. Tommy eventually barged through the door. But he was the team's X.O. So he found a place at the bar. Levi never did appear. Michael hadn't expected him to. He was the boss. His agony had to remain private. "The loneliness of command," Michael blurted.

Hack peered at him through heavy-lidded eyes. "What was that?"

Michael gripped his glass. "I said, never thought I'd have to watch my boys die." As his voice trailed away he tightened his hold on Monica.

THE NEXT morning, tired and irritable, Dragon Team gathered at the terminal prior to boarding a C-17 bound for Honolulu. From there they would catch another C-17 to Andrews, via a refueling layover at a base in Oklahoma.

Sensing his team's resentment, Levi stood apart from them and glanced outside as a ground crew directed an Air Micronesia 737 to a stop near the C-17. Once the mobile stairs were placed snug against the airliner's forward door, a police officer took up a position at the bottom. Levi caught Davis' eye and pointed. "What's with the officer?"

"The Air Mike flights are island-hoppers. They fly from Honolulu to Guam via various islands, dropping off and picking up passengers as it refuels." He gestured outside. "But nobody's allowed off the aircraft. Not here. Not unless they're cleared."

Levi admired the absolute quality of all that took place on this open island of closed secrets. He was about to look away when a rugged-looking man with a ponytail stepped from the 737, then held fast at the top of the stairs as he looked around.

"I'll be a son of a bitch," Levi muttered. "Leo Ryan. Of the *Post*." He turned to Davis. "That guy standing there is a national security risk. I'm not free to explain why. But he mustn't see me or my team when we board our flight." He looked Davis in the eye. "One more thing. His father is Senator Ryan. *The* Senator Ryan."

Davis didn't miss a beat. "Very well. I'll handle this." Now grim-faced, he got Ryan's full name. Stepping away, he picked up a wall mounted island phone and punched four numbers. After a brief discussion he returned. "This won't take long."

Ryan remained atop of the stairs and peered at the terminal building as a fuel truck serviced the 737. The cop remained at his post, bored for all the world to see.

Davis was right. It didn't take long. Six minutes, by Levi's watch.

A police sergeant turned a corner of the tarmac, approached the officer, pointed to the terminal, patted the cop's shoulder, sent him off, then took his place at the bottom of the stairs. Within a minute, one of the hottest women Levi had ever seen hurried from the terminal to the airliner. She was all smiles, waving her arms over her head and shouting Ryan's name.

Ryan stiffened. He looked at her. Deep lines etched his forehead. He pointed at his chest. His mouth formed a question mark. When the woman nodded rapidly, Ryan looked about uncertainly. But he finally descended the stairs at the very instant that the sergeant began examining the pure blue sky. Ryan stepped onto the tarmac. The woman held her arms out as if to embrace him. He smiled uncertainly, took six steps... then reared back in shock as the sergeant whirled and grabbed his arm.

The sergeant slapped handcuffs on a visibly protesting Ryan, then pulled a radio from his belt and spoke into it. A half minute later—as if on cue, in fact—a white patrol car appeared on the tarmac with two black officers. After one got out and positioned herself at the stairs, the sergeant stuffed Ryan inside the car and got in next to him. Seconds later, the driver whisked them both away.

"Nobody's allowed to set foot on this secure facility," Davis said in a monotone. "It'll get a person arrested, just like that." He snapped his fingers and shook his head sadly. "Unfortunately for our *passenger*, it'll take the police the better part of the day to verify his identity. Then they'll bring criminal trespass charges against him. By the time they're finished he'll have missed his flight." He tilted his head at the 737. "Which means he'll have to spend the night in a holding cell."

Davis gave Levi a direct look and spoke at a subdued volume. "I'm as dedicated as the next person. Especially when it comes to stopping an incoming asteroid. If one is coming. Speaking theoretically, of course." He paused. "I have a good idea why you're here. I can deduce what's at stake." He glanced outside. "I'm honored to have met you and your team, and damn proud to have been of assistance just now."

Levi understood the man's mood. In the world of classified information, Davis couldn't let on that he knew more about the asteroid than he appeared to. But he'd given Levi the secret handshake that said, *I know that you know what I know, about what you know*. Levi said, "Thank you for all you've done, Dr. Davis." Turning on his heel, he sat quietly apart from his team.

Michael got up at once and sat next to him. The others followed, then joshed one another until it was time to board their flight.

When the team finally stepped inside the giant aircraft's cavernous no-frills cargo area with its attendant odors of ozone and oil, they accepted the blankets and earplugs that a crew member was offering, knowing from experience that it would get cold and noisy once they reached a cruising altitude.

Monica and Michael found seats next to each other, and the instant the plane went wheels-up they found a dark area near some crates, where they spread their blankets on the cold metal deck and hunkered down together to catch some Z's.

Levi watched her curl up against him, her head on his shoulder, and noted the way in which he wrapped a protective arm around her. They fell asleep at once and Levi thought it was all good. Then he and the others also settled back for some shut-eye, because from Andrews the team would leave at once for Luxembourg.

CHAPTER TWENTY-ONE

· ·

YURI BOGROV leveled the black-haired beauty with a suspicious squint. It wasn't the price; he'd used the escort service often enough to avoid going into sticker shock. What he hadn't expected upon opening the door to his suite was a woman taller than he, and darker in both appearance and attitude.

Two hours later he pressed his lips tight. "Do you call that pitiful masquerade you just put on a service to be paid for? That was not sex. That was rubbish. Now get out."

Swinging his legs to the floor, he put on a robe and waited. Once she was dressed he reached into a pocket and pulled out a wad of Hundred Euro notes. Peeling off twenty bills, he stuffed them in her hand and showed her the door with the admonition to never return. Closing it behind her, he listened to the hurried *click click click* of her heels and grunted. Then he took a long, cleansing shower.

Afterward, he stared at a framed photograph of his son. Touching a finger to the glass and tracing the image, he whispered, "Such a beautiful boy." All at once he clamped a hand over his eyes as the tears welled. Then his body shook as he sobbed for his long-dead son. The main body of tears were from regret that he'd lost him. The rest were out of anger, since even the joy—not to mention the physical release—of sex had been taken from him by the lingering vestiges of death. Now more than ever before, he saw that he could best use the papers by bringing the world to a premature end. But prior to calling a press conference he would still pursue other alternatives—ones that might bring him even more satisfaction out of life and death, not knowing that he was in conflict with himself more than everything else combined.

Finally wiping away the tears, he dressed and entered the living room where a simple breakfast of coffee and two baguettes awaited him on a silver tray. Also waiting for him was Slavko, standing at unconscious attention next to the tray.

Knowing full well that the coffee would be perfectly blended and at the ideal temperature, Bogrov still tested it carefully. It *was* perfect but he turned a sour face to Slavko. "Why is it that nothing is served correctly?" Raising the cup to his lips again, he inhaled the coffee in three gulps, poured a second cup, then grabbed a baguette. Speaking while crumbs fell to the marble floor, he asked Slavko, "Are all preparations in order?"

"Yes. We leave on the noon flight."

Nodding rapidly, still chewing, Bogrov said, "Very well. Two days in Moscow. I shall make phone calls. From there we proceed to the island." He set the cup down heavily enough to make it clatter. "Now then. The men. Have any responded?"

"Only three."

Bogrov growled and said more to himself than to his employee, "That will not do. We must expedite the hiring. For if I do choose to speak to the world, we'll have little chance of preserving our lifestyle without them." He reached for the second baguette.

CHAPTER TWENTY-TWO

· ·

DRAGON TEAM gathered inside the Crystal City SCIF's conference room at 8:00 AM precisely. Each team member had one carry-on and one check-in bag. The carry-ons contained toilet kits, a complete change of clothes including shoes, and valuables such as cameras. They also held three passports: a personal one, an official one, and a private passport issued by Canada—"throw downs" that would shield their U.S. citizenship in case they were compromised by a group hostile toward Americans.

The check-ins contained two changes of clothes, gym shoes, workout shirts and shorts. They also contained a set of clothing suitable for a climate 180 degrees opposite their destination in case they were diverted for some unforeseen reason. Finally, the bags held a seven day supply of socks and underwear. The team could pack so lightly because few people would see them on a daily basis and the members didn't care what the others wore. Clean underwear and hotel irons were what made it possible.

While Tommy passed out the official passports with updated Schengen visas for travel within Europe, Levi made a few remarks. "We're going armed. However, the only U.S. flagged carrier flying into Luxembourg is operated by a European airline."

The team nodded. As in most things, there were always technical difficulties. They were private contractors, but they'd been sworn in as Special U.S. Deputy Marshals under a codicil of the U.S. Code that permits this in certain cases. As deputies, they could carry weapons anywhere within the United States, its territories, and abroad—but not on a foreign aircraft.

Levi continued. "To get us in under the radar while packing heat, we're flying to Luxembourg in a large business jet. It's a regular flight in case anyone—our friend Leo Ryan leaps to mind—is watching." Then he asked in a clipped voice, "Questions?"

Michael said, "Any word on that escapee?"

"Pete? Nothing that's not in the news." He shrugged. "If he's after me, I'll deal with him. If he has other targets in mind? Blue Crew's on your family."

IT WAS late evening by the time they touched down in Luxemburg City. As the aircraft taxied in, the team adjusted their watches for the time difference. Once the engines wound down, the door opened and a conservatively attired man walked aboard.

"I am Stephen Boyd, United States ambassador to Luxemburg." He glanced about the cabin. "Who is in charge, please?"

"That would be me." Levi stepped forward with an outstretched hand and introduced himself. Then he swept a hand at the team. "We're here for you, sir."

Boyd offered a curt nod. "Very good. Shall we?" Gesturing toward the door, he led them from the plane.

PIERRE ROLAND examined the Americans as Boyd ushered them into a VIP room of delicate dark furniture and quiet carpeting. A refreshment area at the far wall was stocked with deli meats, cheeses, and pastries. There were also soft drinks, beers, wines and liquors. And this being Europe, there were bottles of both plain and carbonated water.

He saw that the Americans were alert, their eyes moving here and there as they took in their surroundings. They also remained restrained, and Roland felt a degree of both personal and professional shame for pre-judging them. For while they came from a fat land filled with fat people, these operatives were trim, athletic, and silent. No babbling, no cursing or woo-hooing. They were quiet professionals who reminded him of John Wayne in *The Quiet Man*. Only they were not as big as Mr. Wayne, with the exception of one gentleman who appeared older than the others, and leaving Roland unable to decide whether he resembled the actor Sam Elliot, or the Marlboro Man.

When Boyd introduced Levi, Roland found the tall but slender man's grip to be firm, dry and reassuring. Roland in turn introduced Levi to Dieter. "Herr Hart, I am pleased to introduce *Frau* Dieter."

Taking her proffered hand, Levi said, *"Gutten Abend. Ich freue mich, Sie kennen zu lernen."*

"Danke." She offered an infectious smile. "I am pleased to make your acquaintance as well. Please. Call me Hannah."

Watching this, Roland thought, *an American who speaks at least one other language. This could prove useful.*

Levi introduced the team members and asked, "We're ready to get to work."

Taken aback, Roland said, "You have just traveled a great distance. Do you not wish to check into your hotel and rest?" Thinking that these Americans were indeed not here for recreational purposes, he began to admire them. "You can always, how do you say—catch a few winks?" Proud of his knowledge of slang, he revealed a shy smile.

But the American's mouth became a straight line. "This mission is too critical for rest. There'll be plenty of time for that later."

ROLAND TOOK the inspector aside while the team went through immigration and customs to assure him that the Americans' concealed pistols were authorized. Once the ambassador bade them farewell, Roland took them to a secure meeting room at police headquarters and revealed all he knew of his Tunnel Rippings suspect, adding that he'd placed him under surveillance.

Levi made no apologies when he stressed the top secret nature of their mission. "I can say only this. Your suspect is in possession of stolen documents that are so sensitive, their disclosure could create global panic."

Roland narrowed his eyes. "Then perhaps we should bring Bogrov in for questioning."

Speaking guardedly to avoid accidentally divulging classified information, Levi said, "The short answer is that we don't know if he even plans to reveal anything, or if he does, whether he's awaiting a more opportune time."

"He might've also established an alternate means of spreading the news," Tommy said. "A fail-safe system that'll tell all if he's taken out of action."

"Fail-safe?" Roland cocked his head. "What is this *fail-safe*?"

"Sorry." Tommy explained the USAF term for a system that ensures the ability of bomber and missile crews to receive valid orders to attack their targets. "Bogrov might have directed an attorney or some other trusted individual to divulge the contents of the stolen documents if he's arrested... possibly out of spite."

As Roland nodded, Michael picked up the thread. "Even if our government denies everything, it'll be too late. People today tend to buy into outrageous rumors. Denial will be a futile exercise. If word leaks, the damage will have been done."

Hannah Dieter, who'd been listening quietly, slowly stood in a way that drew all eyes to her. "What we know of Bogrov's emotional profile clearly points toward a tendency to play god. It's why I am in full agreement with Mr. Wilkins' assessment." Glancing at Tommy, she offered a brief smile. "Despite not knowing what the documents might reveal, I believe your fail-safe analogy is quite correct. How so, you might ask? It is because psychopaths are calm and meticulous. They are attentive to details and often have contingency plans in place. Those two facts are givens." She waved a hand as if conceding a debate point.

"But the answer is also founded in our Christian beliefs. Although Bogrov would not pray so much to the deity whom we refer to as 'God', he would pray to his own self. The point is clear, however. As God did when he sent his only son to us, Bogrov will subconsciously mimic that great turning point in world history. He will be sure to leave behind an emissary to carry out his mission if Earth's 'sinners' disrupt his plan, whatever that plan might be."

Roland stood. "I concur. So. We must first determine if he has passed along this information. Following this, we shall seek to establish what automatic means he might have developed for its dissemination."

Roland, Dieter and Dragon Team played point-counter-point a bit longer. In the end they agreed to gather at first light and interview Bogrov at his residence. Roland then took them to their hotel — a typical European one with minuscule rooms that are meant to be used only for sleeping.

Readying himself for bed, Levi lay back but left the blanket bunched at his feet while he reviewed the day's activities. He had trouble getting his mind off the reason they were here — someone had possession of stolen information that could undo the world, and it burned him to imagine what could happen if Dragon Team failed in its assignment. He also pictured Michael's agony after learning the true nature of their mission. Moving on, he had sensed Roland's total professionalism — along with his covert appraisal of Dragon Team. Before falling asleep he recalled Hannah Dieter's assessment of Yuri Bogrov.

MONICA MASTRONARDI couldn't help but admire Hannah Dieter. She wished they could sit and talk shop. Always moving and working within a male environment, she craved an opportunity to speak with another professional capable of communicating on a different level. Settling into her hotel bed, she looked forward to working with her. They might even find time for a sit-down. Her thoughts then turned to Michael. He was suffering inside and while Levi might be his best friend, Michael had told her often enough that she was his next best buddy. She felt likewise and decided to have a sit-down with him, too.

•　•　•

Yuri Bogrov gulped down a second vodka before staggering off to bed. Flopping down, he gamed several options. The first plan centered on his choice of reactions when local authorities arrived to question him—which they were sure to do, if only to justify their costly surveillance. So much for playing a waiting game.

Even so, he would play it cool. The various tunnel cameras would have captured his image and they couldn't help but recognize him. They would *have* to question him.

One option would see him leave within a day or two. Again, it all centered on not altering his everyday patterns. *A routine business flight to manage my affairs.*

Bogrov explored another possibility: venturing into nearby Belgium to sidestep any immediate interviews. But in the end he decided to remain here and set up a series of business meetings to explore the odds of selling the papers—although deep down, the idea of telling-all to the world held the greater appeal. However, he enjoyed the cat and mouse of conducting business too much to forgo it completely. Settling down, he closed his eyes until a gnawing uncertainty began eating at him. Having learned long ago to trust his instincts, he sprang from bed and went down the hall to Slavko's bedroom.

Opening the door, he hit the lights. "Get dressed. Now."

Bogrov then went to the kitchen, where for once he played the servant's role by brewing coffee for the two of them.

"Yes?" Slavko asked a moment later as he trudged in with his wandering eye shifting here and there, totally at odds with the straight line he was walking.

"Pack your things. Include this." He handed over the framed photo of his son. "Next, get the car. Drive to the airport. Park in the long-term lot. Go from there to the terminal and rent a car. Use one of your alternative identities. Pay with one of your phantom credit cards. Inform them that you intend to stay in Luxemburg for one week. Once you've accomplished that, call me on this." He held up a cell phone. "Disposable. Brand new." After handing it to Slavko he provided the number for a second disposable phone—his own. "Now then. After you leave here, I shall walk to a nearby club. I will stay for only a short time. Then I shall go to another at random. That is why you must call me, for I will have to tell you where to pick me up."

"I understand. Do not worry. I shall of course remain alert for the shadows of the policemen." The tall man cocked his head. "What will be our ultimate destination?"

Bogrov didn't mind divulging the answer. "Moscow. By a circuitous route."

Slavko gave a curt nod. "I shall pack at once."

"Excellent." Bogrov offered his servant a cup of coffee, then stared at the front door as if expecting a knock at any moment.

CHAPTER TWENTY-THREE

· ·

YOUNG LEVI BAILEY—The Kid—rapped his knuckles against the door. "Hurry up. It won't stay warm forever."

Jen hurried out of his bathroom. "Okay okay, already." Grabbing a thatch of his heavy brown hair, she gave it a tug. "You're a nut-job, you know that?" She added with a wry smile, "And you were a very naughty nut-job. *And* nice. And *randy*."

He wagged his eyebrows at the raven-haired cheerleader as a coda to their having just showered together in the wake of their five mile jog. They'd been friends since pre-school, homework buddies since age nine, and laid-back lovers since fifteen. Right now they were hungry no matter what their age, and after trading bemused looks they went downstairs to eat.

He'd made tonight's meal for he was quite the chef, having learned to cook at his mother's fine-dining restaurant. Jen often joined him and his bother Nick for dinner and then stayed over—both sets of parents having signed-off long ago on letting them sleep together, feeling it was safer for them to get their raging hormonal needs met with her on the pill and within each other's homes rather than in dangerous lovers' lanes.

After they sat at the table he raised his glass of cabernet. "To us, to Mom, and to Dad." The boys' parents had taught them to enjoy alcohol responsibly and had given them their reigns. As a result of this liberty, neither son had ever over-indulged or taken advantage of their other freedoms. They clinked their glasses and sampled the wine.

But before cutting into his roast beef, the Kid caught the eye of the tall lean man seated in a shadowy corner of the living room with an MP-5 submachine gun on his lap. Raising his glass again and tilting it at the Blue Crew operative, the Kid mouthed "thank you" and smiled when the man gave a smart salute as a way of saying, *don't mention it, Kid*. Young Levi had seen to it earlier that he and the other two stationed outside had had a chance to eat the same meal that he, Jen and Nick were sitting down to. He was grate-ful for their presence, and they saw one another as family. Jen was also at ease around them. The fact that she even knew of his father's job spoke of the depth of trust between the couple. But the Kid's good feelings for Blue Crew were bitter-sweet for the simple reason that he felt more concern for his father's safety than for his own.

· · ·

Hours later — and six zones to the east — Levi Hart shivered despite the dawn sun as he, Roland, and Dieter approached Yuri Bogrov's residence while the others quietly surrounded the simple gray stone building. Levi found it interesting that the nouveau riche Bogrov had acquired an unpretentious home. He also thought his disappearance had come as no surprise. An excellent investigator, Levi knew not to frame suspects within subjective boundaries. Instead, he adhered to the rule that all suspects are capable of all things beyond a mediocre investigator's imagination.

Roland pushed the front door buzzer, waited, and pressed again. After a third attempt he turned to the curb and beckoned to Hacksaw Jones.

Hack hurried over, checked the door and its lock, then said, "No problem."

While watching Hack open a small leather case from which he extracted a tension tool and a pick, Levi wondered at Roland's ability to acquire a search warrant so quickly. The European Community takes a dim view of searching private homes. Roland would have had to assure the judicial authorities that the Tunnel Rippings made the need to search for evidence proportionate to a possible violation of EU Conventions. In this case, Bogrov's midnight vanishing act while under surveillance had sealed the deal.

Hack said to nobody in particular as he inserted the tension tool, "I was in Florida one day. Saw a guy trying to kick-in the front door of a house. Claimed it was his sister's house. Said he'd flown in from Ohio and had used the key she gave him for the door. But he was befuddled when he still couldn't push it open." Hack pulled out the tool and slid the pick in. "I go up, take hold of the knob... an' *pull*. The door opens. No sweat. Why? 'Cause in Florida, you can't kick a door *in*." He twisted the slender piece of metal with a flick of the wrist. "In Florida, by law all doors now have to open outward to keep 'em from bein' blown inward by hurricanes." He tweaked his wrist. There was an audible *click* and the door sprang open an inch. "An' that's how we do things with *this* weird-ass portal of entry, too."

The three men and Hannah stood to either side with hands at the ready. Roland pushed. The door swung wide open.

Four pairs of eyes probed in all directions as they filed in. Out of sight of the public now, they drew their pistols and searched the austere apartment. When all four verbally declared the place was safe, Roland called in the waiting crime scene techs.

While they waited for the techs, Levi stood in the apartment's epicenter to get a feel for the place and its inhabitants. He'd read a file on Bogrov which described his activities as a pimp who'd formed ties to the Russian mafia. The file mentioned the billionaire's chauffeur/bodyguard, who was always at his side. It also noted Bogrov's son and the manner of his death, along with theories that while the Russian's love for his son rang true, the obsessive manner in which he clung to the boy's memory stemmed from a psychopathic view of the son as an extension of his narcissistic self. In short, Bogrov felt only a mimicry of authentic love. Sure enough, while looking about Levi saw nothing to remind Bogrov of his loss—no photos, no keepsakes; nothing.

"He was never the same afterward," Roland said as he approached Levi.

"I can well imagine," Levi replied.

"No, my friend. You do not have to imagine. You see it in your mind's eye."

Turning to Roland, he said matter-of-factly, "My guess is that he'll go to ground."

"To isolate himself further? As you did following your son's death?"

"I fled *my* demons. Why should he be any different?"

"Yet you returned," Roland said. The meticulous detective put a hand on Levi's shoulder. "And I think you do not dwell on this great loss." He gestured at the room. "So. Have you by now acquired a feel for this apartment?"

"A sad place. Almost monastic, despite the expensive furnishings."

"*Exactement.*"

"However," Levi continued, "this sad quality, while troubling enough, is overridden by something even worse. I couldn't place it until you mentioned Bogrov not being the same after his son's death. Now I have it. There's a sense of... degeneracy about this apartment. Not despondency. Degeneracy."

A quick intake of breath, then, "How *extraordinaire*. That is the very feeling I have acquired. Degeneracy. Death. Despair. Yet most of all, resolve."

"Deadly resolve," Levi muttered.

THE CRIME scene techs made quick work of the sparse apartment, discovering among other items strands of long black hair on a pillow atop Bogrov's bed, and a pair of handmade leather shoes with bits of soil and other debris clinging to the heels.

"A man of the city," Levi remarked as a tech held the evidence bag up for him and Roland to see. "But also a child of the farm. Let's not rule out the possibility that he wanders the countryside for therapeutic purposes." After pinching the end of his nose he added in an undertone, "I've read that he visits his father's grave. But cemeteries are grassed over. There wouldn't be much loose soil."

"I agree," Dieter said quickly. "Also, I know the particular cemetery. It is near the American one, where General Patton lies with his troops. No, there is no loose soil in either of them."

They were still playing devil's advocate when Roland's phone chirped. He took the call, listened, spoke in rapid French, finished, and turned to Levi. "Bogrov's ZIL. It has been located at the airport. I've ordered it taken to our headquarters for analysis. My colleagues will review ticket transactions and airport surveillance tapes."

"May I offer a suggestion?" Levi asked.

Roland made a Gallic shrug. "But of course."

"Check the car rental agencies. Bogrov might be attempting an end run."

"That is an excellent observation." Turning to the crime scene supervisor, he gave orders to bring the evidence in for examination. Then he wrapped his fingers around Levi's elbow. "Let us proceed to the office of the medical examiner. They already have the results of the gross toxicology tests of the deceased Swiss guards. However, on the side of caution I have asked them to recheck their findings. Perhaps by now they have something of interest." Making a show of checking his watch, he added, "They begin work in twenty minutes. We shall meet them at the front door."

•   •   •

Bogrov examined the flaking red paint around the glass door of the small cafe and told Slavko, "There. That one." Then he settled against the rear seat as Slavko guided the rented Audi down one of Kaiserslautern's innumerable side streets.

Since crossing the border from Luxembourg into Germany they'd traveled an additional hour and a half and now Bogrov was hungry. The instant Slavko parked, they entered the establishment and took a small table that let them watch the door.

Following a meal of breads, meats, and cheeses, Bogrov put down his coffee cup and leaned toward Slavko. "From here we travel south. We'll transit France and proceed to Zurich, turn east to Zagreb, then north to Budapest. From there? A train to Moscow."

Slavko said as he gulped the rest of his coffee, "Circuitous. As you say."

"First however, I will make a telephone call. A wealthy capitalist lives here… in *Kaiserslautern* of all places. I wish to meet with him." He checked his watch. "Soon."

CHAPTER TWENTY-FOUR

· ·

HAVING OUTGROWN Pierre Roland's cramped office, Levi and his team gathered inside a contemporary meeting room at a nearby annex. The brightly lit space smelled to him of new fabric, and boasted L-shaped workstations of frosted glass and black metal frames. Laptops and stationery were in place at each seat, and a beverage service in a far corner exuded coffee and tea aromas that somehow soothed him.

Going to the head table, he sat in a faux Aeron chair next to Roland and held a pen poised over a notepad.

"Ladies and gentlemen," Roland began. "We are confident that Yuri Bogrov has fled and has most likely crossed Luxembourg's frontier. Common wisdom suggests two possibilities. First, that he is in the German state and is making his way to the Rodina."

Levi mentally translated. When capitalized, the Rodina, or *Родина* in Russian, signified the Motherland. Russian nationalists hold this notion dear to their hearts, just as the Germans of old held the concept of the Fatherland close-in. If Bogrov had gone to ground as Levi theorized, he would make his way to the bosom of his heritage. Levi's instincts also cried out that their now-elusive prey was not taking a direct route, that he would not pass "Go," and would not bother collecting his two hundred dollars. Therefore a hot pursuit by Dragon Team would be futile. They'd sap their energy while Bogrov nurtured his own. It would be far wiser to exercise patience. After all, Bogrov juggled too many business interests to remain hidden for too long. Levi could tap into those interests and search for connections, debts owed to old cronies, and spikes in his trading partners' activities. But if he had to go to Russia and eliminate the billionaire, he wouldn't hesitate.

Roland's clipped voice brought him back to the room. "The second possibility is that he has already reached Moscow by a chartered aircraft. In either event he will remain difficult to pin down. This does not mean we cannot locate him. I have reached out to colleagues throughout Europe and asked that they conduct a quiet manhunt." He paused to let this sink in. "Our next order of business. Bogrov's automobile. It is being processed for evidence. Airport cameras captured images of his bodyguard, *Slavko*. He lives among the shadows. He is never there. And yet he always is. In this case, he stepped in front of a camera to rent an automobile. A black Audi. Of course." He sniffed audibly and made a face. "Nothing but the best for Bogrov."

"Which could prove to be his undoing," Hannah mentioned. "An obvious conclusion, I know. Still, there it is."

"Yes," Roland said. "Now, the autopsy findings." He recited the pathologist's conclusions that not one, but two men murdered the Swiss guards. The angles of the knife wounds showed that a short man killed Johan, while a taller man had slain the older one. The report concluded that the assailants never faltered while driving their knives home, the pathologist having noted the absence of either hesitation or defensive marks on the bodies—marks that would all but shout, *vacillation*. Finally, the killers brutalized the corpses. "But in doing so they erred," Roland told his audience, "For sexual crimes are almost always perpetrated by lone attackers. *"Almost* always.*"

"Just as the Turks during World War I were almost successful in defending Aqaba from a British invasion," Levi said, relying on his master's in history. "The Turks pointed all their guns toward the Red Sea. So T.E. Lawrence recruited a rag-tag band of Arab tribesmen and crossed six hundred miles of hostile desert to attack the Turk's undefended rear. Lawrence lost two men. The Turks? Completely wiped out. 'Almost' can be a very big factor."

Roland shifted in his chair. "Quite so. At any rate, perhaps someone will capture him before he can 'almost' make good his escape."

Now Levi stood. "Monsieur Roland has connections. But I'd like to use any reports that might reach us of Bogrov's travels as separate tools—not just to track his movements, but to keep an eye out for any contacts he might make along the way. For example, has a German industrialist unexpectedly sold off shares of Blue Chip stocks? Has a Canadian steel magnate traveling through Paris put out feelers about dissolving his company?"

"All signs that Bogrov's started a bidding war for the papers," Michael said as he peered keenly at his friend.

"Ah, yes. I see. *Très bien.*"

Hannah regarded her boss. "I have a colleague in the Ministry of Economy and Exterior Commerce. Perhaps I could alert him to also stand a vigil. A discreet one."

"Please. By all means." Roland beamed at her.

They then fell into various discussions until Roland's phone chirped. He listened, ended the call, and announced, "Initial findings from our crime scene specialists. The soil on Bogrov's shoes is sandstone, with traces of plants they've identified as coming from plums and strawberries. Old ones, however. Evidently one crop had been overplanted by another. They also found traces of willow trees."

"The southern region of the Luxembourg Plateau," Dieter said at once. "There are old farms south of the city. Many years ago these farms were found to be rich in iron ore. Various mining companies bought the majority of them for future exploitation. However, other farmers refused to sell. Instead, they left their fields to the elements in the hope that nitrogen would replace the iron ore."

Roland's face lit up. "That would explain the traces of iron ore on his shoes. Also, I was about to report that our specialists discovered the same traces of soil and vegetation embedded in his car's tires. Furthermore, two soiled shovels were inside the boot." He raised an index finger. "Finally, they found traces of excrement in the back seat."

Levi said, "They killed someone and buried the body in a rural field."

Roland nodded like a bird pecking at crumbs. "Of course." He made a call and held a brief conversation. Ending it, he announced, "One of the specialists tells me that willows only grow near riverbanks. She knows of three abandoned farms with iron ore deposits in close proximity to the city—and one of them is near a river."

"I'd say we're about to take a journey," Levi said.

LONG SHADOWS made patterns across the meadow as if they'd sprouted from the fertile soil. At the same time, the air had grown chill. Earlier, a police helicopter fly-over revealed an anomaly in the meadow. A cadaver dog confirmed the presence of a corpse. Now Levi, Roland, and Dieter stood to one side while a medical team exhumed the body.

When they uncovered a woman's dirt-caked corpse, Levi suppressed a rising nausea as the stench of rotting flesh hit his nose like a fist. After they lifted her from the shallow grave and cleaned her off a bit, he saw the probable cause of death. Pointing to the ear-to-ear laceration, he told Roland, "No hesitation marks. Quick. Brutal."

"Final." Roland gestured at the body. "Black hair. Hmm. Perhaps luck will be with us, and we shall find that it matches the hair discovered on Bogrov's pillow."

"Wait," Levi said abruptly. "What's this?" Stooping down, he picked up the left hand and peered at it. "She clutched fibers of some kind. Carpet fibers? Maybe from a car?" Releasing the hand, he stood. "Pending the forensic and autopsy results, and absent any new information, I'd say Bogrov is our chief suspect. And if he did in fact murder the Swiss guards, this is the game changer."

Roland put on a blank television stare. "Why?"

Levi gestured at the body. "He's a careful man but this time he was careless. Not sloppy, but without care. I believe it's why he mutilated the Swiss guards. He must've known it was an amateur thing to do. That's because he wants us to pursue him."

"Again, why?"

"To prove he's clever enough to elude us. He's raising the stakes. This way he draws greater attention to himself. He'll have a larger audience for... later on."

Pursing his lips, Roland asked, "What else is there about him that is pertinent? Or perhaps I should ask, what is more relevant than before this latest homicide?"

"He's not about to be taken alive."

Roland wrapped his hand around Levi's arm and nodded. "*Exactement.*"

"But..." Levi's voice caught. "That means he'll release the information if he's cornered. If not before."

Releasing Levi's arm, Roland knelt next to the body and examined it. "Naturally I do not know what this information consists of. But if it has shaken you then I am shaken. If Bogrov is your enemy then he is also mine."

CHAPTER TWENTY-FIVE

. . . .

LEVI HART believed in the "three-strikes, you're out" rule. His first strike, called by an unseen umpire, occurred a few minutes after dawn when his phone buzzed. One look at the caller ID made him sit up in bed. After thumbing the phone he said without preamble, "You're up awfully late, Mr. President... assuming you're in D.C."

"All the better to chew you out." A slight static belied the expected clarity of a call placed from the White House. In fact, the static was engineered—an element of the phone's encryption system. "Why haven't I gotten any reports from you? For that matter, what possessed me to send you to a spot in the middle of the Pacific Ocean first, before signing-off on your travels to your current location?"

Levi did a mental countdown before he replied. Even so, his knuckles turned white as he gripped his phone. "I had nothing substantive to report, sir. I'm waiting for some additional data, rather than trouble you with a cluster of dog and pony reports. *Sir.*"

President Cohen's response was as acid as Levi's. "Do I need to find someone more suitable to do this job, Mr. Hart? A person with greater qualifications, perhaps?"

"Mr. President. I—" Levi held the phone at arm's length while he got his anger under control. "Mr. President, it is your prerogative to replace me any time you wish. But until you show me the door, give me the time I need to do my job."

Cohen's voice exploded in Levi's ear. "Who the hell are you to talk to me in this fashion?"

"Since you're asking," Levi said evenly, "A man who isn't afraid to tell the emperor he's not wearing any clothes. You want ass-kissers? Sorry. I don't qualify." He said in a softer tone, "My job is to be square with you. Otherwise, poor decisions might be made. I'm a part of your team. My job is to make you look good…"

"You're *job* Mr. Hart is to deliver results." Cohen fell silent. The sound of papers being shuffled came over the phone. "Levi," Cohen began in a more conversational tone. "Have I lit a large enough fire under your butt? Or do I need a blowtorch to get you to move faster."

Levi willed himself down from his anger. "A blowtorch isn't needed, sir. We're making progress. I'll have a report for you within two hours."

"I want results, Mr. Hart. Stat." Cohen ended the call.

Levi tried to place himself in Cohen's position. Something must be up for The Man to come down so hard. Levi could handle "hard." It came with the territory. What troubled him was that Cohen didn't operate that way. He rarely if ever raised his voice. Even worse, he hadn't gone through Baker. This reinforced Levi's conclusion that some unknown trouble must have surfaced—and probably of a political nature.

Levi had always realized that even if Bogrov might enjoy a leisurely timeline of his own choosing to sell or reveal the papers, the team had to remain two steps ahead of him. Cohen's call had served as a reminder. Levi hadn't needed it, but he respected the pressure Cohen must be under. He swung his feet to the floor. He would produce a report and have it on Cohen's desk within the hour. Then he would meet with the team.

STRIKE TWO came forty minutes later when he entered the hotel lobby and spotted Leo Ryan staring at him from a wing chair placed near the front desk.

"Nice move you made on Kwajalein… Mr. Hart."

Levi's face was a burlap bag of confusion. "Kwa-*jellin?*" Then relief flooded his features. "Wait, isn't that the new restaurant in D.C. everyone's talking about?"

Ryan's greeting marked the second occasion within a span of an hour that he'd been referred to by his family name. Levi fought the temptation to turn his hands into fists. Instead, he squinted. "Refresh my memory. Do you work for the Des Moines, Iowa *Post?* Or is it the Dubuque *Post?* 'Cause I'm a bit sketchy on your press credentials."

Ryan slowly clapped his hands. "Bravo. Give the man a see-gar."

Levi moved to within a foot of Ryan and loomed over him while noting the man's Rolex. "You living on daddy's trust fund?" He swept a broad hand at the lobby. "It costs money to travel to Europe and stay in fancy digs."

Ryan said with a set face, "It also costs money to fly to Kwajalein. Unless you're able to hitch a ride on a government-operated aircraft. A C-17, for example."

"Don't know what you're talking about." Levi leaned forward. "Say, do you fabricate *all* your stories? Or only the ones that get you fired?"

Ryan made a show of laughing. "Oh, that's rich. You should try out for a spot on the Comedy Hour. You're a regular stand-up." The smile vanished as an elderly couple passed by. "One thing's certain. I won't have to embellish the story I'm currently on. If you're smart, you'll sit down for a little chat."

"Don't try to play me, Ryan." Levi let an oily smile creep across his face. "Or I'll notify the police that you're wearing the Rolex that was stolen from my room."

"Really? *Really*? Then what? Get them to arrest me?" His eyes turned hard. "Having me locked-up clearly didn't prevent me from tracking you here. And it won't prevent me from calling The Senator if I'm forced to."

"The Senator. My, my. Is *that* what you call 'daddy'? No wonder you're fucked-up. Probably explains why you falsify stories." Squinting, Levi said, "If I do have you arrested? Take it as a hint to leave me the fuck alone."

"Nixon would've been okay if he'd admitted to Watergate," Ryan shot back. "And you're right. I am a trust fund kid but I'm able to connect the dots. Missing Vatican documents. Dead Swiss guards in Lux City. Then you show up."

Levi showed no reaction as he walked off. But he felt in turmoil. First Cohen, now Ryan. He had to act fast before a third strike threatened to take him out of play.

"WELL?" LEVI waited for a reply.

Pierre Roland leaned back in his office chair and studied the cream-colored ceiling. "Yes, I can find a law that will permit me to take this Mr. Ryan to the hoosegow, as your Mr. John Wayne might say."

"But?"

"But why not sit with him? Determine whether he is loyal enough to give leeway. In return, you offer him an insider's story after the fact."

Levi rubbed his long jaw. "Good point. It worked for JFK during the Cuban Missile Crisis. After a news editor caught wind of things, Kennedy appealed to his patriotism. Convinced him to sit on the story until he could address the nation." Then Levi recalled Ryan's reference to Watergate—the scandal did more than shove Nixon into early retirement; it sent patriotism into a spiraling nosedive.

Roland asked, "What've you to lose?"

"Too much, my friend." Levi thanked Roland and excused himself. Entering an emergency exit stairway, he cocked his head and listened until he was satisfied that he was alone. Then he called Heath Baker and discussed his dilemma in broad *I-have-this-friend* terms. After listening to Baker's pro and con arguments, Levi said, "Bottom line? Offering him a redacted carrot might satisfy his needs. But if I do and it fails? Then I'm not averse to taking proactive measures."

"I agree," Baker said. "Too much is at risk. Why not talk it over with your colleagues." Although they were on encrypted phones, Baker still chose his words carefully. "Get their consensus. But in the end it'll be…"

"My call." Levi nodded from habit. "Thanks, boss. I'll keep you posted."

"Wait," Baker said. "A mutual friend called. He described an earlier conversation with you. I jumped on him for not going through me. He pointed out the obvious: that there are other issues involved. I'm out of the loop on what's going on. My best guess? I suspect additional Vatican leaks."

"Leaks, combined with politics. A deadly combination."

Baker grumbled. "It's your call. I won't second-guess you."

"Thanks for your vote of confidence." Levi ended the call, then began contacting the others for an emergency meeting.

Returning to Roland's office, he told the detective, "I'm meeting with my team shortly. Have you anything else?"

"*Oui*. While you were away I checked with some associates. There've been no instances of captains of industry abruptly liquidating assets. Therefore, I propose that you and I pay a visit to a certain person. Tomorrow morning, perhaps?"

MICHAEL'S FACE was hard and pitiless when he responded to Levi's feelers. "End him. Now. Before he creates problems beyond our control."

"I agree," Wild Bill said at once. "Ryan's gotta go."

Levi nodded, then pointed at Hack.

"Delay any decision until you've met with the man."

"Why?"

"Explore and exhaust all possibilities."

"I concur," Monica said. "It's no different than a deadly encounter. You order the adversary to surrender. If they don't, you take it to the next level. A hands-on takedown. Or a taser. But shoot only as a last resort."

Tommy pointed a finger at Levi. "It can't hurt to have a sit-down. We'll remain nearby. Give a signal and we make him disappear."

"For good," Michael said.

Levi looked at each of them. "I agree it's wiser to start at a more benign level. If we have to amp it up—?" He looked at Michael. "—I'll do it."

LEVI KNEW where to find Ryan. Striding through the hotel's main entrance, he spotted the erstwhile reporter's smug look at once.

"He returns," Ryan trumpeted.

"The prodigal son *remains*," Levi fired back. He jutted his jaw toward a bar of dark wood, small tables, and the rarified air of old yet dignified age. "Let's have a talk."

"Let's have it," Ryan said the instant they sat on leather-cushioned chairs.

"Here's what we're gonna do. I'll offer a deal. If there's room for haggling? Fine. We'll explore possibilities."

Ryan's lips curled into a small smile but his eyes remained hard. "And if there's no room?"

"Simple. I go about my business. You run yourself ragged."

A waiter appeared and the men gave orders for a Beck and a St. Pauli Girl. When they were alone again, Levi draped an arm over the back of his chair and waited.

Ryan rested his elbows on the table, and leaned forward. "Okay. Talk to me."

"An exclusive story. After the fact. But it won't come from me."

"No good. I want in on the action."

"Who said there's any action?"

"Because you're an action kinda guy." Ryan pursed his lips. "If he—he being the man at 1600 Pennsylvania—had wanted an accountant type he'd have sent for one. He didn't."

Levi said evenly, "The offer's non-negotiable. The only variables are, 'when do you get the exclusive story, and from whom.' Take it or leave it."

"I'm not buying it," Ryan said at once. "We wouldn't be sitting here now if you didn't recognize the tenaciousness with which I'll pursue this story." He leaned back and folded his arms across his chest.

Levi regarded it as a Mussolini-like act of arrogance, fueled by a mistaken notion of triumph. "We're talking because I'm a reasonable man who recognizes another prize fighter. It's why we're touching gloves. But even prize fights have rules." Levi regretted the words the instant they left his lips.

"Rules?" Ryan didn't even try to suppress his superior smile. "There are no rules. Not where I come from."

Knowing it would be a waste of time to appeal to Ryan's loyalty to his country, Levi tossed some Euros onto the table to cover the cost of the beers which had yet to arrive. Then he walked out while a refrain from his police days ran through his mind: *We take no guff, we cut no slack. We hook 'em and we book 'em and we don't look back.*

He didn't look back. But he did make a decision.

CHAPTER TWENTY-SIX

· ·

COMING TO stiff attention at the bottom step, Levi bobbed his head out of respect. *"Guten morgen, mein Kapitän."*

Koehl stared impassively as he shifted a black, leather bound missal from his right hand to his left before glaring at Roland and saying in English, "You have come at a most inopportune time. As you can see I am on my way to the Holy Sacrifice of the Mass. However — " Turning, he unlocked his door and pushed it open. "Please enter."

"Herr Koehl," Roland began once the door closed behind them, "May I present my colleague, Herr Levi Hart, a representative of the United States of America."

Koehl all but snarled. *"Le*-vi Hart. Humph. Another *Juden.* Like yourself, Herr Roland." He then asked Levi, "Well? Is that not so?"

Levi thought, *Roland insisted on talking to this guy. But I need to tell him to kiss my ass before he'll respect me.* He replied in even words, "With all respect *mein Kapitän,* my beliefs are none of your business."

The tall Swiss pulled himself up to his fullest Charles de Gaulle-stature and stared down as if examining a bacterium.

A protracted silence followed. Finally his countenance softened and he chanced a brief smile. *"Ja.* You are correct. It is not my concern. You are obviously a man of principle—and quite right to put me in my place." He flashed another smile. "Nor do I think you are *Juden.* Or that it would matter, for I am often called 'a true *mensch.*' So. Please wait here. I have a refreshment to offer." Leaving his visitors standing near the door, he disappeared into the kitchen.

Levi heard a cabinet door open and close, followed by a rattling of glassware before their host reappeared with a bottle and three shot glasses. Koehl passed out the glasses. Levi readied himself, for he knew what the bottle must contain: *Rakia,* an alcoholic drink, and refusing a shot despite the early morning hour was a cultural sin.

After Koehl filled all three glasses to the brim, he held his own glass aloft and peered at the clear liquid inside it. *"Rakia.* Made by a colleague in the village of Batina." To Levi he said, "Naturally I do not expect you to know of Batina."

Levi replied in German. "Batina is an old village in northeast Croatia. It sits along the Danube River and is linked to Serbia by a modern bridge. On a bluff overlooking the bridge sits a statue honoring the Russian soldiers who liberated Batina from the Nazis." Locking eyes with Koehl, he raised his glass and gave a Serbo-Croatian toast. *"Živjeli."*

Koehl replied in English with a sudden, ominous tone. "Be careful. The rakia you are holding is ninety per cent by volume."

"Then it will warm the heart on this chilly day."

"Yes. Quite. Well, then… *cheers* to you as well."

Raising the glasses to their lips, the three men ritualistically tossed down the homemade liquor.

Levi managed to keep from making a face. *Damn, this stuff is awful. Worst ever. Feels like its melting the enamel on my teeth.* He wondered why nobody had informed the maker that it was beyond dreadful. But he held the empty glass out as good manners dictated and waited while Koehl refilled it. Raising the glass to his lips again, he tossed his head back and downed the liquor. "Mmm. Best rakia I've had all day. Thank you, Herr Koehl." Then he turned the glass upside down — the polite way to signal that he'd had enough.

The old man took the glass from Levi. "You are a man of many religions and cultures." He came to attention and said, "*Ja. Sehr gut.*" Then he relaxed and gestured toward the chairs that Roland and Dieter had taken previously. "Gentlemen, please." He waited until they were seated before sitting ramrod straight in the chair opposite them.

Levi examined the walls, barren except for Koehl's ebony and ivory crucifix. Meanwhile, Roland lit a non-filter Gauloises and exhaled a cloud of harsh smoke which formed a wreath around his head. Facing their host, Levi absently caressed an inner elbow with his fingertips as he said, "Perhaps Monsieur Roland will honor you by explaining the nature of our impromptu visit."

Koehl nodded once. Nothing more.

Roland dragged deeply at his cigarette again, sending twin jets of gray smoke from his nostrils toward the floor before they curled upward. "There's been another homicide. A woman whom we've yet to identify. However, we've obtained evidence from Bogrov's apartment and his automobile that links him to this latest crime."

Koehl's eyebrows shot up. "What sort of evidence?"

"Shoe prints from two men next to a hastily dug grave. One set matches Bogrov's shoes." Roland looked at Levi. "Herr Hart found carpet fibers clutched in the corpse's hand. They're from Bogrov's ZIL." Roland began ticking off other items on his fingers. "Traces of feces on the car's rear seat were the corpse's. There were two shovels in the trunk. The dirt adhering to them came from the gravesite. The autopsy revealed semen from two men in her vagina." He reached his fifth finger. "Finally, her arms, shoulders, and face were dotted by previous bruises." Roland put the cigarette to his lips but then pulled it away. "I have ample findings to obtain a warrant for Bogrov's arrest. That said, prior to proceeding I wish to know *your* thoughts."

"You will not be able to serve the warrant," Koehl said at once.

"Go on."

"He has fled our Grand Duchy of Luxembourg. While I do not know this to be factual, I can say that flight would be disproportionate with his manner of conducting business... and that is precisely why I am convinced that he's done just that."

Levi jutted a jaw at Koehl. "There's more."

"Yes," he said with a faint glimmer of light in his otherwise dark eyes. "He will isolate himself."

"A knee-jerk reaction to the loss of his son," Levi fired back.

Koehl regarded him with a new interest. "An astute observation. Hmm. Your insight leads me to suspect that you've experienced a similar loss. Is that not so?"

"That is correct."

Roland sent a blue cloud of smoke into the air, where it hung between the men.

Koehl tilted his head and told Levi, "I see you most clearly, you know."

"Wonderful. Now then. Bogrov has just scheduled a press conference. From an unknown site, of course. It's slated to be held one week from today." He leaned forward. "I need to locate and apprehend him before then."

"A clearly defined need." After a brief silence Koehl said, "Very well. I will assist you to the best of my ability." He peered at Levi, then stood abruptly and gazed at some unseen thing. "I have heard whispers in the streets. Mutterings that transcend mere rumors." Pivoting his head to address both men, his next words burst forth as from a machine gun. "Bogrov owns an island. He now seeks soldiers of fortune. They are to keep the island secure. From what, nobody knows."

Roland waited until Koehl sat again before saying, "The Shah of Iran sought mercenaries, you know. To fortify an island. Having foreseen his limited future, he hired 300 men to protect him and his family at this redoubt."

Koehl cleared his throat. "You will never reach Bogrov for the time being. He is either already in Moscow or well on his way. He is cunning and obscure. In any event, you will waste resources trying to hunt him down. Even if he addresses various media, he will do so from Moscow, where the current regime will never give him up." He stared into Levi's eyes. "You have no other choice. Liquidate him. In Moscow. Now."

Levi told himself that President Cohen wouldn't hesitate a second to demand Bogrov's extradition—and he would back it up, no matter what. Levi held Koehl's gaze as an unspoken acknowledgment passed between them.

"However, if he holds his conference from the island—and if you can get to the island, you can get the man. For once he is there he will be accessible to you, while at the same time unable to flee to a neutral corner. Nor will he enjoy the protection of a regime that has rotted from within." He briefly studied Levi, then spoke slowly. "I have contacts. I will get word to Bogrov of a certain gentleman's transparent interest in becoming a member of his private army."

"Thank you," Levi said. But he didn't know Koehl, and tossing discretion aside, he looked at Roland. When the detective nodded, Levi felt better.

Perhaps in retaliation for the carelessness, Koehl skewered Levi with his eyes. "Does Monsieur Roland know that you are a heroin addict?"

Levi's breath came sharp. *Damn, this guy's good. He's also too friggin' intrusive.*

Roland turned and looked Levi over as if for the first time.

Leaning forward, Levi bit off his next words. "I'm not sure *what* he knows. Nor do I care. Now tell me... *mein Kapitän.* How is that relevant?"

"What is relevant is that you and I are similar in so many respects." He sniffed and waved a hand at Levi. "I saw you trace your fingertips along your inner arms." Koehl grew quiet as he traced his own fingertips along an arm.

Glaring, Levi said in a low tone, "We're a pair, you and I. Is that it?"

Koehl faced Roland and smiled indulgently. "Perhaps now you will understand that my *transparent* vow of poverty is in fact not so much by choice but by necessity as I endeavor to support my needs." He set his jaw. "Oh, by the way? Bogrov has a love affair with opium. Perhaps the stress of his latest actions will rekindle that love."

Levi's breath caught. "Hmm. Yes. I can use that against him."

Roland stubbed out his cigarette. "I agree. Your addiction can work in your favor. That is, if you get that across to our Russian friend during a job interview. For after all, what better people for him to surround himself with, than those who also use drugs—for what better soldiers to have, than those who would become subservient in order to get their needs met." He touched Levi's shoulder in a show of respect. "Is that not so?"

"Yes. That's what I'm thinking. As a drug-user he'll want to surround himself with like-minded individuals. Then he can lord it over them. Puts him in a comfort zone, there on his lonely little island."

Koehl said, "I agree. You will prove to be an attractive applicant to the maniac Bogrov, since your taste for opium will support his quest for grandiosity." Narrowing his eyes, he said, "Who knows? He might even invite you to share in his cornucopia. How wonderful would that be, eh?"

Looking beyond Koehl, Levi said, "That won't happen." He faced the former Swiss Guard. "You'll get me that job interview?"

"*Natürlich.*"

"Thank you." Grateful for the opportunity, Levi made a mental vow to work Bogrov and discover what he knew; what he didn't know — what his plans were. Then he'd find those papers and take him down.

Koehl's hands became fists. "It is my pleasure to assist you, Herr Levi Hart. To that end, please remain awhile. We shall use the time to discuss deeper aspects of this Russian mafia scum's character." He hesitated, then said with hooded eyes, "I shall also explain why I am convinced that your addiction grew not out of some personal desire or worse — out of weakness — but as a consequence of your employment. I will add, too, why I knew you are not Jewish — and why I baited you anyway."

CHAPTER TWENTY-SEVEN

· ·

"WE MUST not remain long," Bogrov told Slavko. Closing the door of his lavish Moscow home, he slid the deadbolt into place and surveyed the light, airy main room. Danish furniture had been placed with care—no velvet curtains or stodgy furniture for Yuri Bogrov. Nor were there any sounds beyond the subdued hum of air conditioning. Odors? They were also absent. He did not want to deal with them. No leather smells; no scents of colognes or perfumes, nor the tang of diapers in need of washing.

Bogrov stepped further into his castle. Knowing he would be seeing this place for the last time, his gaze lingered upon this object and that until he found himself staring at a brightly painted wooden rocking horse, so incongruous despite being tucked into a far corner. But he'd handcrafted it himself, and it was the one thing of his son's that he'd been incapable of parting with.

"Gather your belongings," he told Slavko. "One hour. No longer."

"Let me guess," the lumbering chauffeur said. "We will then go on to the airport."

"Of course." A muscle twitched in Bogrov's jaw as he stared at the rocking horse and wondered whether to take it. The perpetually grinning horse mocked him. Yet at the same time it provided a link to his long-dead son. *I can afford this one luxury. After all, I reached* this *place without trouble. No police stopped us. All that remains is to leave. For good.* His decision made, he pointed at the rocker. "Bring it."

The meeting with the wealthy but eccentric capitalist in Kaiserslautern had turned sour. The man refused to purchase any documents until his attorney vetted them. Bogrov explained that this was impossible and encouraged the man to examine the papers. But the old gentleman swept them aside unread.

A similar incident in Zagreb had convinced Bogrov that selling the papers—and divulging their contents anyway at a later date, along with photocopies to buttress his claims—was a useless endeavor. Besides, he'd only wanted to sell them as a means to demonstrate his ability to manipulate others, for he certainly didn't need the money.

Therefore he'd notified various media that he would hold a press conference in a week's time. It was a diversion, however. He would postpone it. Toy with them. Set a new date a fortnight from the previous one. However, that one would take place—even if not precisely on schedule. But it would happen. Now he and Slavko must travel to the island redoubt. Strangely enough, he didn't see himself as a man fleeing the police. That was a coward's way out. From his perspective, this was simply a tactical relocation.

But they needed to reach his business jet before local authorities elected to arrest him in the wake of ever-shifting political promises and paid-for loyalties. At the same time, he'd increased the risk along with the rush that came with it by calling the press conference. Assuming now that he did reach the airport unhindered, he would order the pilot to file an instrument flight plan for Novgorod, where he had a cluster of business interests. Once airborne, he would have the pilot cancel the flight plan and fly without one, as permitted under Visual Flight Rules. They would also turn off the transponder to make it difficult for air traffic controllers to track them. Once they reached the Atlantic Ocean's international airspace, he would have the pilot pop back up on radar and file a revised plan using the tail number of a former associate's business jet.

They left the apartment precisely one hour later. Bogrov had all he needed. That included the rocking horse and, of course, the pope's papers.

· · ·

"Clever man," Leo Ryan muttered beneath his breath as he stepped aboard the flight to JFK. "Clever, indeed." Ryan craned his neck for a last look at the Luxembourg police officer who'd brought him to the airport, with orders to make sure he got on the airliner and remained aboard until it took off.

Ryan hadn't been surprised when two officers arrested him on a vague charge of 'stalking with intent to commit bodily harm.' Nor had he been astonished when offered a choice: leave Luxembourg at once via a direct flight to the United States, or face charges and *probable* incarceration.

As he took his seat near the rear lavatories, with their strong odors and passengers jostling seats while waiting their turn, he vowed to get even with Levi even if it meant losing the story. However, the plan he was forming would let him get both: the story *and* the prize fighter who thought he'd landed a knockout blow. Leo Ryan whispered as he buckled his seatbelt, "That was only round one, Mr. Hart."

• • •

Bogrov blinked against the harsh glare of the Barbados sun sixteen hours later. It had taken fourteen hours flight time plus a fuel stop to reach the Caribbean island. That much had been routine. The trick had been in eluding authorities. It's why he told the pilot to refuel in Casablanca, where the police were lax and willing to look the other way for the right price—and Bogrov had been quite prepared to pay. But nobody in that fabled city showed the least interest in either the biz jet or its passengers. As for Barbados, they weren't staying there, so they didn't have to clear customs and immigration.

From Barbados they had a choice. They could take a small twin engine airplane to Union Island, where they would board a small but luxurious boat for the final leg of the trip to his private island. Or they could board the lavish Sikorsky S-76 helicopter that was waiting nearby, its rotors turning and the lovely pilot watching him for a sign. Bogrov preferred the plane and boat option. However, to reduce the chances of further scrutiny he tapped Slavko's shoulder and pointed at the helicopter. The instant they loaded their suitcases and the rocking horse, the pilot lifted off.

It took less than an hour to complete the overwater flight. As they drew closer to Bogrov's 435-acre sanctuary, he told the pilot to circle the island. She banked the aircraft at once and reduced speed to offer a leisurely inspection. The island's most prominent features were its two hills. The higher one rose to 300 feet. The other topped out at 150. Two bluffs offered vantage points to northern approaches; patches of cleared fields and forests dotted the landscape.

A small herd of cattle were grazing in a pasture. Other spaces had been cultivated for food. Solar panels and wind turbines sprouted from the higher hill, and water storage tanks and utilitarian buildings were scattered among them. Finally, a number of cottages and villas lined the beaches, while atop the smaller hill sat a modest house painted white, with a red tiled roof marred by photovoltaic solar panels. Once the pilot completed the fly-by, Bogrov told her to land on the private retreat he'd dubbed *Isla de la Rusia*—although unknown to him, the region's locals rolled their eyes and referred to Bogrov's habitat not as *Island of the Russian*, but as *esa isla de Rusia*—*that* Russian's *island*.

The subtle variation revealed their contempt for the arrogant owner. Not that Bogrov cared what they thought, so long as the merchants served his needs. Few of the islanders had even been there. Other than a Filipino couple who managed the crops and a handful of North American men and women whom he'd recruited to supervise things, he had imported most of his staff from Russia. Currently there were sixteen residents on Isla de la Rusia. He planned to increase that number by adding fifty fighting men, along with several sexually attractive females—for as he once boasted, what use is an island if not to have fun?

AS THEY stepped from the Sikorsky onto the dockside helipad, Bogrov and Slavko were greeted by the balmy breezes of a languorous late afternoon. Pausing to gaze at the setting sun, the Russian judged it would be another hour before the super-hot orb dipped itself into the ocean's inviting waters. Next, he gestured at the solid Russian woman with a double-chin and eternally flushed cheeks who'd come to meet them. "Well?"

Bronislava lifted both shoulders. "Well, what? Everything is as it should be. Now do we go up the hill? Or have you a need for further conversation?"

Bogrov worked to conceal his merriment. His housekeeper had the manner of a logging-truck dispatcher, a quality that made her the only woman he truly respected. Leaning toward her, he adopted a conspiratorial voice. "To be truth-ful, I thought I would whisper sweet words in your ear." He raised his eyebrows. "Well? Shall we make with the bump-bump?" He pointed to the nearby helicopter hangar. "There, perhaps?"

Her reply was direct: she flipped him off, turned, and trudged up the narrow road to the main house.

Bogrov didn't bother asking why she hadn't brought a jeep to bring them up the long, winding hill. He and Bronislava had a special connection and she'd undoubtedly deduced that he'd want to walk after the long journey. So he picked up the rocking horse and started off with her, leaving Slavko to gather the remaining luggage.

As they reached the hill's summit a house revealed itself from behind coconut palms, an ancient banyan tree, and red bougainvillea. Pausing at the handsome door of Brazilian cherry wood, he waited while Bronislava opened it. He sniffed and made a face. Even with air conditioning, the house tended toward stale air unless someone opened the doors now and then. Thinking that would never be a problem again, he flicked a wall switch and three rows of LED track lights came on at once. Soft and unobtrusive, they were in keeping with the island's energy-conservation needs.

Striding forward, he went to a huge window and pulled the curtains aside. The landscaped gardens captured his eye first. Beyond those lay the powdery white sands of a beach. Placing the rocker until it looked out, he told himself that though the house might smell, it was all about the view. That, and the billions he would gain by selling the papal papers. Or... the billions who would starve after he revealed the papers' revelations to the world. *If I must die, then I must. After all, death is inevitable is it not? Ah, but in this case I shall be the one to call the shots. Not only for myself, but for the pitiful squawking masses of worthless scum that I'm forced to share this planet with. Hah! If only they knew how little time they have left. Well—within a month they* shall *know.*

Turning away from the window, he dismissed Bronislava and rested a hand on the horse's head. *The garden. The beach. The ocean. Da. It is all good. A fitting panorama for my son.* Next, he went to a rear door and stepped outside, for he wanted to see one more thing before he opened a bottle of vodka and drained it.

Making his way along a trail that snaked through clusters of bromeliads, hibiscus and geranium, he followed the cobble stone path that reminded him of the Rodina. The path took him to the opening of a carefully trimmed fichus hedge, where inside a small clearing of well-maintained Bahia grass surrounded the granite marker of his son's grave.

He'd gone to great lengths to bring the boy here. The most difficult part was exhuming the body a few days after he'd been buried. But after smuggling the remains to Isla de la Rusia, he'd known everything would be all right.

Bogrov knew that such sentimentality was his Achilles heel, but this had been his son—a reflection of himself. It's why he'd made sure to keep the real location of this grave something akin to a state secret.

A number of polished pebbles sitting atop the thick marker testified to his prior visits, and he rested a hand atop the cold granite the same way he'd touched the lifeless rocking horse. "I give you greetings, my son." Then he said a prayer—a vestige of his own childhood—and afterward he found a fresh pebble and placed it on the stone. His heart felt lighter. He turned to go, knowing he'd return tomorrow and each day after, and from now until the end of time he would refer to this place not as Island of the Russian, but as *Isla del hijo de Rusia*—Island of the Russian's Son.

CHAPTER TWENTY-EIGHT

· ·

LEVI HART'S auburn hair was a tangled mess, he had a three-day scruff, and a thin veil of perspiration covered his body as he lay naked atop a decrepit bed that all but grew from the wall of a low-rent London hotel room. A solitary window smeared by ancient layers of grime looked out onto a brick wall across the gulf of a narrow alley. The place smelled of tobacco, mildew, vomit, and spent energy. An ancient steam radiator ran full-blast—when *it* wanted to—then banged non-stop until weary of its own cacophony.

Easing the woman's head from his shoulder, he reached for the pack of Richmond cigarettes—a British brand with a dark blue/light blue logo that only the poor bothered to smoke. He pulled one out and lit up.

Levi didn't smoke, but Rocky O'Toole did—and he'd become that person, a high school dropout blessed with a sharp brain who brought knowledge, skills and abilities to whatever table he approached.

He'd adopted the deep-cover role to break into Bogrov's army. Under normal conditions the U.S. government needs six months to approve an undercover op. During this time support personnel are selected, per diems calculated, and overtime budgeted. Vehicles and surveillance apparatus must be allocated, and a Class One authorization to do hard drugs to fit in with certain gangs must be obtained from Justice.

But the present crisis mandated a Herculean effort, and the Bureau accomplished a heroic task akin to the World War II job that was done when the carrier USS *Yorktown* limped into Pearl Harbor after sustaining heavy damage during a running sea battle. With a decisive clash brewing at Midway, Pearl Harbor's damage control experts, welders, and ship fitters swarmed aboard *Yorktown* and made six months worth of repairs in fewer than seventy-two *hours*.

In Levi's case, it helped that Michael had been a street kid-turned Army Ranger. Levi had picked his best friend's brains enough to be able to talk the talk and walk most of the walk. Logic dictated that Michael would be the better choice for this assignment. But Levi had a vast amount of experience in working hard-core, deep-cover assignments, and now was not the time to break-in a new player. And, Levi no longer had a family.

Michael's contributions came as other wheels turned rapidly. Levi even had a passport in Rocky's name courtesy of the Department of State, which overnighted the fake document to him, complete with signs of wear and the usual immigration stamps.

His new identity and passport sprang to life after Koehl made good on his promise to get him an interview for a *special job* requiring certain types of men. Levi, Roland, and Dragon Team took this to mean men who could and would fight—but who also lived life on a broad scale. The deduction was realistic: unlike the politically correct U.S. military which now eschews the sort of raucous behavior that's at the heart of true warriors, other armed forces—the Russian forces in particular—believe that soldiers who don't party like animals won't fight like animals.

Levi—*Rocky*—handed the cigarette to the woman. She inhaled, held the smoke a second or two, then exhaled with a deep sigh before giving it back.

Reclining and causing the old-fashioned bedsprings to squeak, he arched a hairy leg and planted a foot flat on the dingy mattress, then smoked in silence as he studied the ceiling's flaking white paint. He was careful not to stare at the camera lens. He'd spotted the pinhole lens soon after checking into this hotel, having taken it as a matter of faith that he'd be under surveillance. Bogrov had a history of hiring only high-caliber people, and he'd have hired the best to thoroughly screen each applicant. It's why Levi had been instructed to go to this dump—to gauge his reactions; it's why he bought the Richmonds and picked up the woman. Undercover operatives would have avoided both, but a real McCoy smokes and seeks sex from casual pickups or prostitutes. As for the camera, he was indifferent to it—during college he and Michael had supplemented their income by working the ladies club circuit as male strippers.

As an argument between two men in another room filtered through, he glanced at the trail of clothes that began just inside the door and ended at the base of the bed. The stunning blonde of thirty, tall and slender, had been wearing Prada until he stripped her with real purpose, while his own clothes consisted of a second-hand flannel shirt, faded military cargo pants, and old work shoes.

He'd met her hours earlier in the financial district. Knowing he stood out with his scruffy loser-look, he wasn't too surprised when she came onto him, explaining without shame that she'd always harbored a desire to have sex with "a ruffian sort."

"Really?" he'd asked. "Hmm. A woman who knows what she wants." Leaning closer, his nose crinkled. "What's that you're wearing? Eau de Crap?" She answered with a nervous laugh, he saw no wedding band, he was a man and she was clearly a woman—and he took it on faith that she worked for Bogrov and had been sent to evaluate him. So he'd told her, "I'm gonna screw you into next week." Then he took her to the room and gave her the hot, lusty sex she sought—fully aware that they were being videotaped. But he had to infiltrate Bogrov's operation, so despite the revulsion he felt, he'd used her to put on a show that would establish his credentials.

That was then. Now, she puffed at his cigarette once more and nestled against his shoulder. "Mmm, you are sooo delicious." Hooking a long slender leg over his warm thigh, she looked him over. "Tell me about the tattoo on your ankle."

He grunted. "Souvenir of San Quentin."

She jumped a little. "The prison?"

"Is there another San Quentin I don't know about?" He looked at her with jaded eyes—Rocky O'Toole's eyes. "Did six years. Aggravated assault."

She asked carefully, "Is that what you Americans call 'hard time'?"

"Hard as it gets."

"Oh." She fell silent, then began tentatively, "Were you ever…"

"Hey! Do I look like I was ever?" He waited until she averted her eyes. "Are we done playing twenty questions?" When she replied by kissing the base of his sweaty throat, his belly and then his hip bone, he scoffed. "I see. Ex-cons turn you on."

Pausing, she looked up at him. "Hmm. You sure know women."

He belched. "I know fighting. And fucking." Settling back with arched leg and cigarette while she took care of him, yet acting bored by it all by blowing smoke rings, he finished the cigarette and chain-lit the last one. She finally brought him to a grunt and a sigh, but as she entered his arms again, a sudden shout near the door made him shift until he shielded her. Reaching under the pillow, he gripped an untraceable .45 automatic.

His viscera sent a signal. He thumbed the pistol's hammer, ready to cock it.

The door burst open. A large man lurched inside—and fell flat on his face.

Flat or not, Levi prepared to do battle while the woman clutched at him.

Another man charged inside but came to an abrupt halt. "Sorry, mate." A cruel scar marked the bridge of his nose, but the otherwise handsome young lad smiled and gestured at the guy on the floor. "Me and this tosser here, we was havin' a bit of an argument, we was. Not to worry, though. I'll have this bloke out in a jiff." Stepping closer to the moaning man, he stared at Levi's visitor with liquid, woman-loving eyes.

Levi was edging the pistol from the pillow when the young man said affably, "That's quite the lovely lass you've got there. Starkers, as well. Sure, then. I thought I heard some bumpin' an' grindin' going on." He winked, then reached for his friend's arm. "Now you two carry on. We're all but out of here."

Levi said in a glib way, "Don't let the door hit your ass on the way out."

The young man said with great cheer, "Right-O. Good one, there."

But Levi suspected an ulterior motive behind the visit. Letting go of the pistol and not bothering to cover either himself or the woman, he tilted his head at the crumpled pack of Richmonds and the still-burning cigarette next to it, then pantomimed smoking. "Hey, pal. You got one I can bum?"

Laughing heartily, the Brit pulled a pack of Marlboros from a pants pocket and extended it. Levi noted a Virginia tax-stamp on the pack as he pulled out a cigarette and dropped it to the nightstand.

Offering the pack again, the guy shook it. "Go on, mate. Have another. Or two or three, if it suits your fancy. Cheers."

Levi took two more and tossed them next to the other one, then held out a hand. "Rocky."

"Brilliant. Ian's me name." He gave a firm handshake, then pulled his friend from the floor with amazing strength. "Up you go. There's a good chap now."

"Thanks for the smokes," Levi said off-handedly. "Don't forget the door."

"Not to worry, mate." Still hoisting the drunken man, Ian put a hand on the knob and gave Levi a very male grin before shutting the door.

Levi listened until their footsteps faded. "You okay?"

She put her head on his bicep. "My god. I thought my heart would stop. But *you*. You handled him with such *vim* and *vigor*." She laughed nervously. "You're the Natural Man. Every girl's dream."

"A regular Marlboro Man, huh?" He grabbed one of Ian's cigarettes and lit it. Bogrov would want hard-core types. But he'd also want team players, and because the visit probably hadn't been accidental, it's why he put on a show of being sociable rather than coming across as a lone wolf.

As he caressed her long graceful back he smoked the cigarette to its filter as poor people do, then mashed it against the wood floor and pulled her close. In time, the rhythmic *creak creak creak* of bedsprings filled the room again.

She touched his cheek afterward. "You're quite lovely in bed. The way you kiss me, touch me. It's why I'm so dreadfully afraid to tell you that I must leave now."

He nodded and wordlessly pulled on his clothes while she dressed with regal grace. Then he walked her to the nearest taxi stand. But on returning to his room he found Ian leaning against the door.

The Brit grinned. "There you are, mate. Once I got rid of that tosser I thought we'd have a drink. I knocked. Didn't hear any action inside. Thought I'd wait a bit. And here you are." He offered a charming smile. "I'm glad I waited."

"A drink, huh?" Levi stopped an arms-length away, ready to fight. Just in case.

Ian pulled a bottle of gin from his coat and held it aloft.

Although quite certain that Ian had just finished a thorough search of the room, he invited him in. But leery of drinking something that might've been spiked, he got a bottle of Scotch from the bureau and splashed liquor into a pair of water glasses. "Grab a chair," he said in a bored way as he handed one to Ian.

But Ian put down his glass and reached inside his jacket. "Oi. You strike me as a player, you do." He pulled out a vial of white powder. "Well?"

"Thanks. It's not that I haven't done blow. I did, when I was young and dumb." He gestured at the vial. "Haven't done anything harder than booze in at least ten years."

"Right-O. Thought I'd offer." He took a swig of the Scotch.

Levi watched Ian for any untoward reaction, then tossed back half an ounce and felt the slow burn at the back of his throat while wondering what would come next.

He soon found out when Ian said, "That was a lovely lass you had. Not that I'm surprised. I mean, good-looking chap like you." He gave Levi a once-over, then yawned and looked pointedly at the bed. "I didn't realize how late it's gotten. Or how tired I am. Say, do you mind a bit of company for the rest of the night? That's if you could do with sharing that bed." Already undoing his pants, he grinned. "I sleep starkers. You too, I'll wager." Then he unzipped and grew a sly smile. "Well come over here an' have at it. Or if you prefer, I could—" He stared at Levi's crotch. "You do fancy a bit of fun, right?"

"Do I fancy? Sure. With a woman." He stared at Ian.

The Brit's eyes bulged. "What? You think I'm a *poof*? I only meant..."

"Listen," Levi said. "I don't care what puts the whiz in your wick. The way I see it? The more gay guys there are, the less competition there is for the women." He raised an eyebrow. "Are we done now? Because I'd like to get back to drinking."

They had one more drink apiece before Ian remembered the time and left. Levi locked the door behind him, then stripped and plopped onto the bed to think. Dragon Team had done their best to prepare him for this assignment. But left unsaid were two realities: this mission was as big as they get, and therefore he'd have to kill Bogrov. It was the only way. Taking him into custody would give the Russian an opportunity to tell-all in court. Even if he were taken before a military tribunal, someone might talk.

Levi hadn't discussed assassination—not with the team nor even privately with Michael, reasoning that a man must keep certain things to himself, especially when he'll enter a forum where rules don't exist. His last thought before drifting off to the music of gonging radiator pipes was, will I get through this?

When he jerked awake sometime later the room was dark and he was naked and alone and that's when it hit him—he'd never asked the woman her name. Not that it mattered. He'd known when she approached him that she must be an operative bent on assessing his values, virtues, and virility. He felt confident that he'd passed the scrutiny, but he also thought, what a sordid business this is. Reaching for one of the Marlboros, he lit up and smoked in the stifling dark room while the radiator came to life. After finishing it, he ground the stub out against the floor and closed his eyes.

•   •   •

Monica closed her eyes and danced her fingertips like butterflies against the back of Michael's neck while he kissed her goodnight, reveling in his scent which she found to be bold yet gentle; the bed jouncing when he drew away. Now sated, she regarded him anew, his glance lazily content as he ran a hand through her long black hair. She touched his cheek in response and traced a thumb along his lips. "Thanks, Lover Boy. I needed that." He offered a shy smile beneath knowing eyes, then kissed her again.

He'd come to her Luxembourg hotel room earlier to shoot the breeze, for it was how the close friends dealt with the loneliness of long-term travel, the two of them talking while sitting on the bed since it was the only place in the tiny room *to* sit. As he put on his shoes he suggested they meet for breakfast and after she agreed, he left her.

Locking the door behind him, she undressed and slipped into bed. She'd loved him from the start—and not for his striking good looks, which couldn't be denied. But she wasn't in love with him. What she loved was his depth and the fact that despite the childhood terrors he'd endured, he'd kept his soul intact. He had a good heart, and yet he could be hard-core in performing his duties. But most of all he was a dear friend.

If he'd been single she'd have sought a life together and had his children. Now she might never have any, not if that asteroid pulverized the planet into fragments. She knew she should scrub the image from her mind and stay focused. But she was only human, with all of the attendant dreams, joys and fears that come with being one.

Her thoughts turned to Levi. Their friendship also ran deep and she easily recalled the day she met him: devastating charm. Effortless, subdued; lethal. The fact that he'd so deeply loved his wife and son made him more special, for she believed that only a strong man could be a gentle man — and both he and Michael had those qualities. And when Levi saved Michael's life during the White House shoot-out, she'd loved him for that, too.

But now he'd be exposed to great peril at Bogrov's hands and there'd be little that she or the team could do for him. Pushing it aside, she settled in, although doubting that sleep would come — not when she knew that the team had done its best to set Levi up to be slowly tortured by the Russian should he ever discover Levi's true identity.

Unknown to her, in the darkened room where no mirror could show her reflection, her face took on the hard cast of a fighter who'll do whatever it takes to prevent global catastrophe, even if it means taking one or more lives. In her case, she'd killed once already. Then as now, her innate sense of duty was so great that if called upon, she'd trade places with Levi in a heartbeat.

PART III

. . .

London's Heathrow Airport
The Following Day

CHAPTER TWENTY-NINE

· · · · · · · · · · · · · · · · · · · ·

HAVING ARRIVED early at one of London Heathrow's better airport hotels, Levi Hart performed an area recon before rapping his knuckles against the door to Room Twelve. A stern male voice on the other side said, "Enter and secure the portal behind you."

Levi had already spotted the pinhole camera lens where the wall and ceiling met. His clean shave and combed hair were undoubtedly being noted, along with his black leather jacket, white polo shirt, and blue jeans. Drawing a deep breath, he turned the knob and took a single stride through the door—and by doing so he transitioned from elite agent to gun-for-hire. Seconds later he shielded his eyes from a bank of harsh flood lights while he 'secured the portal' as ordered. There would be no turning back. Not now.

A disembodied voice from behind the lights said in a refined British accent, "Step forward three paces, stop, turn completely around, then stand still."

Levi knew they were gauging his ability to follow orders. They were shopping for alpha males, true—but they'd want obedient ones. He performed the task without delay and stood at a slight attention.

"Very well. Take one more step forward and state your name and age."

He stepped forward. "Rocky O'Toole. Twenty-eight." Levi was forty, but experience had proven that he could readily pass for a twentysomething.

"Rocky O'Toole, you have been directed to come to this place. I assume you know why. Describe, therefore, your qualifications."

Levi provided a short biography of a high school dropout who had roamed the streets until he got wise and took a high school equivalency test. After achieving the highest score in Nevada's history he entered the army and did a stint as a Ranger.

"Ranger, huh? Tell me, Mister… O'Toole. Where is 'the ranch'?"

Levi narrowed his eyes. "You're not supposed to know that term."

"Clearly I do. So. Ever been there?"

"Was never invited."

"But you were a Ranger, were you not?"

"A Ranger, yes. But not *Delta* Force, which as you apparently know is…"

"Is headquarted at 'the ranch'. Very well. Continue."

"I was a good soldier but ended up in prison. Aggravated assault. Army gave me a D.D."

"Provide the specifics—victim's name, address of the court; that sort of thing."

"Sure. His name's Brian Hadley. He—" Levi described breaking Mr. Hadley's elbows and both bones of his lower arms. He gave the date and place of the crime and the court's address—where FBI-manufactured police reports, arrest data and court records, plus a dishonorable discharge from the army were in place as of yesterday morning. In addition, a civilian FBI employee had been tapped to play the role of the injured Mr. Hadley. Rocky O'Toole's mug shot and records were also in San Quentin's files and even on its website. "Yeah," Levi finished. "He had it coming."

"No doubt. Continue."

Levi described doing odd-jobs since his release and admitted to experimenting with drugs as a teen. "You know. The usual. Coke. Heroin; dropped acid a couple of times. But only at parties. Never alone." In response to the interviewer's next question, Levi assured him that ten years had passed since he'd done hard drugs.

Then Levi asked off-handed questions that might offer insight into Bogrov and his operation. His queries were met by silence, although the interviewer did tell Levi that the woman he'd bedded and the men who crashed into his room were evaluating him and had given him high marks for bravery, sexual prowess and suitable sexual orientation. "Our lady told us you're quite the swordsman. She rarely offers such a compliment."

Taking the compliment for what it might be—an attempt at gauging his level of arrogance or lack thereof—Levi said nothing.

All at once a bespectacled man in a drab suit appeared from behind the lights. Holding up a BP cuff and stethoscope, he told Levi to strip to his shorts. Then he checked Levi's vitals, listened to his chest, felt for a hernia, examined his arms and feet for illicit needle marks, and asked about the tattoo. Lastly, he drew three vials of blood, muttering that he would analyze the samples for STDs and recent drug use.

Before the presumed doctor retreated, the interviewer told Levi, "Hand over your cell phone. There's a good lad, now. Then put on your clothes."

Levi got dressed. When the doctor reappeared a moment later to return the phone, Levi knew it meant he'd downloaded its address book and call history. They would check the recent callers. The interviewer announced, "This meeting is concluded. You may go."

Levi came to full attention, executed a sharp about-face and marched out.

CHAPTER THIRTY

· · · · · · · · · · · · · · · · · · · ·

BOGROV AWOKE feeling so restless that after performing his morning ablutions he put on a white linen shirt, khaki trousers and walking shoes. Picking up his father's old leather bag, he slung it over his shoulder and ventured outside, only to be further agitated when forced to shield his eyes from the sun's glare. Donning a pair of Wayfarers—the style of sunglasses JFK had worn—he set a quick pace along the trail to the cemetery.

Although the morning air was humid, the trades were moderating the heat and so he barely broke a sweat, walking in relative comfort past small boulders and palms before passing through the hedge that protected the memorial park. Finally kneeling beside the headstone, he ran his hands over the polished granite face that bore his son's name. "Well, Anton. Here we are again. And from this point on, it shall be for eternity."

Turning quiet, he gazed at the hedge as if by peering hard enough, he could see through it to the endless sea beyond. Now it was all about his coming out on top. But he had to perform a chore before putting the next inevitable step in motion, and so reaching into the bag, he pulled out a nine by eleven inch velvet-covered box. Lifting away the top, he inspected an ornate antique icon of Our Lady of Kazan, painted on wood in 1840 and bordered by gold lead. He'd paid $30,000 U.S. dollars for it, and turning it over, he gave it a quick check. Then he put it back in the box.

From the leather sack he retrieved a trowel and a durable zip-lock bag. He put the box inside the bag, moved a vase at the bottom of the headstone, then dug until he created a shallow pit. After setting the icon inside the pit, he filled in the dirt and placed a pebble atop the marker. But as he walked away, he debated once again the merits of putting the papers up for auction, or calling a press conference instead.

THIRTY MINUTES later, Yuri Bogrov brought his jeep to a stop on one of the island's roads and nodded, satisfied by what he'd seen during his ritualistic inspection tour. The narrow roads, the spidery foot paths, and the network of trails provided access to every part of Isla de la Rusia. During the drive he'd seen small birds flitting about, green and red parrots flying overhead, and lizards crawling across fallen palm fronds. Then to his surprise he laughed aloud. *Good God. I live in a wildlife-sanctuary. Why did I not think to import some elephants and rhinos to shoot?* It wasn't idle musing. He'd love to shoot both. But he hadn't brought any species of big game, much to his regret now.

However, he'd had three dozen cottages, plus dining halls and recreation facilities built, with all of them nestled within this paradise setting. And along a hilltop ridge there were arrays of solar panels that would guarantee perpetual electricity for the LED lights and other energy-conserving measures that made the island self-sufficient. Immediately below the ridges were cisterns from which he and his people could count on a constant supply of running water.

Then there were the innocuous buildings placed a quarter-mile from each other. He believed in separate assets, and each building held enough military rations to feed a small army for five years. They also contained fishing nets and tackle for a fleet of row boats housed at the dock. A surveillance radar sat atop the highest hill, while bunkers and other fortified buildings held enough ordnance to keep the world at bay—or to at least discourage an attack once he told all—and until the asteroid hit.

His long-term plan called for him to decide which would come first. But because he looked forward to spending an eternity with his boy, he didn't want to wait too long. It's why he was in a rush to get his army in place, since a leak of the revelations would compel the world to enter into an alliance to overwhelm him. If on the other hand no such alliance could be formed, that would also suit him, since it would give him more fun time before the world's inevitable end. Either way, he would call the shots. He would decide whether to let the world live in ignorance for another eighteen months, or to writhe in death throes while he lived the party life. That's what really appealed to him.

But after taking off his Wayfarers, he squinted at the ocean and vowed to get on with it after all. Yes, that was it. He'd make a few calls today to put out feelers. Then he'd establish a final date to alert the media. It all came down to whim. Bogrov knew this and didn't care, for in the end he would

either have more riches than his father could have ever imagined, or he'd have sent the world into a feeding frenzy of
self-preservation against a certain end. He decided. One
month from today. In one month he would have it all. The
rest of the world? It would have nothing. Both eventualities
left him the ultimate winner.

CHAPTER THIRTY-ONE

. . . .

TWO DAYS later, Levi Hart stepped from an inter-island boat onto Isla de la Rusia's dock. He had to be here. There was no other way—not after Roland tracked Bogrov to the island; not after the detective, Dieter, and Dragon Team debated the merits of sending in a lone operative rather than Delta Force. But after learning that Bogrov had tried to sell the papers in Kaiserslautern, the team realized the futility of mounting a major operation unless and until they developed incontrovertible proof that Bogrov hadn't been able to sell them elsewhere. A third option called for using an electromagnetic pulse to neutralize all electrical power and devices on-island. That would prevent Bogrov from informing the world of the papal papers via something so simple as a laptop.

That idea was nixed when Dentz pointed out the obvious: while an EMP would undoubtedly be effective, its use would alert Bogrov that his enemies were closing in, and taking him out could trigger the fail-safe system that would tell-all to the world—and the Dragons *had* to assume that such a system existed. Besides, in the wake of an EMP, the Russian could easily sail to an unaffected island to 'let the word go forth.'

Consequently, after consulting with Heath who in turn met with the president, the consensus was clear—send in Levi Hart. If he failed or if his mission got compromised, then as Levi put it the fleet would sail, Delta Force would deploy, men would shout, dogs would bark, and mothers would pull their children from the streets.

That's why he'd ended up on Isla de la Rusia, and after taking in the scenery he announced, "Hey, this isn't half-bad."

The look on Slavko's face nearly shouted that he didn't think much of this latest polo-shirted, denim-clad arrival. "You are the new mercenary. Yes?"

Walking toward the towering man with the wandering eye, Levi held out his hand. "Rocky O'Toole. One of the soldiers you guys hired."

"A mercenary," Slavko mumbled. "We will see whether you are true soldier." Blowing air from his cheeks, he pointed to a waiting jeep. "This way."

But Levi hooked a thumb in the waistband of his jeans and stood fast in a way that conveyed a message: *Don't even think for one minute that I'll kiss your ass.* He also used the stare-down to absorb his new surroundings. The boat trip from the nearby island hadn't revealed much beyond the solar panels, wind turbines, and water tanks atop the larger hill. The similarities to the "green" civilization that the Ecos built weren't lost on him, either. Concurrently, the well-maintained dock facilities and richly appointed pier were in line with what he knew of Yuri Bogrov—that with some exceptions such as his million and a half dollar watch, he valued quality over flashiness.

Levi also thought that the weather couldn't have been nicer, especially when compared to Kwajalein's sweltering humidity or London's dismal chill. Here, a clear azure sky accented the Caribbean's patchwork of blues, turquoises, and greens. The coral sand was talcum-powder fine, and facing east he felt the trade's moderating breezes as they brushed his face.

Thinking he could've landed a mission that would've taken him to Antarctica, he said a silent thanks for this small gem in what would undoubtedly be a nasty undertaking. Picking up his knapsack, he slung it over his shoulder and followed the tall guy.

Slavko opened the jeep's tailgate and said, "Put the contents of your bag here." Levi obeyed, then watched Slavko poke through his sparse clothing and toilet kit. Next, the hulking man pulled a small electronic device from a pocket and swept it over Levi's personal effects. When the device emitted no beeps, he had Levi raise his hands. After passing the gadget up and down Levi's body, front and back, he mumbled, "Open your mouth." While holding the device against Levi's teeth, he said, "It fascinates me to see the manner in which transmitters can be made to resemble a tooth." When no red flags appeared, Slavko grunted. "Very well. Pack your things and get in."

The security precautions were par for this situation. Levi had expected nothing less, since psychopaths seek to control other people's abilities to communicate. It's why he'd had to assume that the rich Russian would have ringed his island with emission detectors to alert him if anyone made an unauthorized cell phone call—assuming they could even get reception. But Levi could not be incommunicado, so he and the team had brainstormed an idea that was already in action.

At this very second a Predator unmanned aerial vehicle was flying high overhead. The Bureau and Dragon Team were watching Levi in real-time. They would monitor him all the way to his quarters, then lock-in its GPS coordinates. Later tonight, a SEAL squad would deploy from a submarine and plant a satellite phone in a place of Levi's choosing.

The iridium SAT phone he'd get was the size of a smart phone. Of military-grade durability, it also boasted a rugged high-gain antenna and enhanced SMS and email messaging. It had hands-free capability and a GPS tracking function complete with a panic button for emergency situations. Whenever Levi typed a message and tapped the SEND button, the device would instantly encrypt the message and transmit it as a micro-burst that would be immune to emission detectors. It could also receive coded messages.

LEVI STOOD outside Bogrov's home minutes later, and when the Russian walked outside Levi made an initial assessment of his nemesis: *bulk in proportion to height, outsized hands from life on a farm, and he's constantly looking around with a wolf-like alertness.* Levi's gut told him that this guy radiated pure evil. But when Bogrov drew closer, Levi poked a friendly hand at him. The Russian smiled with his facial muscles as they shook. Levi thought he was an oily snake but said aloud, "I promise to give you all I have." With chin up and shoulders back, he added, "That's my vow to you."

Bogrov bobbed his head. "*Khorosho*. That means, *good*. I hope you will hear this word often, for to hear it coming from my lips means that your performance has pleased me. To hear me say *da, khorosho* signifies *great* happiness." He glanced at Slavko, who waited patiently nearby. "Let us hope you will make me happy, Mr. O'Toole."

"Please call me Rocky." While covertly noting a large middle-aged woman standing just inside the door, he added, "Thank you for hiring me."

Bogrov opened his mouth to reply, then shut it and squinted. "You remind me of somebody. I am not yet sure who, but it will come to me." Craning his neck, he called out in Russian to the woman.

Her eyes narrowed as she peered at Levi. Finally she said, "*Nyet*."

Bogrov told Levi, "That is Bronislava. She has been with me for many years." Then he said, "I am told you enjoy a woman's skills in the bedroom. *Khorosho*. That is mark of good soldier. It is why I also hired many single women to work here. This is good, da?" Bogrov paused and fixed his gaze beyond Levi's shoulders. All at once he barked, "Roll up your sleeves."

Levi complied and said while Bogrov examined his arms, "Like I told that guy in London… I haven't done anything hardcore since I was a teen."

Tapping Levi's arms, Bogrov smiled and told Slavko, "This one will do." He chewed at his lower lip, then said in a low growl, "Enjoy what there is of life, Rocky O'Toole. Feast on it, for not much time will remain once my soldiers are all in place."

Levi's insides turned cold. Did this mean Bogrov intended to act sooner than anticipated? Soldiers are not to question their commanders. And they shouldn't kill them. But Levi knew he would transcend both proscriptions, beginning by asking questions. "Is there anything I need to know, sir? That is, to protect this island?"

Bogrov's face suddenly flushed red; an artery stood out in his forehead. But his anger subsided in a heartbeat. "Da. You ask good question. It is question of clarification of orders. Khorosho." He offered a more gracious smile. "There is nothing you need to know. Not yet." A new, genuine friendliness formed on his face before he nodded once. Then he turned to go.

Levi now had to work even faster to determine what Bogrov knew, who he'd shared the information with, and what he'd done with the pope's documents. If he failed, the world would go insane, the Kwajalein project would be threatened, and all could be lost. He watched Bogrov enter the house and thought, I'm gonna cancel your ticket, and soon. Then he climbed into the jeep.

Slavko drove down the long driveway, and on reaching an east-west road he spun the wheel to the right and drove on. Levi asked permission to smoke and when the Serb nodded, Levi offered him a Lucky Strike. But Slavko made a face, so Levi lit up and smoked while taking everything in — warehouses, observation posts manned by bored sentinels, and pillboxes nestled behind shrubs. Slavko finally stopped in front of a contemporary villa on a white sand beach graced by a fresh sea breeze.

Levi grabbed his gear and followed the silent man to the door. But when Levi twisted the knob and found it wasn't locked, he looked questioningly at Slavko.

"We have no need of locks," he intoned. "We are secure here."

"Good to know." Real good to know, he thought as he pushed the door open and walked inside. Clean floor tiles shone even in the dim natural light. When he turned on the LEDs they illuminated a well-equipped kitchen, a richly appointed living room of wood panels and crown molding, and hurricane-resistant sliding glass doors that looked out onto the Caribbean. Finally, he saw a bedroom on either side of the central core.

Slavko pointed to the one of the left. "Yours. For the moment the other remains unoccupied." He cleared his throat. "While off-duty you may dress as you wish. You will find that everyone is quite casual here—even natural, as it were. On-duty you will wear a uniform. It is now 1130 hours. I will return at 1430 hours to bring you to the supply hut."

"Three hours," Levi said while checking the cheap Timex on his arm. Then he discreetly looked around again, trying to spot the surveillance cameras that he had to assume were in place and already monitoring him.

"Put away your things. Rest awhile. Swim in the ocean if you like. But beware of predators." Slavko's sudden show of white teeth came unbidden. "Beach umbrellas and chairs are in there." He pointed through the glass doors to a small pastel-painted shed.

Levi thought the colors shouted, 'Welcome to the Caribbean,' and he imagined hearing steel drums. But Slavko was the type to hide an ace or two, along with a blade or even a shark. Hoping to hear steel drums after all, he touched his ear and listened.

•   •   •

Michael's lips brushed the eye-catching redhead's ear. "I want you. Here; now." The swim goggles hanging from his neck jounced as he deftly undid her bikini amid the hotel pool's swirl of warm water, gurgling filters and chlorine odors. After grinding against her until she whimpered and begged him to *do it,* he held still while she peeled away his blue Speedo and hooked a leg around his waist. Then, slowly rolling his hips, he had her gasping and arching her back in anticipation, only to sob when he hastily backed off. "The pool boy sees us. Okay. Wait here. I'll make sure my wife's gone, then come get you." She clung to him but he shook his head doggedly. "I said, *wait.*"

Hitching the Speedo back in place, he got out and put on his terry-cloth robe, then padded into the hotel that he'd checked into after the team flew to Barbados to support Levi's deep-cover op. Stepping inside an elevator, he punched the fifth floor button.

Earlier, after stowing his things and phoning Wild Bill who was in Luxembourg to meet with Koehl, Michael had gone to the pool and was finishing a mile when the redhead appeared. They chatted amiably until she blithely propositioned him. "No," he said. "I'm married." But when she abruptly fondled him, he resolved to drive home what *no* means by stringing her along to within a millimeter of actual contact and then leaving her pre-empted. It was cruel. It was overkill. He didn't care. She could rot while waiting for him. *I told her I'm married and that's that.*

Once inside his room he tossed the robe, ditched the Speedo, and pulled on black nylon running shorts. Shunning a shirt and grabbing his shoes, he placed them at the door but then frowned. *Time to break this habit.* He put them in the closet instead, then went to the mini-bar. It was scarcely noon but big boy rules applied, and after snatching a local beer he stepped through the French doors and settled onto a balcony chair. Then while taking in the ocean view and inhaling the fresh salt air he drained half the bottle, decided it wasn't half bad, and examined the label. Another gulp. He stared out to sea. Bathers cavorting in the waves brought back memories of playing with his young sons in the surf.

All at once he wanted to phone home. But he was in OPSEC mode; calls can be tracked. If that escapee *was* out for revenge it served as another reason not to call, even if Blue Crew were protecting his family. For that reason—but also because he was spending too much time away, he wondered if it might be time to leave the team at mission's end.

In point of fact, he'd grown terribly lonely and concerned with the fate of the world. Although confident in the team's ability to complete *its* task, the asteroid-busting project troubled him, and despite seeing the gadget close-up, his heart didn't trust it and he feared that all the people he knew and loved could soon be dead.

His own eventual death didn't trouble him so much. What he didn't handle well were the deaths of those close to him. The first to go had been his mother. Michael had been born into poverty so dire that his unwed mom couldn't even afford to circumcise him; so poor that he pocketed every penny and automatically took off his shirt, shoes and socks upon entering the trailer in order to stretch the lifespan of the few clothes he had. But he also left the shoes at the door so he'd at least have footwear whenever his sicko sadistic step-father came at him with either a bat in his hands or lust in his eyes.

His mom died on his fourteenth birthday, shattering his heart and making him easy prey to the step-dad. So he fled the bastard only to end up on the streets, fighting off predators and evading pimps until one of the latter sporting a purple velvet running suit cornered him in a dark alley. Holding a .25 caliber pistol to the boy's temple, the pimp offered a choice: work for him, or die. Hanging his head, Michael stifled a sob and admitted, "Right now I'll do anything for food. *Anything*. Even gay porn." But when the pimp lowered the pistol, Michael went wildcat. Bared his teeth. Tore into him. Broke his jaw. Grabbed the gun. Took off running. Didn't stop till he reached Vegas.

But desperation for food and shelter drove him into selling his body after all, to the women whose eyes met those of the beautiful boy standing near the casinos. They were striking women who convinced themselves that the tall boy with hair the color of lemons, gorgeous brown eyes, and beguilingly haunted look *had* to be eighteen. Jailbait or not, they'd invite him to their rooms where he'd make them glow with his kid-from-the-wrong-side-of-the-tracks rhythm. On leaving the hotel with four Ben Franklins in his pocket, he'd stuff a fifty into the waiting hand of whatever doorman had looked away as he walked in with his client. Then he'd turn another trick before going to a seedy hotel whose owner cut him a break on the room, so long as he serviced her.

Michael spent the next four years hustling women. In lean times he also hustled men willing to fork over two bills just to give the skinny young slum boy blowjobs inside of restroom stalls that reeked of disinfectant. All the while he dodged a string of white, black and Latino pimps who to their credit read the boy for what he was — a fighter whose eyes glazed over into a stare that said they'd be wise to move on toward a soft target. He also had that first pimp's pistol — just in case.

Yet despite a growing fear of the dark and even darker nightmares, he never let his trials affect his soul; never sneered at the tricks as a way to shield what he'd become from those who came onto him. Refusing to let anger subjugate him, he made attentive love to countless women, while wanting only to love and be loved.

Resolving to obtain his goals, he sat for a GED exam and got Nevada's highest score ever. Next, he enlisted in the Army, took the $80,000 he'd banked from turning tricks, and turned it into a college fund. He also turned into a Ranger and saw combat in Mogadishu. Three years later he entered college and shared a room with Levi Hart, the son of loving parents and a product of prep schools. As Levi unselfishly mentored his intelligent but poorly-educated friend, they formed a brotherly bond. After college they got hired as cops. In time, Levi went to the FBI and rose rapidly through the ranks to become Assistant Special Agent in Charge of the San Diego field office.

Michael meanwhile married Nadia and fathered the two sons he adored. Since he was neither ashamed of nor secretive about what he'd done to survive, the boys were well aware of his past and they loved him all the more for what he'd endured. He also instilled in them a healthy outlook toward sex. "It's natural. It can be playful and passionate; sassy and sweet. But more than anything, it's about life. Life, and in time, death." And, death being ever-present, he eventually got that phone call in the middle of the night.

Levi's voice had been lifeless. "They're dead, Michael. Both of them. Dead."

Shaking his head to clear it of sleep, Michael thought he must be referring to a pair of his agents. Levi wasn't. While he was away on assignment, a young addict in search of money broke into his home. Levi's wife Anita confronted him at the door. He shot her twice in the chest. When eight year old Michael charged down the stairs with both fists flying to defend his mother, the addict put a bullet in the boy's brain. The drug-ravaged killer was still in the house when police arrived. He confessed, described the boy's bravery, and even voiced regrets at shooting him.

A few days later, Michael and Nadia stood with Levi in the stern of a boat as he scattered the ashes of his wife and son atop the crest of a Pacific swell. In the days that followed, Levi appeared stoic but grief had seized him in a vice-like grip. One day he abruptly resigned from the Bureau and went to Baghdad to find the terrorists who were setting booby traps for U.S. troops. From there, he went to work for Heath Baker.

Michael drained the beer and was contemplating another when he heard a knock at his door. He grimaced. *Better not be the redhead.* But when he checked the peephole and saw a heavily perspiring Monica attired in running clothes, his mood brightened at once. Opening the door, he ushered her inside.

"Hi, Lover Boy. Mind some company?" Entering his arms, she kissed his mouth and patted his butt, then lay her head on his naked shoulder. All at once her nose crinkled. "Gawd. You reek of chlorine." Then she chortled. "As if I don't stink from running."

"Bathroom's got a shower. There's a fresh robe next to the towels."

"Yeah? Sure, why not?" Giving her head a toss that sent her black hair flying, she turned around and craned her neck. "Help me with this?" After he undid the clasp of her sports bra with a practiced flick of the wrist, she held it in place and faced him. "You're welcome to join me, you know." Hooking a finger inside his waistband, she tugged at it. "Well? How about it, Romeo?" Now inching the shorts down, she raised an eyebrow.

He grew an instant smile, and drawing her close he nuzzled her ear. "Mmm, baby. You know I want to. The thing is, I have to do my nails. Can ya gimme a rain check?"

She laughed along with him, for theirs was a world of taunting daredevil games. "Tell you what. Let's just break out the booze and have a ball." With a puckish look that signaled her awareness of his boundaries, she gave his waistband a resounding snap.

He winked and swatted her rear as she walked off, then grabbed two beers and stretched out on the chaise lounge to wait.

When she appeared in a robe minutes later smelling of fresh soap and a citrusy shampoo, he held out his arms and the lounge creaked as she snuggled against him with a kittenish quality that he loved. After they clinked bottles he asked about her jog, then idly ran the pad of his big toe up and down her silken calves as she talked. Next, he told her about the pool episode. Then while the surf murmured as if only to them, the friends spoke in low tones under a robin's egg blue sky. But over a second round of drinks he studied her upturned face. "You're worried about him."

"Of course."

"So am I." His earlier funk returned full blast. He swigged some beer. "I also feel sick at heart about my family if, you know, the worst should—" He stroked her cheek. "Babe? I'd do anything to save them." Spotting the redhead stalking the pool area with hands on hips, he felt haunted; hunted. "Anything," he whispered.

•   •   •

Levi stowed his things, then changed into swim trunks and stepped outside to do a walk-around of the villa. He saw no cameras, and after deciding on the shed as the best spot for the phone, he stepped onto the beach. The sands were scorching, but singed soles were low on his list of priorities. Standing still, he held both arms out and turned in a small circle—a guy happily taking in the sun, sand, and surf of his new home. In fact, he was telling the high-flying Predator's pilot to pay close attention. Next, he went directly to the shed and stood beside it for sixty solid seconds. Definition: *put it here*. Then he plunged headlong into the ocean and its swirl of colors. The meaning: *end of message*.

But *end of message* proved to be more than he'd bargained for when he got snared by a rip current. Using a side-stroke, he swam diagonally to escape it, then put on a show of languishing in the warm water in case Slavko was watching from afar—although he'd rather get busy by digging into Isla de la Rusia. But he had to pace himself for now.

After swimming parallel to the shore with practiced strokes for three hundred yards, he saw a nude couple entering the surf. Recalling Slavko's comments about the island's casual dress code, he noted this level of freedom because although clothing-optional bathing is common in Europe, this local freedom could reveal the lengths to which Bogrov had gone to keep his troops happy. Reversing course, he beached himself amidst skittering sandpipers and stretched out on the damp sands. The sky was blue, the hills green, and palms with long brown trunks and extended fronds lined the edge of the white sand beach. Closing his eyes, he tuned in the ocean's rhythm and drifted into battery-charge mode. He worked best this way. It helped him to think and plan.

"YOU MUST be a new arrival."

Levi's eyes snapped open.

"Better get out of this sun." The lilting voice had an Italian accent. "You'll burn easily in these latitudes. Especially with your fair skin and lovely blue eyes."

Realizing he'd fallen asleep, he propped himself on an elbow and examined the striking woman standing next to him. Tall, slender and in her twenties, she wore a bikini, a broad sun hat, designer sunglasses, and a bright smile.

Standing, he saw that her breasts were high and full, and she appeared sure of her powers to please. Watching the breeze tease the ends of her hair, he offered his hand. "I'm Rocky. Rocky O'Toole."

She took his hand, then removed her sunglasses. Her eyes were gentle, unguarded. "I think you are very handsome man, Rocky O'Toole."

He flashed a smile. "Thanks. You? You're gorgeous. But you already know that."

"You are an American, I think. Yes?"

"Yes."

She showed gleaming teeth. "I am called Sophia, as in Sophia Loren."

"The actress, huh? Nice."

"My mama, my papa—they grew up with Sophia Loren in their hearts. Then Sophia married the director Carlo Ponti. My papa is also called Carlo—Carlo Loren. So he and my mama decided to name me, their first daughter, 'Sophia.' Now here I am. Sophia Loren."

"The *beautiful* Sophia Loren," he corrected, thinking he'd never learn her real name because prostitutes never use them. And he had no doubt that she was one—and that she hadn't appeared at his side by chance.

Sophia took off her hat, and when a gust sent her long black hair flying, she ran careless fingers through her mane before pointing at his ankle. "You were in prison, no?"

"I was in prison, yes." He lifted his foot to let her inspect the barbed wire tattoo.

"Hmm. I do not care for it. But you have nice eyes—*kind* eyes—so I think perhaps you are a nice man."

"I'm nice to ladies." Then he stupidly added, "That includes working ladies."

Sophia's smile vanished. "You think I am 'working woman'?"

"I, well…"

"I am mistaken. You are not nice man. You are vulgar man." Turning on her heel, she strode off.

"Wait." He jogged to keep pace with her. "I didn't mean anything by that. I…"

"Oh?" Putting hands on hips, she leaned into him. "Just what did you mean?"

"Why don't we start over?" He touched her arm.

She reared back. "No. I came out here to greet my new neighbor." She pointed to the villa next to Levi's. "That is my home. I must now return to its safety, to shield myself from you." With that, she put on her sunglasses and turned to go.

"Sophia, wait. Listen. Soldiers screw up. You're one, right? So you know."

Her sudden laughter was light and lyrical as she walked away. "Soldier? No. I am not soldier. *I* am pilot of Yuri's helicopter."

He grimaced. Bogrov's personal pilot? She could be a vein of gold, a source that never stopped giving so long as he tapped it. But he'd alienated her, and now had to win her over. "I'd like to see you later," he said to her retreating back. "I'll make dinner for you. At your villa. You'll see that I'm not the loser I've just come off as."

This time she stopped, and facing him she took off her sunglasses and regarded him as one might an insect. "I have no wish to ever see you again. Much less to share a meal with you." Turning once again, she marched off.

He'd kick his own ass right now if it were possible. Bad enough he'd offended her. Now he'd have to work doubly-hard to offset his gaffe before he could even think of mining her for intel. But while that vein might seem lost to lesser men, he ranked among a different breed. As he trudged back to his villa he formed a plan to make amends.

He was still fifty yards away when he spotted a young woman standing in front of the sliding doors. She was blonde, slender, and dressed in casual island clothes. "I am Lara," she began in a sing-song, Russian-accented voice. "I am told you are called Rocky. I take care of the island's food supplies. I heard of a new arrival." She stepped closer to him.

He found her sexiness appealing, and if it meant hopping in the sack with her to gain any insight she might have, he would do it. But not now. Checking his watch, he told her he had to leave soon, then made a date to go snorkeling. After she walked off he went inside and stripped off the swim trunks. Unfortunately, he'd forgotten about the lack of locks. As he started for the shower, a bare-assed Lara stepped next to him.

When the jeep's brakes squealed at precisely 1430 hours, he dashed outside with shirt and flip flops in hand while a still-nude Lara blew him kisses from the doorway. The Serb regarded Levi anew, grunted, and stepped on the gas.

After a brief drive they turned onto a road flanked by shrubs and Bismarck palms, their fronds swaying below a high sun. "The rules are simple," Slavko abruptly began. "You shall protect Mr. Bogrov from all eventualities. The next order of priority is island defense. Lastly, you shall defend its inhabitants. How you will carry out your orders is simple. Killing is killing. There is no room for pity or the weak knee." He faced Levi while the jeep's tires kicked up a rooster tail of dust. "Be ruthless, as you were when you broke that man's arms. For which you went to prison."

"Don't worry. I will. But who protects you?" Levi looked at him and waited.

Slavko stood on the brakes, nearly throwing Levi against the dash as he brought the jeep to a shuddering stop. Staring through Levi, Slavko said in a voice devoid of light, love, or life, "Do not ever think that you or any other man must protect me as if I were some woman. And do not ever cross me. Or I shall torture you without mercy until you beg me to kill you, which I will not do until it pleases me to do so."

Levi put on a bored look and lit a cigarette. "Save it. So, what're the other rules?"

"While off-duty you may indulge in whatever pursuits you wish. If you prove to be true soldier? I shall look the other way for certain—things." He looked pointedly at Levi's arms. "But do not become incapacitated to such the degree that you cannot go to battle on short notice."

A minute later they arrived at a small brick building where Slavko outfitted Levi with jungle combat fatigues and boots. He also issued a helmet and rain gear. After Levi loaded everything in the jeep, Slavko took him to a larger building. "The primary armory," he explained. "We have a total of six."

Once they were inside, Levi's flip flops slapped against the concrete floor as he browsed, noting the rows of racked assault rifles and wooden ammo crates with Russian markings. Against one wall were RPGs and 81mm mortars. Farther back he spotted several dozen MANPADs—man-portable air-defense systems—and he guessed that unlike the Stinger missiles the US gave Afghanistan decades ago, Slavko undoubtedly ensured that these missiles received regular servicing by trained technicians.

Slavko handed two weapons to Levi. The first was a Russian AK-47. The Serb observed closely as Levi pulled back the bolt to check that it was unloaded, then let it slam home with a loud *thunk* that marked the smart, experienced motions of a weapons expert. Next, Slavko issued a Beretta 9mm pistol. Levi disassembled it in 2.3 seconds flat, examined its parts for cleanliness, then met Slavko's stare in a way that said *yeah, I friggin' know what I'm doing so kiss my ass.* Slavko showed no outward reaction as he issued the appropriate ammunition, magazines, and pouches. Lastly, he opened a gray metal box and handed over four hand grenades.

"You will store everything in your living quarters. Keep your equipment battle-ready at all times. Is that understood?"

Levi, not about to play the pushover, looked sidelong at him. "Hey. I'm on it."

"Humph. We shall see. Very well. Let us continue."

Levi put the weapons and gear in the jeep and hopped in. Slavko then took him on a tour of the island, sometimes offering comments while other times pointing silently at a building or a place that required no explanation. But during the tour he also pointed out three overgrown dirt roads, and each time he sliced the knife-edge of his hand through the air. "Do not go down that road. It is off limits." Levi shrugged after every admonition, but he pinned the locations to memory so he could return to discover what constituted "off limits" on a tiny island that lacked locks.

During the remainder of the tour Levi assessed potential redoubts that he might need to reach if he had to trade shots with one or more of the others. One in particular caught his eye as Slavko drove along the road that led to Levi's villa—a narrow path that was isolated, yet close to home. He added it to his list of things to investigate further.

Slavko showed Levi the recreational facilities and introduced him to the on-duty soldiers. He finally came to a bone-shaking stop in front of the villa, where he watched impassively from behind the wheel as Levi unloaded his gear. "I'll be here at 2200 hours to bring you to your post. Be ready." He roared off without waiting for a response.

●   ●   ●

The combat swimmers emerged one by one from *USS Dallas'* escape-trunk and flutter-kicked at once to the SEAL Delivery Vehicle—the SDV—that was mounted atop the hull in a special dry dock shelter. The squad worked quickly and efficiently to deploy it, and once all were aboard the pilot waved farewell to the soon-to-be deactivated *Dallas*.

The pilot then set course for Isla de la Rusia. After navigating below the surface, he settled the SDV onto the seabed a hundred yards from where the surf was breaking. He would stay with the vehicle while the other five went ashore.

The men swam quickly, their closed-system rebreathers leaving no tell-tale trail of bubbles. When they rose silently from the surf in the pitch-black shore, the lead SEAL checked the area with a night vision device. Satisfied that all was clear,

206 · RICHARD CRAIG ANDERSON

he signaled the others and they removed their swim fins. Clipping them to their arms and with automatic weapons at the ready, they moved forward.

The team leader found the shed readily enough and crouched at its darkest corner. While the others covered him from all directions, he pulled the iridium SAT phone from its waterproof container and concealed it beneath two inches of sand. Then he waved the others back to the surf, covering their six while wiping away their tracks as he went.

On reaching the SDV they climbed aboard and headed back to *Dallas*. Two hours later, the SDV secured, the team inside the sub and their debrief completed, they pursued their typical 3M lifestyle while aboard a submarine—a meal, a movie, and a mattress; mission complete, bring on the sleep.

• • •

Michael jerked awake drenched in sweat, his heart thudding against his chest like a trip hammer. His younger son had been calling out. "Dad! The asteroid! It's coming!" He read the clock. A bit past three. He closed his eyes. The redhead popped into mind. She'd tracked him to the room while he and Monica were having their drinks. He and a robed Monica stood arm-in-arm as he told her to bug-off. Then he'd shut the door in her face. But being hunted down can trigger PTSD-induced nightmares. In this case it involved his child. He blew air from his cheeks.

• • •

Levi's breath came short the instant he spotted the SAT phone. He knew of course that SEALs would deliver it, but he still felt warm and fuzzy knowing he had this level of support. That, and the fact that they'd come ashore as phantoms, never-to-be-seen, had impressed him. Being careful not to leave fingerprints, he sent a micro-burst message detailing the island defenses he'd learned about so far. Once he received a reply he powered-down and secreted it beneath a floorboard in the shed. Then as the sun rose above the horizon he went inside, only to find Lara awaiting him in his bed.

CHAPTER THIRTY-TWO

. . . .

WHEN LEVI knocked on Sophia's door later that day, she speared him with her eyes but he pushed on. "Look, I screwed up. How about letting me prepare dinner. You'll see. I'll prove that I'm not the scumbag I came across as."

She regarded him with a calm detachment. "Perhaps you have confused me with Lara. Should you not be inviting *her* to dinner, then back into your bed?"

He said in a kind manner, "Since you know she invited herself into my bed, then you must be aware that I showed her the door five minutes after getting home."

This was true. Lara had handed him a *fait accompli*. But needing to play both ends in case she might prove useful, he'd feigned nausea rather than give her the heave-ho. "Must be the water," he'd told the Russian girl, who then rushed off to her job.

"But you have been intimate with her? Yes? No?"

"That's between her and me." It was a gentleman's way out. He wasn't disclosing anything, but neither was he concealing a truth that Sophia clearly had knowledge of.

Even so, the Italian beauty sniffed. "She spoke well of you. Perhaps *she* should be your friend."

"I want you for my friend. Lara's just—" He smiled. "See you at six?"

Following a protracted silence, she nodded. "Six." But she did not smile.

At least he'd acquired an opening. His instant thought: dinner tonight—exploit her for intel later. Manipulative as it might be, he didn't care. He had a job to do.

Levi reappeared that night wearing what passed as island formal: a polo shirt, trousers and shoes. After air-kissing each other, he stepped into her kitchen and began putting on a show—for Levi knew food and wine. With Sophia perched atop a stool to watch, he cleaned, sliced, diced and prepared appetizers of mini tacos filled with carnitas and chicken topped with cilantro and guacamole. There were also platters of hummus, tomato bruschetta drizzled with balsamic glaze, and a three-olive tapenade with feta cheese that he served with baked garlic toast.

The kitchen already teemed with sharp odors by the time he started the entree and its heavier, lingering smells: beef stroganoff with mushrooms and egg noodles, with a sour cream gravy. Desserts were next—a vanilla gelato in honor of her Italian heritage, with fresh blueberries and a nut puree that he placed in the freezer. Then he set the dining table and filled wine glasses with a 2007 *M. Chapoutier Belleruche*. He'd found the Rhone wine among the island's extensive stock of alcohol. In fact, it had inspired the beef stroganoff in the first place, since the wine of 80% Grenache and 20% Syrah is difficult to pair with very many foods. But of course Bogrov was Russian, so the bottle's presence on-island made sense—as did the meal itself, since he not only needed to gain her respect, he had to capture her heart if she were to provide him with even the slightest edge in taking down Bogrov.

Over dinner they ate and talked beneath soft romantic lighting, and when her signals came clear, he held her chair while she stood. Then to hell with the desserts—he took her hand and they went to her bedroom.

Afterward, they spoke in low tones until he segued into relevant conversation; relevant to his needs, that is. "I haven't heard any helicopter sounds since I arrived. Does Bogrov only use it to check the scenery?"

She showed fine white teeth. "Once a week I ferry a solicitor back and forth from St. Lucia. I bring her here. She meets with Yuri. They have dinner. I fly her home."

"She?"

She laughed. "Yes, Rocky. We women have broken into the professions."

"I didn't mean it that way." He put on an innocent face. "What I really wanna know is... how well stacked is she?"

Raising her eyes toward the ceiling, she mock-shouted, "I knew it. Already you want to rid yourself of me." Her eyes sparkled. "Yes, she is quite lovely. Not as lovely as I, of course..."

"I was about to say that."

"Nor is Lara," she taunted, but then she smiled. "So. This solicitor—she and Yuri have been friends for long time. He even brings her to the grave of his son."

Levi's pulse quickened. Bogrov's son had been buried near Moscow. "His son?"

"Oh, yes. He is buried here. It is a great honor, to be taken to his grave." She got a mischievous smile. "Now I shall be grave if you do not get for me some coffee, yes?"

Remaining calm, he nodded while thinking about this lawyer. She could have a special standing with Bogrov. His friend; his frequent guest. Then it hit him and he all but gasped. She might be his fail-safe system—a local attorney, with instructions to release the papal papers if something untoward befell her client.

Levi asked carefully, "Does this lawyer have a name?"

"Ho-ho-ho, you do want to leave me for her, yes?" She turned serious. "Okay. I tell you now. Her name is Katia. Katia Lagunov, Private Solicitor. There. See? When you have legal problem, you let me know. I shall introduce you to her. Then you will decide who is the more lovely. Yes?"

"There can be no woman lovelier than you." He smiled pleasantly, then got up naked to make coffee for her. Back in bed, they talked as they drank, and later they kissed and touched until their bodies joined together of their own accord.

That morning he made their breakfast, and after a bit of talk he excused himself and returned to his villa, where he ventured into the shed and transmitted a message to the team about Katia Lagunov. He told them what actions they were to take—although he felt bad for Michael—then added that they should send Wild Bill to the island.

Sophia Loren appeared at his door around noon and over a glass of wine she told him, "Yuri wants me to be his woman." She shuddered as if she'd seen a roach. "I do not want this. I want to be with you, only." She said quickly, "I don't mean as a refuge. I, um, well... you are not only the stud in the kitchen and the chef in bed, you warm my heart."

Seeing an opening, he took it. Having her as his live-in provided an excuse to quit Lara without ruffling her too much. And, he truly liked Sophia. Half an hour later he was helping her hang the last of her clothes in his closet. Then he was helping her undress.

After they made love in their new home, he suggested a walk on the beach. It was a romantic thing to do, but his real purpose was anything but—he wanted to scope things out in greater detail, and Sophia might add useful insights.

Plenty of off-duty soldiers and women were cavorting along the beach, many of them nude. Sophia waved to some of the men and most of the women, whom she described as assistants who'd been brought here to keep the men happy. "All the time with the sex and the booze." A fully-clothed Lara was among them. Her face lit up and she called out to Levi, sprinkling the air with her fingers before giving Sophia a withering look.

As they walked on he noted the narcotic quality of the island life that Bogrov had built, for it provided his men with a motive to fight with deadly resolve against any threat to their nirvana. *Yeah, this Land of Lotus-eaters is quite an operation—and I'm gonna bust Bogrov's little world wide open.*

However, the time allotted to the mission was finite. He had to crack Bogrov's shell and unlock the mysteries before either Delta Force or a Marine task force appeared on the horizon. Delta Force was preferable. They could do a HALO—a High Altitude Low Opening parachute jump from aircraft flying at 30,000 feet, then use GPS to guide their descent to the fields dotting the island. Two hundred or more Delta Force operators would easily take control of the island. Or, a squad of SEALs could execute a stealth entry of Bogrov's house, kidnapping him and the Serb and delivering them to a CIA interrogation team before getting back to their 3-M activities.

But utilizing either option could spell disaster. If Bogrov had a fail-safe system, all would be lost. Even if he didn't, the media would eventually learn that a Delta Force "training exercise" had actually been a highly classified raid of some kind. They might even catch a whiff of a SEAL "extraction of two adverse principals." Self-styled experts would then expound at length about the pontiff's papers and the killer asteroid. To maintain ratings and newspaper sales, they would conclude that the big rock could not be destroyed or even diverted, "regardless of scientific claims to the contrary." The end result: fear and panic in the streets. It was why, deep in a corner of that dark room that inhabited his soul, Levi acknowledged that any pretenses to the contrary, he'd come here to assassinate Bogrov—and he remained fully prepared to do just that.

CHAPTER THIRTY-THREE

· ·

THAT EVENING Levi put on his BDUs—Battle Dress Utilities—and gathered his weapons. Then he kissed Sophia Loren goodbye and stepped outside. Slavko arrived promptly at eleven and brought him to the dock area, where Levi watched how the Serb conducted roll call for a midnight shift consisting of six soldiers and a sergeant.

The sergeant mentioned that a recently-hired soldier had gone missing. "The Pole. What's-his-name… Kaczmarek. Nobody's seen him. He's not in his quarters, either."

Slavko grunted. "He is not missing. I know where he is—and it is not here. He decided to return to his *Polonia.*"

The sergeant lit a Camel and exhaled a gray cloud. "Fuck him, then."

Afterward, three soldiers climbed into Slavko's jeep for a ride to their posts while Levi and the others went to the sergeant's jeep. Minutes later the sergeant dropped him at an observation bunker atop the northern cliff and sped off into the darkness.

It took Levi a few minutes to adjust to a black moonless night with only the quiet surf sounds a hundred feet below, and the calls, clicks, and croaks of night creatures to keep him company. But when the wind shifted and he heard a high keening that sounded so human-like that he shuddered, he cocked his head. There it was again, carried on the back of the wind, a murmur almost, desiccated and fleeting yet very real: *Muhhhhhh.*

What the hell?

The winds died. The sound went away. Minutes later he heard it again. *Muhhhh.* But that was followed by, *maaa.* Levi waited awhile longer, then reached into a cargo pocket and got out his earpiece. After plugging it into his belted radio, he grabbed the bunker's night vision goggles—the NVGs—and set off to investigate.

The sound came from the south. Perhaps not coincidentally, it originated from one of the paths that Slavko had declared off limits. Levi meant to check it anyway. Now he had an imperative. He put on the NVG and thumbed the switch. Night became day in the form of a green TV-like image in the eyepiece. After a quick look-around to make sure he was alone, he started down the trail. But the dense vegetation kept the wind at bay, so he quickly broke into a sweat. Then a mosquito began worrying his right ear, and after a few more steps he reared back after blundering into a cloud of no-see-ums. Undaunted, he continued along the path while being careful to stop every few feet to look, listen and feel for any signals his viscera might send.

Then the wind moaned again. *Muhhhh.* Except, it wasn't the wind.

Levi took ten more steps before his stomach clenched and the fine hairs on the back of his neck stood up. He flipped the NVG to infrared and scanned right and left. Nothing. But when he scanned to the center his breath caught and everything inside went dead. *Is that what I think it is?* He heard it again. *Muhhhh… maaaaaa.*

Switching the NVG back to normal, he took a few more cautious steps and froze. It was a body. Kaczmarek's body, impaled on a dozen wooden stakes that had been fixed to a long and flexible tree branch. He'd been snared in a booby-trap. Levi figured he'd tripped a wire that sent the stake-studded branch springing back and impaling his torso. The Pole was quite dead. Probably a blessing, Levi decided.

But then he heard it, and there was no wind at all this time: *Muhhhh… maaaaaa.* A shudder ran through him. Kaczmarek *wasn't* dead. Then Kaczmarek's mouth opened and from it came, "Muhhhh maaaaaa."

Mama.

Levi's guts twisted. He wanted to help the man. But mission parameters stopped him. Then he studied Kaczmarek again. Now the NVG's garish green haze picked up a black smear between the man's legs—a black smear that in natural light would be red—blood red. It didn't take a genius to figure out that he'd been emasculated. That alone should've caused him to bleed out and Levi wanted to recoil in horror, but he had to stay focused. Why had Kaczmarek suffered this fate? More importantly, who did this to him?

Just then a jeep's motor sliced the silence like a sword, followed by a squeal of brakes near the opening to the path. Levi quickly hid behind a clump of low shrubs and flicked the AK-47's safety off as footsteps crashed toward him. By remaining still he might escape detection—unless whoever it was had their own NVG. But if that proved to be the case, Levi would cancel their ticket before they could even fart.

When a flashlight's beam flared, Levi lowered his eyelids to shield his night vision. The beam remained fixed on the trail, with no hunter's side-to-side sweep in search of prey. This told Levi that whoever it was, they knew where they were going. He held his breath as cold trails of perspiration rolled from his armpits and insects buzzed about his face. There were chirping sounds and boots crunching foliage, when Slavko suddenly appeared in the green haze of Levi's NVG. He was carrying a small shovel, and he went directly to Kaczmarek.

Levi was already riled when Slavko muttered something in Serbo-Croatian, but when he burst into laughter and made the cooing sounds of a man taking pleasure in seeing someone's wounds, Levi wanted to kill. That notion grew when Slavko pulled a knife from a pocket—and when it sprang open with a sharp *click* and Slavko put its point against the Pole's right eye, Levi seriously considered killing him.

Especially when Kaczmarek moaned.

A chill ran down Levi's spine. *Holy mother of God*—

Laughing gleefully, Slavko plunged the blade into the Pole's eye and viciously twisted it until the eyeball popped out.

Kaczmarek writhed against his bindings. "Muhhhh, maaa... *Muhhhh* maaa!"

Then Slavko cut the other eye from its socket and Kaczmarek retched, spewing vomit and causing Slavko to swear until he grabbed the Pole's shoulders and yanked him free of the wooden stakes with a single brutal tug. Though near-death, Kaczmarek still screamed in agony. Slavko responded by driving a fist into the man's mouth before letting him plop face-first onto the ground.

That was grisly enough. But what Slavko did next shook Levi to the core. Using the shovel, he dug a shallow grave. Then he rolled Kaczmarek in and buried him alive.

Levi was at the point of putting a bullet through the Serb's brain. But of course he couldn't. Instead, he watched Slavko rig the booby-trap to snare anyone else who dared to venture down the forbidden path and suffer a lingering death until Slavko moved in for the kill. Kaczmarek probably wasn't the first victim, and Levi figured Bogrov knew about Slavko's penchant for torture but sanctioned it. After all, it was a way to keep the Serb happy and willing to do his bidding. Levi thought, here in Lotus Land the soldiers get wine and women. As for Slavko, he gets to torture men into slow agonizing deaths. The wind kicked up again.

Muhhhh, maaa.

It had to have been the wind. After all, the Pole was buried. But Levi kept his weapon trained on Slavko and almost wished the sadistic son of a bitch would discover him—it burned him that much to see this man getting away with this. *Christ, is this what we're trying to save the world for? To keep it viable for depraved lunatics?* It was an academic question. He knew full well that Dragon Team had accepted the mission to save the world's children—and they included Michael's children.

Settling down now, he watched Slavko lumber back down the path to the road. Then he waited until the jeep roared off before carefully venturing from the hiding place and starting back to his post.

This alone made him resolve once again to take care of Slavko for good, because leaving Kaczmarek to smother to death was Levi's most difficult decision ever. He could barely imagine the terror Kaczmarek must be experiencing. Alone. Friendless. Dying; no mother to comfort him. He was even denied Levi's proximal presence, as if by remaining nearby he could offer Kaczmarek a spiritual connection.

But Kaczmarek had known the job was dangerous when he signed-on, and in the grand scheme of world events his agony couldn't off-set what would happen if Dragon Team failed in its mission. Feeling sick to his stomach, Levi turned his back on the man.

"Muhhhh... maaa."

Oh, God. Levi clamped his eyes tight and pressed on without looking back, hating himself and hating Slavko and Bogrov that much more. When he finally reached the road he hustled toward his post, only to come to a screeching halt when he spotted Slavko's jeep parked next to the bunker. Stepping quickly into the tree line, he stuck a cigarette in his mouth, turned away to cup the flame as he lit it, then intentionally crashed through the underbrush on his way to the post.

The Serb all but barked when Levi appeared from the trees. "Where were you?"

Levi drew himself up to his full height. "Hey. Deep cleansing breath." He flicked an insolent ash and jerked a thumb over his shoulder. "Had to answer a call of nature. Didn't wanna stink up the place." He made a show of shrugging before locking eyes with him. "So what can I do for you?" He wanted to add, *you bloodless bastard.*

Slavko looked at him with an animal intensity before glancing in the direction of the path. "Show me this place where you answer the call of nature."

Levi scoffed. "You want something to see?" He pointed in a general direction. "Be my guest. Thirty paces. It's where I left a present for you." He stared at him with hard eyes and blew a rude cloud of smoke his way.

"A present, huh?" Slavko grunted, then pointed a finger. "Range practice. In the morning. I'll pick you up. Be ready." Climbing into the jeep, he fired it up and drove off.

Levi muttered while watching him go, "Don't worry, pal. I'll be ready." The wind picked up. Levi felt sick at heart. Worse still, he couldn't stop staring at the path.

THE DUTY sergeant drove up an hour later for a routine post inspection. After a brief chat he off-handedly added that Slavko had retired for the evening. Levi waited ten minutes after the sergeant left before grabbing the NVG. A minute later he was hyper-alert and stepping carefully as he drew near the shallow grave. While eyeing the trip-wire Slavko had set, he slowly brushed dirt from the grave, hoping Kaczmarek was already dead. But when he uncovered the final layer of dirt, the Pole's mouth twitched.

"Muhhhh… maaaaaa."

Clenching his teeth, Levi put his palm against the man's forehead. "I'm right here," he whispered. "You're not alone, and I'm not going to leave you."

"Ma… ma." Kaczmarek released a long sigh. Then his chest rose and fell rapidly. Seconds later, it stopped.

Levi slid his fingers to the Pole's carotid artery. Nothing. He put a finger beneath the nostrils. Zip. There were no eyes to check—just blood-encrusted depressions covered by eyelids. Levi patted Kaczmarek's forehead and said a silent prayer, then covered him over before cautiously making his way out of there.

MUCH LATER, a brisk breeze carried pungent sea smells past the villa's open window and into the bedroom, where Levi caught a whiff of a sharper-than-usual lacing of salt. He'd come home at dawn and laid next to Sophia, and as the breeze picked up he didn't have to look to know the sky must be overcast and that it would be raining by lunch time. Still haunted by what last night's wind had brought, he studied the ceiling.

When Sophia stirred at his side, he watched the steady rise and fall of her chest and his heart felt lighter. He'd done the right thing last night. Now it was time to move on. So he gently shook her awake and said he had to go to the range. She smiled at him, and as they talked he realized how much he'd come to care about her. If things were different, who knew what might develop?

Finishing their pillow talk, he donned clean BDUs, shined his boots, gathered his gear, and stepped outside just as Slavko slid to a tires-on-gravel stop inches from where he stood. Levi studied the psychopath's face for any sign of his activities last night, and wasn't surprised when he found nothing there.

THE SMALL range was on the island's lee, which would at least provide them with a marginal protection from the chill wind, and getting there would require a bumpy ride over the island's spine. But as they crested the summit, Levi could see the whole of Isla de la Rusia and its surrounding waters.

He could also see the island's coastal surveillance radar—and knew that Bogrov had invested wisely in this best of the commercially available surveillance systems.

The hilltop location provided a commanding 360° view of the sea, and the radar boasted both X- and S-band capabilities. Generally speaking, detection of targets as small as rigid inflatable boats in good weather isn't all that challenging. But in heavy rainfall or high seas the situation changes dramatically. A radar then requires a high gain antenna with narrow beam width to reduce rainfall and sea clutter return. This system had both features and it could detect wooden, metal, and even fiberglass boats—including the high speed inflatable boats that SEALs used. And it could simultaneously track the boats alongside larger ships—a destroyer, for instance. Or that Marine Corps task force.

As they drove past the radar dish, Levi wondered if it had picked up the boatload of new-hires who were due in today. It should arrive soon and he hoped Wild Bill Dentz would be on it. But if his hopes sparked a ray of light, a sudden squall squelched it, but while he ignored the rain pellets that began lashing at his face, Slavko cursed and pulled over. After leaping out, he put the canvas top in place. He might've saved himself the trouble. As they rounded a sharp bend, they popped out under gray but dry skies.

A moment later Slavko spun the wheel and braked to a stop at the shooting range. Twenty or so new-hires milled about. Some were tall. Others were short. A few of them sported pot-bellies while others were slim. But all of them were squared away, and none were the type that meeker men would care to encounter in a dark alley.

Bogrov was also there, resplendent in tailored BDUs and polished boots.

Slavko told his boss, "Everyone is here." Then he nodded at the range master.

The range master in turn called the men to the seven-yard line to shoot pistols at milk carton-size targets. As the men got going, Levi proved that not only could he cook, he could shoot—and shoot amazingly well. He consistently drew a holstered pistol and fired within a split second, and put holes through the target's exact center each time. His rounds were so precise that Slavko had to use calipers to show that they'd all punched through the initial hole he'd made—an ability that even won him a modicum of Slavko's respect in the form of a nod. Levi thought, the man might be a total psychopath but he does respect talent.

In point of fact, Levi ranked among the top 1% of the world's shooters—people who could literally draw from the hip and hit tiny targets within tenths of a second. It required a great deal of money to reach this ability, but Baker demanded the best and he'd paid top-dollar to provide his people with the finest instruction. On the downside, Levi was forced to explain his prowess by claiming to have honed his talents while serving as an Army Ranger. At least it served as a credible explanation.

He demonstrated a similar skill with his AK-47, shooting on the run and spinning out of various vantage points to hit his marks dead-on, and earning contemplative nods not only from the new soldiers but from Bogrov.

So despite ominous clouds and gathering squalls rolling in from the sea, he was in good spirits when Bogrov clapped him on the shoulder and told him they must have a drink one of these days. Levi instantly pounced on the opening, using it to talk openly with Bogrov, but while being careful not to come across as overly familiar.

Everything appeared in order until Bronislava arrived in a van and summoned Bogrov to her window for a hurried conversation. Then the passenger door opened. Levi paid little attention to the clean-shaven but heavily tattooed behemoth who stepped out. But when Levi took a second look it was already too late. He went dead inside as Bogrov called everyone to gather around to meet the newly-arrived soldier.

It was Pete, formerly of Levi's skinhead gang and currently an escapee from Super-Max. All at once the skies opened up.

CHAPTER THIRTY-FOUR

· ·

LEVI'S PISTOL had one round in the chamber and fifteen more in the magazine. He also had two spare mags, for a total of forty-six 9mm hollow points—more than enough to take out everyone, provided he acted first. Which he might have to do. For as the rain came down in torrents, Pete locked eyes with him. But the huge ex-skinhead said nothing and showed no reaction while Bogrov, unmindful of the deluge, introduced them.

Bogrov said to Levi, "I am told the boat brought only two men. This one will share with you your quarters." Then he turned to Pete. "This is Rocky O'Toole."

The giant held out a bear paw-sized hand. "How's it going... Rocky?" He glanced sidelong at Levi. "Looks like we're bunking together. I hope we can be friends."

Levi gripped Pete's hand. "I'm sure we will be."

The Russian beamed. "You are making with the acquaintances already. Very good. That will ease the chore of *team*-building." He threw back his head and laughed. "Team-building. What will those American eunuchs think of next? Perhaps they will teach men to wear makeup and keep house, yes?"

Pete grunted. "Yeah. Maybe." Although his eyes were fixed on Levi, he showed no outrage and gave no sign of seeking revenge by outing Levi in front of everyone.

Levi wondered, what's his game?

HE FOUND out an hour later as they stood inside his villa — *their* villa, now that Pete would live here. With rainwater dripping from their clothing and forming puddles in the entryway, Pete was putting down his belongings when Sophia appeared.

Levi told him, "This is my woman. Her name's Sophia." After they greeted each other, Levi said, "Come on. I'll show you the beach."

Always presuming that the villa was bugged, he brought Pete to the wind-swept beach so they could speak privately. At the same time, he was emotionally *and* physically prepared to kill Pete with a single blow to the throat if the massive enforcer even hinted at blowing his cover. For Levi, the stakes were that high.

Once outside under gray skies, Levi radiated sunburned health as he lit a Lucky Strike while leading Pete behind a dune where he could kill without being seen. He even had a motive ready, one that Bogrov wouldn't dispute: he would claim that the big man had tried to grope him. "Here, this'll do." Levi stopped and faced the giant.

Pete squinted at him. "Soon as I saw it was you I done some fast thinking. We was friends, me an' you. More than that. You was like my brother."

"That's true," Levi admitted. "We sure partied a lot, didn't we?"

"Humph." His features softened. "I can't be pissed at you. Hell, you was just doin' your job." Then he met Levi's eye. "Plus, I heard you done put in a good word for me during sentencing."

That was also true. Levi believed in taking a stand but then extending a hand. In his view it's the best way to develop informants. Also, a cop never knows when he might need a hand extended to *him*. It's one reason why, in the aftermath of the White House attack, he met with the U.S. Attorney and put Pete's role in the grand scheme of things in perspective. Though it ultimately did no good, news has a way of reaching a defendant's ears. To men like Pete, this level of loyalty is a supreme virtue.

Pete shuffled his leather boots in the sand and fixed Levi with a stare. "Don't worry. I ain't gonna say nothin' to nobody. Fuck, I don't even know why this Bogrov punk even needs an army. But I wasn't 'zactly in no position to be askin' too many questions when I heard 'bout the job. Anyhow, here I am an' I don't need no problems." He cleared his throat. "I figger you're working some sorta operation." He gazed at the mist-shrouded horizon. "I just want us to get along, 'cause even if you close this place down next week, it ain't gonna matter 'cause this gig ain't gonna last forever no how."

Levi's breath caught. "What do you mean? Why wouldn't it?"

Vigorously rubbing the end of his nose, Pete said, "Don't you know?"

Levi made a motion as if to a card dealer and said, "Gimme."

The behemoth shrugged. "Bogrov done told me an' the other new guy that soon as his army's put together? The shit's gonna fly. Said that'll be in about four more weeks. He said even if we survive any rough stuff, the contract still ends in eighteen months."

Levi thought, this is going down sooner than I imagined. Christ, I need to crack Bogrov *now*. Outwardly though, he remained unruffled. "You're right. It could end soon. So where's that leave us?"

"Here's the deal. Until it's over and it's time for the fat lady? Me an' you are gonna get along to go along. There. That's easy enough, right" Putting his hands on his hips, he leaned into Levi. "But before you answer, listen up. I might not be much. But my word's always been my bond."

Levi nodded. That's how he'd always regarded the man. Now he had to decide. He could exercise the first option and kill him. Or he could sign a treaty and look over his shoulder for the duration. His choice made, he nodded. "We have a deal."

The relief on Pete's face was palpable. "Good." Then he said affably, "How's my artwork doin'? The one I left 'round your ankle?"

"Still there, still getting a lot of attention."

"Ha. Warms my heart to hear that." He buddy-punched Levi's shoulder. "Hey, I can order some tools. Tatt you up all over again. You looked good all inked-up. I can also put your name across the top of your woman's ass. Whatever you want."

Levi kept his reply light-hearted. "Hmm. Yeah, maybe." He finally felt a degree of genuine relief. He'd learned long ago that Pete was a simple man who lived for the moment. But even so, Levi could never drop his guard.

The skies were clearing as they started back. He was anxious to get to his SAT phone and alert the team to Pete's presence, and to ask if Wild Bill Dentz had been sent along and would turn out to be today's only other newcomer.

"THERE YOU are, mate." The handsome man with the cruel scar on his nose held up a bottle of Scotch and said *sotto voce*, "I have some quality nose candy as well."

"Ian," Levi said after recovering from the shock of seeing who had knocked at the door after he and Pete returned. *Christ, it's the old strike one, strike two thing again. What's next?*

Pushing himself inside in the way in which people who never feel the need for an invitation do, Ian held out his hand. "I'm told that you're now aware of the true nature behind my visit to your hotel room—although bollocks, I certainly didn't fancy putting one over on you. Or playing a poof's role."

Levi had close friends in the LGBT community. But he had a role to uphold so he prodded Ian as men often do. "Tell me, big boy. What would you have done if I'd said, 'assume the position and let's get it on'?"

"I—" Ian's mouth worked silently until he grinned. "You tosser, you." Then he winked. "I should think we'll never know the answer to that one, will we now?" He grinned and jangled the bottle in front of Levi. "Well?"

"I'd love to. But I gotta work tonight."

"There it is, then. Bad luck, that. No matter. We'll have plenty of opportunities later. To drink, that is." Ian flashed a smile, then cocked an eye. "You could at least do some nose candy with me. They won't detect *that*. Well? Shall we, then?"

"No way. Not when I'm working." He was looking to change the subject when Sophia appeared with impeccable timing, and in the time that it took to make the introductions, Ian had dropped the idea of getting high.

And yet the day brought yet another surprise—as if Pete and Ian weren't enough, when Slavko stopped by to inform Levi that he'd been promoted to sergeant.

"You are transferred to the day shift. These men here," he pointed at Ian and Pete. "They are assigned to your squad. One more thing. Mr. Bogrov wishes to see you. In one hour. Informal attire is approved. You will walk there, yes?"

It wasn't a question. Not really. Levi acknowledged him.

After Slavko drove off, Ian went to his villa, Pete went to his bedroom for a nap, and after Sophia got back to the novel she'd been reading, Levi went to the shed and sent a text message. He started with Pete, added a sentence about Ian, asked the team to check out the Brit, and instructed them to brief Wild Bill about both men. After requesting an update on Katia, he thumbed the SEND button and sent the message in a micro-burst. Turning it off, he hid it beneath the floorboard, checked his watch, and calculated the time it would take to walk to Bogrov's house.

LEVI RAPPED his knuckles against the billionaire's door exactly one hour later. Bronislava opened it, mumbled in Russian, gestured at his flip flops, then pointed to a place near the door. This was SOP in Eastern Europe, where vacuum cleaners are in short supply. Stepping out of his footwear, he followed her into the main room where Bogrov sat in a green leather club chair. A rocking horse placed next to the window appeared to be looking outside. Finally, a black leather sofa with matching end tables supporting graceful Scandinavian lamps dominated the room's center. A stranger was seated on the sofa with his back to Levi.

But Levi didn't need to see the man's face to know who it was—not after he spotted the pony-tail.

Just then Leo Ryan turned, smiled, and raised a glass of vodka in salute.

CHAPTER THIRTY-FIVE

· ·

There it is. Strike three. Only, it's Ryan who'll soon be out. And we're talking permanently. Levi ignored the smirking Ryan and looked to Bogrov for an introduction.

"Ah, Rocky. I have visitor, no?" He tilted his head at Ryan. "Mr. Leo Ryan, of the *Washington Post*."

Levi noted Ryan's leather shoes. The fact that he had them on sharpened the clear line of demarcation that existed between them: Ryan was a guest. Levi was no more than hired help.

Bogrov said to Ryan, "Please to meet Rocky O'Toole. He is among the best, as I myself saw today. Also, he is now sergeant. I trust he will meet with your needs."

"Indeed he will," Ryan said, the amusement in his eyes now impossible to ignore as he stood and offered his hand. "Rocky. Hmm. Intriguing name. Not one I'd forget." He chuckled. "All I have to do is think about a prize fighter."

"One who wins," Levi fired back.

Bogrov cleared his throat. "Rocky. You are off tonight. So please to help yourself to the drink, *da?*" He waved an imperial hand in the general direction of a mini-bar that sat off to the side.

"Thanks, Mr. Bogrov. I'm honored." He went straight to the bar.

"Ah, well. You see, this reporter for great United States of America newspaper requested interview with me. He arrived a short time ago, by special boat."

Levi said idly, "Is that so?"

"Da. Mr. Ryan wishes among other things to speak with my best men. You are one of them."

While sloshing two fingers of Johnnie Walker Green Label into a Salviati crystal tumbler, Levi decided the time had come to cause Ryan's lasting disappearance. He had plenty of ideas, too. In fact, his biggest problem was in selecting the best option.

Bogrov said, "Mr. Ryan tells me he spends time in the islands. He grew curious about Isla de la Rusia. He questioned the merchants who support us. He learned it is I who owns this island, and asked for interview. Now I show him how secure we are from the cocaine cowboys who raid small islands. Plus, I am billionaire. All the more reason for pirates and cowboys to take shots at me." Bogrov grinned.

Levi saw why. The Russian had been handed an unexpected gift in the form of an opportunity to provide an innocuous rationale for his lavish security posture, one that made total sense for an island residence. But it would also let him taunt the world even more through the appearance of respectability and endorsement he'd have once a fawning story about him appeared in the *Post*.

After listening to a few more pleasantries while tossing back the Johnnie Walker, Levi turned to Bogrov. "Perhaps Mr. Ryan would enjoy a short tour." He jutted his jaw toward the large window overlooking the ocean. "Why don't I begin by showing him the beach? We can talk along the way."

Bogrov's facial muscles coaxed a smile. "A wise recommendation."

LEVI SAID to Ryan minutes later as they stood on a narrow sand spit, "Talk to me."

Pulling himself up to his full height, Ryan jabbed a finger at Levi. "No. You talk to me." He narrowed his eyes. "I've got you, Mr. *Hart*. You're clearly working a case. Now do you give me a story, or do I blow your cover? And I mean *right* now."

Levi let loose with a low whistle. "Wow. Hmm, I need to think about that one. Let me see. You blow my cover, and any case I might be working goes south. Then you go straight to prison for interfering with a federal agent. Is that what we're talking about?"

"Freedom of the press, my friend. I have a right to look into things."

"Sorry, pal. You're not an accredited reporter. And national security trumps free speech." Levi was bluffing. He'd stepped into a gray area that had a certain precedence in the wake of the well-known actor who interviewed a notorious Mexican drug lord. Gray area or not, he had a black and white plan and the time had come to use it. "I offered a deal in Luxembourg. You should've taken it. Would've saved yourself a lot of effort."

"What, an exclusive story *after* the fact?" Ryan forced a laugh. "Sorry. But this kid goes after the story *while* it's unfolding. And that is *non*-negotiable. '

"Non-negotiable, huh?" Levi stared out to sea as if considering his options. In fact, he'd purposely told Bogrov he was bringing Ryan to this particular beach as the opening gambit in the plan he'd formed while still in the house.

A part of that plan called for him to appear fatigued and at a dead-end. As the wind ruffled his hair, he began stroking Ryan's vanity in a bid to gain intel. "I have to say, I'm impressed that you tracked me here. How'd you do it?" He held up a hand before Ryan could answer. "I have a reason for asking. One that'll interest you."

"How? Hell, it was easy. Remember — my Vatican source told me about a theft. A pair of Swiss guards turned up dead in Luxembourg. Then you're suddenly no longer in Washington. I do the math, fly to where the action is, find out that Yuri Bogrov also happens to be in town, *and* that he's a suspect. As the numbers begin to tally he does his own vanishing act. Then you disappear again." He snapped his fingers. "I learned about this island and wrangled an invitation from our Russian friend."

"Huh. Gotta hand it to you, Ryan. That's excellent work." Levi meant it. Shifting gears, he regarded Ryan with hooded eyes. "Ever think of coming to work for us?"

"By 'us' you mean…"

"Never mind who. Well? Are you in?" Levi arched an eyebrow. "Helluva way to impress The Senator. It'd certainly be better than relying on discredited stories."

Ryan didn't even hesitate. "Sorry. I don't work for anyone who can wave a wand of authority over me."

"You've had your fill of The Overbearing Senator. Is that it?" Levi scoffed. "I see. You want a win-win solution. Very well. But, it'll take an hour to explain what's behind the Vatican theft and I told Bogrov we'd only be gone a few minutes. So here's the deal. I'll meet with you here, tomorrow, at 0900 hours. Then I'll talk."

Ryan's nose crinkled. "What's that I smell? Cheese?" He shook his head. "Sorry. I'm not buying it. We'll talk now."

"Negative." Levi locked eyes with his nemesis. "My story, my call. Take it, Ryan. You won't get another chance. If you blow my cover, you'll win a battle but lose a story that your grandkids will be telling *their* grandkids." He stepped closer and laced his next words with steel. "Do not test my resolve in this, or you'll face an oblivion of obscurity that will last even after you die. *Your* call."

Ryan's eyes darted about for a long moment. "Okay," he finally said. "It's not as if you can run. We are on an island, after all."

We sure are. And I'm gonna use it to my advantage, and your detriment. "Great. I'll see you tomorrow. 0900 hours. Right here." But Levi still needed to lock down a final detail for his plan to come together. "Where should I come calling if you're late?"

Ryan beamed. "Me? Easy. My host was kind enough to put me up in his home."

"Yeah? Hmm, that is nice. I hear he's got a splendid guest room."

"It is. Extra fine."

Levi squinted. "The good room. The one on the southeast corner. Right?"

"Yep. That's the one."

"Fine." Levi exhaled loudly. "I guess we'd better get a move on before our host sends a search party." Then as they headed up the hill, he provided Ryan with a synopsis of the island's security, in case Bogrov quizzed either of them later.

SLAVKO WAS nowhere in sight when they returned. Levi noted this, helped himself to more of the Johnnie Walker Green, tossed it down, then thanked Bogrov and left so as not to overstay his welcome. After reaching his villa, he greeted Sophia and suggested they take advantage of the nice weather by going for a swim. But while pulling on swim trunks he told her, "Give me a few minutes to check the waves and get some chairs."

Leaving at once to get the SAT phone, he was stepping through the sliding doors when he saw that the shed door was open. While his pulse shot to one fifty he edged closer, then stepped inside and almost suffered a heart seizure when he found Slavko standing in the middle of the small space with the electronics detector he'd used to sweep Levi the day he arrived.

Levi frowned and put hands on hips. "What're you doing here?"

"Routine," Slavko said almost as an aside as he moved the detector in a broad arc.

"If it's so routine, where's your jeep? Looks to me like you snuck over here."

The big man stopped and stared at Levi with one eye while the other appeared to roam the shed's interior. "Do not pose questions to me as a prosecutor might." He made a fist and thumped his chest. "I ask the questions. Not you." He regarded Levi in silence until he said, "But you are good man so I will tell you. It is parked beyond the curve in the road. In front of Sophia's former villa. Where I started my search. I will go to your *other* woman's villa next. Yes. Lara. She is still yours, is she not?" He arched an eyebrow and waited.

Levi shrugged. "Whatever. Listen, finish what you're doing so I can grab some chairs." A man with something to conceal might deny a relationship, or else add a line about going for a swim. But offering too much explanation will only arouse suspicion. Fortunately, he had on his swim trunks and saw that Slavko was indeed looking him over. To Levi's great relief, Sophia appeared in her bikini. Although initially taken aback upon seeing Slavko, she recovered so quickly that the visit must be routine. Or maybe not. Slavko had given Levi just such a stare the night of the moaning man.

"I am finished here." Slavko thumbed off the device and stepped past them. Levi watched him trudge down the beach toward Lara's villa.

A FULL hour passed before Levi could retrieve the SAT phone. He saw nothing to suggest the floorboard he'd hidden it under had been disturbed, and since he always powered the phone down, it couldn't have emitted anything to trigger the detector. But he thought the Serb was wily enough to have left some other detector in the shed. So taking the SAT with him to the dune where he'd spoken to Pete, he fired it up and sent a priority text about Ryan and what needed to be done. He also stressed the absence of locked doors on Isla de la Rusia. Turning the phone off, he put it back inside its waterproof bag and buried it near the base of a coconut palm.

Three hours later he checked the phone and saw a message icon, and after entering the password he reviewed the response to his earlier text. Satisfied by what he read, he turned it off and slipped back into the villa.

HE EASED OUT of bed at zero dark thirty and told Sophia, "I'm feeling antsy. Think I'll go for a walk." Kissing her before she could ask to come along, he got dressed and grabbed a bottle of tequila as he swept through the kitchen. Once outside, he looked up at a moonless sky, nodded, then began walking to the coastal surveillance radar center.

Although the radar antenna sat atop the island's highest point, its operators were housed in the island's comm center, which was located on the leeward side halfway up the hill to protect it from floods and prevailing hurricane winds. After a fifteen minute hike under partially obscured skies, he reached the center and knocked on the steel door.

A pale, morbidly obese Hispanic in his fifties opened the door. "Ah, *mi amigo. Como estas?*"

"I'm fine, *Buey*. Just out walking. Trying to shift gears after working midnights, ya know? Thought I'd stop by and—" He held up the tequila. "What do you think, Hector? A little something to help pass the time?"

Levi had befriended Hector the Ox during his first night shift. When he discovered Hector's taste for tequila, he found a bottle and returned to give the large man some shots of the drink with the small worm. Hector had been grateful; sitting alone in a comm center at three in the morning can be torture and he'd welcomed Levi's visit. Hector now waved him inside.

The room had a faint ozone-odor from the green, red, and blue lights that glowed from various electronic arrays. Pouring a couple of shots while watching the radar screen, Levi put the next phase of his plan to get Ryan off-island into play. "*Salud,*" he said while raising his glass.

Thirty seconds later, Levi offered the toast again. And a third time...

THE U.S. Air Force C-130 skimmed low over the warm Caribbean waters. It was twelve miles east of Isla de la Rusia and flying with a mere one thousand feet showing on the altimeter. The pilot had been briefed that he would pass by an island where a radar was tuned to detect targets—but only to within six miles—and so he'd turned off the four-engine cargo plane's nav lights long ago. Now approaching the drop point, he added power and when he pulled back on the control wheel, the C-130 lurched upward until he leveled-off at 2,500 feet. After checking his bearing, he told the co-pilot to drop the loading ramp. Seconds later a whir of electric motors caused the deck to vibrate while the greasy ramp opened.

As warm air rushed in and filled the cargo space, the crew chief signaled the SEALs to stand up.

A green light glowed. The crew chief pushed a pallet containing a deflated rubber Zodiac down the ramp. It vanished into the black void, its parachute deploying automatically.

Next, eight SEALs dove head first off the ramp, their night vision clearly showing the route that the raft was taking. Adjusting the risers of their chutes to follow the raft down to the surface of the sea, their Heckler-Koch MP-5 submachine guns were in place against their chests, the holsters for the Beretta 9mm pistols secure, all eight men lined-up in a stack.

Meanwhile, the C-130's pilot, having hopped across the water before popping up to deploy the SEALs in a classic "hop and pop," raised the ramp while simultaneously lowering the nose to get back down to a thousand feet.

At the same time, the lead SEAL checked the GPS mounted to his wrist and verified they were on course. Then — splashdown. Twelve miles from shore. The eight men joined ranks and bobbed in a slight chop next to the FC 470 Zodiac raft. They got it inflated, climbed aboard, rigged its 40 horsepower outboard engine, and hunkered down while the coxswain started the motor and set course for Isla de la Rusia.

"BUEY," LEVI began, "I've got it. Go take your thirty winks."

Hector looked at him with gratitude, and rising unsteadily, he shuffled to the illegal cot he'd set up in the far corner and plopped down.

Levi waited until Hector's chest began to rise and fall in a steady cadence before taking a seat at the screen. His first task was to kill the alarm that would sound if the radar picked up a target closing in on the island. Next, he glanced at the clock and watched the screen in earnest. It didn't take long. *There they are. Such a small blip… but it would be bigger than a 747 for someone with Hector's watchful eyes.*

THE SEAL coxswain eased back on the throttle and killed the engine. The rush of wind died at once as the bow wallowed. Seconds later, the keel scraped the sandy bottom.

All eight SEALs wore NVGs. They waited for the lead's signal. When he slashed a hand toward shore, they slipped into the shallows, gripped the raft's handholds and whisked it ashore, then turned it seaward before covering it with palm fronds. They'd been briefed that the operative who'd requested the exfiltration had scouted the area, and that this was the most isolated beach to land on.

LEVI NO LONGER saw the blip on the radar screen. He peered at Hector, listened briefly to his soft but steady snoring, and checked the time. *Okay, guys. You're on the clock. Twelve minutes. Good luck.*

THE LEAD SEAL studied Bogrov's house through his NVG while his men got into position behind him. *There it is*, he told himself. *EP One.* Turning slightly, he pointed at the main door. Entry Point 1—the squad's designated access point. Under normal conditions the team would have a secondary Entry Point—an EP2. But the lead had decided that the operative on this island knew his tradecraft, and hadn't questioned the lack of a secondary—or the fact that the Entry Point would double as their Exit Point. Making a fist, he extended two fingers to the others while mouthing, "EXP." Exit point. They'd discussed this during the briefing while studying an outline of the house and the location of the target's bedroom. But the carpenter's rule applied: measure twice, cut once.

The lead ventured forth—low, slow and quiet; standard stealth entry. They'd been told there would be no locks or cameras. They looked for them anyway. Once all eight SEALs were hunkered down at the Entry Point, they brushed their footwear with their gloved hands to avoid leaving sand trails. Next, the lead cocked his head and listened. Satisfied that all was quiet, he pointed at the door.

Seconds later they were inside. Each man had a piece of the pie to protect—an area inside the structure to observe for threats. The lead went directly to the guest room. His NVG let him discern the figure atop the bed. Caucasian male. Thirties. Pony tail; the target also matched the photo they'd studied during the briefing.

The lead reached back without needing to look and tapped the operator behind him. Then he clamped his hand over Ryan's mouth and nose while the other SEAL stuck a syrette loaded with 150 mg of midazolam into Ryan's upper arm. The sedative is the same one given to condemned inmates once they're strapped to the gurney. It takes five seconds to do its job—three on a good night. If they'd been out to execute him, they'd have followed-up with a lethal chemical cocktail.

The gods favored them this night. Ryan stopped struggling almost at once. But the sedative, in addition to having few side effects, also wears off fast. The SEALs got busy, bagging and tagging him—blindfolding him, taping his mouth shut, and cuffing his wrists. Seconds later, three of them lifted the semi-conscious, underwear-clad Ryan from bed and silently but swiftly hustled him outside. This method was easier than knocking him out completely. Too much dead weight to carry. Meanwhile, a squad member found Ryan's trousers and swept them up. With the others watching their slices of the pie, the lead started for the Exit Point.

Three minutes later they were loading Ryan into the Zodiac while the SEAL who'd grabbed Ryan's trousers folded them neatly and left them atop the sand. Then they pushed off beyond the breakers and clambered aboard.

LEVI NOTED the time while watching the tiny blip as it moved away from Isla de la Rusia until it faded entirely. Flipping the alarm back on, he shook Hector awake. "*Buey*. Time to wake up." After the ox took his place at the screen, Levi made small-talk before stretching his arms and stifling a yawn. "I'd better get my ass ready for my new day as a sergeant… with all the ruffles and flourishes that accompany the honor." The big man smiled and winked as Levi gathered the tequila and waved farewell.

USS DALLAS, along with its SEAL Delivery Vehicle, had departed the region long ago. So it hadn't been available on such short notice for this mission. But *USS San Juan* was in the area, and the SEALs arrived at the rendezvous point on schedule and watched the sub surface. While half of the squad got Ryan below, the others deflated the Zodiac and pulled it aboard.

After the lead SEAL got Ryan sequestered and sedated anew in sick bay, he and his men sought their 3M's: meal, movie, and mattress. In the meantime, the *San Juan's* commanding officer passed The Word to his crew: "You didn't see anything, and the men you thought you saw were never here." Then he ordered the officer of the deck to submerge and set course for a point twelve miles east, and to make sixteen knots.

An hour later *San Juan* surfaced a hundred yards away from an *Arleigh Burke* class destroyer. The destroyer's whaleboat came alongside the submarine's gleaming black hull within minutes, and after its crew took a still-sedated Ryan from *San Juan*, the coxswain headed the boat back to his ship while the sub vanished beneath a swirl of water. The destroyer's SH-60 Blackhawk took off soon after and set a course for the former U.S. Air Force base on Antigua, where the crew transferred the blindfolded, unresponsive passenger to a waiting civilian aircraft that bore the corporate markings of an entity that was actually a wholly owned and operated subsidiary of the CIA.

AT DAWN a few short hours later, a BDU-attired Levi stepped from his villa just as Slavko's jeep skidded to a stop. The Serb's face was unreadable as he announced, "We have lost our guest."

Levi's eyebrows nearly came together. "Guest? You mean, the reporter?"

"Yes. We found his pants at the beach…"

"Beach?"

"The one you took him to. Yesterday. They were folded. He must have gone for a midnight swim." Slavko shook his head. "Stupid man. To swim in the ocean. Alone. At night. With all the predators…"

Levi slowly shook his head. "What a dumb fuck."

Slavko handed him a paper bag. "His effects. Wallet, watch; clothes. See to it that they are shipped to his family." Frowning, he drove Levi to the briefing area.

The instant Slavko roared off, Levi checked Ryan's effects. They included a smart phone. Fortunately, he hadn't password-protected it. Levi checked for messages or notes that might reveal his true identity, but wasn't surprised when he found nothing. Ryan struck him as the type who kept things close-in. Levi checked the wallet and rummaged through Ryan's other effects but came up empty. Even so, he took grim pleasure in knowing that Ryan wouldn't be able to bother him for a long time to come—and even if free to do so, Ryan wouldn't want to unless he was totally insane.

•   •   •

The instant Leo Ryan stirred next to the underage girl in the Tijuana brothel, she left the *Norte Americano* lying naked atop the bed and tip-toed to the door. Beckoning to her pimp, she said, "I think he has awakened."

The pimp snorted and opened the decrepit hotel's front door. Almost as if on cue, six officers of the *Municipal Policia* stormed inside. Their captain took one look at Ryan and another at the underage girl. Then with a wry smile he ordered his men to arrest the *gringo*. As they handcuffed Ryan and took him away, the captain mentally counted the cash he'd been given to arrive in front of the brothel, "in the nick of time."

CHAPTER THIRTY-SIX

· ·

"YES, SIR. I understand." Tommy pocketed his phone and stared at a blank space on his four star hotel room wall. Heath Baker had called to inform him that the National Security Advisor had urged the president to initiate a pre-emptive move against Bogrov, rather than sit idly by. Baker explained that while cooler heads had prevailed, Levi had to make substantial progress. Baker added, "The people you visited on a small strip of land have achieved sudden progress of their own. They're now confident that their gizmo's potential has risen from 68% to 76% effectiveness."

A SHORT DISTANCE away and at roughly the same time that Tommy finished his call, Michael Bailey was settling his long, lanky frame onto a beach lounge and adjusting his Speedo—normal attire for St. Lucia, an island first colonized by the French. The team had been here for three days, ever since Tommy repositioned them after receiving Levi's order to check out Katia Lagunov. But despite being in paradise Michael had his family in mind—no easy task in view of the admiring looks he was getting from eye-catching women, and now from a very good looking young man who was passing by.

"*Bonjour,*" the lad ventured. "*Je suis François.*"

"*Enchanté,*" Michael said, adding in fluent French that his name was "Mark."

He invited François to stay and they talked awhile. Wasting no time, the young man made it clear that he found Michael attractive. The Dragon Team operative didn't mind. He'd had gay friends all his life and François proved to be good company. But Michael was out to attract one person only: Katia Lagunov, Solicitor — so after a few minutes he yawned to signal the young man that it was time for him to leave.

On cue, Monica strolled past as François walked off. When she continued on, he gathered his things and went to his hotel room, where he showered and put on shorts in time to answer a gentle knock at the door. After checking the peephole, he let Monica in and they sat at a small round table. Then as gentle ocean breezes washed through the open windows, she told him that Heath had just notified Tommy that in light of Pete's presence on Levi's island, he'd pulled Blue Crew from their protective duties. Michael nodded. He'd have done the same if he were in charge.

Next, Monica reported that Katia had remained at her office instead of visiting the beach as she'd done each noon the past three days, adding that Tommy and Hack were currently watching her. From there, they got on with planning the night's activities.

"It's Friday," she began. "We know she leaves her office precisely at five."

"Not what you'd call a hard working attorney, huh?"

"She might not *have* to work hard. Not if billionaire Bogrov's paying her bills."

"Okay. I'll plan on bumping into her when she leaves. If my timing's off? No sweat. I'll approach her at that restaurant she's been frequenting."

Monica rested a hand on his forearm. "Are you still prepared to do it?"

"Prepared? Yes. Reconciled? No. Probably never. But…"

"Don't worry. She'll understand."

He pressed his lips tight. "Nadia must never know."

LATER THAT day he dressed in a dark Prada polo, khaki trousers, and black Hermes shoes. Then he slipped his expensive Mont Blanc wallet and fake ID into a hip pocket to become Mark Miller — successful day-trader, millionaire, and unabashed lover of the ladies. After taking a moment to settle into his new persona, he walked to the business district only to be forced into dodging a flurry of quitting-time office workers moving pell-mell along the sidewalks. Then there were the tourists, attired in pastel T's and shorts that fit corpulent bodies far too tightly. Food stalls and eateries where everywhere, and they teemed with the odors of ocean reefs, inland plantains and everywhere chicken. Horns tooted as taxi drivers negotiated the traffic and friends called out to one another. And yet the air also enjoyed a stillness. Working his way east until he reached a gift shop next to Katia Lagunov's law office, he stopped to peer inside a display window.

HE SPOTTED her the instant she stepped from her office door. Young and lithe with hair the color of midnight, she had on a sheer blouse that flattered the intense quality of her high breasts. She also wore a look of absolute confidence, making her his type of woman. But when she turned west as she'd done during previous recons, he chose that moment to step back from the window directly into her path.

"Idiot," she snarled as they collided.

"I'm so sorry," he gushed. "Look, it's my fault. Please let me make it up to you."

Katia looked him over. Her glare softened. Then her Russian accent sweetened the air. "Oh, but it is not necessary. It is, how do you say, accident of the simple variety."

"All the more reason for me to offer you a coffee. Or better yet, dinner." He put on his most infectious smile. "I'm Mark."

"Ah, *Mark*." She regarded him anew. "Yes, how do you do? I am called Katia."

"What a beautiful name! You are from Eastern Europe, no?"

"I was born in Lithuania." Then she stood taller. "But I am *Russian*."

"How nice. I've been to Moscow. It's wonderful, especially in the summer."

While studying him, she asked, "But did you not find it difficult to get around? The Metro, it's—" She rolled her eyes. "Terrible, the Metro. Is it not?"

She was testing him. He shook his head. "I didn't find it bad at all. Quite the contrary. I found it easy to use. Other than not running 24 hours a day, I…"

"I know of good restaurant," she said at once. "It is nearby. I was on my way there when you—we—bumped into each other." She showed gleaming teeth. "Come. We go there now."

Michael flashed a winning grin as they walked a short distance to the same trendy restaurant that Hack had followed her to the last three nights, where a tall, old and very black waiter greeted her by name before leading them to a corner table with a splendid view of the quaint downtown buildings.

"Champers for me," Katia told the waiter.

Michael ordered a Guinness and engaged her in small talk. The waiter brought their drinks, along with a starter of fried gnocchi with strips of jerk pork in a sweet pea sauce that he thought was otherworldly. Later, as they dug into main dishes of battered king fish fillets with grilled asparagus, aromatic roasted peppers, and a tomato and mushroom salad, he glanced often at her, and when after a few more drinks she tapped her shoe against his, he tapped back—then held his against hers.

WHILE MICHAEL and Katia thrust and parried, Tommy and Hack made their way down a shadowy alley near her office. Hack had seen a young man park his motorbike there twice already, and fortune favored them tonight because it was there, secured to a large water pipe by a case-hardened steel chain. After looking over his shoulder, Hack used a shim to open the bike's locked gas cap. Next, he shoved a strip of cloth into the tank, then held it and looked at Tommy.

The team's assistant leader spoke quietly into his hands-free mic. "Clear?"

Monica replied at once. *"Clear."*

Tommy did a final look-around and whispered to Hack, "Looks good," adding, "Poor slob's never gonna know why his bike had to be sacrificed."

Hack shrugged, flicked a lighter and touched the flame to the cloth. Then he and Tommy jogged toward the street. There were only a few pedestrians present when Hack nudged Tommy's ribs. "Should be about…"

Boom!

Shouts filled the air. People ran helter-skelter toward the alley, now bright with the orange glow of a roaring fire that was sending up thick black smoke.

While a crowd ran toward the scene, Hack slid a tension tool into Katia's locked office door. When Monica gave the all-clear from her vantage point across the street, he got past the lock and the men slipped inside while everyone else gathered at the fire.

In a perfect world they'd have waited until Michael got Katia to her home. But they couldn't count on that happening, so they had to do their work while the opportunity presented itself. Hack went for the file cabinet. Tommy attacked the desk. Seeing a cell phone sitting atop it, he got out his laptop and connected its USB port to the phone. After downloading the phone's files, he put it back exactly as he'd found it and studied the desk drawers.

An experienced cop can tell at a glance when a professional criminal commits a burglary. The pros open desk and file cabinet drawers from the bottom up, searching each in turn but never closing them. When they've finished, all of the drawers are left open. This reduces the chances of leaving prints by pushing them back in, and saves seconds when spending too much time on-site increases the risk of discovery.

But this was a different matter, and as Tommy searched each drawer for any proof of a fail-safe system, he closed each one afterward. Katia must never know that someone had searched her office. He was opening another drawer when his earpiece tingled.

"*Company.*" Monica said in a calm, clear voice.

Tommy acknowledged her and tapped Hack's shoulder, then pointed wordlessly at the office closet. Stepping inside, they gripped their holstered pistols.

MICHAEL SAID, "I thought we were going to your place for drinks." Pulling Katia close, he pressed against her to make his needs known, all in a desperate bid to keep her from entering the office and finding two black men in the middle of a black-bag job. But she was determined to retrieve her cell phone—the one she'd left on her desk.

"It takes not a rocket surgeon to understand that I am *solicitor*. I need my phone. *Da?*" But she kissed him hungrily before pulling back and smiling.

"It can wait until tomorrow," he argued. Then he began working his hips against her with sensual male hunger until Monica crossed the street and walked by with a finger to her ear to signify that she'd alerted the crew. But Katia was not to be dissuaded.

They stepped inside the office. She snapped on the light. And froze.

Michael went on high alert, glancing at the closed closet door and watching Katia as creases erupted across her forehead.

All at once she gasped. "Mark! Something is not right."

He said while easing her toward the door, "You'd better wait here while I..."

"No, no." She waved her hands in frustration. "My attaché case. I left it on the floor, there next to the desk. But it is gone. I—" She slapped a hand against her head. "I must be like the retard. It all now comes back. I placed it in the closet."

"I'll get it," he said while stepping quickly past her. Shielding the closet door with his body, he edged it open and after trading looks with Hack, he plucked a black attaché case from the floor and held it high. Then he looked at her with bedroom eyes. "Now let's go, shall we?" Without giving her time to answer, he waited until she grabbed her phone, then ushered her through the door and onto the street.

TOMMY AND HACK remained in place until Monica gave the all-clear. Then after wiping a broad hand across his brown forehead, Tommy blew air from his cheeks and returned to the desk, while Hack went back to work on the file cabinet.

MICHAEL BAILEY stared wide-eyed at Katia's condo. He thought it was spectacular, and because he and Nadia were worth six million dollars, he knew wealth's trappings. But Katia's condo went beyond expectations. And yet it's why he'd chosen to present himself as being independently wealthy, to circumvent any suspicion that he would establish a relationship to live off her wealth. *Which she obviously has an abundance of. This place certainly wasn't acquired on an attorney's wages.*

He thought this alone fortified her connection with Bogrov—a man who wasn't about to spend a fortune on an investment without a substantial return. He also decided that Bogrov's relationship with Katia wasn't a sexual one. Nor an intellectual one, for she'd shown no depth nor any grasp of world events. And like many women who are so beautiful that most men don't dare approach them, she was also lonely. Perhaps that was the void Bogrov filled for her—that of companionship. Michael would find out.

While standing at her side in the living room, he watched as she poured Louis XIII Rémy Martin cognac into crystal snifters. *Hell. The empty bottle alone has a resale value of $800.00.* When she finished pouring she led him to a balcony that boasted a splendid view of a small city at its night-time best, and he was genuinely taken in by the palms, the white strip of beach, and the sea beyond.

She swept a hand at a pair of teak lounges, and after they were seated she rested a hand on his knee while they talked and swirled their snifters and laughed, until finally she asked, "Why don't I show you the bedroom?" Standing, she grazed the back of his neck with soft fingertips and stepped inside.

Michael loved his wife. He hadn't been with another woman in the eighteen years they'd been married. But he would do whatever it took to boost any chance of holding world disaster at bay. Feeling sick at heart, he got up and followed.

AT THE SAME time seven blocks away, Hack looked up from the file drawer he was searching and muttered, "She sure doesn't have what you'd call a plethora of clients. The bottom drawers are nearly empty. Top ones hold a dozen files. That's it." A moment later he moved on to the closet, while Tommy began inspecting the backs of the certificates and photos that were hanging from the walls.

MICHAEL BURST from the hotel elevator just before noon the next day, marched down the hallway, and found Monica waiting at his door.

"Nothing," she said as he pushed it open.

Once inside he plopped onto the bed and crossed his ankles, then draped an arm over his eyes. The breeze through the window was desultory. So were the dull sounds of passersby below. He lay quiet amid conflicting emotions, yet certain of three things: he'd done his duty, he loved Nadia completely, and he could never hurt her by revealing that life's circumstances had forced him into prostitution again. In this case, it was not only for the survival of his family, but of his very soul had he balked at using all the resources at his disposal to keep them alive.

Monica settled next to him and began without deliberation. "This is a job where a lot of rules don't apply. They can't apply, because this job often wrecks the lives of good people in their quest to avert calamity." She hesitated, then pushed on. " Nadia will understand. She…"

"Monica? Shut the fuck up." Lowering his arm, he looked at her. "I don't need to rationalize, *okay*? I can compartmentalize with the best of them. Don't worry. I won't start with the *mea* fucking *culpas*, 'cause that just doesn't work."

"You're right," she said without rancor. "I don't have to worry. I only have to be your friend. Especially now, when you're pissed at the world."

He exhaled, then gently squeezed her hand. "I'm sorry." A hesitation. Then, "Nadia told me long ago that if I'm ever so lonely that it hurts, then she'd understand if I needed, well, a friend. This thing with Katia was… is… work-related. Still—" He grimaced, then squeezed Monica's hand again. "So they found nothing, huh?"

"No. But Hack planted the listening devices. Maybe they'll produce."

Tommy had requested the bugs, along with a backstop for Michael's new role as Mark Miller. The FBI had sent a courier with the devices that very evening.

Michael looked at her. "Katia's asked me to move in with her for the duration of my 'vacation.' I said yes, of course."

Her hands turned to fists. "Sure. Great opportunity to see if she knows what Bogrov's all about."

He snorted. "Jesus, look at me. Back to hustling. Once a whore always a…"

"My turn." She raised up on an elbow. "Shut up." Satisfied, she lay her head on his chest. "I can hear your heart beating. I love that sound. '

"Thanks." He grunted. "Yeah, guess I'll become a male Mata Hari. Woo her. Win her heart." He adopted a deep, female Teutonic voice. "She shall be like putty in my hands. I shall play her, then toss her aside. But gently, if I find she is only Bogrov's pawn."

"See? You're still spiritual, even after being forced to be corporeal."

He touched her cheek. Then despite the duty-oriented anguish, he said what he felt. "I wish you and I could be lovers. After all, we are… friends." When her breath caught and their eyes met, he hesitated but then nodded.

MICHAEL GOT up naked sometime later and padded into the bathroom where he splashed water on his face. If the sex had been awkward the first time, by now it was great. It all had to do with seeing her as a friend—the *her* in this case being Katia, whom he'd gone to after his soul-cleansing talk with Monica.

Walking from the bathroom and returning to bed, he kissed her and got down to business. The key to obtaining intel lay in her heart, so he began asking those questions that the lovelorn inevitably focus upon: where had she been raised? What schools did she attend? What were her pet peeves and favorite foods?

She ate it up as he'd hoped she would, so he expressed a rush of feelings for her. But when he touched her intimately, she demurred.

"Darling, even on the Saturday I must go to the office." But her eyes sparkled. "Is okay. I return soon. Then you and I will make the love again. Yes?"

Not about to give up, he offered an infectious smile that caused her to open her arms—and more—to him. Later, once the door closed behind her, he leaped from bed and phoned Monica. "Elvis has left the building."

"I'm on her. Yeah, she's going to her office. Hack'll pick it up from there."

Ending the call, he pulled on a pair of shorts and went to work. An hour later he laughed aloud when he found a thumb drive hidden behind the frame of a bucolic scene of Gorky Park done up in garish pastels. *Humph. Always in the last place you look.*

Acting quickly, he inserted the thumb drive into his laptop and found several pages of instructions in Russian. The drive also contained copies of papers written in Latin. Since Latin is as much a Romance language as French, he deciphered enough of what he saw to realize he'd hit pay dirt. After saving everything to the laptop, he sent a virus to the thumb drive that would corrupt it—along with her credibility if she ever tried to disclose what it once contained.

Now he had to determine whether she'd read any of it, or knew anything else about Bogrov's plans. That meant being her lover for a week or even a year, if that's what it would take.

For now, he put the thumb drive in its hiding place and went for a walk, during which he chanced upon a small man of Congolese descent. Michael, always the friendly sort, engaged him in casual conversation—and once Hack heard what Michael had to say about the thumb drive, the former locksmith sauntered off to inform Tommy of the discovery, along with Michael's future plans with the solicitor.

"I WONDER if they ever knew?"

Tommy finished sending a coded message about Michael's findings to Heath before he looked at Hacksaw. "Who? And what?"

"The general population of Ecos; the pending astcroid. Imagine," Hack mused. "An advanced civilization *eons* before ours." He made a steeple of his fingers and held it against his lower lip. "There was a movie. *The New World*. Ever see it?"

"That the one with Colin Farrell?"

"Yeah. About the first English settlers of Jamestown, Virginia. *My* Virginia. More specifically, the Tidewater region of that *singular* commonwealth, along with Captain Smith an' Pocahontas. The year is 1607 or roundabouts." Hack tapped his fingertips against his teeth. "Thing is, the English were sooo advanced compared to the Powhatan tribes that'd been living there in the *utmost* harmony with nature for who knows *how* long." He let the steeple collapse. "The tribes never saw the pending English onslaught."

Tommy closed the laptop cover and frowned. "But enough of the *Ecos* knew about the asteroid. Or there wouldn't have been a rocket to the moon with its 'we were here' jazz."

"But the population as a whole?" Hack insisted. "Do you think *they* knew? Truth be told, would *you* wanna know?"

"NO. I DON'T think I'd want to know," Michael said in response to Monica's identical question. They were seated at the sidewalk cafe where he'd gone to meet her after seeing Hack. Now he looked past her at the beach and frowned.

"I would," she said. "I'd find great peace in knowing when and how I was to die."

"If it were only me? Maybe. But I don't care to know when Nadia will buy it. Or my kids. Or you."

"Or me." She looked into his eyes. "We're such good friends, you and I."

"We are. And we'd make beautiful babies. If I weren't married, I'd…" All at once he jumped to his feet. "Gotta go. Katia might come home early." Turning on his heel, he said over his shoulder, "I hope Levi's making inroads… and not in any danger." His last words were almost lost to the sea-breeze. "Or sick."

CHAPTER THIRTY-SEVEN

. . . .

LEVI BARELY made it to the toilet before he vomited.

Two days earlier, following the arrival of Pete and Ian, he'd stood outside his villa at first light while waiting for Slavko. It would mark his second tour as the early shift sergeant. He had used the first day to good advantage by making friends with the island's civilian workers, since they often knew what was going on behind the scenes. But when Slavko arrived, lazy eye and all, the Serb grunted. "Yuri wants to see you." Levi hopped in. Minutes later the jeep was grinding its way up the long driveway to the house.

Slavko pointed at a corner near the door. "Leave your weapon there."

Levi leaned his AK-47 against the wall and removed his boots without waiting to be told. He also undid the harness that carried his hand grenades and ammo pouches. But he kept his pistol on—just in case.

Slavko showed little emotion but he did mumble, "Excellent. This way."

Levi followed him into the main room and found Bogrov staring out an open window, the rocking horse at his side.

A cooling air from last night's rain blew in, making the sheer curtains flutter like leaves. The air also brought the intoxicating scents of golden gardenia, frangipani, and moss into the house.

Bogrov turned and clasped his hands behind his back. "I have finally realized who you remind me of."

Levi tensed. *Has my cover been compromised? Good thing I kept the pistol.*

Bogrov fairly glowed. "Yes, Rocky. It is the shape of your face, along with the color of your hair and eyes. For you see, it is the face my son might have grown into had he survived childhood." He pointed at the rocking horse. "My son's. I crafted it myself."

Levi's heart actually went out to Bogrov. He might be a psychopathic murderer, but he cared about his kid. *Gotta give him that much.*

Bogrov patted the horse's head. *"Da. Khorosho.* Now you and I shall have recreational experience. Yes?"

"Recreational experience?"

"Please, call me Yuri." His upper lip curled as if by habit. "I am in command of this island. You? You are soldier. But you are good soldier. That makes the difference with me. My father, he too was the good soldier." He grunted. "Not that we were so close. We were not. Even so, I respect a man who can handle the weapons as you do. This skill can capture the hearts of women, da?" To Levi's puzzled look, he said, "The people who hired you. They spoke highly of your adventure with their, how do you say in America—their operative. Da. So I also respect you." He gestured grandiloquently at the ornate coffee table in front of the leather sofa.

Levi looked. It held a vast assortment of drugs and paraphernalia.

"Rocky, you told my people that you have experimented with the heroin during your youth. Is that not correct?" He squinted at Levi.

"Yes. That's right." Levi noticed a faded track mark on Bogrov's arm.

"Then please to sit and demonstrate your ability to use the needle. Perhaps I will then join you. A syringe has been prepared with five milligrams of excellent heroin. It is a small dose. But then, I do not want you to become addict, da?"

"No, you don't want that." Staring warily at it, Levi knew he couldn't do even a small amount of heroin without wanting more. But he'd come here to pry secrets from this leering Russian, and his own well-being meant nothing when measured against the catastrophic results that could occur if he failed in his mission.

However, he couldn't tolerate responding to Bogrov's play book. He had to get Bogrov to react to *him*. But compromises are the rule in life. Right now he'd have to defend against Bogrov's new gambit. However, he would turn tomorrow into a day of his own choosing. First, he had to get going with the dope.

Plucking a yellow surgical rubber tourniquet from the table, he pulled it snug around his left bicep and clenched its bitter tasting end between his teeth, the familiar rituals of his old habit alive again. Next, he probed the space inside his left elbow until he found a suitable vein. After smacking at it until it bulged, he swabbed the site with an alcohol pad, grabbed the syringe, examined its dirty brown contents, put the needle against the engorged vein, and pushed steadily until it went in with a soft *plop*.

He was aware that Slavko had quietly moved behind him—to take aggressive action if Levi wavered. He needn't have. Levi had gone to war. The bugles had sounded. His heart was racing. But it raced for the wrong reason as synapses in his brain, sensitized by his previous undercover drug use, clicked-in. All at once he was drooling as he put a finger on the plunger, wanting the drug for real now, easing down with rising excitement, only to frown as the first cold drops hit his bloodstream. There was something wrong. He pushed again but still didn't feel the indescribable contentment that should follow. Staring at Bogrov with a WTF expression, he said, "If this is heroin, it's gone bad."

Levi detected a hint of a smug smile on Bogrov's lips and instantly grasped what the cautious psychopath had done: he'd provided a fake solution to see if Levi really had used heroin. A true *veterano* would discern the real from the unreal. But a phony might moan and keen as if he'd felt a rush that couldn't exist—thus raising any number of red flags. Levi thought, this bastard's mega-careful as only his kind can be. It also made sense that he hadn't been vetted this way during the hiring process, to guard against possible undercover cops arresting the interviewers for possession.

"Slavko," Bogrov barked. "Come here." As the dark-featured man shambled from behind the sofa, Bogrov snapped at him. "What is wrong with you? I ask for proper dose. Yet you give us the shit. *Bah*. You are incompetent. Leave my sight at once." He waved his hand dismissively. Then as his anger subsided he turned to Levi. "Please to excuse the lapse.

Now if you will be so kind as to wait, I will prepare proper dose. From now on too, I will invite you into my home with frequency. Then we both will do the heroin."

"Sure thing." Levi paused intentionally, then cocked his head. "Yuri, I tried drugs as a kid. But the only drug I use now is alcohol." While letting this sink in he stared at the dope that was still spread atop the coffee table and wet his lips as if he couldn't wait to shoot up—and deep in his cortex, it's what his brain was screaming at him to do. But that wasn't an option. So to get past it he focused on attacking Bogrov's plans. "Don't get me wrong. I loved doing heroin. Who wouldn't? Hell, I'll gladly shoot up with you as often as you want." He closed his eyes and smiled. "Mmm, yeah. It's sooo good, isn't it?" He snapped his eyes open. "But I want to be a good soldier, so I'd better play it slow."

After turning his arm to reveal the track mark that had already formed from the fake dose, he jutted his jaw at the bottles of liquor atop the mini-bar. "But booze? It never screws me over." He looked at Bogrov to make his point, then waited to see if his bid to remain a good soldier rather than a junkie would work.

Unable to conceal a growing smile, Bogrov bobbed his head. "You know who you are. That is good thing. Yes, after you arrived I heard how it was with you and the women. Two of them threw themselves at you. Others among the women want to be with you as well. The men respect you. As do I. As would my son, whom you resemble."

Levi could see Bogrov coming down from his need to shoot up and clenched his hands in triumph. Now he wanted to paint a bulls eye on the bastard's forehead and score in a different manner.

"From now on," the Russian went on, "it will be as you say. We shall not each day do the drugs. For you are right. I do not wish to have the zombie army." Bogrov fell silent and stared with unseeing eyes. "Now I desire to introduce you to someone."

Levi's heart pounded. *Yes. Say it, Bogrov. Say your son's name.*

"I shall take you to meet my son. Not this moment. But soon." After flicking his eyes at Levi's track mark, he pressed his lips tight and went to the mini-bar where he got a bottle of *Grey Goose* vodka and two shot glasses.

Smiling inwardly, Levi knew he'd scored a major victory. But now he had to do a series of shots. *Whatever it takes...* Half a minute later he was shuddering from the splendid warmth that flooded through him after a tumbler of the good vodka. After the tenth shot he barely made it to the toilet in time to vomit. But at least he'd won out over his host, who'd gotten sick to his stomach first.

PART IV

· · ·

St. Lucia

CHAPTER THIRTY-EIGHT

· ·

WHILE MICHAEL squired Katia Lagunov, the team investigated her personal life. Hack gave the manager of Katia's mail drop a thousand dollars to inspect her mail, while Monica made discreet inquiries into the solicitor's character. Tommy assigned himself the task of chatting it up with local merchants to determine if any of them were delivering supplies to Bogrov's island.

· · ·

Michael and Katia drew plenty of veiled glances from other pedestrians as they walked arm-in-arm to her restaurant of choice. Hack also admired the handsome couple, albeit from afar—part of the 24/7 surveillance they were keeping over their star player.

For tonight's outing Katia wore Givenchy—a black and white contrasting band sweater that she'd paid almost three thousand for, and a black ruffled skirt with red borders which had set her back another three grand. She'd dressed him in Versace. He had on seven grand in shirt, trousers, and shoes. The thin gold bracelet on his right wrist alone cost fifteen grand, which she'd paid without hesitation.

In short, he was a kept man whom she was using to accessorize herself in public, and to satisfy her lust in private. But perhaps reading his thoughts, she'd told him that his personal wealth precluded any need to lavish him with presents. But she gleefully bought gifts anyway, for she'd clearly grown to like him. A lot. And she'd told him so.

In any event he wasn't out to dicker over dollars. His sole cold analytical concern centered on the headway he'd made into her heart. It's what drove him. *The deeper I get her to fall for me, the deeper I can probe.* A measure of his success had come last night when she brought up the idea of living together and even having children. "You told me that you are the day trader. Splendid. You can do your day trading from here, yes?"

He'd jumped at that, since by gaining total access to her condo he could search it more thoroughly than he had previously. He was also out to determine what she knew of Bogrov, and he'd opened the door to that last night as they walked home after seeing a movie about a pending Apocalypse that he'd purposely chosen, since it would give him a chance to ask an innocent opening question: "What would you do if the end of world was upon us?" But she'd laughed and said, "All talk of Apocalypse is rubbish."

So tonight he would use her largesse as a key in probing further for any secrets she might have. Then he would call Tommy and relay anything he'd learned. That's why as he and Katia enjoyed a superb meal accompanied by a fine wine, he smiled winningly at her and said without preamble, "You know something? I'm the luckiest guy on Earth. I mean, here I am having dinner in a fabulous restaurant with a beautiful woman." He all but swore that she smelled of Catalina island, causing her to break into a radiant smile. He ventured further. "A brilliant, gifted woman."

"Stop it." She got busy pushing a few flaky bits of a sea bass around on her plate, but her glow revealed her pleasure.

"I mean it. Listen, I've been around. I recognize class when I see it. You're no trust-fund kid. You earned your money the same way I did—the hard way."

She blushed. "Perhaps I have, how do you say, secret admirer."

"Oh?" It's what he'd hoped to hear. Going deeper in-role, he held his fork poised in midair and frowned. "Tell me his name. I guarantee he won't dare cross my path."

Obviously flattered at the notion of two men fighting over her, she sprinkled the air with light laughter. "No, I do not think you would want to meet him."

"Yeah?" His frown deepened. "Listen. I fear no man."

Looking quite pleased with herself, she turned to taunting him. "Perhaps you might, if I told you it is none other than Yuri Bogrov."

His nose crinkled. "*Who?*"

She reared back in mock indignation. "No. Tell me it is not true, that you do not know this name... this Yuri Bogrov."

"Never heard of him. Who is he? A rich uncle?" He sipped the viognier wine he'd ordered for her rich, oily fish. "I'm kidding. Of course I know who he is." He settled back in his chair. "So, you and Yuri."

"Do not become jealous." She was in good spirits. "He is a client. Not the lover. We are mere friends, just as you and I..." Realizing her error, she fell silent.

"Katia," he said with great alarm. "Aren't we more than friends?" He raised a palm toward the ceiling. "Because my God, I'm all about *you*."

Her face lit up. "Really? Oh, Mark. You make me most happy."

"Good." He sniffed, sat back and looked sidelong at her. "So this work you do for Bogrov. It's honest work?"

"Honest? It is all honest. I give him the legal advice. I handle his regional bills." She rolled her eyes. "I swear, sometimes he is like the idiot. With his money, I think."

"Hmm. Interesting. What other tasks do you perform?"

"Well, there is something else." Her eyes danced with a new light and her smile knew no bounds. "He has made me *executrix* of his estate."

His pulse raced as he cut into his fresh brook trout and waited. *Here it comes.*

"Yes. I have list of special instructions."

"Really?" He put down his fork. "I'm intrigued. What are these instructions?"

"I have not the idea. He gave to me a thumb drive. But he was clear. I must never read what is on it unless he is, how do you say, incapacitated."

"Aw, come on. Don't tell me you haven't even glanced at it?"

Her sudden, inward breath and the cloud of all-consuming fear in her eyes said it all. "Never. He has told me several times, as if I am cretin, never to disobey his order; never to ask what is in this thumb drive and to conceal it." She clutched his wrist. Her lower lip trembled. Then she said barely above a whisper, "No. I would never. *Never*."

Michael decided she had no idea what was on the drive because she plainly feared an unimaginable punishment if she ever opened *that* Pandora's box. Armed with this knowledge, he resolved to fly to St. Vincent tomorrow, where the rest of the team would relocate. "I'm ready to go home," he told Katia. Then he folded his linen napkin and dropped it next to his half-finished plate of fresh fish.

AS THEY GOT into bed he told her, "I have to leave in the morning. Remember?"

"Yes. I do. However, I umm…" Turning pensive, she put splayed fingers to her belly and looked at him with large eyes. When his breath caught she said hurriedly, "Is okay. You did not put into me your baby. But I was having the hope that you had. Or that you will, for I am so soon with the deep feelings for you. Now I am with the fear that you do not feel similarly toward me."

He saw the eagerness in her eyes, alongside the terror of being rejected. He gave her a disarming smile. "You know how I feel about you. But I do have to leave. I have to handle my affairs." When she pouted he lifted her chin. "I *will* be back. Okay?"

Her eyes sparkled. "You make me so happy to hear this, for not only do I have for you the love, but you are only man who knows how to fuck out my brains." With a pixyish smile she reached between his legs. "Also, you are clearly not the fucking Jew."

Nadia was Jewish. He ignored the slur. Besides, Katia wasn't all that bright.

She chewed at her lip, then carefully asked, "You would marry me? You would give to me the children?"

"Yes. I'll marry you and yes, I'll put my babies in you. How's that sound?"

Wrapping long slender arms around his neck, she covered his face with kisses. "Now we make love. Tomorrow, you go. But come very soon back to me. Okay?"

.   .   .

"You're one shit-hot operator," Tommy said the next day as he and Michael ate lunch in a St. Vincent cafe. "Yes, sir. Levi must've been thrilled to hear she's clueless." He picked up his beer and drained a third of it, then regarded Michael. "Listen, my friend. I can't even begin to plumb the depths of the personal costs."

"Save the 'for king and country' speech, Tommy." He gulped some beer. "We're at war. I sold my body to help us win. I'm not the first to do it. Won't be the last."

LATER, HE MET Monica along a wind-swept seaside promenade. She had on a white blouse and jeans. He was a poster of suntanned health in a black shirt, maroon shorts and black flip flops. But all that was belied by haunted eyes, and as an elderly couple shuffled past, images of living in the streets washed over him: unloved, unwanted; uncared for—a loneliness so devastating at times that he turned tricks just for someone to talk to. Now isolation descended upon him yet again and he said in the way grieving people do, "I did what had to be done. But—" He moved a shoulder disparagingly. "Monica? I wasn't lonely while I was with her." His brows came together. "Am I making sense?"

"Michael, don't." She put her fingertips to his mouth. "Don't try to explain. The world could end. We've been all over that. But we're a team. More than that. We're friends who share our problems. So we press on. And after? After, we go home."

"Christ. I need a drink."

They went to a tiki-hut bar and ordered rum and Cokes. There were no words. None were needed. By the third round she asked, "Exorcised your demons?"

"More or less." He got to his feet, then looked at her.

"You're leaving the team." She stood, and with arms akimbo she waited.

"Yes." He ran both hands through his thick blond hair. "At mission's end."

Monica flinched. "We're not even going to discuss this?"

"We?" He waited while a passing teen regarded Monica with an appreciative eye. "What do you want me to say? Look, I've got other priorities."

She scoffed. "Who're you trying to convince, Lover Boy? Me? Or, yourself?"

He turned on her, his eyes ablaze. "Don't patronize me."

She bit off the next words. "When's the happy going-away party?"

"Kiss my ass." His mouth opened and closed. Finally he touched her forearm. "Monica? There's something else. You see, I could use a friend until then."

"A friend." Her eyes searched his. "And after?"

"After, we go home." He gave her a look. "Okay?"

Seconds swept past. She put a palm to his cheek. "Let's go for a walk. A very long one. And after? After, we move in together."

Returning to the hotel, they brought her luggage to his room. Then they went to a nearby restaurant that offered sidewalk seating and seaside vistas. The talk was strained and both were nervous. But when they returned and he took off his shirt out of habit, it all fell into place. He kissed her, holding it long and sweet, then unbuttoned her blouse while her fingers grazed his long bare back before moving to undo his shorts.

"Just friends," he said as they fell in a clump around his ankles. "Right?"

She nodded, then eased his black Calvin Kleins off.

LATER, THEY strolled along the ocean's edge beneath a canopy of glittering stars. Wrapping a possessive arm around her waist, he cleared his throat. "Monica, listen…"

"Don't start beating yourself up."

He bridled. "I'm not fragile, damn it. It's just that, well, you were right. About how some rules don't apply. I mean, we're not like other people. We're different and we're *here*, thrust into a swirl of world events and cut off from loved ones."

"And good people suffer when they set out to avert calamity," she reminded him.

"True. It's also a self-justification meant to soothe the inevitable consequence."

"Stop it. You said Nadia would bless anything… if it's based on friendship."

He drew a deep breath and let it out. He needed Monica, true. But he wasn't about to use Nadia's authentic dispensation as an excuse. He could only pray that she really would understand, as Monica certainly did. "Come on. Let's go to bed."

A GENTLE breeze ruffled Tommy's business-casual clothes the next morning as he waited at the far end of a quay for the others. As Michael and Monica turned a corner hand-in-hand, he noted a change in them and figured it out. When Hack showed, Tommy discussed Katia and set an agenda: Michael would manipulate her by phone while the others searched for mail drops and talked to locals. The goal: pick up on any talk of the papal papers and if there was talk, find out if the papers were being offered for sale.

After that he told them, "FYI, The Senator got his boy out of Tijuana's jail." He raised both palms toward the sky. "Next order of business. Wild Bill met with Bogrov's people. He's waiting to see if they'll hire him." He opened his mouth and closed it.

Michael frowned. "What else?"

Tommy cocked his head. "Exactly one week from today, either Delta Force will move in, or the fleet will sail. And I can assure you that the U.S. friggin' Marines have orders to storm the island *unless* Levi provides a reason not to." He worried the end of his nose. "The thing is, we've not heard from him in two days, and nobody's sure why."

Michael clenched his fists. "Then we're going there to find out why."

"Absolutely," Hack and Monica said in unison.

Tommy stroked a non-existent beard. "I see we're on the same page. Now that we've made a detached, unemotional decision to act, here's the rest of it. Nobody knows if he's even still alive."

CHAPTER THIRTY-NINE

. . . .

LEVI CRACKED open an eye, wondering if he was alive or had died and was now emerging from that long tunnel of brilliant light. He almost wished he were dead, since that state would be preferable to the torture he was now being subjected to.

A new onslaught of pain doubled him over as the monster inflicted another series of lashings. But there could be no pleading with this particular ogre, as booze knows nothing of sympathy. Curling into a fetal position, he waited until the pains wracking his body subsided. But even that holiday would be short-lived; a brief respite before a new bout of agony slammed him.

His current spiral began after another round of vodka shooters with Bogrov. Levi had finished his day shift when Bogrov invited him to his home. After leaving his boots and rifle at the door, he found the Russian waiting for him with a fresh track mark, a full bottle and two empty glasses. Then they tossed back Grey Goose shooters until Bogrov stumbled into his bedroom. Levi, barely able to walk, crashed on the sofa.

Awakening to a raging hangover sometime after the sun had set, and smelling a steak being broiled, he walked unsteadily to the kitchen and found Bronislava at the stove. He'd hoped to make small talk with her in case she might let something slip, but she only spoke Russian.

He was turning away from her when Bogrov appeared looking refreshed and relaxed. "Ah, Rocky. There you are. Perhaps we have some more of the vodka, da?"

Levi thought, this man's hardcore... but so am I. He forced a smile. "Sure. I'm up for it." He wasn't, but drinking beat the alternative: doing heroin.

So they went to the living room and after they each tossed back a glass, Levi moved a mental chess piece in a new gambit. "Did you know I lost a son?"

The Russian peered at him. "Can this be so? Tell me."

"His name was *Anton*."

"Oh my God. How did you come to give him that name?"

"The mother... the woman I knocked up, she was from Ukraine."

Bogrov's eyebrows arched formidably. "Anton. A good name. *My* son's name."

Levi knew that of course. "She killed him. My son, that is."

"Killed?"

"She left him alone and went next door to her girlfriend's to get tanked."

"Tanked? Yes, I know the meaning of this word." With a smug smile he tossed back another shot and then poured another with quick, raw movements.

Seeing the Russian's eyelids fluttering, Levi pressed the attack. "She'd left food cooking on the stove. It caused a fire." Levi finished in a rush of words. "Anton died from the smoke."

"The smoke," Bogrov repeated. Then he made a fist and slammed it against his thigh. "*Da!* Tomorrow I shall do what I promised. I will take you to see *my* son's grave."

"Grave," Levi echoed while the Russian refilled his glass. But then he considered the grave communications problem he'd been having: his SAT phone was dead. He'd checked the battery and its innards, but came up with nothing. At least he had a fall-back plan: he could use a hand mirror to send Morse code to a spy satellite that was keeping watch for just such an eventuality. But it would be risky. Someone might see him. Clouds could prevent the satellite from picking up the flashes—and it had been totally overcast the past four days. He hoped the skies would clear by tomorrow.

• • •

Tommy Wilkins eased back on the throttle and brought the sleek, 46' Beneteau yacht to a smooth stop a mile off-shore of Isla de la Rusia. Then the former sailor nursed the throttle into station-keeping mode to hold the sailboat in place against the current. He was well aware of Bogrov's surface surveillance radar, so he'd kept their signature small by taking in the main sail and furling the Genoa while still several miles out, then using the 54 horsepower Yanmar engine to bring them closer. If a radar operator painted them as a target at all, Tommy hoped he might write it off as sea-clutter return.

Out here in the pitch black, without so much as a whisper of a moon or any lights showing on the yacht—not even the navigation lights required by law—he could barely make out the base of the low-lying clouds that had been blanketing the region.

The island was a different matter, revealing itself through twinkling lamps and blinking red nav lights. Inside the darkened cockpit he set the autopilot to keep the vessel stationary while he and Monica got Michael and Hack overboard. After a final check of the GPS and the chart plotter he'd used to triangulate a station-keeping position in reference to Levi's villa, he took a final bearing and grabbed the binoculars.

Handing them to Michael, he sucked in a lungful of sea air. "It's two o'clock in the morning and the bars are closed. Parents, do you know where your children are?"

"Let's find Levi," Michael muttered. He put down the binoculars and went to the aft ladder, where small waves were lapping against the fiberglass hull.

They'd rented the yacht after their quay-side meeting. They also rented four sea scooters, two waterproof sport GPS devices, and a submersible night vision monocular. The yacht alone cost $950 per day, plus another two grand in rental fees and security deposits for the other items.

Michael was a natural for the night swim. As for Hack, he'd grown up in the Virginia tidewater region and claimed to be a water rat. Both had on dark swim trunks and were now donning fins, masks, and snorkels. Michael also clipped a fanny pouch around his waist. It held a substitute phone for Levi if it turned out that his had gone bad. It also carried the night vision monocular and one of the two GPS devices. Tommy would keep the other GPS in case he and Monica had to go to their rescue.

The men slipped into the water and Tommy lowered the 32 pound sea scooters. Their two hour battery life and 3.3 mph speed would get them to shore and back. But as the two men were about to go, Michael tapped Hack's shoulder. "Don't make any sudden movements when the sharks come around."

Hacksaw's eyes turned huge, their size distorted further by the thick glass of his mask. "You *are* kidding... right?"

"No. I didn't mention them earlier because it would've eaten at you." Michael paused. "Sorry, bad choice of words. Look, they're night hunters. They might nudge us while we motor along. But they're only sniffing to see if we're on their menu—which we're not. So don't go all wildcat and start thrashing around, or they won't bother sniffing. They'll just charge." He gripped Hack's arm. "Okay?"

"Man, I ain't never done nothin' like this." And yet his teeth gleamed in the low light. "Oh, well. Let's go before I change my mind."

"Remember," Tommy said as they started off. "Don't take any chances. If you see Levi in the cottage, you see him. If not, don't go on safari. We'll return tomorrow night."

"That's right," Monica said. "The mission comes first. Levi knew the risks. If something's happened, we go to Plan B and get that motherfucking Russian."

MICHAEL AND HACK were still half a mile from shore when the first shark attacked. Its sleek gray dorsal fin appeared as if by magic and sliced the surface as the shark lunged for Michael. But he knew that it was likely going for the sea scooter's whining engine, which probably attracted the shark's acute sensors in the first place.

At the same instant, Hacksaw reared back. "Holy fuck!"

Michael cocked an arm. Slammed his fist against the shark's snout. The animal twisted and writhed. Its tail slapped Michael's shoulder. His arm shot out again. The shark thrashed a bit, but swam away.

Hack swore between his teeth. "Gud-*damn!*"

"Settle down, brother." Michael gripped Hack's wrist and urged him closer. "Stay by me. Don't worry—I'm right here. I'll keep you safe."

"You're there, he's some*where,* an' I feel like I'm goin' nowhere *fast.*" He drew a deep breath. "Okay. Let's get goin' before my joints lock-up from freakin' *fear.*"

But they'd gone barely fifty yards when Hack said, "Whaddya want?" When Michael looked quizzically at him, Hack frowned. "You tapped my shoulder. You..." All at once he gasped. "Fuck! Another shark!"

Michael turned in time to see a fin break the surface thirty feet away. Larger than the first, it was headed directly for him. "No you don't," he muttered. Turning the sea scooter, he charged straight at it. The fin turned ninety degrees. Michael turned back and got next to Hack. "Sometimes," he said through clacking teeth, "... sometimes ya gotta play chicken with 'em."

They emerged from the surf twelve minutes later. Both men were shivering, but Michael ignored the shakes as he got out the night vision device and scanned the area. The NV's optical viewer lit the night in a bright green glow. He didn't expect to find anyone out in this dreary weather but he didn't take shortcuts. Finding the area deserted, he still flipped to infra-red and did another scan. Seeing no threats, he checked the GPS to confirm their location. Then with his mouth gone dry and his heart slamming against his chest, he ripped off his mask and fins. But he would carry them SEAL-style while he did the recon. Hack would remain at the shoreline to safeguard the equipment.

Crouching, Michael took off at a slow run across the darkened beach. The sand was cool beneath his feet, but its powdery texture slowed him down. The bedroom to the left was lighted. Levi's was on the right. Still, he went toward the brighter room and did a quick-peep inside. A bear of a man was sitting on the bed, smoking either crack, meth or heroin. Michael shook his head. *Your mug shot did you justice, Pete.*

Ducking down, he made his way to the living area and brought the NV device to his eye. Nothing. Then he went to Levi's darkened window. Peering inside, he saw a woman asleep in the bed. He couldn't tell her hair color through the scope's green haze, but she was stunning—definitely the type Levi would hook up with. Scanning further, he spotted a pressed military shirt draped over the back of a simple wooden chair. It could mean that she expected him to return sometime soon.

But he didn't see Levi. That left three possibilities: he was working, out partying, or dead. Though concerned for his best friend's safety, he kept Tommy's orders in mind and made his way to Hack.

TOMMY HEARD the high, tinny whine of the sea scooters as the men materialized from the gloom. Seconds later, he and Monica were wrestling the scooters from the water and placing them on the deck.

Michael urged Hack toward the ladder. "You first."

Monica grabbed Hack's hand and helped him aboard. After wrapping him in a blanket, she offered one to Michael as he stepped away from the ladder.

"I'm fine." But his teeth were clacking and after they shared a private glance he turned to Tommy. "I spotted Pete in his bedroom. Looked like he was smoking crack. Checked Levi's room. Saw a woman in his bed, plus a clean shirt on a chair that looked ready to wear. I think he's okay. He just wasn't there."

Monica all but shouted, "I just know he's all right."

Tommy said, "I think so, too. Great job, guys." He shook their hands and pointed to the cockpit. "We've got a pot of hot coffee going… and a bottle of Jack Daniels."

Michael shook his head and went below. Tommy shrugged and adjusted a control. A moment later the engine, idling all along in station-keeping mode, kicked into a new pitch. Then the yacht shuddered as the prop bit into the water. But once it settled into a rhythm and the vessel slowly built speed, the vibrations ceased and Tommy set a course for St. Vincent.

Monica and Hacksaw joined him. The locksmith's hand trembled as he tried to pour coffee. Giving up, he grabbed the bottle of Jack. "Man, I ain't lyin' when I'm sayin' how plumb scared I was out there."

Tommy said, "You're a braver man than I, Gunga Din. You'd have had to hold a gun to my head to get me in that water."

"Tell me about it." Hack got quiet. Then he began speaking in the rolling rhythms of his Tidewater home. "I can assure you that if not for the *dire* need to check on Levi,

I would not have gone in with *sharks* around. Not even at gunpoint. An' that's the Lord's truth." He tossed back some of the Tennessee whiskey and shook his head. "Didn't faze Michael none. How do I know?" He described the first shark incident, ending with, "He done punched that sucker in the head and kept on going like *Joshua* toward *Jericho* so as to *fit* that battle. An' I ain't lyin'. No, sir. Not one bit." A violent shudder coursed through him and he took another slug.

"Wow." Tommy altered course slightly and asked, "What'd you do?"

"Me? I got real close to my main man—too scared to go back alone, too scared not to an' too plumb scared to leave his side. An' it's a good thing I didn't, 'cause another of them mothers came at us. But Michael drove that one off, too." He grimaced.

Tommy regarded him carefully. "You are a brave hombre, Hack. I mean it. But I need to test myself, too. So I'll go with him tomorrow night." He didn't think Hack bought the honorable out he'd offered, but Hack's silence revealed his relief.

Throttling up while Monica poured a cup of coffee, Tommy altered course five degrees and checked his watch. They'd been cruising at ten knots for thirty minutes. Now he eased back on the throttle, which made the yacht wallow as it settled down. But as he trimmed the prop the boat ran true again.

Michael finally emerged in a black polo and blue jeans, and he made a straight line for the bottle of Jack. After pouring a healthy shot he braced his bare feet wide on the polished wooden deck and moved his body in time with the rolling, pitching boat. Monica went to him, and after joining his rhythm they spoke in low tones.

Later, when Tommy decided they'd put a safe distance between themselves and the island, they worked to raise the main and unfurl the Genoa. After trimming the sails, Tommy killed the engine and they sailed the rest of the way to St. Vincent in silence, each of them keeping their private counsel, the hull hissing as it cut into the water, the trailing edges of the sails fluttering and snapping, the sea air invigorating.

THE INSTANT they docked, Michael rushed Monica into their room and tore her clothes away, then shoved her against the wall, wrists pinned over her head, breasts flattening against his chest, Monica undoing his jeans and urging him on, their bodies straining to join of their own accord, both of them panting and groaning, till finally he hoisted her onto his hips, and once she locked her legs around his back he slowly moved against her, raw and relentlessly, taking her completely, driving himself against her, their moans growing louder, until in time they simultaneously surged against each other and released long-held cries. They rested, then went at it again. And then once more.

THE FOLLOWING evening Tommy accompanied Michael to the foreboding shore. In a repeat of the previous night, Michael inspected Pete's room and then the living area before going to Levi's window.

But there he hesitated. His gut all but yelled, *something's not right*. He checked all around with the NV. He listened carefully. Finally standing, he put the NV to his eye and peered inside the room. It was empty.

He was pulling the NV away when a hand clamped over his mouth from behind. He went to DEFCON One until Levi whispered, "It's me."

Michael's body went limp as he turned and whispered, "I don't know whether to kiss you or slug you into next week for scaring me." His eyes darted about as he kept up a constant lookout. "We hadn't heard from you…"

"My phone," Levi replied. "Deader than my grand dad's pecker."

"Thought so." Michael grew quiet, overcome by emotion. Not trusting himself to speak, he handed the replacement phone to Levi, then bent his head to find the zipper on the fanny pack. But when he looked up Levi had vanished as silently as he'd appeared. After getting control of himself, he made his way back to Tommy.

Half an hour later they were tossing back some Jack while Monica and Hacksaw stowed their gear. Then Tommy executed a 180° degree turn for St. Vincent.

CHAPTER FORTY

· ·

SPURNING HIS normal island attire of t-shirts and shorts, Levi appeared at Bogrov's door in a polo shirt, trousers and shoes as part of his bid to drive the show and bring Bogrov to a destination of *his* choosing—beginning with a trip to the son's grave.

"Good morning," Bogrov said in a robust voice while his face formed a large question mark. "Now explain yourself. Why do you come to my home uninvited?"

"But you did invite me," Levi began. "To visit your son."

"My son?" Bogrov cocked his head. Lines popped from his forehead as he glared at his employee. All at once they vanished. "Da. You are right. Yesterday I tell you we will pay visit to the place where he rests. I see that you dress appropriately. It is sign of respect. For me; for my son. Good. We go. Right now."

Levi followed him along a winding path bordered by bougainvillea, bromeliad, Bismarck palms and frangipani, until they reached a ficus hedge. He figured it guarded the gravesite—a sentinel standing between the insanity of a chaotic world and the harmony of a sanctified place. They stepped inside.

He felt it at once. "My God—" This small plot of land, isolated as it was from an island which was itself insulated from the world, radiated a sense of peace so profound that his jaw dropped. Everything about it was perfect: the pleasant odor of grass and moss; the scented plants that met his nostrils with the grace of a baby's breath against its parent's cheek; the calm embracing air; the brilliantly blue sky. And since it was well above sea level, a cooling breeze swept the enclosure, keeping it free of mosquitoes and virtually anything else that might defile the resting place of a young boy who'd never done anything to offend anyone.

"For God so loved the world that he gave his only son."

"Huh?" Stirred from his reverie, Levi turned to see Bogrov watching him intently.

"For God so loved the world that he gave his only son," the Russian repeated. "It is what Christians so often say without understanding what it is they say."

Levi silently mouthed the words that Hannah had spoken in Luxembourg.

"Come," Bogrov said, urging him forward. "Please to greet my son. Please introduce yourself to Anton."

Clearly moved, Levi edged closer to the grave marker and unconsciously placed his right hand over his heart. "Hello, Anton. I am Le—" Realizing his error at once, he swallowed as if stifling a sob and began over. "I am *leading* a good life I think. I want you to know how honored I am to meet you."

Levi hadn't expected Bogrov to reveal any emotion—he was too much the Joe Stalin-like beast to harbor sentiments. But to his great surprise, Bogrov patted Levi's shoulder and it made sense: the Russian regarded his son as a narcissistic extension of himself, and Levi would play on that—two fathers from opposite sides of the world, but united by a mutual grief and now bonded by an unbreakable trust.

And Levi vowed to use that trust like a dagger and drive it through this ruthless bastard's heart if he got in his way; drive it like a '67 Mustang… like a friggin' 18-wheeler. Then he'd go after Slavko. *If only Wild Bill were here. Sure would make it easier, since everyone knows that two assassins are better than one.*

● ● ●

A blast of frigid air from the polar vortex that had been lingering over Maryland for a week now greeted Michael Bailey's older son Levi and his girlfriend Jennifer as they left a cinema. It was early evening and unrelenting winds were whipping the odors from a nearby Burger King into a frenzy. Holding her close in case she slipped on an icy patch, he shook his head. "You'd think someone would toss some salt on the friggin' sidewalk."

"No sense getting upset. Life's messy sometimes." She looked at him as they laughed at their private joke—one of many they'd developed since they were kids.

"You're right." In fact, he thought that most things were right in the world. Yet he also felt a deep sense of foreboding, and his stomach clenched whenever he thought of his father or Uncle Levi. "I'm scared as shit," he told her.

"About?"

He kissed her cheek. "My dad. My uncle."

She squeezed his hand. "I wish I knew what to say. I don't."

"Not much anyone can say." He smiled bravely. Then out of habit he looked for his Blue Crew detail before remembering that they'd been pulled. He missed them too, because he'd grown to see them as an extension of his family.

As they drew closer to the black late model Mustang that he'd saved and worked for, he guided her to the passenger door. Then as he'd done ever since the days when they rode together in their parents' cars, he opened it for her. Jen got in and said while adjusting her seat belt, "After we meet Bethany and Rob for burgers? Let's go home."

"Your folks know you're sleeping over?" He arched his eyebrows.

"Well—" She gave him a sly look. "I told Daddy, at least."

"Long as he doesn't come after me with a shotgun." Laughing, he closed her door and got behind the wheel. A minute later they drove off.

A SILVER TAURUS followed from a distance. Inside, Ryan vowed to get his story even if he had to coax it from the mouths of these two babes. Patting his waist, he felt the Taser's reassuring lump. But if things got out of hand he also had a pistol for protection, although from whom he didn't know. But he'd had enough of Mr. Hart's tricks; enough of waking up in that Tijuana brothel; enough of being raped in the holding cell before Dad could get him out. This time he would succeed. This time he'd show Mr. Hart.

CHAPTER FORTY-ONE

· ·

LEVI HART would've bet good money that someone had sandpapered his eyes. He had the sweats and the room wouldn't stop spinning, all because Bogrov had challenged him to a drinking contest. Naturally, Levi had accepted the dare.

Feeling Sophia shift against him in her sleep, he nudged her. "Babe?"

She opened her eyes slowly, only to spring up on an elbow and hover over him with a frightened expression. "You look terrible." She put a cool hand to his forehead. "You are not with the fever, though. That is good."

"Or not," Levi mumbled. At least the cause of his discomfort hadn't come from sticking a needle in his arm. Summoning his energy, he got to his feet and stumbled into the bathroom. Turning on the sink's cold water, he soaked his head while groaning inwardly at his next move—saving the planet. After pulling on nylon shorts he told Sophia, "I'm going for a run. Best way I know of to get rid of a hangover."

"Wait. I will come with you." She started to get up.

"No." He held her arm with a firm hand. "I need some alone time. Okay?"

Turning on his heel before she could reply, he went outside and jogged along the shoreline, while sea birds hovering overhead scolded him with their raucous cries. But his authentic hangover wasn't the raison-d'être behind his need to get outside. He needed to send a message. So after doing a quarter-mile he reversed course and trudged through softer sands to arrive at the palm tree where he'd hidden the new SAT phone.

Sweeping it up, he thumbed the power switch and composed an activity report. He added a query about Wild Bill, then pressed SEND. Once he got confirmation that the encrypted micro-burst had been received, he wiped the phone of prints and hid it away.

When he got home and entered the bedroom, Sophia's eyes opened and she smiled a North Star smile. "I love you, Rocky. Very much."

His heart went out to her, for he knew the pangs of unrequited love. He kissed her forehead, then held her in his arms and told her how much he loved her. The fact was, he didn't. But he couldn't say this because he still had to work her. And yet he saw her for the tremendous woman she was, and at any other time he might've nurtured their relationship. They might even marry and have children. But not now, and he felt a deep remorse for using her. But as he'd once explained to Michael's sons, life can be messy.

CHAPTER FORTY-TWO

· ·

ALTHOUGH THE MORNING rustling of foxtail palm fronds sweeping past the balcony door sounded like music, deep lines etched Tommy's forehead. He was sitting in his hotel room and reading a message on his laptop. When he finished, he left-clicked the mouse to exit the secure email site and looked at Hannah. She sat quietly on the bed with her legs crossed and with one running-shoe clad foot jouncing. Pierre Roland sat next to her, and Tommy met his eyes next.

Roland and Hannah had flown in the previous evening to discuss new evidence they'd developed. They hoped it would let them extradite Bogrov—barring the one big technical glitch: that he was on a heavily defended island from which he could easily resist the whole of the Grenadine Island chain's meager military resources.

Tommy said, "I need to round up the others."

THE TEAM gathered thirty minutes later on a lone, palm-sheltered strip of sand. Tommy raised his voice above the surf's roar. "Wild Bill checked out of his hotel. New-hires go to Bogrov's island by boat, but he hasn't shown up at the departure point."

Pierre Roland cleared his throat until all eyes turned to him. He wasn't difficult to miss. He had on a white shirt and khaki trousers, and his sole surrender to the beach were Birkenstocks—which he wore with long black socks. "We should send one of our number to see if he arrives, yes?"

Monica shifted her bare feet in the sand. "I'll go."

Hacksaw Jones shook his head. "No way. It's my turn at bat."

Michael cleared his throat. "Tommy, any news from Levi?"

"Just getting to that. In his last message he said we should be ready to roll at a moment's notice. So with that in mind I wanna run something past everyone." He began talking in hushed tones about the pair of twin-engine Augusta helicopters that had been pre-loaded with the team's BDUs and weapons. They were on standby alert in Puerto Rico. Tommy felt they should come to St. Vincent. This way the team could reach Isla de la Rusia in thirty minutes. "They can stay in the international arrivals area. That way they're off-limits to customs inspectors, so our weapons will be safe. Once we board the aircraft, we can change into BDUs and weapon-up en route."

The consensus was that he should order the helicopters in.

MONICA'S FINE white teeth worried her lower lip as she and Michael walked off. When they were out of sight of the others she stopped. "Hold me, Lover Boy?" Entering his arms, she clung to him. "I can't say why, exactly. But I'm worried sick about Levi."

He waited while a group of kids with gleaming teeth and brown faces swept past. "Me, too." A breeze fanned his hair as he looked out to sea. "That first night on the yacht. The two sharks. The fear I suppressed in not knowing if I'd find his body; it's why I went below to decompress. I—" Draping an arm around her shoulders, he urged her toward a cafe that was emitting sizzling burger smells. "Levi's an operator. He'll get through it. Especially now that Wild Bill's gonna have his back."

HACKSAW JONES stepped off the inter-island commuter flight and went to the small terminal's arrivals area to wait for Wild Bill. After scanning a flight status monitor for incoming flights, he shook his head and approached a young female ticket agent. "I'm supposed to meet a friend," he explained.

She said without looking up, "You missed the last flight by one half of an hour."

His forehead creased. "It's not even scheduled to *arrive* for ten more minutes."

Throwing her hands in the air, she glared at him. "*Backsides.* What you tink, mon? That you in New York City? These da islands. Time means nah-tink here."

"Did you at least notice if a tall white guy got off? Big moustache?"

Nodding rapidly as she shuffled her papers, she said, "Yes yes yes. I see this mon. Look like de actor. He go with two other white dudes to the ferry boat. Now if you don't mind?"

Hack thanked her and checked the status board again. The final flight of the day wasn't scheduled to arrive for another three hours. He decided to wait for it. Stepping outside, he found a coffee vendor and ordered a large cup. "Cream, if you please."

The old man working the stall said as he handed over a steaming coffee, "There you go, mon. That should do the trick, yes?"

CHAPTER FORTY-THREE

· ·

"THERE, MATE. That should do the trick." Ian's tongue searched the corner of his mouth as he eased the needle into a bulging vein atop Pete's hand.

"Dude. Hurry, will ya?" Pete swiped at the cold sweat trickling down his neck.

Ian had come to Levi's villa to do heroin with Pete, but the behemoth hadn't been able to raise a vein. Fortunately for him, Ian had been a Royal Marine medic and he was able to find one in Pete's hand. Now that he had the needle in, the Brit winked and pushed down on the plunger, giving Pete all twenty mills.

"Mmm," Pete said, closing his eyes and writhing as the rush enveloped him.

Levi's heart beat a staccato as he recalled how great heroin had made him feel, and all too easily he found himself envying Pete. So he tossed back a healthy amount of his rum and Coke to distract himself. But it did no good, and now he was salivating as he watched Ian inject himself. Then as if someone had flicked a switch he convinced himself that it wouldn't hurt to shove a needle up his arm—just this once, of course.

A lesser man might have. But Levi had exercised iron discipline to put a cap on his addiction during rehab, and he slammed that cap back on. Tearing his eyes away from Pete and Ian as they moaned from their places in Nirvana, he thought about what a good job Bogrov had done in putting this island together. *He wants to keep his men happy and he's succeeding. But he's also cutting it too closely by giving tacit approval to indulge in so much sex and drugs. Then again, it'll ultimately make my job easier.*

Padding away finally to join Sophia on the patio, it occurred to him that Bogrov's largesse might mean that he was planning to escalate things sooner rather than later. *One more reason why I have to stay a step ahead of this maniac.*

After sitting next to Sophia, they spoke in low tones while they drank. Then he probed. "When are you going to St. Lucia again? To pick up that solicitor, I mean."

"In three days. Maybe." She shrugged. "Yuri sometimes skips a visit."

Levi acknowledged her, but his mind was on the heroin again and it wasn't long before he broke out in a cold sweat. He licked suddenly dry lips. Shifted a bit. Thought about the rush some more. *Mmm. Why not? Sure. Just a little…* His hands turned to fists. To break the spell he focused on making small talk, telling Sophia that he'd always wanted to learn the game of golf.

It had the desired effect by getting her going. She spoke of her doting parents, of her pleasant childhood and her desire to fly, and he found himself listening eagerly as she described becoming a pilot at an early age. She'd then worked as an instructor, and later as a corporate pilot. But the company failed. Jobs became scarce. After far too many doors were slammed in her face, she called a banker who knew a billionaire in search of a helicopter pilot.

"And that is how I came to work for Yuri Bogrov. Now I am happiest woman in the world. Why? Because I find the most amazing heart inside the man I am with right now." Putting down her wine and locking her arms around his neck, she covered his face with kisses. "Let's make a baby," she said.

She was being playful, so he acted shocked. "Darling Sophia, love of my life, do you know how much trouble they are? To begin with, you have to pick a name—"

"SO WHAT should we name it?"

It was the day after he and Sophia played the baby-naming game. He and Bogrov had been mainlining heroin. The Russian had insisted. Levi had no choice this time and he agreed—albeit a little too eagerly as his heart began beating faster and faster. But he'd faked it by discreetly mixing his own dose—a dummy one with the characteristic burned band-aid smell and all—although it nearly killed him to do it because his brain cells screamed at him to shoot up with the real stuff. In the end, his need worked in his favor when he moaned so deeply that the false rush rang true.

Finally seeing his chance when Bogrov got the nods, he'd said, "Yuri? You've never told any of us why we're here. What I mean is, it looks as if we're preparing for the end of the world."

Bogrov appeared to study the fresh track mark on Levi's arm before he smirked. "End of the world. Hah. Good one, Rocky O'Toole. You make good joke."

Levi's trained eyes detected a hint of pride in that smirk—like the one Bogrov had flashed after testing Levi's familiarity with heroin. And this instant pride convinced Levi that Bogrov *wanted* to tell him of his plans; that he *had* to tell him, so he goaded the Russian into talking. "Come on. I'll never tell a soul." Settling in for what would be a long process of seducing Bogrov into telling all, he waited.

But this proved to be one of those rare instances when Levi misjudged his prey, because his host did start talking and it all came out in a rush—the stunning revelations of a long-dead advanced civilization and its abrupt demise, followed by news that another killer asteroid was on its way. He mentioned the pope's papers, then bragged about how he and Slavko had butchered two men to gain possession of them.

Levi let out a low whistle. "Damn. I guess you and I are the only ones who know this." When Bogrov told him that Slavko also knew, this is when Levi shook his head and suggested they come up with a name for the papal papers.

"So… what should we name it?"

"Name? Hah. Who ever thought of such a thing as this?"

"It has to have a name, Yuri."

Bogrov blinked his eyes rapidly. "Huh? What is this thing you say?"

"A name. It'll add to your bragging rights." Levi began bringing his argument full circle. "Like the atom bombs they dropped on Japan. *Fat Man* and *Little Boy*. The big bang bombs."

Bogrov's eyes revealed a glimmer of admiration. "Yes. Big bang." He flung his arms wide open. "Boom! *Da?*"

"*Da. Khorosho.*" Levi thought Bogrov could have been lifted straight out of a Gilbert and Sullivan comic opera—or, from one of Bergman's darkest nightmares.

"So tell me, Rocky O'Toole. What name shall we choose for the little child?"

Turning serious, Levi spoke the name at once. "Anton." When he saw the Russian's eyes glaze over, he pushed harder. "It's perfect. You have the biggest bomb ever. So it cries out to have your boy's name. That way he'll live forever."

"Forever," Bogrov said as if walking in his sleep. "Into eternity." All at once he drew a deep breath and peered at Levi. "Your son shall live as well, Rocky O'Toole."

Levi nodded with deep gravity, then pointed to a blank space on the wall before bringing the motive behind assigning a name into play. "You should frame the papers and hang 'em from the wall. Like a picture." He paused to let the drugged Russian digest this. Then he did a full court press. "Hell, get the papers and we'll hang 'em right now."

But Bogrov shook his head doggedly. "They shall remain out of sight."

Levi pushed. "Can I at least see them? I mean…"

"*Nyet.*" Bogrov thumped his chest. He might be high, but he was alert. "Nobody else shall see them, for they will have an unutterable effect upon the world."

Nodding while rubbing his chin, Levi used this as a cue to speak in general terms about devising a fail-safe system in case Bogrov met with some disaster—insurance against someone other than Katia Lagunov being in possession of a thumb drive.

"Why should I need this fail-safe?" He turned his palms upward. "Such a thing would do me no good."

"Why?"

Bogrov's eyes darted about. "Because I must be alive when I tell the world, for only then can I know that I have succeeded in bringing my son back to life."

The Russian rambled on, but the more he denied the existence of a back-up plan after what Michael had found on Katia's thumb dive, the more Levi came to believe that he'd devised a redundant system. It's what sharp people did—and this Russian was one sharp son of a bitch. Levi prodded him further. "That part about telling the world... when will you do that?"

"When?" Bogrov edged closer to Levi and dropped his voice. "You pose interesting question. At first I planned to say nothing. Let the asteroid come. We will live the party life until that day. It is why I wanted small army—to keep the *hoi polloi* from my island."

He sniffed. "Then I think, why not tell the world now? Why not watch them go to pieces while we have big party here?" His eyelids fluttered as he tried to focus on Levi. "To answer your question, I will tell the world soon. In one week. But first I must deal with a problem." He smiled and patted Levi's shoulder. "Tomorrow I will reveal this problem, for I want *you* to handle it for me."

Levi kept a poker face while running some numbers. With only a week left, he gave himself three days to find the papers. That would provide a buffer in case the ever-erratic Bogrov called an earlier press conference. *Three days. Then I signal the team to send in the troops. Once they're en route I'll kill*

Bogrov and Slavko. He wanted Wild Bill's assistance more than ever now, but that clearly wasn't going to happen unless he was on tomorrow's boat. He waited until Bogrov nodded off, then he idly tapped his new track mark while wondering what the next day would bring. Finally he closed his eyes.

CHAPTER FORTY-FOUR

. . . .

"WHA...?" MICHAEL'S eyes snapped open. He sat up.

Monica gripped his naked thigh. "What is it?" Her bare breasts brushed his ribs as she turned on the bedside lamp and peered at him through sleep-heavy eyes.

"I, um... nothing. Bad dream."

Settling back, he wondered if it was PTSD when all at once a deep dread gripped his soul: somehow, his older son was at risk. He wanted to call Nadia, but not at this early hour and certainly not with Monica in his bed.

He felt a sharp stab of guilt about that, but as Nadia had intended, he no longer felt lonely. So after pulling Monica into his arms he told her about the dream. Then they spoke of other things until she dozed off. Feeling a renewed gratitude for her friendship, he anchored an arm around her waist and fell into a deep sleep. And he dreamed again. It was different from the first, but no less disturbing.

MONICA FELT Michael stir in his sleep. It was late; she was late. Thinking back, she guessed that stress or fatigue must have altered her body's rhythms. Maybe she should tell him now. Maybe not. But as the a/c kicked in she kissed his chest, then put a hand to her belly and imagined how it would look in nine more months.

TOMMY WAS having brunch with Hannah and Roland when his cell chirped. A red icon alerted him to a priority text from Heath. Firing-up the encrypted laptop, he read it, frowned, drafted a reply, added his own concern, sent it off, then went to Michael's room.

He knocked. The peephole darkened. Then the deadbolt turned with a *click*. Michael opened the door. He had on nylon shorts and gripped a sodden T-shirt while Monica stood at his side in running clothes but with one shoe already off. They were sweat-streaked and smelled of spent energy, and a whispering shower awaited them—its misty fingers curling around their heads and drawing them in to add to the steam. Tommy noted the rumpled bed and her things in the room. He'd known of course, and had known why. Anyway, it wasn't an issue.

"Michael," he began. "Ryan confronted your son and his girl at a gas station a short time ago. Ryan had a Taser. Told them to get in his car. The Kid shielded his girl with his own body and told Ryan to get fucked. Ryan was repeating the order when the Kid spotted a pistol in our dear friend's waistband. The Kid went ballistic. Decked him. Knocked him flat on his ass. Then he and a customer held him down until police arrived. Your boy and his girl were a bit shaken but are otherwise okay."

Michael nodded, a mixture of relief and pride flooding his face.

"The Kid called Nadia. She got in touch with Heath. He called the Maryland State Police Superintendent. Told him Ryan's got mental issues. The troopers filed a slew of criminal charges, and are now taking him to a state hospital for a psych eval."

"They'll keep him a minimum of three days," Michael said. "After that? Who'll pay attention to the ravings of a discredited and mentally disturbed child-stalker?"

"That's the thinking." Tommy knuckled his jawbone. "Even so, Heath put Blue Crew back on your family and Nadia's getting a restraining order."

"Good." Michael turned quiet. When he spoke again, he was reflective. "I had this strange dream last night. About The Kid, in fact. But then I had another dream."

Tommy squinted at him. "Anything to do with our friend to the south?"

"Yeah, as a matter of fact. Why do you ask?"

"Because I've got a bad feeling about..."

"That's it," Michael barked. "Call the helicopter crews to battle stations. We can be ready if he sends a mayday." He tore off the shorts and reached for a pair of jeans.

"Don't worry," Tommy said. "I've already made that call."

•   •   •

Heath Baker grumbled as he moved about in a futile attempt to find some relief. Still in his pajamas and propped in bed by an avalanche of pillows, he briefly pinched the bridge of his nose before following up on Tommy's reply to his earlier message. Then he pulled up his phone's contact list and thumbed the green CALL button. A White House operator answered at once. Heath's voice was rattled by phlegm but he said with absolute authority, "This is Mr. Baker. Put me through to the President." Then he uttered a code word that meant, *I don't care what he's doing, he needs to take my call right now.*

"Yes sir, Mr. Baker," the operator said. "I'm putting you through."

Baker listened to a soft hum for the few seconds it took to make the connection. "Mr. President," Heath said when the phone picked up. "We're unable to reach our man on that island, and he's failed to check-in with us. We've also lost track of another of my men. Per protocol, I'm requesting a fly-by of Bogrov's island by that pair of Hornets at Naval Air Station Key West." He listened. "Yes, sir—the ones that have been briefed to make two sonic booms near the island—our man's signal to call-in, ASAP."

He paused and then said, "We have no hard evidence that something significant is underway. But these two events are consistent with established criteria for mobilizing Delta Force. Therefore it's my recommendation that you get them en route. Dragon Team will also deploy to determine if anything's going on." He listened. "No, a SAT recon isn't feasible. My man down there said it's overcast. It's why the team will eyeball the place, and issue a recall order if Delta's not needed." He pressed the phone harder against his ear, listened and then nodded. "Very well, Mr. President. Thank you."

Tossing the phone aside, he pressed a button on his nightstand. When his wife of fifty-six years appeared, he turned wearily to her. "Send the attorney back up, my love. And dearest? Have him bring that bottle of *Laphroaig,* along with a couple of glasses." He smiled bravely. "That should re-light my fire."

•   •   •

Levi Hart shifted his stance to redistribute the weight of his gun belt as he peered up at the morning sky. There were high clouds from horizon to horizon, but they could easily vanish in these latitudes. As the day-shift sergeant he had the duty jeep to inspect the guard sites. He'd already seen Pete, and although Levi remained wary of him, the fine line that existed between them had been holding. Now he was at the island's westernmost observation post, where he and Ian were discussing—what else—women.

All at once Ian nudged Levi and showed him a vial of cocaine that he'd brought along. To Ian's raised eyebrows, Levi waved a flat hand through the air. "Negative. Not while we're working. Now put it away." He started to add something when he cocked his head at the distinctive sound of military fighter jets flying at high speed.

•   •   •

Commander Keith "Runkman" Runk checked his six and nodded. His wingman, Lieutenant (j.g.) Gary Smith was astern and slightly to the left of Runkman's F/A 18 Hornet. The two Naval aviators of Strike Fighter Squadron 106, aka the "Gladiators," had taken off from their TDY duty station at N.A.S. Key West, and were currently at four thousand feet on a heading of 161°. The Hornets could carry a variety of bombs and missiles, including air-to-air and air-to-ground.

They also had 20mm Vulcan cannons. Powered by twin GE F404 turbofan engines, the fighters could reach Mach 1.8.

Right now their Mach meters were pegged at 0.9, and as they skirted the edge of Bogrov's island, Runkman thumbed the radio transmit switch and told Smith, "Tally ho. Target in sight. On my mark, go to afterburners and increase speed to Mach 1.1." He checked his target, nudged the joystick to the left, eased down on the left rudder pedal, watched his heads-up display, and finally announced, "Mark!"

The two aviators firewalled their throttles. Full WEP—war emergency power—a seldom-used term that Runkman still loved to throw out there. The thrust slammed both men against their ejection seats. As the fighters went transonic, flow-induced white vapor cones trailed in their wake.

Runkman knew that he and his wingman were rattling someone's dishes on the deck. He didn't know *why* they'd been ordered to break the sound barrier and he didn't want to know. Although he was a maverick of wide repute, he also understood when not to question a command. *Sometimes ya just gotta do what ya gotta do, and keep it zipped.*

As the island receded he pulled up sharply on his joystick and went into a ninety degree vertical climb, the Hornet's thrust-to-weight ratio turning the aircraft into a rocket. The high-g, high angle of attack pull-up created powerful vortices at the wings' trailing edges, which showed as white extensions as the fighters climbed rapidly through warmer air and into colder air. At eight thousand feet, and still well below the cloud deck, Runkman pushed forward on the joystick and nosed back down into horizontal flight.

Thumbing his transmit switch, he told Smith, "Turn one-eight-zero degrees. Slow to Mach 0.9, and let's head to the barn." He settled in. At their speed they'd be on the ground and sitting in post-flight within the hour.

• • •

Levi put on a look of annoyance for Ian's sake when the sonic booms slammed the observation post. But his pulse raced. He had to contact Tommy. He was about to shove off when he cocked his head at the sound of an approaching jeep.

"Ah, here is Rocky," Bogrov said as Slavko stopped next to the O.P. Two soldiers whom Levi had checked on earlier sat in the jeep's open back seat and they were rolling their eyes. Bogrov snorted. "What sounds just now, yes? American fighter pilots, no doubt flexing their muscles." Then he told Levi, "Please to follow us. I will now show you the problem I mentioned just yesterday."

Although anxious to get to his SAT phone and make that call, Levi jumped into his jeep and trailed after them. The morning air smelled of sweet island growth and parrots flew overhead as he bounced along narrow roads. Slavko finally parked in front of a small cinderblock building—one of a string of solar power transfer stations.

Slavko pushed open the metal door. A blast of cold air hit Levi as he entered the dimly lit room. Reaching to one side, Slavko hit a switch. Overhead lights turned bright.

The first thing Levi saw was the jail cell. The next thing he noted was the bruised, battered, bloody-faced man sitting inside it and staring back at him. But Levi had to step closer before he was able to recognize Wild Bill Dentz.

CHAPTER FORTY-FIVE

. . . .

"THIS MAN you see before you is an agent," Bogrov said over Levi's shoulder. "He applied for a position here. However, my people discovered anomaly in his story."

Unable to help himself, Levi glanced at the spot between Bill's legs to see if he'd suffered the same fate as Kaczmarek. Everything appeared to be intact.

But Slavko gave Levi an eerie look. "Yes. The prisoner retains his manhood."

A chill ran down Levi's spine. *Had he seen me, but kept quiet until he can use it against me? Or is he fishing?* He grimaced as if he'd bitten into a lemon and ignored the Serb. Then he exchanged a look with Wild Bill, whose black and blue eyes were nearly swollen shut. At least he still had eyes. He also had a broken nose, his lips were split, and pinpoint burns on his neck might've been made by electrodes. His fingers were the size of dill pickles, likely after being jerked backwards one by one until they'd snapped, and his fingernails had evidently been pulled out with pliers. Levi figured he probably had several broken ribs, too.

Bogrov made a sound. "As I say, we discover glitch in this man's story. He came to us with straight-up demeanor, that of Navy SEAL turned soldier of fortune."

"But?"

"Ian pays unexpected visit to this man in London. Ian was Royal Marine."

Levi's stomach flip-flopped at the idea of Ian playing Wild Bill for a fool — and in his own hotel room. He thought, the bastard's done his job too well.

"Ian has good eye. Good memory. He looks at this man in hotel and thinks, 'I have seen this man before'."

"And?" Levi's back and forth had a purpose — to buy time while he devised a host of contingency plans. But he'd also gone to high alert in case Bogrov had already made a connection between him and Wild Bill.

"Ian is part of old boy network. He recalls photograph shown to him by other Royal Marine. Ian points to this man here and says, "He looks like actor in western movies. So Ian's friend tells him he was SEAL who joined private U.S. company of covert operatives. We decided to bring him here. To deal with him in our own way."

"And?"

"Slavko has interrogated this man for two weeks now."

Slavko cleared his throat. "He remains steadfast."

Bogrov glared at his employee's intrusion. "So. We cannot say with certainty."

"But?"

"But we do not leave anything to chance on Isla de la Rusia." He grunted. "So. He is problem. We cannot afford problems. Therefore we must dispose of him." He smiled like a monkey in a banana tree. "You shall have the honor."

Cold trails of perspiration ran from Levi's armpits. The game had just morphed. Now he had to get to his phone, *and* find those papers. But how? An idea leaped to mind. If he could convince Bogrov to leave Bill alone for a few days or even for a few hours, he might be able to complete the tasks. He glanced at Wild Bill. The SEAL's eyes told Levi what he needed to know: that the man trusted him totally—even if it meant dying by Levi's hand if that's what it took to maintain mission integrity.

Levi told Bogrov, "Yeah, That'd be great. Leave this son of a bitch to me."

"Ah, well. Do it then." Bogrov gestured at Levi's holstered pistol.

Levi glared at him. "What, shoot him through this... this *cage?*" He flung his hands in the air. "What do you think I am? A fuckin' coward?"

Bogrov looked at Slavko with an 'I told you so' expression. "Ah. It is good you feel this way. It is why we have not already disposed of him. We are careful men. But we are still men. We do not act in cowardly fashion. However, he must die. This is final."

Levi knew from Bogrov's expression that it would be useless to argue. He tried anyway. "Why kill him? He might still break if we question him long enough."

"Nyet. He will die." Turning to Slavko, he spoke in rapid-fire Russian. Slavko nodded and reached for his pistol.

"Wait," Levi said. "I only meant that we might gain some intel. Hell, I'd love to take care of him."

Bogrov drew himself straighter and peered into Levi's eyes. "So. How shall you deal with this problem?" He stabbed a finger at the two soldiers. "I brought them here to have firing squad if you wish. That is sign of honor. But if you think he does not deserve this tribute, then we will hang him."

"Or," Levi began quietly, "we can burn him alive."

Slavko actually smiled as he went to the door, where Levi saw a large brass cell key hanging near the light switch. "Hold on," Levi said. "I have an even better idea."

Slavko paused. Furrows erupted across his forehead as he examined Levi anew. "Better than burning alive? Hmm. I am intrigued. What is this better idea?"

Levi smiled malevolently. "You brought me to my quarters the day I arrived. You showed me the beach. Remember?"

"I remember."

"You told me to be careful of the predators." Levi figured the cut-throat bastard had already figured it out, but said for Bogrov's benefit, "We wait till dusk. Feeding time. I take this turd and a bucket of chum off-shore in one of the boats. I stir up some sharks and give 'em a nice big meal to sink their teeth into—live, of course. Problem solved." He could also escape in the dark with Wild Bill. He looked to Bogrov for approval.

A snake crawled onto the Russian's lips, and curled itself into a smile. "*Da.*"

"I will go along," Slavko said, smiling for perhaps the third time ever. "I wish to watch the show from the ringside seat." The soldiers laughed and gave Wild Bill their best "see you later" looks. But Slavko went back to studying Levi's face.

Sensing impending disaster, Levi got busy improvising a plan he'd been devising the instant Bogrov made it clear that Wild Bill would die—a plan that would utilize his surroundings to deal with the three-fold problem he faced. Of course, he could just shoot Bogrov, Slavko and the soldiers right now. All four were off their guard. But then he might never find out what Bogrov had done with the papers.

Until now, his original scheme if he'd failed to find the papers was to signal the cavalry to come to the rescue. Once the bugles had sounded and they were en route, he would find Slavko and kill the sociopath. Next, he would confront Bogrov and break the two hundred and six bones in his body one by one until the Russian told him where the papers were. Then Levi would assassinate him and get the papers if they were even on-island, race to the dock, commandeer a motorboat, and make his escape.

But even if he shot all four men now and forfeited the papers, the day shift lieutenant would eventually ask about the two soldiers—and Levi had to help Wild Bill. That wouldn't be easy. Levi would never get him past the guard at the marina without killing him—which would send the others in pursuit. And he absolutely wouldn't leave Bill to be butchered by vengeful soldiers before the cavalry arrived. However, he could hide him—at least temporarily.

That's why he'd decided to buy enough time to send a message, eliminate his two targets, get the papers, and still get Wild Bill to safety. So as they all turned to go, Levi shot Wild Bill a look. When the ex-SEAL cursed him, Levi knew he would be ready and waiting to be rescued.

As they stepped outside under clearing skies Levi recalled a joke he'd heard: *the best plan is to have no plan at all—that way nothing can go wrong*. It sounded absurd but it spoke a universal truth—things do go wrong. It was simply a matter of when and by how much. In Levi's case, his plan began to unravel at once.

After Slavko closed the door—and after Levi recalled that there were no locks on this island—Bogrov directed the soldiers to remain and stand guard. *Strike one*. Strike two came when the Russian told Levi, "Leave your jeep with the men. They can use it to get their lunch. You will go with us." The third strike fell when Bogrov grinned at Levi. "I feel it is time for some vodka. *Da?*"

With his timetable now in shambles, Levi made a show of tapping his foot against a stone. "That sounds great. But I need to take care of my men, first." He swept a hand at his jeep. "I'll finish my rounds, stop back here, and hoof it to your place."

"*Nyet.*"

Levi got ready to argue until Bogrov said, "Make your rounds. Return *here*. Have one of these men *drive* you to my home." He added with great cheer, "See? I too take care of my men." Then he nodded to Slavko, and as they started off he called over his shoulder, "I will see you soon. We will have much vodka. Then we shall see the fun." He tilted his head at the building, and was still laughing as the jeep vanished around a corner. Getting into his own jeep, Levi tossed the guards a wave and drove off.

LEVI RETURNED to the cinderblock building minutes later and told the guards, "Change of plans. Bogrov wants to feed the sharks *now*. Come help me carry the bait from his cell." Jutting his jaw at the jeep, he told them to put their AK-47s in the back.

Once they complied, Levi went inside and hit the light switch. Grabbing the key, he opened the cell and told the guards, "Get his ass out and sit him in the front seat. You guys will hold him from behind. Now be gentle; we want live bait."

The bait screamed in agony anyway as they carried him out, but fell silent after they got him in the jeep. Then the moment the guards were distracted, Levi unholstered his pistol and said in a low, even voice, "Drop your weapons." The men had murder in their eyes, but they did what he'd ordered.

Wild Bill said in a raspy voice, "You got back sooner than I expected."

"Yeah. I forgot about those five bucks I lent you at that bar in Rio. Figured I'd better collect now, know what I mean?" With the pleasantries over, Levi took the men's radios and locked them in the cell while they hurled epithets at him.

After pocketing the key and closing the main door, he gave Wild Bill some water and set about tending to his injuries. But the raw-boned man shook his head and told Levi to get moving. Levi hesitated, then nodded and started off for his villa. It was the best option—use Sophia's declared love for him to make things happen. She could also minister to Wild Bill while he handled Bogrov and Slavko, although it might require a great deal of convincing on his part to get her to help. And yet when he pulled up in front of the villa, she stepped outside as if expecting him.

She glanced nervously at Bill. "What is going on?"

"You know what this is about," he said. "I'm here to deal with Bogrov. Now will you help me? Or not?"

She didn't answer right away. Finally she wet her lips. "Maybe you have for me the love. Perhaps not. But Yuri? Yuri gave me position as pilot. This is true. But he hates women." Her eyes went out of focus. "He has also told me that I am to leave you and be *his* woman. That I cannot allow." A shudder coursed through her. "And? I love you."

Levi had sharp antennae when it came to reading people, and saw that he could trust her. "Okay. Gather anything you can't live without. Pete's got some Oxy in his room. Grab it." Once she took off, he told Wild Bill, "I'll be right back."

Leaping out, he ran the short distance along the beach to the palm tree and got the SAT phone. He didn't have time to call in, so he thumbed its panic button to send an automatic SOS. Pocketing the phone, he reached the jeep at the same instant as Sophia.

"I found the Oxy," she said while holding up a white plastic bottle.

"Good." He wanted to take her and Bill to where the helicopter was hangared. But that was at the dock. They would never get past the sentry. Settling instead for a hidden trail near the dock that he'd discovered while exploring the island, he drove to it, shoved the transmission into reverse, and backed in until undergrowth concealed the jeep. Then he shut off the engine. But he left the key in the ignition.

Turning to Sophia, he wiped the sweat from his face and told her who he really was. Then he asked, "Do you know how to handle an AK-47?"

"Of course. Yuri trained all the women here. Just in case."

"Excellent." Reaching behind the driver's seat for the weapons he'd taken from the jail guards, he grabbed an AK, a pistol, ammo, and eight grenades. "For you."

Next, he pulled one of Wild Bill's bootlaces free. "Maybe your fingers won't function, but you need a fighting chance." Grabbing the other AK, he worked the bolt and chambered a round with a loud *clunk*, and placed it atop Wild Bill's lap. Then he tied one end of the bootlace to Bill's right wrist, and the other end to the AK's trigger.

"Now then," Levi began. "This is Sophia. She'll give you some Oxy. It'll kill the pain but still leave you alert. I should know. I…" All at once it hit him. A new twist in his plan to deal with Bogrov and Slavko.

Shaking his head in wonder, he said to Bill, "Fate sure does have a funny way of working. First it gets you hooked on heroin, then Fate offers it as a tool." He squinted in the general direction of the Russian's home, then put iron into his next words. "Stand by, Mr. Bogrov. You too, Mr. Slavko."

The SEAL's eyes flashed with anger. "Send that Serb bastard to me." Then he softened and faced Sophia. "Wild Bill, ma'am. An' I'm right pleased to meet you."

Her eyes burned with a new passion. "I will take good care of you."

Gripping Sophia's arms, Levi told her, "I have to take care of something. Then I'll neutralize the dock sentry. Once that's done I'll return for you and Bill. You'll fly him to St. Vincent." Then he gestured at Bill. "If things fall apart before

I get back, do whatever it takes to escape. We *must* get the word out. That's primary. No matter what. Is that clear?"

"Clear, boss."

. . .

Dragon Team—along with Roland and Hannah—gathered at the edge of the tarmac while the pilots prepped the twin-engine Augusta helicopters. When there'd been no call from Levi, Tommy made the decision—they would fly to Isla de la Rusia and act like dumb tourists who'd landed on the island by mistake, while counting on Levi to be among the first to investigate the disturbance. Otherwise, as he and Baker had already discussed, he'd let Delta Force come in.

. . .

Levi nodded at Wild Bill and grabbed his own AK-47. After removing the magazine, he nudged the first bullet out, turned it around, and shoved it in backwards. If anyone tried to use the weapon against him, operating the bolt would cause the weapon to chamber a "stovepipe round," jamming it and preventing it from firing. But if Levi had to put the weapon in play, he would simply pull the cocking lever all the way back and then slightly forward, then smartly back again to eject the bad round. That would make room for the next round, which would be correctly faced. He checked his watch: 9:24 AM. He had only a short time to find the papers. Failing that, he would settle on partially saving the world by ridding it of Bogrov and Slavko.

Setting out on foot, he reached for his SAT phone and thumbed it on. He'd sent the SOS. Now he needed to call

Tommy in response to the sonic booms—not to mention sending a concise message concerning the latest developments. The mission had turned into an ever-changing tactical environment, and he needed help.

He thumbed the power button twice. Nothing. The phone was dead. He stared at the brand mark. *Piece of crap. Same as the one before it.* No wonder he'd gotten no response after hitting the SOS button. He considered reciting a prayer but that would take time—and he had no more to spare.

CHAPTER FORTY-SIX

. . . .

LEVI BANGED on Bogrov's door until Bronislava opened it. Setting the AK-47 in its customary corner, he removed his boots and followed her into the living area.

Slavko stood against the far wall, and tilting his head at Levi he asked, "Why did I not hear any sounds when you were driven here?"

Levi said as if speaking to a dull child, "Because Lindstrom dropped me off at the bottom of the hill? Because I hoofed it up the driveway?"

"What does it matter how he arrived?" Bogrov asked from the leather sofa. Then he held up a bottle of Grey Goose. "Shall we?"

"Sure. Let's do it." Levi was all smiles, but he was actually dropping back to punt. "Boss? I wouldn't mind mainlining. Just sayin'."

The Russian's eyes lit up. "You wish to shoot up with the heroin?"

"Sure. Or... we could chase the dragon."

"Chase? Hmm." A few seconds passed in silence before he nodded once. "Da. Why not?" He exchanged a conspiratorial grin with Levi. "I shall get what is needed."

Bogrov got a candle going within minutes and patiently held a piece of foil containing a chunk of heroin over the flame. When the drug started giving off fumes he said, "Khorosho." Then he grabbed a glass tube to draw the fumes into his lungs. After taking a hit and exhaling, he offered the tube to his guest.

Levi's entire body yelled, *Do it! Do the heroin. Drift into that Nirvana you've visited in the past.* Steeling himself while his hand hovered over the inviting vapors, he jammed the open end of the tube into the fumes and drew in all he could, his throat clutching at them; his brain shouting, *Go on. Pull 'em in.* But he exhaled the whole lot and gave the tube to Bogrov. Then Levi had it again. Inhaling. Exhaling. Passing it back. Fake smoking it. Not realizing that with each inhalation he was drawing more and more of the fumes in, until in time the heroin's hypnotic, sensuous qualities lulled him into its trap. His eyelids fluttered. Then he moaned. *Mmm, feels sooo good. Yeah, gimme some more.* He reached for the glass tube. Inhaled. Held it as his body demanded that he finish what he'd started. *Mmm, yeah. Here we go…*

But while trembling with excitement he paused. Then after making a devil's pact to mainline for real once he took care of business, he exhaled everything and studied Bogrov with fresh eyes.

At a point, heroin induces tranquility while retaining alertness. Too much will induce lethargy. So he urged Bogrov to chase more of that dragon until the Russian finally slumped back against the sofa. Faking his own high, Levi plopped into a chair. But when he saw Slavko leave the room and then heard the jeep cough to life, he knew he'd better work fast.

With Bronislava rattling dishes in the kitchen, an energized Levi eased Bogrov into conversation. "Yuri, I've been thinking about those papers."

"Papers?" Bogrov's eyes stared at some unseen thing.

"Papers. What if something happens to you? You should tell me where they are in case you're taken out of commission."

Bogrov glared at the tile floor. "Taken out?"

"Right. Suppose you suffer a heart attack? I could get the papers and still tell the world what's in them."

"Do not be the idiot. That is why I have Slavko." He swept his hand in a grandiose arc. "He can figure things out."

"He is a smart hombre," Levi admitted. "Not someone I'd want to cross."

Bogrov's eyes went wide and his voiced trembled when he said in a low tone, "Nor I."

Really? Damn. That's good to know. Jesus, even Yuri's afraid of Slavko. He told Bogrov, "I only want to be of help."

The Russian tried to focus his eyes. "Why would you do such a thing for me?"

"Because you treat me like a son."

"Son?" Bogrov's head lolled. "What do you know of my son?"

"I know his name. Anton. Same as my son."

Bogrov's face contorted in rage. "*Bah.* You know nothing of my son."

"Sure I do. I..."

"My son! He is all that ever mattered. That is why I must deny the world a chance to live as it has been living. It must fall into chaos for the few months that remain. It is the only fitting tribute to the loss of my Anton... for God so loved the world that he gave his only son." A weird light lit Bogrov's eyes. Then as if a switch had been thrown, he lapsed into a stupor.

Levi's face crumpled in confusion. "For God so loved…" Then he was staring at the rocking horse and whispering, "Of course."

Rising unsteadily from a very real but nevertheless low-order high, he rapped his knuckles against its wooden sides. Solid. A dead end. Then it hit him. He knew where to go. With a glance at his AK and boots—and bearing in mind Slavko's abrupt departure—he stumbled through the rear door.

The skies had cleared but the late-morning sun had turned the trail's confines into a stifling tunnel. At least the moss beneath his socks felt soothing, and it helped lift the heroin fog that still shrouded his brain. Overhead meanwhile, a pair of kookaburra that Bogrov had imported from Australia called out with echoing sounds that mimicked human laughter, and the thought occurred to him that they might easily have been mocking him.

HIS STEPS were brisk as he passed through the hedge's muted entryway and into the sanctum sanctorum. There it is, he thought, knowing what he would find. Falling to his knees in front of the granite marker that stood vigil over the dead boy, he whispered, "Sorry, kid. But I have to do this." Then he dug into the soft, forgiving soil, gathering it with cupped hands and flinging it aside, scooping and tossing until his fingers struck a hard object, then digging further until the sun glinted against a silver frame.

Grasping the icon with his hands, he tore open the zip-lock bag and yanked the testament to Bogrov's son from its protective barrier. Turning the icon over, he opened the back—and there they were. The pope's papers. He gasped in spite of himself, for here was evidence of what had been, what was, and what could be.

Settling back on his heels, he unfolded the parchment-like papers and scanned them. He knew enough Latin to decipher their gist, and when he finished he knew that his discovery marked the end of one journey and the start of another, for now he could neutralize the people who sought to capitalize on what the pages revealed. But first he had to get Sophia, Wild Bill and himself off this island.

And he had to do these things now.

Except that when he looked up, there stood Bronislava with a neutral expression on her face but a very potent AK-47 in her hands—and its barrel was pointed accusingly at Levi's nose.

LEVI TOOK it all in. The AK. The stout woman. Her impassive features as her finger tightened on the trigger. Never taking his eyes from that finger, he noted a tiny nick in the trigger guard that identified the AK as his. What he could not know was whether she'd already worked the bolt—and if she had, whether she'd discovered the reversed bullet. But he knew one fact—it's easier to raise a barrel for accuracy, than it is to lower one simply to blast away for shock effect.

He flung the papers at her. Instinct made her rear back. Then time slowed. He dove for the ground. Saw every blade of grass. His hand went to his holstered pistol. He rolled to his right—*her* left. She tried to bring the muzzle to bear. But lowering it and swinging it caught her off-balance. But she did swing it—and he could see inside its barrel; could count its lands and grooves. His hand found the pistol. He drew it in a single fluid movement, his eyes on her forehead. Then time sped up as she trained the muzzle of *her* weapon on *his* forehead.

Craaack.

A neat hole appeared in the center of her head, then blossomed red as her finger tightened against the trigger in a cadaveric spasm. The AK's signature *rat-a-tat-tat* ripped the air. Spent shell casings flew in a straight arc from the ejection port, sending a flock of green parrots squawking in protest and taking flight with a furious flapping of wings.

Then total silence. The air stank of spent gunpowder and raw earth.

His instant thought—she was good. She saw the sabotage. Fixed it. Came for me. His next thought: but I was better.

Holstering his pistol, he scrambled amongst the shiny brass casings for the papers. After gathering them, he put them in the zip-lock and slipped it inside a pocket. Next, he swept up the AK and checked the mag. It still had six rounds. With a quick-look at the dead woman, her eyes open in surprise and her mouth slightly parted, he smoothed the dirt back over the grave. Then he started toward the house, determined to kill Bogrov and retrieve his ammo, hand grenades, and boots before setting a trap for Slavko.

Levi went partway up the winding trail before stepping off and blending in with the plants and palms to keep from being seen from the rear window. Keeping his eyes moving from side to side, up and down, every detail alive and etched indelibly in his mind, he wondered if the burst of gunfire had roused Bogrov from his heroin-induced daze. But experience told him to expect an energized Russian, for Levi had seen how well the man handled his booze and drugs.

After traveling another fifty yards he stopped at the edge of the tree line and studied the house. A single dash forward would bring him to the front door. His eyes darted about as he slowly walked from the trees, using his soles to feel for twigs or other debris that might snap and give him away. But just as he dug his toes in to sprint ahead he heard a jeep roaring up the hill, so he moved back into the foliage as brakes squealed in protest. Three seconds later the front door of the house banged open, then slammed shut.

There could be only one explanation—Slavko's killer intuition had taught him to trust nothing and nobody. Suspicious after not hearing Levi being dropped off, he'd gone to the jail cell. Levi cocked his head and listened with feral intensity, and seconds later his worst-case scenario was confirmed when he heard the guards he'd locked up speaking in quiet tones from the jeep.

Things happened fast after that. The front door burst open, and Bogrov's outraged voice filled the air as he unleashed a torrent of obscenities. Then two pistol shots shattered the morning calm, followed by thuds as a pair of bodies hit the ground.

Go ahead, Levi thought. Kill my adversaries for me. Reaching into a pocket, he pulled out his earphone and fixed it in place, then he turned on the radio in time to hear Slavko issue orders to the day shift lieutenant, who replied that he'd already alerted his men after hearing gunfire. Levi did some math: Bogrov had fifty soldiers. There were fourteen on today's roster. Removing himself from that list and subtracting the two that Bogrov had just killed, then painting a big question mark over Pete's head, that left ten soldiers for him to deal with—in addition to Bogrov and Slavko.

· · ·

Tommy Wilkins checked his watch. 10:45 AM. He glanced skyward. Clear blue. Not a cloud. Not even high-level cirrus. The temperature hovered in the mid-eighties and a pleasant breeze whispered in his ear. Everything was perfect. It's why he turned to the team and barked, "Mount up."

CHAPTER FORTY-SEVEN

. . . .

"CHANGE OF PLAN," Levi muttered to himself. He had to get word of his situation to the team. But he was incommunicado. His only chance might be in finding a phone inside Bogrov's house. In the meantime Bogrov and company were sweeping the island, and given sufficient time they would find him, Sophia, and Wild Bill.

So the instant Slavko's jeep started down the hill with Bogrov shouting his rage, Levi made a dash for the house. He needed the ammo and wanted his boots, but he was willing to trade both for a functioning phone. Reaching a white stucco wall near the front door, he pressed himself against it and listened.

Hearing nothing, he moved in stealth mode to the door and put his ear to it. Not a sound. Finally drawing a deep breath and with his finger ready on the trigger, he opened the door and looked left and right. Nobody. He stepped inside and instantly moved to the left so as not to silhouette himself in the open door. His grenades, ammo and boots were there, but he ignored them and rushed into Bogrov's bedroom where an empty SAT phone charger told him everything—there were no land lines and Bogrov probably had the SAT. Hurrying back to the foyer, he grabbed his gear and hustled outside.

With little time to waste, he performed a tactical reload by exchanging the AK's nearly depleted magazine for a fresh one. After shoving the used mag into a cargo pocket, he put on his boots and sprinted down the hill. When he reached the bottom he hugged the tree line and took off at a run for the hiding place where he'd left Wild Bill and Sophia. In the meantime Slavko was bellowing orders over the radio, rallying the troops into beating the bushes for the traitorous Rocky O'Toole.

Halfway to the hiding place he heard a jeep and dove behind some trees. Within seconds a jeep carrying five soldiers with their weapons held at the ready rounded a curve. Fortunately for Levi, the jeep continued in the direction of his villa. Bursting from the hiding place, he ran on despite his protesting lungs and the sweat that was rolling down his forehead and blurring his vision.

Reaching the trail, he plunged into its opening, but neither the jeep nor Wild Bill or Sophia were there. *What the*—? A chill ran down his spine. Had Bogrov stumbled upon them? Had he killed them? Or was he holding them as bargaining chips? The game of probabilities and outcomes, he thought. Take action, don't take action, or split hairs by punting. But as he resolved to produce an outcome of his own choosing, he knew it meant going to his villa where they were probably waiting.

And he'd have to cover the half mile distance in the open, because creeping through the woods would take too much time. Jogging back to the road, he turned north and set his priorities: eliminate Bogrov and Slavko, then rescue the hostages. But no matter how he figured things, he doubted he'd live to see high noon.

He set off but had gone fewer than fifty yards when he heard a high-pitched whine. When it increased in pitch and volume, he recognized what it was: turbo-whine. *Wild Bill must've given Sophia her marching orders. Now she's firing up the helicopter. But it'll take a couple of minutes for the engines to spool up. Anything can happen before she's able to take off.*

Changing course, he started for the dockside helipad. He was almost there when he heard a jeep approaching. Dodging behind a large palm, he got ready. Sure enough, the earlier jeep with its crew of five rounded a bend, clearly racing toward the helipad.

Levi took aim at the driver and opened fire. The AK bucked as he fired in bursts. *Rat-a-tat-tat... rat-a-tat-tat.* Slugs ripped the driver to shreds. The jeep careened to the left. Hit a shrub. Levi fired at the front passenger. *Rat-a-tat-tat.* Spent shell casings flew. Gray-white smoke belched from the muzzle. A gunpowder stench swirled around him. The passenger's chest erupted.

But the three guys in back were bringing their arms to bear.

Levi pulled out a grenade. Yanked the pin free. Let the spoon fly. Heard the loud *pop* as the fuse ignited. He heaved it. Time slowed. He watched the grenade sail through the air. Saw the three men follow it. Heard the thunderous *bang* as it exploded over their heads. He charged forward. Was still ten feet away when a soldier moved. Levi fired a burst.

The guy's head exploded like a watermelon dropped from a high tower.

He reached the jeep, and after confirming the five kills he performed a tactical reload. Then he began yanking bodies out. Levi knew them all and he even liked two of them. But this was a hard-core business and too bad for them. Hopping behind the wheel, he jammed his foot against the accelerator and rocketed down the road.

Reaching the pad as the Sikorsky's jet engines roared louder, he saw the sentry's body in the middle of the small parking area. The mangled remains told him that Sophia had run him over with the jeep. Levi had partied with him. But he and the others had come to Isla de la Rusia as mercenaries. They'd known the risks. "Tough titty," he muttered.

The roar of the engines was now deafening as he hopped from the jeep. When Wild Bill poked his head from a window, Levi yanked the zip-locked papers from his pocket and tossed the bag through the opening. "Go," he said above the whirl of rotor blades. "Get those papers to safety. Call for help. Me? I've got unfinished business." He was turning to leave when Wild Bill squinted at something.

Levi spun. A soldier named Rolf Gunderson stood forty feet away, his AK trained on Levi.

Time crawled. Levi dodged left. Bullets tore chunks from the pavement. A second burst. Echoes almost, because his hearing had shifted into auditory exclusion when his primal instincts for survival went from *flight* to *fight*. He charged forward. Stopped. Leaped to the right.

Another burst. Bits of pavement flew. Gunderson closed the distance. Levi put the AK to his shoulder. Heard gunfire. Saw Gunderson's head vanish. *Wha*—?

He whirled and spotted Wild Bill's AK in the window, barrel still smoking. As Sophia lifted off, Bill held up his wrist with the bootlace around it. Then the helicopter's tail lifted high as its nose pitched down. Sophia ran it forward like an airplane building speed on a runway to provide maximum lift. All at once she pulled full collective. The Sikorsky jetted skyward. She's a damn fine pilot, he thought.

As the Sikorsky became a dot in the sky, the radio broke squelch. The day shift lieutenant had found the five dead guys. He shouted, *"Find him.* Kill *him!"*

Levi ran a mental checklist: Bogrov had killed the two jail sentries. Levi killed the five in the jeep. Sophia ran over the dock sentry. Wild Bill just canceled Gunderson's ticket. That left Ian, Pete, the lieutenant, and two others. But there were also Bogrov and Slavko—plus any number of men being called out from their homes, along with the weapons they'd all been ordered to keep at the ready.

Hearing another jeep, he vowed to wage this next fight from a location of his choosing—and it was the place where he knew Bogrov would go. Bulldozing through the undergrowth, he scrambled uphill to the field of battle, and while making his way to the tiny cemetery he muttered, "Yuri? Ya wanna die next to your son? Fine. I'll grant your wish."

But he hadn't gone far when he heard a twig snap, followed by a grenade's *pop*. He hit the deck. An explosion threw dirt in all directions. Dazed, he heard another *pop*. He rolled right. A thunderous blast. Shrapnel ripped his head open. He couldn't see, couldn't hear. Then everything went black.

"GET UP."

Hands tugged at him.

"I said... get up. We ain't got no time."

Levi cracked open an eye. "Huh...?"

Someone lifted him. Someone strong enough to sling him over a shoulder like a sack of onions. Levi soon realized that his head and shoulders were drenched with dark, viscous blood. A hand to his head came away red. *Fragment must've torn a chunk.* Then he felt nauseous—a bad sign where head injuries are concerned. Things began to spin and he began fading in and out as his unknown rescuer crashed between trees and shrubs. He reached for the AK. It was gone. But he had his pistol. And the grenades. Whoever was carrying him finally put him down. Levi looked up. Pete towered over him.

"It was Ian what fragged you," the behemoth whispered. "An' I killed him deader than graveyard dead for doin' it. Now I gotta shove off or they'll know it was me." He locked eyes with Levi and nodded, then blended with the bushes.

Levi touched his scalp and grimaced. If he lived he'd end up with a helluva scar. After wrapping a field dressing on the wound, he rose on unsteady legs and started for the cemetery. But blood loss had sapped his strength. He still had fifty yards to go when the trees, the sky and even the dirt began spinning. His knees buckled. This wasn't good. He tried to shake it off. He vomited. Projectile vomiting. Even worse.

An insistent buzzing in his ears began to fade. He blinked. *Jesus, I must've passed out. But for how long?* He drew a series of deep breaths, but the acid in his mouth from all the vomiting made him retch. He touched his head. The bandage had fallen away. *How much more blood did I lose?* He couldn't think clearly. Then his vision faded.

HE DIDN'T know how long he'd been out — only that when he came to it was blistering hot — and blinking against blinding sunlight, he saw that he had company.

Slavko stood over him with a pistol, smiling cruelly in a way Levi had seen often during a career dealing with every form of depravity. This one especially chilled him to his core. But he was still in the game; still determined to kill Bogrov. "Where's Yuri?"

"Yuri? Bah. That… peasant. That self-styled nihilist. Delusional *dreamer*. He wants you taken alive. He wishes to challenge you to a duel. Imagine."

Though Levi now had to struggle to speak, he remained flippant. "Imagine."

"Ah, so you agree. How charming." Then Slavko snarled and kicked Levi's ribs. "Yuri is an imbecile. He has looked down on me all these years, never dreaming that I'd acquired the numbers to his financial accounts. Once I've fed his body to our friends the predators, all this will be mine." He swept an arm around the small clearing. "*His* island. *His* money. The women he brought here. All of it. Mine. For eternity."

Levi listened to him ramble. The man needed to talk and Levi needed to amass his strength. Blood loss had sapped his energy. He tried moving anyway, but couldn't.

Slavko finished his monologue. But what he asked next made Levi wish he hadn't stopped. *"Rocky.* Do you know why I decided to check on the prisoner? The answer is simple. I saw you with Kaczmarek." He paused for effect. "Yes. I saw you with him. Such sentimental hogwash. Bah!" He got another smile, more terrifying than the first. Then it came. "So. First, I shall do to you what I did to him. I shall take away your eyes."

Holstering his pistol in a fluid motion, he drew a long knife from a pocket and placed its point against Levi's right eye. "Such nice blue eyes you have. So nicely aligned. While mine? Mine have always drawn the sneers, the stifled laughter. The women, they go to you with great eagerness. While I? I must go to the prostitutes." Slavko's wandering eye was devoid of any soul as his mouth formed a straight line.

"Now say farewell to your eyes." Slavko bore down on the knife.

Levi didn't breath. And he didn't blink. "Fuck you."

Slavko hesitated. "A brave man. Very well. I shall concede that point." Pulling the knife away, he looked sidelong at his prey. "At least you tried to help Kaczmarek."

Levi voice was barely above a mumble. "You butcher."

Slavko's face turned purple. He backhanded Levi. Blood burst from his nose. Then the henchman yelled, "Have you no fear?"

"Not of you."

"No?" Slavko squinted, then slowly pulled the knife away. "Very well. You do have fortitude. So let us play another game."

Something about Slavko's voice sent a shudder so deep through Levi that it paled when compared against the Serb's earlier vow to blind him.

Now Slavko's lips drew back, as if pulled by a string into a leering smile. "Hmm, yes. I shall cut your throat like that of a pig. Then I will butcher you and eat your liver."

Levi tried to reach his pistol but he was too spent. The human body can endure only so much, and he'd been hit hard. Still, he tried. But it did no good.

Slavko laughed as he grabbed a handful of Levi's blood-caked hair. After pulling his victim's head back, he pressed the knife against Levi's neck, just beneath his ear.

Levi's skin erupted in goose bumps. Yet he could do nothing.

It was over in seconds. Slavko drew the knife in a quick, sharp motion.

He did it! Squirming, twisting, yet somehow feeling detached as blood ran down his neck, Levi almost laughed when he realized that Slavko had only made a shallow cut. But he snapped back when Slavko made another cut. He'd go for the jugular soon, and in the seconds that remained he grasped the sadist's goal—he was taking his time in order to see the fear in his prey's eyes.

Levi wasn't about to give him the satisfaction.

Slavko's warm breath washed across his eardrum as he taunted him. "Still no pleas for mercy? Very well. I will add to the plan. I shall give you a Columbian necktie. This way I take advantage of the slit I made above your external jugular. But that incision is a mere three millimeters deep. I will deepen it by slicing through the external jugular, while sparing the internal one. You will bleed—but not enough to die. Not yet."

Levi thought, this bastard has his tradecraft nailed. If it all went south he might still clamp a hand against the incision to prevent a bleed-out. That might work.

"Yes, then I will continue. I'll sever the arteries surrounding your thyroid and listen to you gurgle as you flop about like a fish. But you will still be alive and you will know what is taking place. I shall work quickly. I will cut open your throat. Then I'll reach inside and pull your tongue through the opening. It will hang there. A necktie. You will still be conscious as I begin cutting off your arms and legs to feed the dogs with. As for your eyes, I will cut them out and send them to your loved ones… by U.P.S." He laughed, low and deep. "Well? What have you to say?"

Slavko clearly needed to hear Levi plead for his life—which he would never do. But his reserves were gone. Better to die with dignity. Then the cold steel blade was in place against his neck. He took a few deep last breaths and awaited the knife's cruel caress. *This is it.*

And it was. Slavko drew the knife in one quick motion.

Levi knew the end had come. The external jugular parted. Warm blood gushed and flowed down his torso. He struggled. But helplessly.

The henchman laughed. "Hah! There you go! Already flopping like the fish!"

Levi heard the blood roar in his eardrums. His eyes rolled wildly.

Slavko yelled, "Now die!" Then he began going for the thyroid arteries.

Levi felt a searing pain. Gulped blood. Struggled to breathe.

Bogrov's underling only laughed. "Ah, here we go!"

Still not about to give up, Levi reached into his very soul for strength.

But too late. The blade was already nicking the carotid artery. Then...

...*Pop*.

And Levi said, "Now who dies, you sick bastard?" With that, he slipped the grenade into Slavko's pocket and curled into a fetal position as the Serb took off running.

Levi counted. One second; one and a half. Two...

...*Boom!*

Shards of bone, brain matter and viscera splattered Levi just as a burst of automatic weapons fire erupted nearby. Jamming a hand against his neck to stop the bleeding, he wondered if it was Pete doing the shooting.

Still keeping pressure on his neck, he rallied his strength and finally managed to get to his feet. Drawing his pistol, he staggered toward the hedge and paused to catch his breath. Then he passed through and found Bogrov—Euro-trash billionaire but keeper of the key to the world's demise, standing near his son's grave with his pistol pointed at the ground. Bronislava's body was nowhere to be seen.

A wave of nausea hit Levi. His vision blurred. But he was still able to train his pistol on the Russian.

Bogrov spoke. "Rocky. You have not disappointed me. You have arrived for our duel. *Da. Khorosho.* Now you will lower your weapon, as I have done. Then I will count to three and we as men will see who shall win and who shall die. So. One. Two..."

Levi scoffed and squeezed the trigger twice. The Beretta barked. Two 9mm slugs tore into Bogrov's heart.

"Double-tap," Levi said without emotion. Then he finished the shooter's cadence. "Two to the chest... and one to the head." He fired. The round slammed into Bogrov's forehead.

The expression on the Russian's face said, *What do you do? You do not fight as a man.* Then he toppled over.

Levi said to the corpse, "Sorry, but the Marquis of Queensberry rules don't apply 'cause I didn't come here for a boxing match. I came to kill you. *Da. Khorosho.*"

All at once his eyelids fluttered. Then his knees buckled. He dropped to the ground. And it was then that he saw something he'd missed at first. He even smiled at the sight of the wooden rocking horse fashioned by the hands of a loving father that was now standing vigil over a little boy's grave.

Then blood began gushing from his head. He already had one hand clamped against his neck. Dropping the pistol, he jammed the other against the head wound.

It did no good. Too much had already escaped.

Levi fought hard. He had so much left to do. He had to send an after-action report. Had to assure President Cohen that Bogrov had failed, that the U.S./Saudi effort could move ahead as scheduled.

He clung to life. But he was fading. Now his heart was booming rapidly. He gasped for air but came up short. Then his respiration rate went hyper—a bad sign. He struggled to remain alert. *Can't close my eyes... can't go to sleep...*

He was nodding off anyway when he heard the sounds. *A helicopter. No, two of 'em. Flying an approach path. Engines changing pitch. They're landing.*

Sometime later—he wasn't sure how long—he heard shouting. A burst of shots. More yelling. Increased gunfire. Bogrov's men were crashing through the shrubs. But he had nothing to defend himself with—no pistol, no strength.

So cold... I'm sooo cold...

His hand fell away from his neck. Warm blood flowed, sticky; unstoppable. The crashing came closer, then stopped. He heard whispering. Michael's voice. Tommy's, too. Levi called out. *Guys! I'm here!* But the words were only in his head. None escaped his lips. *I have to wait for them. They'll find me. They will. I know they will... .*

Now he felt even colder. He gasped for air. His heart beat a rapid staccato. *No. I can't go. Not like this.* He struggled to hang on but his life was slipping away.

WHEN THE END CAME he took a great final breath. Then a profound sense of peace enveloped him. *At least I beat 'em. At least... I... won...*

His body went limp. The death rattle issued from his throat. Finally the light abandoned his eyes. And that's when he saw them. *Anita,* he cried out. *Michael! You're alive! Oh Michael my son, my son... oh, Michael my son. Where have you been? I've been looking everywhere for you! Michael... my son, my son!* Seeing the boy reaching out to him, Levi took off running to gather him in his arms. *Oh, God. You're here and your mommy's here, and I'm so happy... sooo happy... sooo hap... .*

CHAPTER FORTY-EIGHT

. . . .

"WATER... PLEASE."

Monica grabbed the Styrofoam cup and held the straw to Levi's lips.

He drank greedily before thanking her with his eyes. He was exhausted. Even opening his eyes required effort. His hair had been shorn and his scalp shaved. Sutures secured the wound caused by the grenade fragment. Others closed the lacerations in his neck. Three I.V.s were running blood and fluids. He had an oxygen cannula. Wires from sticky pads on his chest snaked to a cardiac monitor. A cuff around his left arm inflated automatically with a hushed whir every few minutes to monitor his BP.

It had been nearly seven hours since the Delta Force surgeon arrived at his side. They'd flown him by helicopter to Puerto Rico where he regained consciousness inside a trauma facility. Once he was moved to the ICU, Michael, Tommy and Monica gathered at his side.

Michael now filled Levi in on the events. "We were already en route to you when we came across Wild Bill riding shotgun inside some sweetheart of a lady's Sikorsky. He raised us on a common aircraft frequency. Told us what was going down. We called Heath. He said Delta Force had already been dispatched. Tommy told him to send in the Marines, too.

"We were landing at the helipad when Delta parachuted in," Michael continued. "All of us—Roland and Hannah included—we were locked an' cocked an' loaded for bear. When we heard gunfire coming from a hill, Monica insisted that's where you must be."

Tommy stepped closer. "We fought our way to you, buddy. You shoulda seen Michael go at 'em. He killed three of 'em. Hack, another two. The rest of us got…"

"One kill apiece," Monica said. Her voice showed that she didn't feel proud that she'd taken a life—the second in as many years.

Michael said, "Then we found you." He grew quiet. "Covered in blood. Pupils fixed. Dilated. Skin white. Cold to the touch. Couldn't find a pulse. You weren't breathing, brother. But you… had a smile on your face."

"A smile," Levi echoed. His forehead knotted, the lines of concentration drawing in toward the center. All at once his eyes brightened and he said in a hoarse, haunted voice, "I saw them. I saw Anita. I saw my son. I… *saw* them. I tried to catch up to 'em. My boy's arms were outstretched. I…"

Monica gripped his arm. "Oh, Levi."

After a brief pause Tommy said, "We started CPR. Monica got on the horn. Told Delta to get us a surgeon, pronto. He showed up within minutes. Started an IV. Pushed some epi in. Zapped you twice with a portable defib. Didn't think we'd get you back." His voice caught. "We have the documents you gave Wild Bill." He patted Levi's knee. "You beat 'em, boss. You won."

Levi's voice was barely audible. "Guys. You saved my life." He looked into Michael's eyes. "Brother…"

"I won't say who did the mouth-to-mouth," Michael said to lighten the mood.

Levi managed a tiny smile. "Long as it was Monica."

She kissed his cheek. "Thank God you're okay."

"Hack went with Wild Bill," Tommy said. "They had a military jet whisk him to Andrews. From there a waiting chopper flew him to Bethesda. Hannah and Roland are still on-island. They're processing the place for evidence."

Finally, he gave Levi the word on Pete—how he fired into the air while charging a Delta trooper who had no choice but to cut him down with a burst of automatic fire. Levi thought it a fitting end for a fighter who knew he'd be sent back to Super Max, and chose to go out on his own terms.

Monica took his hand, careful not to disturb a large-bore IV catheter inside his elbow. "President Cohen called. First, to offer a prayer. Then to say that once they translated the papers, they came up with a shocker."

Levi grimaced as he sometimes did when preparing to hear bad news.

"Turns out Nixon neglected to include a paragraph in the presidential briefing book. Fortunately it got passed along—possibly inadvertently—to the Pope." She glanced around, ensuring privacy, then leaned closer. "The stolen pages included the fact that the Ecos had developed a scientific theory to divert *their* asteroid, *and* the one that's coming. But at the time they lacked the technological ability." She paused so Levi could absorb this. "Cohen got on the horn to Kwaj. He spoke with Davis, who according to Cohen all but did a back-flip over the phone. Said it's one hundred per cent workable—but they'll need five months of R&D before it's ready."

Michael nodded in affirmation.

Levi said weakly, "Whoa. Great news." Then he met Michael's eyes and offered a tired smile.

"And," Tommy began, "we have another mission on the horizon."

Though drained of energy, Levi forced a thumbs-up. "We did it, guys. We kept the hope. We followed Apollo. All the way. To the moon. And it's sure gonna look different from now on." Left unsaid was that after seeing his wife and son, he could now let go of them. He could look for love, unhindered and with renewed hope.

. . .

ACKNOWLEDGMENTS

• • •

I want to thank my long-time editor Jean Jenkins for the wisdom and patience she brings to her craft. She's the best.

I'm also indebted to Levi Bailey, Tommy Wilkins, Michael DuFour, Quenton Josey, Mark Cohen and Keith Runk for lending parts of their personalities to this tale.

Hannah Montague, Rick Geist, Colleen Pallamary, Michael Shevock, Joe Ross, Barbara Sack and Eric Briggs gave me considerable help with their spot-on beta readings, and William Martinez and Simon Mayeski were kind enough to offer insight that helped me through a couple of rough spots. Thank you, everyone.

ABOUT THE AUTHOR

RICHARD CRAIG ANDERSON started out as a fire fighter in 1971, became a highly decorated Maryland State Police trooper, and went on to accept a position as a counter-terrorist operative. An accomplished aviator, world-class scuba diver and global traveler, Rick has enjoyed a life well lived thanks to the relationships and friendships he's forged along the way.

• • •

hellgatepress.com